DIABLO®

THE SIN WAR

DIABLO®

THE SIN WAR

BOOK ONE
BIRTHRIGHT

RICHARD A. KNAAK

BLIZZARD
ENTERTAINMENT

© 2019 Blizzard Entertainment, Inc. All rights reserved. Diablo and Blizzard Entertainment are trademarks or registered trademarks of Blizzard Entertainment, Inc., in the U.S. and/or other countries. No portion of this book may be reproduced or transmitted in any form or by any means without written permission from the copyright holders.

ISBN: 978-1-945683-47-3

First Pocket Books printing: November 2004
First Blizzard Entertainment printing: March 2019

10 9 8 7 6 5 4 3 2 1

Cover art by Bill Petras

Printed in the USA

DIABLO®

THE SIN WAR

PROLOGUE

The world was young, then, and only a few knew it as Sanctuary or knew that not only did angels and demons exist, but some of them had caused Sanctuary to be in the first place. The names Inarius, Diablo, Rathma, Mephisto, and Baal—to name a powerful and often dread few—had not yet been whispered on mortal lips.

In this simpler time, ignorant of the eternal battle between the High Heavens and the Burning Hells, people struggled and prospered, lived and died. They could not know that even then, the eyes of both immortal sides would soon covet their potential and thus begin a conflict that would spill over into the centuries to come.

And, of all those most terribly ignorant of Sanctuary's awful destiny, Uldyssian ul-Diomed—Uldyssian, son of Diomedes—could be said to have been the most blind. Blind, though he would be himself at the center of what scholars of the world's secret history would come to call *the Sin War.*

It was not a war in the sense of men-at-arms—though there were those, too—but rather a trying, a testing and taking, of souls. A war that would forever eradicate the innocence of Sanctuary and those inhabiting it, changing all, even those not aware.

A war that was both won . . . and lost . . .

From the Books of Kalan
First Tome, Second Leaf

One

The shadow fell across Uldyssian ul-Diomed's table, enveloping not only much of it, but also his hand and his as-of-yet-undrunk ale. The sandy-haired farmer did not have to look up to know who interrupted his brief respite from his day's labors. He had heard the newcomer speaking to others in the Boar's Head—the only tavern in the remote village of Seram—heard him speaking and prayed silently but vehemently that he would not come to Uldyssian's table.

It was ironic that the son of Diomedes *prayed* for the stranger to keep away, for what stood waiting for Uldyssian to look up was none other than a missionary from the Cathedral of Light. Resplendent in his collared silver-white robes—resplendent save for the ring of Seramian mud at the bottom—he no doubt awed many a fellow villager of Uldyssian's. However, his presence did nothing but dredge up terrible memories for the farmer, who now angrily fought to keep his stare fixed on the mug.

"Have you seen the *Light*, my brother?" the figure finally asked when it was clear that his potential convert planned to continue to ignore him. "Has the Word of the great Prophet touched your soul?"

"Find someone else," Uldyssian muttered, his free hand involuntarily tightening into a fist. He finally took a gulp of his ale, hoping that his remark would end the unwanted conversation. However, the missionary was not to be put off.

Setting a hand on the farmer's forearm—and thereby

keeping the ale from again touching Uldyssian's lips—the pale young man said, "If not yourself alone, think of your loved ones! Would you forsake their souls as—"

The farmer roared, his face red with a rage no longer held in check. In a single motion, Uldyssian leapt up and seized the startled missionary by the collar. As the table tipped over, the ale fell and splattered on the planked floor, unnoticed by its former drinker. Around the room, other patrons, including a few rare travelers passing through, eyed the confrontation with concern and interest . . . and from experience chose to keep out of it. Some of the locals, who knew the son of Diomedes well, shook their heads or muttered to one another at the newcomer's poor choice of subjects.

The missionary was a hand taller than Uldyssian, no small man himself at just over six feet, but the broad-shouldered farmer outweighed him by half again as much and all of that muscle from day after day of tilling the soil or seeing to the animals. Uldyssian was a square-jawed man with the bearded, rough-hewn features typical of the region west of the great city-state of Kehjan, the "jewel" of the eastern half of the world. Deep-brown eyes burned into the more pale ones of the gaunt—and surprisingly young—features of the Cathedral's proselytizer.

"The souls of most of my family are beyond the Prophet's gathering, *brother!* They died nearly ten years ago, all to plague!"

"I shall s-say a prayer for . . . for them—"

His words only served to infuriate Uldyssian, who had himself prayed for his parents, his elder brother, and his two sisters constantly over the months through which they had suffered. Day and night—often with no sleep in between—he had first prayed to whatever power watched over them that they recover, then, when that no longer seemed a hope, that their deaths would be swift and painless.

And that prayer, too, had gone unanswered. Uldyssian, distraught and helpless, had watched as, one by one, they died in anguish. Only he and his youngest brother, Mendeln, had survived to bury the rest.

Even then there had been missionaries and even then they had talked of the souls of his family and how their particular sects had the answers to everything. To a one, they had promised Uldyssian that, if he followed their particular path, he would find peace over his loved ones' losses.

But Uldyssian, once a devout believer, had very vocally denounced each and every one of them. Their words rang hollow and his refusals seemed later justified when the missionaries' sects faded away as surely as each season on the farm.

But not all. The Cathedral of Light, though only of recent origin, seemed far stronger than most of its predecessors. Indeed, it and the longer-established Temple of the Triune seemed to be quickly becoming the two dominant forces seeking the souls of Kehjan's people. To Uldyssian, the fervent enthusiasm with which both sought out new converts bordered on a strenuous competition much in conflict with their spiritual messages.

And that was yet another reason Uldyssian would have no part of either.

"Pray for yourself, not for me and mine," he growled. The missionary's eyes bulged as Uldyssian easily hefted him by the collar off the floor.

The squat, balding figure behind the counter slipped out to intervene. Tibion was several years senior and no match against Uldyssian, but he had been Diomedes's good friend and so his words had effect on the furious farmer. "Uldyssian! Mind my establishment if'n you can't mind yourself, eh?"

Uldyssian hesitated, the proprietor's words cutting through his anguish. His gaze swept from the pale face before him to Tibion's round one, then back again.

A frustrated scowl still on his face, he let the figure in his grip drop in an undignified heap on the floor.

"Uldyssian—" Tibion started.

But the son of Diomedes did not wait to hear the rest. Hands shaking, he strode out of the Boar's Head, his heavy, worn leather boots clattering hard on the well-trod planks. Outside, the air was crisp, which helped soothe Uldyssian some. Almost immediately, he began to regret his actions within. Not the reasons for them, but that he had acted so before many of those who knew him . . . and not for the first time.

Still, the presence of the Cathedral's acolyte in Seram grated on his heart. Uldyssian was now a man who only believed in what his eyes showed him and what his hands could touch. He could see the changes in the sky and so tell when he needed to rush his work in the field or whether time enough remained to complete his task at a more moderate pace. The crops his work brought forth from the soil fed him and others. These were things he could trust, not the muttered praying of clerics and missionaries that had done nothing for his family but give them false hope.

Seram was a village of some two hundred folk, small by many standards, of reasonable size by others. Uldyssian could have paced its length in as many breaths, if that much. His farm lay two miles to the north of Seram. Once a week, Uldyssian went into the village to get what supplies he needed, always allowing himself the short break for food and drink at the tavern. His meal he had eaten and his ale was lost, which left only his tasks to complete before he departed again.

In addition to the tavern, which also acted as an inn, there were only four other buildings of consequence in Seram—the meeting house, the trading station, the village Guard quarters, and the smithy. All shared the same general design as the rest of the structures of Seram, with the roofs pointed and thatched, and the bodies wooden planks over a frame whose base was built of several layers of stone and clay. As was typical in most areas under the influence of Kehjan, the windows of each were arched sharply at the top and always numbered three on a side. In truth, from a distance it was impossible to tell one building from another.

Mud caked his boots as he walked, Seram too provincial to have paved streets or even stone ones. There was a small, dry path to the opposite side from where Uldyssian trod, but at the moment, he had no patience for it and, besides, as a farmer, he was used to being one with the soil.

At the eastern edge of Seram—and thus nearest to Kehjan—stood the trading station. The station was, other than the tavern, the busiest of places in Seram. Here it was that locals brought in their goods to trade for other necessities or to even sell to passing merchants. When there were new items in stock, a blue banner would be raised by the doorway up front, and as he approached, Uldyssian saw Cyrus's night-tressed daughter, Serenthia, doing just that. Cyrus and his family had run the trading station for four generations and were among the most prominent of families in the village, although they dressed no more fancy than anyone else. The trader did not look down on his customers, who were also, for the most part, his neighbors. Serenthia, for example, was clad in a simple cloth dress of brown, cut modestly at the bodice and whose bottom hem ended just above the ankle. Like most villagers, she wore sensible boots designed for both riding and walking through the muddy ruts in the main street.

"Something of interest?" he called to Serenthia, trying to focus on other matters in order to forget both the incident and the images from the past it had conjured up.

Cyrus's daughter turned at the sound of his voice, her thick, long hair fluttering about. With her bright blue eyes, ivory skin, and naturally red lips, Uldyssian felt certain that all she needed was a proper gown to allow her to compete with the best of the blue-blood females in Kehjan itself. The unadorned dress did not hide her curves, nor did it detract in any way from the graceful manner in which she somehow moved regardless of the terrain.

"Uldyssian! Have you been here all day?"

There was that in her tone that all but made the farmer

grimace. Serenthia was more than a decade younger than him and he had seen her grow up from a child to a woman. To him, she was nearly one of the sisters that he had lost. However, to her, Uldyssian evidently seemed much more. She had turned down the attentions of younger and more affluent farmers than him, not to mention the flirtations of several visiting merchants. The only other man in whom she showed any interest was Achilios, Uldyssian's good friend and the best hunter in Seram, but whether that was because of his ties to the farmer, it was difficult to say.

"I arrived just past the first hour of day," he replied. As he neared, he caught glimpses of at least three wagons behind Cyrus's establishment. "A fair-sized caravan for Seram. What goes on?"

She finished hoisting up the banner, then tethered the rope. Gazing over her shoulder at the wagons, Serenthia said, "They got lost, actually. They were bound for passage through Tulisam."

Tulisam was the next nearest habitation, a town at least five times as great as Seram. It was also more on the route from Kehjan proper to the sea, where the master ports were.

Uldyssian grunted. "The handler must be a novice."

"Well, whatever the cause, they've decided to trade some. Father's trying to hide his excitement. They've got some beautiful things, Uldyssian!"

To the son of Diomedes, beautiful things generally consisted of strong, sturdy tools or a newborn calf that had its health. He started to speak, then noticed someone walking by the wagons.

She was dressed akin to a noble of one of the Houses that sought to fill the gap of leadership caused by the recent infighting between the ruling mage clans. Her lush golden hair was bound up behind her head with a silver band, allowing full view of the regal, ivory face. Glittering green eyes surveyed her surroundings. Slim, perfect lips parted as the woman, the shoulders of her flowing emerald gown covered by a fur, viewed the landscape to the east of Seram.

The bodice of the gown was cinched tight and although her clothing was the epitome of the ruling castes, it left no doubt that she was very much female.

Just as the arresting figure began to glance in Uldyssian's direction, Serenthia abruptly took him by the arm. "You should come inside and see for yourself, Uldyssian."

As she steered him toward the twin wooden doors, the farmer took a quick look back, but of the noblewoman he saw no sign. Had he not known himself to be incapable of such elaborate fancies, Uldyssian would have almost believed her to be a product of his imagination.

Serenthia all but pulled him inside, Cyrus's daughter shutting the doors behind them particularly hard. Inside, her father glanced up from a conversation with a cowled merchant. The two older men appeared to be haggling over a bundle of what the farmer thought rather luxurious purple cloth.

"Aah! Good Uldyssian!" The trader prefaced everyone's name save those of his family with the word, something that always made Uldyssian smile. Cyrus did not even seem to notice that he did it. "How fare you and your brother?"

"We . . . we're fine, Master Cyrus."

"Good, good." And with that, the trader went back to his business. With but a ring of silvering hair around his otherwise clean pate and his scholarly eyes, Cyrus looked more like a cleric to the farmer than any of those wearing such robes. In fact, Uldyssian had heard far more sensible words from the man. He respected Cyrus greatly, in part because of how the trader, more educated than most in Seram, had taken Mendeln under his wing.

Thinking of his brother, who spent more time in this very building than he did at the farm, Uldyssian glanced around. Although Mendeln would have been clad in garments akin to his brother's—cloth tunic, kilt, and boots— and resembled his brother somewhat in the eyes and broad nose, one look at him by anyone would raise the question of whether he was actually a farmer. In truth, although he did help out at the farm, working the land was clearly not Mendeln's calling. He was always interested in studying *things*, be they bugs burrowing in the ground or words in some parchment loaned him by Cyrus.

Uldyssian could read and write, too, and was proud of that achievement, but he saw only the practical aspects of such a thing. There were times when pacts had to be made that required writing things down and then making certain that they said what they were supposed to. That, the older brother understood. Simply reading for reading's sake or studying merely to learn something of no use in their daily tasks . . . such a desire evaded Uldyssian.

He did not see his brother, who had this time ridden in with him, but something else caught his attention, a sight that brought back to him fully and painfully the memory of what had happened in the Boar's Head. At first glimpse, he thought the figure a companion of the missionary he had accosted, but then, as the young woman turned more in his direction, the farmer saw that she wore an entirely different set of robes. These were of a deep azure and had upon the breast a golden, stylized ram with great curled horns. Below the ram was an iridescent triangle whose tip jutted up just below the animal's hooves.

Her hair had been shorn to shoulder length and the face that the tresses framed was round, full of youth, and highly attractive. Yet there was, in Uldyssian's mind, something missing that removed for him any desire for her. It was as if she was an empty shell, not a whole person.

He had seen her like before. Zealous, an absolute believer in her faith. He had also seen the robes before, and the fact that she was alone made him suddenly eye the room with dread. They *never* traveled alone, always in threes. One for each of their order . . .

Serenthia was trying to show him some feminine bauble, but Uldyssian heard only her voice, not her words. He considered trying to back out of the chamber.

Then another figure joined the first, this one a middle-aged man of strong bearing and patrician features who, with his cleft chin and strong brow, would have appealed to the fairer sex as much as the girl would have the males. He wore a tight-collared golden robe that also bore the triangle, but this time above it was a green leaf.

The third of their band was nowhere to be seen, but Uldyssian knew that he or she could not be far away. The servants of the Temple of the Triune did not stay separated long. While a missionary from the Cathedral often worked alone, the Triune's acolytes acted in concert with one another. They preached the way of the Three, the guiding spirits—Bala, Dialon, and Mefis—who supposedly watched over a mortal like loving parents or kindly teachers. Dialon was the spirit of Determination, hence the stubborn ram. Bala stood for Creation, represented by the leaf. Mefis, whose servant was missing, was Love. The acolytes of that order bore upon their breast a red circle, the common Kehjan emblem for the heart.

Having heard the preachings of all three orders before and not wanting to risk a repeat of the debacle in the tavern, Uldyssian tried to shift into the shadows. Serenthia had finally realized that Uldyssian no longer listened to her. She put her hands on her hips and gave him the stare that, when she had been a child, had made him give in to her way.

"Uldyssian! I thought you wanted to see—"

He cut her off. "Serry, I've got to be going. Did your brothers gather what I asked for earlier?"

She pursed her lips as she thought. Uldyssian eyed the two missionaries, who seemed engrossed in some conversation. Both looked oddly disoriented, as if something had not gone as they had assumed it would.

"Thiel said nothing to me or else I'd have known you were in Seram before. Let me go find him and ask."

"I'll come with you." Anything to avoid the dogs of the Triune. The Temple had been established some years before the Cathedral, but now the two appeared more or less even in their influence. It was said that the High Magistrate of Kehjan was now a convert of the former, while the Lord General of the Kehjan Guard was rumored to be a member of the latter. The disarray within the mage clans—often bordering on war of late—had turned many to the comfort of one message or another.

But before Serenthia could lead them into the back, Cyrus called for his daughter. She gave Uldyssian an apologetic look.

"Wait here. I won't be long."

"I'll go look for Thiel myself," he suggested.

Serenthia must have caught his quick glance at the missionaries. Her expression grew reproving. "Uldyssian, not again."

"Serry—"

"*Uldyssian*, those people are messengers of holy orders! They mean you no harm! If you would just open yourself up to hearing them! I'm not suggesting you join one or the other, but the messages both preach are worthy of your attention."

She had reprimanded him like this before, just after he had stood up in the tavern after the last visit by missionaries from the Triune and gone on at length about the lack of need for *any* of their ilk in the lives of the common folk. Did the acolytes offer to help shear the sheep or bring in the crops? Did they help wash the mud-soaked clothes or lend their hands fixing the fences? No. Uldyssian had pointed out then, as he had on other occasions, that all they came to do was whisper in the ears of people that *their* sect was better than the other sect. This to people who barely understood the concept of angels and demons, much less believed in them.

"They can say all the pretty words they want, Serry, but all I see is them contesting against one another, with how many fools they can brand as their own as what decides the winner."

"Serenthia!" Cyrus called again. "Come here, lass!"

"Father needs me," she said with a rueful look. "I'll be right back. Please, Uldyssian, behave yourself."

The farmer watched her hurry off, then tried to fix his attention on some of the items for sale or barter in the station. There were tools of all sorts that could be useful on the farm, including hoes, shovels, and a variety of hammers. Uldyssian ran his finger over the edge of a new iron sickle. The craftsmanship was the best available in a place such as Seram, although he had heard that in some estate farms near Kehjan proper a few lords had their workers wielding ones tipped with steel. Such a concept had far more impact on Uldyssian than any words concerning spirits or souls.

Then someone quickly strode past him, heading into the back. He had a glimpse of golden hair bound up and a hint of a smile that the son of Diomedes could have sworn was directed toward him.

Without at first realizing it, Uldyssian followed. The noblewoman vanished through the back door as if the station were her own home.

He slipped through a moment later . . . and at first saw no sign of her. What he did see was that his wagon was indeed full. There was no sign of Thiel, but that was not uncommon. Serenthia's eldest brother was likely assisting with some other labor.

Having already dealt with the matter of payment, Uldyssian headed toward the wagon. However, as he neared, he suddenly saw a flash of green by the horse.

It was her. The noblewoman stood on the other side of the animal, murmuring something to it while she caressed the muzzle with one slender hand. Uldyssian's horse appeared mesmerized by her, standing as motionless as a statue. The old male was an ornery beast and only those who knew him well could approach him without the danger of a bite. That this woman could do so spoke volumes about her to the farmer.

She noticed him in turn. A smile lit up her face. To Uldyssian, her eyes seemed to glow.

"Forgive me . . . is this your horse?"

"It is, my lady . . . and you're lucky still to have more than one hand. He likes to bite."

She caressed the muzzle again. The beast continued to stand still. "Oh, he wouldn't bite me." The woman leaned her face close to the muzzle. "Would you?"

Uldyssian half-started toward her, suddenly fearful that she would be proven wrong. However, again, nothing happened.

"I once owned a horse that looked very much like him," she continued. "I miss him so."

Suddenly recalling where they were, Uldyssian said, "Mistress, you shouldn't be here. You should stay with the caravan." Sometimes, travelers journeyed with merchants in order to make use of the protection of the latter's guards. Uldyssian could only assume that this was the case with her, although so far it seemed that she was without any escort. Even with the protection of the caravan, a young woman traveling alone risked danger. "You don't want to be left behind."

"But I am not going with the caravan," the noblewoman murmured. "I am not going anywhere at all."

He could not believe that he had heard her correctly. "My lady, you must be joking! There's nothing for you in a place like Seram . . ."

"There's nothing for me in any other place . . . why not Seram, then?" Her mouth curled up in a hesitant smile. "And you need not keep calling me 'my lady' or 'mistress.' You may call me Lylia . . ."

Uldyssian opened his mouth to answer, only to hear the door swing open behind him and Serenthia's voice call, "There you are! Did you find Thiel?"

He looked over his shoulder at her. "No, but everything's here, Serry."

His horse suddenly snorted, then shied from him. Grabbing the bit, Uldyssian did his best to calm the cantankerous beast. The horse's eyes were wide and his nostrils flared; to his master he seemed startled or frightened. That made little sense, for the creature liked Serenthia more than he did Uldyssian. As for the noblewoman, she—

She was nowhere to be *seen*. Uldyssian surreptitiously surveyed the area, wondering how she could have possibly slipped away so quickly and without a sound. He had a fair view for some distance, but all he saw were a few other wagons. Unless she had climbed into one of the covered ones, the farmer could not possibly fathom what had happened to her.

Serenthia walked up to him, mildly curious at his behavior. "What are you looking for? Is something you needed missing, after all?"

He recovered enough to answer, "No . . . as I said, it's all here."

A familiar—and undesired—shape slipped through the doorway. The missionary glanced around as if searching for something or someone in particular.

"Yes, Brother Atilus?" asked Serenthia.

"I seek our Brother Caligio. Is he not in here?"

"No, brother, there's only the two of us."

Brother Atilus eyed Uldyssian without the usual religious fervor the farmer was accustomed to seeing from his ilk. Instead, the missionary's gaze held a hint of what seemed . . . suspicion?

Bowing his head to Serenthia, Atilus withdrew. Cyrus's daughter turned her attention back to Uldyssian. "Do you have to leave so soon? I know you feel uncomfortable around Brother Atilus and the others, but . . . couldn't you stay and visit with me a bit longer?"

For reasons that he could not explain, Uldyssian felt unsettled. "No . . . no, I've got to head back. Speaking of looking for someone, have you seen Mendeln? I expected him to be with your father."

"Oh, I should've told you! Achilios stopped by just a short time earlier. He had something he wanted to show to Mendeln and the two of them headed off for the western forest."

Uldyssian grunted. Mendeln had promised that he would be ready at the proper time to ride home with him. Generally, his brother was very good about keeping his word, but Achilios must have come across something unusual. Mendeln's greatest weakness was his incessant curiosity, something the hunter should have known better than to encourage. Once started on one of his studies, the younger son of Diomedes lost all track of time.

But although Uldyssian would not leave without his one remaining sibling, he did not want to be anywhere near the Triune's followers. "I can't stay. I'll lead the wagon out to the forest and hope that I find them. Should Mendeln somehow return here without me seeing him—"

"I'll tell him where you wait, yes." Serenthia did not attempt to hide her disappointment.

Feeling uncomfortable for a more normal reason, the farmer gave her a brief—and merely *friendly*—hug, and climbed aboard. Cyrus's daughter stepped back as he urged the old horse on.

He looked back in her direction as the wagon moved and the intensity of his expression made Serenthia's own countenance light up. Uldyssian paid her reaction no mind, for his thoughts were not on the trader's raven-haired daughter.

No, the face that had burned itself into his thoughts was that of another, one whose tresses were *golden*.

And one whose caste was far, far above that of a simple farmer.

Two

Mendeln was well aware that his brother would be angry with him, but his curiosity had complete rein of him now. Besides, it was all Achilios's fault, truly, and Achilios, at least, should have known better.

There was a good nine years' difference between the surviving sons of Diomedes, enough that in some ways the pair might as well have been considered other than brothers. Uldyssian often acted more like Mendeln's uncle or, indeed, their *father*. In fact, from what Mendeln could vaguely recall of his sire—combined with what Cyrus, Tibion, and a few elders had told him over the years—Uldyssian could have passed for Diomedes's twin in both look and manner.

Mendeln shared some of his brother's features, but was half a foot shorter than Uldyssian and, while strengthened by the necessities of farm life, was not nearly as mighty, either. His countenance was narrower and longer—from his mother's side, he was told—and he had eyes that were black and glistened like dark jewels. From where those had come, no one in the village could say, but Mendeln had learned early on that, if he stared, he could unsettle most anyone save his brother and the man now with him.

"What do you make of it?" Achilios muttered from behind.

Mendeln forced his gaze from the hunter's fascinating discovery. Achilios was a blond, wiry figure nearly as tall as Uldyssian. Unlike Mendeln, who was clad virtually

identically to his brother save for the darker shading of his
tunic, Achilios was dressed in a green and brown outfit
consisting of jerkin and pants that allowed him to blend
well into their present surroundings. He had soft leather
boots designed for padding as silently through the woods
as any animal. His slim frame hinted of his swiftness but
belied his strength. Uldyssian's brother had tried to string
and fire the great bow that was Achilios's pride and joy,
tried and failed. The hawk-faced archer was not just the
best at his craft among Seram's inhabitants, but—at least in
Mendeln's estimation—superior to many a hunter elsewhere. He had watched Achilios match skills against veteran guards from passing caravans and never had seen
him lose.

"It . . . looks ancient," was all Mendeln could finally
answer. He felt some embarrassment; even Achilios had
noticed *that*.

But the hunter nodded as if listening to a sage. Although
more than half a decade older than Mendeln, he treated the
youngest son of Diomedes as if Mendeln were the fount of
all the world's knowledge. That was one of the few points
of frustration between Achilios and Uldyssian, who saw little practical use in most of his sibling's learning, but did at
least tolerate it.

"The thing is . . . " The archer ran a hand through his
thick, almost leonine mane. " . . . I've been through this area
many a time and I swear that it's never been here before!"

Mendeln only nodded, his attention once more upon his
companion's find. Achilios had an eye such as he could
only envy, Mendeln's own vision often forcing him to peer
close at parchments in order to make out the words he so
cherished.

And at this particular thing, he peered especially close, for
the symbols etched in its face were, in many places, worn
almost clean away by weather and age. Some of them he
could not have made out even if his nose had been pressed
against the stone. Clearly, the object before him had suffered

long the effects of nature, and yet, how could that be, when it had, by Achilios's declaration, only just appeared?

Kneeling before it, Mendeln estimated the dimensions. Just over the length of his foot on each side of the square base and, had he been standing, a hand's breadth below his knee. The flat top was roughly half the dimensions of the base. In size alone, the stone carving should have been impossible to miss seeing.

He touched the ground before it. "Nothing of recent change in the surroundings?"

"No."

Mendeln traced his fingers almost reverently over some of the more legible symbols. Legible only in that he could see them, not understand them. One prominent marking seemed to loop in and around itself, giving it no end. As Mendeln touched it, he had a sense of incredible age.

He involuntarily shook his head. *Not age,* Uldyssian's brother thought, *but agelessness.*

Mendeln's mind paused at that sudden notion, never having conceived of it before. Agelessness. How could such a thing be possible?

The stone was black, but the markings glittered as if silver. That also fascinated him, for they did not appear to have been painted so. The skill with which the entire thing had been carved bespoke an artisan far more sophisticated than could be found in Seram or even in any of the larger settlements in the entire western region.

Belatedly, Mendeln realized that Achilios was shaking him by the shoulder. He wondered why. "What?"

The archer leaned warily over him, his brow furrowed deep in concern. "The moment you touched it, you seemed to still! You didn't blink and I'd swear you didn't breathe!"

"I . . . did not notice." Mendeln was tempted to touch the artifact again, fascinated to see if the same thing would happen. However, he suspected that Achilios would not like that. "Did you touch it earlier?"

There was a noticeable hesitation, then, "Yes."

"But the same thing did not happen to you, did it?"

Achilios's complexion went pale with memory. "No. No."

"Then, what? Did you feel anything?"

"I felt . . . I felt an emptiness, Mendeln. It reminded me of . . . of *death*."

As a hunter, the blond man dealt with death on an almost daily basis, usually because of the animals he killed, but occasionally because of close scrapes with wild boars, cats, or bears, where for a time he became the prey. Yet, the manner in which Achilios spoke of death now gave it a new and far more ominous connotation, one which, oddly, stirred further curiosity, not fear, in the heart of his companion.

"What *about* death?" Mendeln asked almost eagerly. "Can you describe it better? Was it—"

Achilios, expression suddenly guarded, cut him off with a sharp slash of his hand. "That's all. I went for you right after."

Clearly, there was much, much more involved, but Uldyssian's brother did not push. Perhaps he could slowly gain the information over time. For the moment, he would satisfy himself with the stone artifact. Mendeln seized a small broken branch and scraped the ground near the bottom edge. The mysterious relic appeared to be planted deep in the soil, but how far? Was there more beneath the surface than above? Again, the temptation came to touch it, this time grabbing hold with both hands in order to see if he could move the piece at all. How much more useful it would be if Mendeln could take it back to the farm so as to study it at his leisure.

Mendeln's head shot up. *The farm! Uldyssian!*

He leapt to his feet, startling the generally unperturbable Achilios. The stone's discovery seemed to have upset the archer in a way Mendeln had never seen before. Achilios was known for his fearlessness, but now he seemed to look to Mendeln for reassurance, certainly a first.

"I have to get back," he explained to the hunter. "Uldyssian will be wondering where I am." Mendeln did not like disappointing his older sibling, even though Uldyssian would not have shown any such emotion. Nevertheless, Mendeln lived with the memories of the terrible burdens Uldyssian had taken on with the sicknesses and, later, deaths of their loved ones. The younger brother felt beholden to the older for that reason, not to mention many other, lesser ones.

"What about *that*?" Achilios grumbled, gesturing at the stone with his bow. "Do we just leave it like that?"

After a moment's consideration, Mendeln replied, "We shall cover it over. Help me with it."

The two of them gathered loose branches and bits of leafy shrubbery. Yet, although they quickly had the artifact hidden from sight, Mendeln felt as if it still stood naked to the world. He considered covering it further, then decided to make do with what they had already done. The first opportunity he had to return to it, he would.

As Mendeln focused on the path back, he belatedly noticed that the weather had taken an odd and very sudden turn. The day had been fairly clear and bright before, but now clouds began to gather in earnest to the west, as if in preparation for a major storm. The wind had also begun to pick up.

"That's odd," murmured Achilios, also evidently seeing the change for the first time.

"It is, yes." Uldyssian's brother did not understand the wind and weather in terms of hunting, as his companion did, but rather in measurements of currents and such. Mendeln constantly saw the aspects of farm life in such terms, and while Uldyssian—who knew weather only in how it affected his crops and his animals—constantly shook his head at his brother's ways, he could not deny that once in a while Mendeln had come up with some idea that had helped ease their tasks a bit.

The clouds rapidly thickened. Mendeln said nothing more to Achilios about the strange weather, but at one point when the archer moved a step ahead, Uldyssian's brother glanced back in the direction of the stone.

Glanced back . . . and wondered.

* * *

Uldyssian, too, noticed the peculiar shift in the weather, but chalked it up to one of those quirks of nature to which a farmer had to grow accustomed. He hoped that Mendeln would return soon from wherever Achilios had dragged him. Even then, it was likely that the two brothers would have to make part of the journey home in the rain. The sudden accumulation above hinted at a particularly powerful storm brewing, but Uldyssian hoped that perhaps it would hold for a time before unleashing its full force. If he and Mendeln could at least make it past the low fork, where the trail often flooded, then they would be all right the rest of the way.

Hands clutching the reins, he sat on the wagon eyeing the direction in which Serenthia had indicated the pair had gone. Both Mendeln and Achilios surely had sense enough to see what he did and react properly . . . at least, Achilios did.

As he waited, his mind drifted back to a face framed in gold. Even though Uldyssian had seen her only two brief times, he knew that he would not soon forget the vision of her. It had been due to not merely her beauty—memorable enough by itself—but the manner in which she had talked and acted. There had been something about the noblewoman that had instinctively made Uldyssian want to protect her as he had no other, not even his brother at the time of their family's deaths.

Lylia. The farmer ran the name over and over in his thoughts, savoring the almost musical beauty of it.

The sky rumbled, finally jarring him back to the present. Recalling Mendeln, Uldyssian stood up in the hope of getting a better view. Surely the two had to be almost back in Seram by now.

A flash of green caught his attention, but not the green that made up part of the hunter's woodland garments. Rather, it was an emerald green that instantly caused Uldyssian to jolt to attention, his brother and friend utterly forgotten.

Lylia slowly strode into the woods beyond, leaving the

safety of the village. From her passive expression, it seemed very likely that she did not even notice the potential threat from the sky. In this region, the storms could suddenly grow so vicious as to uproot trees without warning.

Leaping down, Uldyssian secured the wagon, then headed after her. Although the farmer mostly ran after Lylia out of concern, excitement also filled him. He had no illusions about his chances with one of her blood, but at the same time his heart pounded at the thought of at least speaking with the noblewoman again.

Uldyssian caught sight of her again just as the wind doubled. Despite the worsening conditions, Lylia still appeared not to notice. Her lips were pursed and her gaze was fixed groundward.

Despite the swift pace Uldyssian kept, he did not manage to catch up to her until well into the woods. The towering farmer started to reach out a meaty hand, then thought better of it. He did not want to take any chance of frightening her more than he had to. Whatever weighed on her thoughts clearly weighed heavily.

Seeing no other option, Uldyssian cleared his throat.

Lylia straightened sharply, then looked behind her. "Oh! 'Tis you!"

"Forgive me, my lady—"

A shy smile immediately came to her lips. "I told you. To you, I am Lylia. What I once was, I can never be again." As his expression turned to one of confusion, she added, "But what do I call you, sir farmer?"

He had not realized that he had never introduced himself. "I am Uldyssian, son of Diomedes." A rattle of thunder reminded him of their current circumstances. "My—Lylia, you shouldn't be out here. There's what seems to be a fierce storm brewing! Best if you seek shelter, likely in the tavern. It's one of the strongest of buildings in Seram."

"A storm?" She glanced skyward and for the first time appeared to register the change. The clouds had thickened to the point that day had almost turned to night.

Daring her disdain, he finally took hold of Lylia by the wrist. "There doesn't look to be much time!"

But Lylia instead turned her gaze in another direction . . . and a breath later let out a small gasp.

Uldyssian followed her eyes, but saw nothing. Nonetheless, the noblewoman stood frozen, as if whatever had caught her attention shocked her senseless.

"Lylia . . . Lylia, what is it?"

"I thought I saw . . . I thought . . . but, no . . ."

Even when he stood next to her, the farmer could see no cause for her alarm. "Where is it? What did you see?"

"There!" She pointed at a particularly dense area of the woods. "I . . . think . . ."

He was tempted to simply take her back to Seram and return after the storm, but the intensity of her reaction made him worry about what lay out there. Mendeln suddenly came to mind. Mendeln, who was still missing.

"Stay here." Uldyssian started forward, at the same time drawing his knife.

The brush thickened and at times the wild grass rose as high as his waist. How Lylia had seen *anything* was beyond him, but he trusted that this was no wild-goose chase.

Then, as he neared the area in question, Uldyssian's hackles rose. A sense of dread rushed over him, nearly causing the stalwart farmer to backtrack.

A faint but sickly scent wafted under his nose. It brought back memories of the plague, of his family . . .

Uldyssian did not want to take another step closer and yet, he did.

The sight before him made the farmer fall to one knee. It was all he could do to keep his last meal in his stomach. His knife slipped from his hand, utterly forgotten in the face of the horrific revelation before him.

What had once been a man—at least, from the height, Uldyssian decided it must be so—lay strewn across the patch of ground at the base of the first trees. His entire torso had been expertly sliced open, much the way the farmer would have done to a cow after slaughter. Blood soaked everything in the immediate vicinity and had turned the dirt in some places to crimson mud. Part of the victim's own stomach had poured out of the cut and flies already clustered over the tremendous, stench-ridden bounty.

As if cutting open the body had not been terrible enough, the throat had been slit open sideways, the gap large enough to admit a fist. The face was covered with blood from the wounds, and leaves and other refuse decorated it like some bizarre festival display. After a long study, Uldyssian finally determined that he did not know the man, who was roughly his age and with black hair now caked with gore.

It was what remained of the shredded garments that finally identified the unfortunate figure for the son of Diomedes. The robes's coloring alone was sufficient in itself, but the symbol of the missionary's order left no doubt whatsoever.

Uldyssian had found Brother Caligio, the missing acolyte from the Triune.

A gasp from behind startled him. He spun about to see Lylia, eyes wide, taking in the awful sight.

She suddenly went pale. Her eyes fluttered upward, showing only whites . . . and then she began to fall.

Pushing himself to his feet, Uldyssian managed to catch her just before she could strike the ground. He held her prone body for a moment, at a loss what to do. Someone had to be told about the murder, likely Captain Tiberius, chief of the Seram Guard. Dorius, the village's leader, would also need to know.

In his arms, the noblewoman moaned. Uldyssian decided that, first, he had to take care of Lylia.

Fortunately, it took little effort for the towering farmer to carry her. Uldyssian moved at as swift a pace as he could without risking his precious burden. He had to watch his footing at all times, fearful that one false step would send both of them crashing.

It was with great relief that Uldyssian reached the edge of

the village. The sky continued to thunder loudly, but the storm so far held back.

"Uldyssian!"

He stumbled at the sound of his name, nearly tossing Lylia away in the process. The farmer managed to steady himself, then looked to the source of the call.

A great fear lifted off his chest as Mendeln and Achilios came rushing up to him. They had clearly just arrived themselves. Mendeln was slightly out of breath and Achilios had a pale expression that the elder son of Diomedes suspected mirrored his own . . . even though Achilios could not yet know about the grisly discovery.

As the pair came up to him, he immediately growled, "There's a body out in the woods behind me! Near where the forest first thickens!"

Eyeing the farmer's burden, the hunter muttered, "An accident?"

"No . . ."

Achilios grimly nodded. He pulled a bolt from his quiver, notched the bow, and without hesitation went off in the direction Uldyssian had indicated.

"What of her?" Mendeln asked. "Who is she? Is she harmed in any way?"

"She fainted." Uldyssian felt unusually anxious. He kept hoping that Lylia would awaken, but she remained a limp bundle in his arms. "She saw the body, too."

"Should we take her to Jorilia?" Jorilia was Seram's healer woman, an elderly figure some believed half-witch, but who was respected by all for her skills. It was she who had given the brothers the herbal mixtures that had at least eased some of their stricken family's agony. To both Uldyssian and Mendeln, she had done far more than all the prayers combined.

Uldyssian shook his head. "She just needs to rest. She must have a room at the Boar's Head." He hesitated. "But we can't bring her through the front door like this . . ."

"There is a back way near the steps leading to the upper

rooms," Mendeln said with far more calm than the situation would have warranted for most other people. "You could take her through there while I go and speak quietly with Tibion in order to find which one is hers."

His brother's suggestion made perfect sense. Uldyssian exhaled gratefully. "We'll do that."

Mendeln studied him for a moment, perhaps reading deeper into his brother than Uldyssian preferred. As far as the younger son of Diomedes was concerned, Lylia was a perfect stranger, yet clearly she was not so with Uldyssian.

Rather than explain all now, Uldyssian hurried on. A moment later, Mendeln caught up. They spoke no more, intent on their efforts.

Owing to the inclement shift in the weather, they were not hindered by any startled passersby. That both pleased and frustrated Uldyssian, who wanted Lylia safely in her room but also wanted to let someone of authority know about the acolyte's heinous slaughter. He finally satisfied himself with the knowledge that Achilios would certainly contact the Guard or the headman.

Mendeln left him as the pair neared the Boar's Head. Slipping around the back, Uldyssian found the other doorway. With some manipulation, he managed to get the noblewoman inside without losing his grip on her once.

Inside, he wasted no time heading up the wooden staircase. Fortunately, most eyes in the tavern section had turned to his brother, who had apparently timed his entrance to coincide with Uldyssian's. As Uldyssian raced up, he heard Mendeln greet a couple of those seated with a slightly louder than average voice.

At the top, he waited. After what seemed an eternity, his younger brother finally joined him.

"She had no quarters," Mendeln explained. "So I had to arrange for some, with our credit. Was that all right?"

Uldyssian nodded. He looked at the five doors. "Which?"

"This one," his sibling replied, pointing to a lone door farther from the rest. "More private."

With a look of grim approval, Uldyssian had Mendeln open the way for him. This being Seram, the room was fairly austere. Other than a framed bed with down comforter and a table and chair near the single window, there was no furniture. There were hooks on the wall for cloaks and such and a space for a traveler's bag or trunk.

Mendeln noted the last before Uldyssian could say anything. "She must have belongings with the caravan. Shall I go to Serenthia and take care of it?"

While he hated involving Cyrus's daughter in this situation, Uldyssian could see no other choice. "Go ahead."

Mendeln paused at the door. Meeting his brother's gaze, he asked, "How do you know this woman?"

"We met by chance," was all Uldyssian would return. After a moment, Mendeln finally nodded and left the room.

Gently placing the noblewoman on the bed, the farmer paused to look at her. Again, he was struck by the perfection of her face and wondered what could have sent her wandering alone in the world. Certainly, Lylia could have found a good marriage with many a wealthy noble. Was she related by blood, perhaps, to one of the losing mage clans? That might explain the matter . . .

As he pondered this, her eyes abruptly opened. Gasping, Lylia bolted into a sitting position.

"What . . . what happened?"

"Do you remember the woods?"

Her hand went to her mouth as she stifled another gasp. "It was all . . . all true, then? What I . . . saw?"

Uldyssian nodded.

"And you . . . you brought me here . . . where *is* here?"

"The Boar's Head. It's the only inn in Seram, miss—Lylia. We thought you likely had a room here."

"But I do not—"

He shrugged. "My brother took care of that; then we brought you up here. After that, Mendeln went to retrieve your things from the caravan."

She stared long and hard into his eyes. "Mendeln and your brother . . . they are the same person, I gather?"

"Yes."

The noblewoman nodded to herself, then asked, "And the . . . the body?"

"A friend is looking into it. He can be trusted to deal with the matter properly. Achilios will alert the Guard, then our headman."

Lylia drew her knees up to her chin, then hugged her legs. That she badly wrinkled her elegant gown, she did not seem to care. "Was the . . . was the man we found also a friend of yours?"

"Him?" Uldyssian shook his head. "A damned missionary . . . from the Temple of the Triune. His companions were looking for him earlier." He considered. "They came with the caravan. Did you—"

"I saw them, yes, but never spoke. I have little trust in their teachings . . . or that of the Cathedral, for that matter."

This admission, so near to his own thoughts concerning the two sects, inexplicably lightened Uldyssian's heart. Then the farmer quickly berated himself. However much his calling repelled Uldyssian, the man had not deserved such a monstrous end.

Thinking of that, Uldyssian knew that he had to go and see to the situation. As the one to initially come across the dead missionary, it behooved him to tell the village officials what he knew.

His brow arched as he considered the noblewoman. He would avoid speaking of Lylia as much as possible. She had already been through too much.

"I want you to stay here," he commanded, inwardly stunned that he should talk to a lady of high caste so. "Stay here and rest. I have to see those who'll deal with the body. You needn't come."

"But I should be there . . . should I not?"

"Only if necessary. You merely saw what I saw, after all. And you didn't know him, either."

She said nothing more, but Uldyssian had the clear impression that Lylia knew that he risked his reputation by protecting her so. The noblewoman leaned back on the bed.

"Very well. If that is what you wish. I will wait until I hear from you."

"Good." He started for the door, already formulating his explanation.

"Uldyssian?"

He looked at her.

"Thank you."

Face flushing, the farmer exited. Despite his size, he moved silently down the steps. At the bottom, he glanced into the tavern. Everyone he saw acted as if nothing was wrong, which meant that news of the corpse had not yet filtered inside. Achilios could be thanked for that discretion. Seram would be in shock soon enough, the last murder having taken place more than four years ago and that due to a drunken altercation between old Aronius and his stepson, Gemmel, over farming rights, with the latter coming out the loser. Once sober, Aronius had pleaded his guilt and had been driven off by wagon to the great city to dutifully pay for his deeds.

But the butchery Uldyssian had witnessed had not been due to strong drink. This looked more the work of some madman or beast. Surely an outsider, some brigand passing through the region.

Growing more certain of this with each breath, Uldyssian vowed to bring it up the moment that he spoke with the headman and the Guard commander. The men of Seram would be more than willing to volunteer to search the area for the bastard. This time, the crime would be handled locally; a good strong rope would end the matter as it should. It was all such a fiend deserved.

He opened the back door and slipped out—

"There! That is the man of whom I speak!"

Uldyssian retreated into the doorway, startled. Before him stood Tiberius—a beefy man against whom the farmer had wrestled during festival events and *lost* to more than he had won—and gray-haired, vulpine Dorius, who was staring at Uldyssian as if never having seen him before. Behind them stood more than a dozen other men, most of them from the Guard, but also Achilios . . . and the two other acolytes of the Temple. The older male was, in fact, the one who had spoken and now stood pointing accusingly at the perplexed farmer.

Recovering, he looked to the hunter. "Did you tell them everything?"

Before Achilios could answer, Dorius interjected, "You're not to speak to him, hunter. Not yet. Not until all the facts be known."

"The facts *are* known!" declared the Triune's emissary. His female companion nodded over and over as he spoke. At the moment, there seemed nothing pious or peaceful about the pointing figure. "*You* are the one responsible! Your own words brand you! Confess for the sake of your soul!"

Uldyssian fought to keep his distaste for the acolyte from overcoming his reason. If he understood the man correctly, then the farmer had just been accused of the very murder he had been trying to warn them about.

"Me? You think *I* did it? By the stars, I should take you and—"

"Uldyssian . . ." murmured Achilios anxiously.

The son of Diomedes regained control. To the archer, he said, "Achilios! I told you where to find the body! You saw my expression and—" He halted, not wishing to draw in Lylia. "—and you know me! Dorius! You were friends with my father! I swear by his grave that I'm not the fiend who so foully slew this jabbering fool's comrade!"

He would have gone on, but the headman waved him silent. His expression stern, Dorius replied, "'Tis not *him* we speak about at the moment, Uldyssian. Nay, we speak of the other . . . though it might very well be that we'll need to be returning to that before long, as I don't believe in no coincidence."

"'Other'? What other?"

Captain Tiberius snapped his fingers. Instantly, half a dozen men—half a dozen men whom Uldyssian had known from childhood on—moved to surround the farmer.

Achilios tried to intercede. "Dorius, is this necessary? This is *Uldyssian*."

"Your word's respected, young Achilios, but this is duty." The headman nodded to the man in the circle. "I'm certain that it'll all be working out, Uldyssian. Just let us do what the situation demands!"

"But for *what?*"

"For possibly murdering a man," grunted Captain Tiberius, one hand on the sword at his side. Uldyssian had seen the Guard commander carry the weapon only a few times in all the years he had known him, with all but one of those being for the aforementioned festivals and other special events.

The lone exception had involved the murder of Gemmel.

Shaking his head, the farmer roared, "But I told you that I *didn't* slay his companion!"

"'Tis not him we're talking about," Dorius declared. "But it's one of a similar calling, which makes this worse, young Uldyssian. It's the one hailing from the Cathedral of Light who's been found slain . . ."

"The one . . ." Uldyssian trailed off, his thoughts in turmoil. *But I just spoke to the man a short time ago! Less than an hour, if even half that!*

Spoke to the man . . . and *threatened* him in the process before several witnesses . . .

"Aye, you recall him, I see. Yes, young Uldyssian, the honored emissary of the Cathedral was found with his throat cut open . . . and 'tis your *knife* jutting out of the gap made!"

THREE

Uldyssian had never paid much mind to the interior of the Guard building. It was one of those places the farmer passed constantly, but, as he had never been arrested for drunkenness or fighting, there had been no reason for him to ever enter it.

But now he sat in one of the two barred rooms in the back quarter. To reach them, visitors—and prisoners—had to enter an inner wooden door and walk down a short corridor. Uldyssian, sitting in the first cell, felt entirely cut off from the world. A worn wooden bench acted as chair, table, and bed. Uldyssian had lived here for four days now, two days in which his farm had been left all but unattended. The crops needed weeding and irrigating and the animals had to be cared for. Mendeln had promised to see to everything, but Uldyssian feared that his brother was not up to such a task on his own, especially while also worrying about his elder sibling. Moreover, while the earlier storm had, ironically, blown itself out fairly quickly and with little violence, the clouds had remained over Seram since then and Uldyssian feared that another tempest—and perhaps a greater one—might follow. The farm had been fortunate the first time, but a second assault might throw it into a turmoil from which it could not survive.

He knew that the farm should have been the least of his worries. The situation involving the murders had grown even worse than Uldyssian had imagined it could. With both victims members of the leading sects, Dorius had felt

compelled to send word to Tulisam, where the Cathedral
and the Temple had a permanent presence. He had
requested that representatives from one or both come to
help oversee the matter. The two surviving missionaries
had ridden along with those messages, supposedly in
order to give testimony to their particular masters. In addition, while the headman continued to promise Uldyssian
that all would turn out well in the end, he had insisted that
Captain Tiberius keep the son of Diomedes locked up for
that time, lest there be some question as to Seram's notions of
justice for the victims.

Uldyssian remained dumbstruck by what had happened to the second missionary. According to a more
detailed story told him later by the erstwhile Guard commander, the Cathedral's emissary had been found on his
back, his face contorted in what Tiberius freely called
"absolute" fear and the farmer's knife—upon whose
wooden handle Uldyssian had made his mark—thrust
deep into the rib cage.

Compared with the corpse that *he* had discovered, the
second body had barely been touched. That, however, made
the crime no less terrible. In fact, no one could recall such a
multiple tragedy since the plague had swept through . . . the
same plague that had taken Uldyssian's family.

Serenthia came to visit him each day, giving him hopeful
word from many others unable to do the same. The consensus by those who knew him was that Uldyssian was utterly
innocent. Achilios had already blackened the eye of one
man who had suggested otherwise.

As Uldyssian sat with his head in his hands, he thought
not of himself, but of Lylia. She had not come to him once
since his incarceration, not that he had expected her.
Indeed, the farmer hoped that she would continue to stay
away, lest she somehow be drawn into the madness. Soon,
he kept promising himself, soon he would be released and
then the two of them could meet again.

If she even remained in Seram . . .

Thought of never seeing the noblewoman again fueled

Uldyssian's already tremendous anxiety. His entire life seemed to have turned into some nightmare. He had not even felt this way when his family had died, but now those memories, too, added their terrible weight to his already overburdened shoulders.

Not for the first time, the walls of his tiny chamber seemed to close in on him. Uldyssian had been born and raised on the farm. He had never known anything else but freedom. When his mother had perished, Uldyssian had run out into the fields and shouted out his agony, aware that only his brother was there to hear him.

I've got to get out . . . I've got to get out . . . The words ran through his mind over and over, swelling in significance with each repetition. Uldyssian stared bleary-eyed at the door to his cell, unable to accept the bars and the lock. Animals were kept locked up in pens, not *him*. Not—

There was a slight groan and a click.

The cell door swung back with a metallic squeal.

Uldyssian threw himself against the back wall as it happened. He watched in utter amazement as the door swung completely around, clanging against another part of the barred front.

The entrance to the cell stood wide open before Uldyssian, but the farmer made no move whatsoever toward it. He had no idea what had just happened, and despite his deep desire to be out of this place, the doorway enticed him not in the least.

At that moment, the wooden door down the hall also opened. Tiberius and two of his men marched down the halls toward the cells.

When he saw Uldyssian's cell, the captain came to a jarring halt. "What the—"

Recovering, he snapped his fingers and the two guards leapt into the cell to cover the prisoner. As they kept Uldyssian at bay, Tiberius inspected the door.

"No scratches, no damage at all." He glared at the farmer. "Search him for anything that could be used for a key."

The guards did so. However, they came up empty-handed, just as Uldyssian knew that they would.

Tiberius stepped up to his prisoner. Waving the guards back, he leaned close and whispered, "I don't like having you here any more than you like being here, Uldyssian. You may not believe this, old friend, but I don't think you any more guilty than I am for what happened to those two."

"Then, why—"

"This may only be Seram, but I'll run the Guard here like it's Kehjan itself! My father served in the Guard there for three years and then ran things here! I'll not dishonor his memory by failing in my duty. We do this as decreed, however disdainful it may seem."

While Uldyssian could respect Tiberius's position, it did nothing to assuage him. "I just want this over with! I've done nothing!"

"And that'll be proven. You'll see." The captain gestured at the door. "But that'll only make matters worse . . ."

"I didn't do that! It just opened on its own."

Tiberius looked disappointed. "I expected better of you, Uldyssian. There's nothing wrong with that door. I checked."

"I swear by my father!"

With a deepening frown, the captain grunted, then turned away. He stepped out of the cell, the guards following. One of the men shut the door, then tested it to make certain it would stay shut.

"It's locked tight," the man declared to his commander. Nevertheless, Tiberius checked it himself by seizing the door with both hands and throwing his full weight back. The entire cell wall rattled, but held firmly in place.

Captain Tiberius let go. Despite the display, he leaned against the bars and said to the farmer, "Don't do it again. I might have to give an order I wouldn't like to see fulfilled. Just be patient, Uldyssian."

The anxious—and thoroughly baffled—prisoner could only nod. Satisfied, the captain led his men off.

One of the guards came back a short time later with a

bowl of stew. He tested the door yet again, then, with a nod, slid the farmer's meal through.

As he ate, Uldyssian tried to ponder once more what was taking the matter so long. He was clearly innocent. He also wondered how the true murderer could have moved so swiftly. It had only been a short time between the moment of the first grisly discovery and when the Cathedral's missionary had been slain. The fiend would have had to almost fly from one to the other the moment that he had the farmer's knife. Uldyssian ruled out Achilios as the possible madman; the hunter was not only too good of a man, he was a true friend . . . and he had also been with Mendeln during the entire incident.

Then . . . who?

Footsteps echoed down the corridor, but footsteps much lighter, more delicate, than the tramping boots of Tiberius and his men. Uldyssian looked up . . . and beheld Lylia nearing.

"I had to see you," she murmured, her smile hesitant. Clearly she feared that he would be angry about her disobedience.

But at this point, Uldyssian could not reprimand her. She had waited a long time. He was even grateful that the noblewoman had not simply fled Seram, abandoning him to his fate.

Still, he started his greeting by saying, "You shouldn't be here."

"I couldn't stay in my room any longer. This is wrong! It's happening all over again!"

"What do you mean?"

She pressed herself against the bar. Uldyssian put down the bowl and went to her. He had a great urge to crush her in his arms in order to comfort her. He felt as if *she* were the one in danger, not him.

"You were kind to a stranger," she whispered, her hand reaching through the bars to touch his. "A stranger with nowhere to go. Do you know why?" Lylia looked down.

"Because of the game between the Cathedral and the Temple!"

"The *what?*"

Her eyes shifted up to his, their beauty seizing his gaze. He wanted to drown himself in those eyes. "The *game*. This is all a game to them, with the winner being the one who survives. They will let nothing and no one stand in their way and one thing that both despise is a heretic."

Uldyssian did not like where the conversation seemed to be heading. "What . . . what do you mean, Lylia?"

She glanced back toward the door leading to the cells, then, maintaining her whisper, replied, "This has happened before. With my family. We had influence and wealth, both of which the two sought for their own. But we rejected them publicly . . . and then our world turned upside down! There was violence, the burning of a minor temple, with many of the faithful injured terribly. The fire spread to other buildings nearby. Afterward, it was somehow found that the tragedy had been of human making and that *my* family had some tie to it."

He gaped.

"All lies!" she quickly added, clearly taking his shock for belief in her family's guilt. However, Uldyssian by no stretch of the imagination suspected Lylia of such horror . . . and, by extension, her loved ones, either.

"I believe you," he quickly told her. "I believe you. Go on."

"While we had rejected them, there were others, far more powerful, who had embraced one or the other sect. Accused without true proof, my family was nevertheless stripped of *everything*. My father and mother were dragged off, never to be seen again! My brother was sent to the dungeons and my sister forced to wed one of the Cathedral's most prominent supporters! A similar fate was intended for me, but I took what money I could get and fled from the city . . ."

"And that's how you ended up in Seram?"

"Not at first . . . and certainly not in the company of those serving the very evil I sought to escape!" She bit her lip. "I've told you so much . . . now I suddenly fear that you might think that *I* might be responsible for what happened to the two!"

Uldyssian immediately shook his head. "That's hardly possible! This was done by someone much stronger and certainly more monstrous than you could *ever* be! It makes more sense that they would suspect *me!*" But something dark occurred to him. "Tell no one else this, though! They might think that I did it on your behest!"

She put a hand to her mouth at this realization. "I did not think—"

"Never mind. It'd be best if you leave and don't come back. Things will be all right—"

"But they won't be! I heard at the inn! There are Inquisitors from the Cathedral of Light arriving tomorrow and someone hinted of Peace Warders from the Temple soon after! It's happening just the same as with me!"

Her announcement jolted him. He had been told nothing of Inquisitors or Peace Warders coming to Seram. The arms of justice for each of the two sects, the two groups acted as judges and guards. True, this involved the slaughter of their own, but where Uldyssian was concerned, there was hardly a need for either element.

The farmer stood there for a moment, trying to think. It was the noblewoman, however, who spoke first.

"We made the mistake of letting them act before we did, Uldyssian! You cannot let that happen! They will twist everything around, so that even if you are innocent, your guilt will be obvious to all! You have to stand up to them! Speak out defiantly, as you have always done! Your friends will rally to you, I know it! Neither the Cathedral nor the Temple will be able to use your hatred of them against you, then!"

"I—" There were points he would have argued, but they faded to nothing under the arresting beauty of those eyes. He finally decided that Lylia was right; Uldyssian would make use of the lesson of her family to save himself . . . and her, too.

"You must do it . . ." she breathed. "Please . . . for our sake . . ."

Without warning, the noblewoman pulled his face close to the bars, then kissed him. As the farmer stood there, completely at a loss, Lylia, her face scarlet, fled the area.

Uldyssian watched her vanish. Blinking, he suddenly recalled the door. As the guard had done, the farmer tested it. The door held, as it should have.

To Uldyssian, that settled everything. Lylia was absolutely right. He needed to stand up for himself. The Inquisitors—and the Peace Warders, assuming that they, too, were on their way—would be looking for guilt, not innocence.

He would do his best to leave them disappointed.

Serenthia pulled back out of sight of the Guard headquarters as Lylia passed. She had no real reason for doing so, save for what she realized was likely jealousy in what to her had been a ridiculously short time, Uldyssian had clearly fallen for the blond woman. She had been able to do with her mere appearance what Serenthia had for years often hoped of doing. Even as a child, she had been fascinated by Uldyssian's perseverance, his inner strength, especially the way in which he had managed the terrible deaths in his family.

Lylia vanished in the direction of the Boar's Head. Cyrus's daughter waited a few moments more, then stepped from behind the corner of the smithy—

At which point she collided with Achilios.

"Serry!" he managed. "Where did you—"

"I'm so sorry!" Serenthia felt her face flush. While she had spent much of her life pursuing Uldyssian, Achilios had done the same in regards to her. It was not unflattering, either, for he was handsome and well respected and treated her the way a woman wanted to be treated. Common sense said that the trader's daughter should have accepted his courting with pleasure, but although Serenthia welcomed the hunter's company, she could just not yet give up on her dream of gaining Uldyssian's love.

Of course, that had been before the arrival of Lylia.

"I was looking for Mendeln," Achilios finally managed, his own countenance somewhat reddened. "But this is a happy accident!"

His cheerfulness did not suit her at the moment, not with Uldyssian locked up for foul deeds he could never in his life have committed. Her annoyance with Achilios's pleasantry must have shown, for the hunter quickly sobered.

"Forgive me! I didn't mean to be light! Were you on your way to see Uldyssian?"

"Yes . . . but I didn't wish to disturb him. He had another visitor."

"Oh?" The hunter's brow arched. "Ah! The fair Lylia . . ."

It made matters worse to Serenthia to hear Achilios also mention her in such terms. Yes, the noblewoman was beautiful, but Cyrus's daughter knew that she could attract the attention of men, too . . . with the exception of the one she wanted.

"She just left. I think I saw her return to the inn."

Achilios rubbed his chin. "I wonder how that went over with Uldyssian. He said that he wanted her to stay away, so that she wouldn't be drawn into the situation any more than necessary."

Serenthia had a twinge of hope that perhaps Lylia had angered Uldyssian with her visit, but immediately after suspected that such was not the case. Like most men, he had surely forgiven her once she had gazed up at him or smiled.

She recalled Achilios's question. "I haven't seen Mendeln. In fact, I haven't seen him in two days. Has he been to his brother, even?"

"Not since early three days ago, from what I know," answered the archer, much perturbed now. "And when I rode out to the farm, I found young Justivio—Marcus ul-Amphed's second son—doing the chores there. He said that Mendeln paid him for the work without explaining where he planned to go."

Serenthia could understand why Mendeln might have left the farm in the hands of someone more competent than himself, but that he had not ridden to his brother's side immediately after—and then stayed there—she could not fathom. Mendeln was very loyal to Uldyssian and when he had heard the news concerning his brother he had denied the charges with far more vehemence than any would have expected from the scholarly sibling.

"I worry about him, Serry," Achilios went on. "I doubt that he can imagine the world without Uldyssian—which is not my way of saying that Uldyssian is in any danger of being condemned for those awful crimes! No, I'm speaking only of Mendeln. He's not been the same since we—since that day."

It almost sounded to Cyrus's daughter as if Achilios had been about to speak of something other than the murders, but what could possibly compare, she could not say.

"It could be that he is with Father," Serenthia finally suggested. "I haven't been there since this morning."

"Perhaps . . . I wonder . . ." The hunter's gaze shifted away, as if something else had come to mind. He gave a minute shake of his head, then added, "You should go on with your visit with Uldyssian, Serry. I'll find Mendeln soon, I'm certain. You just don't—"

His mouth snapped shut and his eyes now stared wide and disturbed at something beyond his companion. Fearful that she already knew just what that might be, the black-tressed woman followed his gaze.

The party of riders had just reached the edge of the village. They rode slowly and confidently, looking as if they owned all they surveyed. There was no mistaking them for what they were, the glistening silver robes and breastplates obvious sign enough even without the golden sunburst set in the center of the latter to definitively mark them as of the Inquisitors of the Cathedral of Light. All wore round, crested helmets atop their heads save for the lead rider, whose thick gray mane was draped by a golden hood. Behind him flowed the rest of the shimmering cloak, the bottom hem nearly blinding the horse behind his own. The cleric was clean-shaven, as were all those who served directly under the Prophet. This was not mere personal choice, but a purposeful decision. After all, the Prophet himself himself wore no beard . . . and, if rumor be true, looked young enough to be this cleric's grandson despite supposedly being much older.

The party numbered a dozen at least, a number that startled both onlookers. Dorius had given every indication that he had expected two at most and none of them of such authority as he who now dismounted.

The Master Inquisitor—Serenthia knew that the distinguished figure could have no lesser role—surveyed Seram as if uncertain that this backwater could be his destination. He suddenly noted the pair and immediately signaled them to approach. Well aware that this man held much sway over Uldyssian's fate, Serenthia obeyed instantly, with the archer but a step behind.

"I am Brother Mikelius!" boomed the Master Inquisitor, as if seeking to announce it to every inhabitant within a mile. "Is this then Seram, the scene of such terrible doings?"

"This is Seram, yes, Holiness," Serenthia responded meekly, curtsying at the same time. Unlike Uldyssian or Achilios, she had some belief in the teachings of both the Cathedral and the Triune, but had yet to decide which was her preference. The Triune taught of the power of the individual, while the Cathedral preached that it was Humanity's combined efforts that would best see it achieve its ultimate destiny.

"Who is in charge? We were supposed to be met."

"Our headman is Dorius, who—"

Brother Mikelius cut her off. "Never mind! You!"

He pointed at Achilios. "You know where the body of our unfortunate brother lies?"

Following Serenthia's example, the hunter bowed. "I believe I know where he was buried." When the Master Inquisitor frowned, Achilios added, "It's been several days, Holiness. Both bodies had to be put to rest or else they . . ." He spread his hands. "Well, you understand."

"Of course, my son, of course. Lead us to the grave, then."

"With due respect, Holiness, it would be proper if Master Dorius or Captain Tiberius led you to—"

"We are here," declared Brother Mikelius firmly. "They are not. We shall speak with them at first possible opportunity . . . and the barbarous heretic, too."

Serenthia stifled a sound at this description of Uldyssian. She wondered what Dorius's messenger had relayed to the Master Inquisitor. Brother Mikelius sounded certain that the true murderer had already been caught.

"Your Holiness—" she began.

But Brother Mikelius had already started past her, four of his guards accompanying him. The rest of his party began fanning out as if preparing to attack Seram and, in truth, they looked capable of winning such a battle, even outnumbered as they were.

"It's this way," Achilios said with a tone of surrender.

The Master Inquisitor paid Serenthia no further mind, but at the same time he also did not keep her from following. Cyrus's daughter wanted to run to Uldyssian and warn him of the Cathedral's arrival, but she also did not want to miss whatever Brother Mikelius might say or do, even if Achilios was also there to witness it.

Several villagers, perhaps alerted by the Master Inquisitor's loud voice, stepped out to see what was going on. Brother Mikelius acknowledged them with an occasional wave and pious nod as he strode commandingly toward the burial sites.

The sky rumbled, but otherwise the late day seemed oddly calm. There was not even the least wind, something unusual. As Serenthia entered the village cemetery behind the others, she felt as if the spirits of the dead all stood hushed around them.

A dank, stone wall waist high surrounded the grounds, here and there broken areas speaking of some neglect. It was not difficult to find where the victims had been buried, for not only were they the only fresh graves, but they were in a corner far from the rest. Unspoken by all the villagers was the hope that their interment was only temporary and that the Cathedral and the Temple would claim their own and thus allow Seram to forget what had happened.

Whether or not her village would ever forget, Serenthia saw that it was indeed Brother Mikelius's intention to do something with the body of the dead acolyte. He gestured at a pair of shovels set next to the side wall and two of his armed escort immediately went to retrieve them.

"This will be far enough for you," the Master Inquisitor said to Achilios . . . and by way of that, to the trailing Serenthia. "This is now a matter for the Cathedral alone."

The hunter wisely bowed, then stepped back. Crudely etched into the wooden markers over each of the graves was the sign of that victim's calling. Brother Mikelius sniffed at the one signifying the Triune, then proceeded to the other. The two guards wielding shovels followed at his heels.

The Master Inquisitor went down on one knee before the marker. He ran a gloved finger over the symbol on the marker, then, muttering under his breath what Serenthia supposed was a prayer, set his hand on the top of the mound.

And almost immediately thereafter, pulled it back as if scorpions had suddenly sprouted out of the dirt in great numbers.

His countenance more grim than ever, Brother Mikelius leaned forward again, then removed from around his neck a chain that his robe had hidden. At the end of the chain was a golden medallion in the shape of a sunburst. The centerpiece was a clear gemstone that glistened even despite the cloud cover.

The cleric held the medallion over the spot in question, muttered for a moment more, then drew back, once again seemingly aghast.

Eyes blazing, Brother Mikelius turned on the two. "Who has done this? Who dares this sacrilege?"

Achilios looked at her, but she had no explanation for him. The Master Inquisitor stood straight, then pointed at the grave. "You! By your garments and that bow, I gather you to be a huntsman!"

"That I am."

"Then, you have a practiced eye. Use it! Come close and tell me what you see!"

Achilios reluctantly obeyed. Under the watchful glances of the Inquisitor guards, he stepped up to the mound.

"Look close," demanded Brother Mikelius.

As Serenthia watched, Achilios knelt just as the Master Inquisitor had. He even ran his hand gently over the same location touched by the former.

And, just as Brother Mikelius had done, the hunter could not help momentarily jerking his hand back.

This was all the robed figure evidently needed to verify his suspicions. "Yes, you see it, also, do you not, huntsman?"

Cyrus's daughter started forward, but a breastplated guard easily blocked her way. She watched in utter confusion as Achilios slowly rose to face the Master Inquisitor.

"Perhaps . . . a small animal, Holiness. Seram is, after all, surrounded by woods for—"

"This was done by no animal," Brother Mikelius fairly hissed.

A suspicion concerning what they spoke about flashed through Serenthia's thoughts, causing her to gasp. Brother Mikelius turned his glare her direction.

"Who was it?" he demanded, as if she knew the answer. "Who has done this?"

"Holiness," Serenthia managed. "I don't understand—"

Achilios sought to intercede. "She couldn't—"

He would have none of either protest. The Master Inquisitor's arm cut the air sharply as his imperious eyes looked down at both. "I will say this succinctly and clearly only one more time!" The guards suddenly shifted position, surrounding the pair as if they were criminals. "*Who* has desecrated the grave and body of our murdered brother?"

FOUR

Mendeln's head throbbed horribly and not for the first time since his brother had been wrongly accused of the deaths of the missionaries. Uldyssian's brother leaned against a tree in the woods deep to the north, one hand against his temple as he tried to fight down the pain.

But worse than even the pounding was that this was the *third* time now that he had blacked out for a period of time. The last he recalled, he had been on his way from the farm to see his brother.

Putting his fingers to the bridge of his nose, the younger son of Diomedes squeezed his eyes shut. He hoped that the action might relieve some of the pressure—

The image of a robed man screaming filled his head.

With a grunt, Mendeln stumbled from the tree trunk. He looked around, certain that what he had seen was taking place before him at that very moment.

But the woods were empty. Mendeln gradually realized that, while the man's mouth had been open, no sound had come from it. Mendeln recalled hearing the wild rustling of the grass and even the sound of thunder, but not the voice.

A momentary nightmare? A figment of his overwrought imagination brought on by the heinous murders? Mendeln could believe the experience nothing else . . . and yet, it had seemed so very *real*.

The throbbing abruptly renewed its assault. His eyes shut again as the pain overcame him.

And, once more, Mendeln was assailed by the image of the man, only this time the figure lay sprawled helpless on the ground as something loomed over him. Utter fear covered the missionary's face and he sought in vain to crawl on his back away from whoever approached.

Mendeln opened his eyes . . . and the scene vanished.

This time, though, Uldyssian's brother understood that what he witnessed was neither a figment nor an event of the present. He was indeed alone in the woods. No, this time, the glimpse had lasted long enough for him to recognize the garments of the screaming man, if not the man himself.

It had been the garb of an acolyte from the Triune . . . and the man had been the emissary who had been so brutally slaughtered.

Mendeln shook. What did it mean? Why was he suddenly having these monstrous visions of the missionary's murder?

There had never been any talk of witchcraft in either side of the family and Mendeln himself doubted that such was the case. There had to be a more reasonable, honest explanation.

His nose itched. Mendeln realized that there was something on the bridge. He brushed at it and was rewarded with several bits of dirt in his palm. In fact, for the first time, he saw that fresh dirt covered most of his fingers.

When had *that* happened? Uldyssian's brother had not been at the farm, much less working in the fields, for some time. He had been too concerned about helping his sibling. Had he for some reason fallen while riding? That might explain both the latest blackout and the dirt.

"What is . . . *happening?*" Mendeln muttered. His life had always been an utterly normal—and even boring—one. Now, everything was turning on its head. These blackouts, Uldyssian's dire predicament, the ancient stone—

The *stone.*

Mendeln was no believer in coincidence. He had not started to have these blank moments until after touching the artifact. Somehow, it had affected him in a manner that he could not fathom. Oh, Mendeln had heard stories in his childhood about magic places and creatures, but those had been just *that,* stories.

Then it occurred to him to wonder why he now specifically saw the murder of the acolyte. The first notion that entered his thoughts drained the blood from his face.

No . . . I did not! I could not! Had the reason that he had seen the murder . . . and from such a frontal angle . . . been because *he* had somehow been responsible?

But common sense prevailed. Mendeln had been with Achilios at the time that the murders had taken place. Therefore, he was innocent of the nefarious events, just as Uldyssian surely was.

However, that still did not answer for the dirt on his hands nor his odd and lengthening periods of memory loss. The aspects of those frightened Mendeln greatly.

He thought again of his brother, a prisoner. The image of Uldyssian in the cell steeled Mendeln. He could concern himself with his own troubles when time permitted; what was most important was seeing that Uldyssian languished in the cell no longer than he had to.

Straightening, Mendeln headed back to Seram. However, as he did, he cautiously wiped his hands clean of any further residue. Perhaps the dirt meant nothing, but he did not want to take any chances. Too many unsettling things were happening and innocent bits of soil might just hint at some new and dire deed. He could not help his brother in the least if he suddenly became suspected of another crime.

Mendeln grunted at his foolish thinking. Of *what* crime could dirt-covered hands condemn him in a farming region?

Nonetheless, Uldyssian's brother continued to wipe his palms and fingers against his clothes all the way back to Seram.

A pair of guards came for Uldyssian just as he finally managed to drift off into a troubled slumber. As he stirred, one of them rattled the cell door, then unlocked it.

"Come with us," barked the taller of the two, a plain-faced younger man whom Uldyssian knew as Dorius's nephew. "Don't give us no problems, huh?"

In response, the farmer quietly placed his hands behind his back and turned so that the guards could secure his wrists. When they had done so, they led him out.

Tiberius met them at the door leading outside. The captain made no attempt to hide his disgruntlement, although he did not bother to explain to Uldyssian the reason for his mood. The farmer could only assume that it boded ill for him.

And sure enough, as he stepped out, Uldyssian knew that matters had gone from bad to worse. He sighted the senior figure from the Cathedral of Light immediately and knew him to be more than simply a priest from the nearest town. This was a Master Inquisitor, one of the higher-ranking officials of the sect. Worse, the imperious-looking man was accompanied by several brooding guards . . . and a very distraught Serenthia and Achilios.

The priest strode up to him. Gazing down his nose at the farmer, he declared in a much-too-loud voice, "Uldyssian, son of Diomedes, know that I am Brother Mikelius, Master Inquisitor of this region for the great and golden Prophet! I come to ascertain the depths of your guilt and thereby judge that which is needed to redeem your soul!" He paused, then added, "And, after that, the soul of whatever miscreant desecrated the grave of our emissary, too!"

Uldyssian went white. Brother Mikelius had left no doubt that he considered the matter of a trial moot. This was not what Dorius had promised!

Before he could even open his mouth to protest, the Master Inquisitor turned from him to where the headman himself looked on with less enthusiasm than Uldyssian would have liked. "With your permission, Master Dorius, we shall make use of your quarters for questioning of this one. I apologize for the inconvenience, naturally!

The Cathedral loathes such inquiries, but they on occasion become necessary, you understand."

"I wrote also to the Procurator General in Kehjan," Dorius replied, trying to regain control of the situation. "I haven't heard word, but surely he'll be sending a proper authority—"

Brother Mikelius shook his head. "Through the Prophet, blessed be him, I carry the proper authority myself for this situation! The Procurator General will rely on my good word . . ."

And from the Master Inquisitor's tone, thought Uldyssian, *Dorius and the rest were to rely on it, also, whether they liked the fact or not.* The farmer grimaced. Considering how Brother Mikelius had so far handled the matter, Uldyssian also doubted that he would be allowed to say very much at his own defense . . . unless he chose to confess.

"There is also the matter of the Triune," Dorius added. "As one of their own was also a victim—"

"The Cathedral is here; the Temple is not. If the Triune is sloth in seeking justice for its children, it is their own failing."

Defeated, the headman quieted. Uldyssian bit back an epithet. Brother Mikelius would not be denied.

Uldyssian tried to console himself with the fact that at least Lylia had not been drawn into things. That, the farmer could not have stood for. She had already suffered too much at both sects' hands—

Even as he thought that, out of the corner of his eye, the telltale emerald green flashed. The farmer shook with dismay. Without meaning to, Uldyssian glanced in that direction.

Unfortunately, so did the Master Inquisitor.

Lylia stood like an animal caught in a trap. She appeared to have crept from around the back of the Boar's Head to watch things unfold and no doubt her fear for Uldyssian had made her forget his warning.

Brother Mikelius could obviously see that she was not a

local. That in itself might not have mattered, but there was that in his gaze which, when it met hers, seemed to Uldyssian to register some recognition.

The robed figure thrust a condemning finger at the noblewoman. "You there! You—"

The sky thundered, this time with such vehemence that several people, including Brother Mikelius, had to cover their ears.

The wind suddenly rose up, howling like a hungry wolf. People were thrust back by the intensity, even several of the Inquisitor guards unable to keep their positions. Only three figures remained unmoved—at least momentarily—by the fearsome gale.

Brother Mikelius, Lylia, and Uldyssian.

But the Master Inquisitor had to struggle to maintain his place. He tore his eyes from Lylia, returning them to the prisoner.

Brother Mikelius's expression was terrible to behold. He eyed the farmer with what seemed both fury and . . . *fear*. "By the Prophet! What are—"

A savage bolt of lightning struck the village center . . . *and* the Master Inquisitor.

He had no time to scream. A sickening, burning stench filled the air, spread quickly by the wind. The bolt left barely a charred mass. Uldyssian had seen the results of other strikes, but none with the intensity of this.

A second bolt hit near the first. Someone let out a cry. People began scattering in every direction. The wind continued to howl through Seram, bowling over those not holding on to something solid.

Uldyssian looked for Lylia, but she was nowhere to be found. A piece of rubbish flew up at his face and the farmer instinctively blocked it with his arm.

Only then did he notice that he was again free. The cuffs dangled loosely on one wrist and when he tugged at them, the remaining one unlatched as if never locked.

Not wasting time questioning the carelessness of his

guards, Uldyssian focused on what to do next. However, Brother Mikelius's escort decided matters for him by trying to reach the freed prisoner despite the terrible wind. Three of them were already nearly in weapon range, with a fourth not far behind.

But as the foremost reached him, from out of the gale flew a thick wooden bench that Uldyssian belatedly recognized as usually sitting in front of the tavern. Almost unerringly, the bench collided with the guards, sending one sprawling and the other flying off with the makeshift missile.

Some distance behind the sprawling figures, Lylia reappeared. Holding on to the corner of the smithy with one hand, she waved for Uldyssian to come to her with the other.

Without hesitation, the stunned farmer ran toward the noblewoman. All around him, loose objects darted through the air. People scurried into buildings. Another bolt struck near the village well, tearing apart most of the surrounding stone wall.

Despite the many threats, though, Uldyssian made it to Lylia unscathed. Other than a few loose strands of golden hair, the woman, too, appeared untouched.

Concern for her overwhelmed all other thought. "Lylia! You need to find shelter—"

She seized his arm, but instead of coming with him to the smithy entrance, Lylia tugged Uldyssian toward the woods. Her strength was surprising, and rather than risk a struggle that would leave both of them out in the open for much too long, the farmer allowed her to guide them both beyond Seram. He knew that common sense better dictated that they hide in some building, but Uldyssian still somehow convinced himself that they would surely find just as safe a location in the wild.

Indeed, the wind seemed to lessen as they rushed deeper into the woods. Refuse still swept past them, but, miraculously, nothing greater than a leaf ever touched them.

From the direction of Seram came a now-familiar crackling sound. The sky momentarily lit up as if the sun had suddenly burst through the cloud cover. Uldyssian started to look over his shoulder, but Lylia tugged him forward.

Thunder continued to rumble as if the horses of a thousand riders trampled over the land. That made the farmer think of the Inquisitors and the unfortunate Brother Mikelius. The guards would surely be after Uldyssian once the weather settled, especially after the unsettling death of their superior. While Uldyssian blamed the cleric's horrific end on the mercurial aspects of nature—even though never in his life had the farmer witnessed such a bizarre and deadly shift—he did not doubt that somehow Brother Mikelius's fate would somehow be tied to him, no matter how ridiculous that might seem.

"Keep running!" Lylia called, gazing over her shoulder at him. "Keep running!"

But in her concern for him, the noblewoman did not pay attention to her own path. Uldyssian saw the dip in the landscape just before her foot settled into it. He tried to give warning, but by then his companion was already flailing.

Her grip on Uldyssian slipped. A short-lived cry escaping her lips, Lylia tumbled forward. As she landed, she twisted around.

Stumbling, Uldyssian went to her side. Lylia lay there, her eyes open but momentarily unseeing.

"Lylia!" All fear of the unnerving weather or the Inquisitor guards vanished utterly. All that mattered to the farmer was the figure sprawled before him.

To his great relief, the noblewoman blinked. Her eyes focused again. She looked up at Uldyssian and her expression made him redden.

Trying to cover up his embarrassment, Uldyssian gave her a hand. However, as Lylia tried to stand, she let out a moan and her right ankle buckled.

"I think . . . I think it may be twisted," she managed. "Could you see?"

He wanted to refuse, but knew that he could not leave her in pain. Mumbling an apology, Uldyssian pushed the long skirt away just enough to reveal the ankle.

It was black and blue and already a bit swollen. When the farmer put a gentle hand to it, Lylia gasped again.

"I need to bring you to a healer," he muttered.

"No! If you do, then you'll be captured again! I won't let them do that!"

Uldyssian frowned. What had she expected to eventually happen? He could not very well just run off. This was his home. His family had lived in Seram for generations, possibly even since its beginning. More to the point, there were those he could not leave behind, especially Mendeln. Mendeln would surely pay if his brother could not be found. There was also Achilios, known to be Uldyssian's best friend, and even Serenthia possibly risked being involved.

But at the same time, how *could* he return? The Inquisitors might eventually leave, but Tiberius would assume it his duty to arrest Uldyssian on the spot if the farmer reappeared. There was also the possibility of the Peace Warders of the Temple also still arriving to make their own judgment of the murders.

Uldyssian knelt there, the hand over the ankle forgotten as he tried to think about what to do. Lylia's fate concerned him as well and at least matters would have been a little easier if her ankle had not been injured—

"Uldyssian . . ."

He paid her no mind, still caught up in his concerns. Perhaps he could carry her back to the farm, then from there send her by horse to a neighboring settlement. She could get the aid she needed in one of the larger ones, then be on her way. At least then the noblewoman would be out of risk.

As for Uldyssian himself, that was another—

"Uldyssian!"

Although Lylia kept her voice low, there was no mistaking the sharp emphasis in it this time. Uldyssian glanced around, certain that they had been discovered. However, there was no sign of anyone else, especially the Inquisitors or the Guard.

"Uldyssian," she repeated. "Not that. My ankle . . . the pain is *gone.*"

Her hopeful words only fueled his worries. If she felt no pain, it was likely that the ankle had gone numb, not a good sign. He pulled his hand aside, fearful of what he would see—

And finding instead that the ankle now looked perfectly healthy.

"But—" Uldyssian stared at the limb, certain that he saw wrong. At the very least, the ankle had been bruised badly . . . and now was not.

He looked to Lylia, and the way in which she gazed at him only made Uldyssian more uncomfortable. There was awe, incredible awe, and what almost seemed . . . *worship?*

"You turned away . . ." the noblewoman murmured. "But you left your hand near my ankle. I knew . . . I knew you were not touching it, but I suddenly . . . I felt a wonderful warmth and the pain . . . it just went away . . ."

"That's not possible . . . there must be a reasonable explanation! An injury like that doesn't just *heal.*"

"*You* did it."

At first he thought that he had not heard Lylia correctly. Then, when her words at last registered with him, Uldyssian could scarcely believe that the noblewoman would even consider something so outrageous.

"I'm no mage or witch!" he insisted, taken aback. "Your ankle was obviously not hurt after all! That's the only answer!"

She shook her head, eyes filled with something that should have gladdened his soul but only unnerved him more. *Adoration.* "No. I know the pain I felt. I know what I sensed from your hand . . . and I know that all the pain then disappeared as if it had never been."

Uldyssian stepped back from her. "But I didn't do it!"

The blond woman rose, then stepped toward him. Lylia moved without the least hint of injury.

"Then who? Who performed such a miracle?"

The last word sent shivers through him. He would not hear her. "We've no time for such foolishness!" He looked up. The sky seemed calmer, at least by them. Thunder yet roiled in the direction of Seram. Another bolt flashed over the village. "The storm—" Uldyssian had no other word for the peculiar weather. "—seems to be stalled. Praise be for that bit of luck!"

"I do not think it was *luck*," the noblewoman murmured.

"Then what—" The farmer cut off, his face now blanching. "No, Lylia . . . don't even jest—"

"But do you not *see*, Uldyssian? How timely was that wind! How righteous was that bolt that struck the arrogant Brother Mikelius just before he could condemn you for murders you did not commit—"

"And now you'd claim I've powers that *did* slay a man! Think of that, woman!" For the first time since he had met her, Uldyssian wanted to be nowhere near Lylia. It was not that he did not still find her desirable, but surely she suffered from some dementia. Perhaps the strain caused by her family's misfortune had finally taken its toll. That had to be the explanation for her behavior . . .

But what explained the injury that Uldyssian had seen? He did not consider himself of an imaginative nature. How, then, could his mind have conjured up such an elaborate delusion?

"No!" the farmer snapped at himself. If he followed such reasoning, he would find himself believing Lylia's outlandish suggestion. If that happened, it would be better for Uldyssian to turn himself in to the Inquisitors or the Guard before he truly *did* endanger someone else.

A soft, warm touch on his hand stirred him back to the moment. Lylia stood barely an inch from him. "I *know* it was you who healed me, Uldyssian . . . and I believe that it is you who summoned the wind and the lightning in our time of need."

"Lylia, please! Listen to the absurdity of what you say!"

Her flawless face filled his vision. "You want me to believe otherwise? Then prove me wrong." The noblewoman gently took him by the chin and turned his gaze so that it fell upon the direction of Seram. "The lightning still falls, bringing justice and retribution with it. The sky still roars its anger at the false accusations made against you. The wind howls at the presumption of those who would judge you when they themselves are guilty!"

"*Stop* it, Lylia!"

But she would not. In a firm, even defiant voice, Lylia said, "Prove me wrong, dear Uldyssian! Will with all your might for the sky to quiet—nay, even clear—and if it does not, then I will gladly admit that I was sorely deluded." Her lower lip stiffened. "Gladly . . ."

Uldyssian could not believe that Lylia was so deluded that she could even imagine that something like she suggested was possible. Still, if the noblewoman meant what she said, it was the quickest and easiest way to snap her back to reality.

Without another word, the farmer turned toward the turbulent heavens. Although he could have simply looked at them and pretended to be concentrating, Uldyssian somehow felt that doing so would be a betrayal to his companion even if he knew nothing would happen.

And so, the son of Diomedes squinted and thought. He wished the violent weather to vanish and the clouds to clear away. He tried to take the situation as seriously as he could, even if only for Lylia's sake.

But he was not surprised when everything remained as it was.

Certain that he had given Lylia's delusion as much chance as anyone could have, the farmer wearily turned back to her. He expected the noblewoman to be distraught, but Lylia instead looked only patient.

"I did what you asked and you saw what happened . . . or didn't," he said soothingly. "Now let me take you away from here, Lylia. We've got to find a place where you—where we can rest and compose our minds . . ."

Unfortunately, instead of agreeing, Lylia continued to stare past him expectantly.

Uldyssian's own patience finally came to an end. Lylia had swept his heart up the moment that he had first seen her, but he could not tolerate her delusion any longer just because of that. It was for her own good, if nothing else. "Lylia, you've got to pull yourself together! I did what you asked and—"

"And it came to pass . . ." she murmured, her face suddenly glowing with renewed adoration. Lylia gently took hold of the farmer by his arms and turned him back toward the village.

Uldyssian, about to reprimand her further, stopped. His mouth hung open.

The sun shone over Seram.

The Grand Temple of the Triune—located two days' ride south of Kehjan—was a sprawling, triangular edifice with three high towers, each situated at one of the points. The pinnacles themselves were three-sided, with each face marked by one of the holy orders. Triangular windows lined the towers from bottom to the top.

Nearly all things concerning the structure were of a similar triple nature. To reach the entrance—which faced Kehjan—pilgrims needed to ascend three levels, with each level consisting of thirty-three steps. At the entrance itself, three massive bronze doors—also triangular—allowed the faithful into the vast welcoming hall within.

Worshippers were, naturally, greeted within by glorious effigies of the three guiding spirits. Bala the Creator loomed on the left, the androgynous figure clad in the robe of its order. In Bala's hands were a mystical hammer and a bag, which the clerics preached contained the seeds of all life.

Both nature and the architectural triumphs of Humanity were under the auspices of this spirit.

Dialon hovered to the right, the marble statue much akin to the first save that this figure held to its breast the Tablets of Order. Dialon brought purpose to Humanity, and the tablets taught how to achieve blessedness. As with Bala, Dialon wore the colors associated with those following the principles of Determination.

And in the center stood Mefis, who carried nothing but cupped its hands as if cradling the most tender of infants. Without Love, Creation and Determination could not thrive, so taught the Grand Priest—the Primus—who some said surely had to be the child of Mefis, so caring was he of his flock.

Under each of the giants, another bronze door gave way to the grand chambers of the various orders. Pilgrims and novices who found one preferable over the other would enter through these and listen to the words of that particular high priest. Peace Warders, cowled guards in leather who wore the symbols of all three orders on their chest, guided newcomers to their most likely choice. Within each chamber, several hundred could kneel in prayer at one time.

And when the Primus himself made an appearance, the walls between the three orders—walls which, although they had the facade of stone, were made of wood—were slid back into hidden niches so that *all* could bask in the Grand Priest's noble presence. Upon an elevated dais before his followers, the leader of the Triune would bring forth the word of the Three.

Today, however, the faithful came to make their own prayers, for the Primus was in council with his three most beloved, the high priests of each order. Chief among them was the tall, athletic Malic, senior of those of his rank. He had risen from an eager acolyte to his venerable role through determination, creative thinking, and devotion to his master.

He was, even the other two knew, the right hand of the Primus.

The private chamber in which they met was a small, almost empty place. The only furniture at all was the Primus's regal chair, the back of which rose high above his head and featured the triangular symbol of the sect. Twin torches set in wall niches illuminated the oval chamber, not that there was anything else to see but the chair's occupant . . . which was exactly the point.

The Primus gazed down at the three as he quietly spoke words for their ears alone. Of all, Malic and his counterparts knew the innermost secrets of the Triune as no one else did.

The Grand Priest's voice was pure music. His face could have been chiseled from marble, so unmarred was it. He had long, flowing hair of silver, with a short, well-trimmed beard that matched it. His features were very angular and his eyes were of a gleaming emerald. He was taller and stronger-looking than most men, but despite his commanding appearance, moved at all times with a practiced gentleness.

Until now.

Only Malic, surreptitiously lifting his gaze up, noticed the sudden and very slight tremor. Under his dark brow, the high priest of the Order of Mefis watched with concealed concern.

But the Primus evidently saw that concern despite Malic's attempts. Completely recovered now, the Triune's beloved leader made a single gesture of dismissal, to which the mustached Malic quickly alerted the others with a tap of his own hand. The three senior priests, heads kept low, quickly retreated from the private chamber.

The Primus sat silent, his eyes apparently staring at the empty air before him. The flames of the torches suddenly flickered madly, as if a strong gust of wind briefly danced about the room.

And as the torches returned to normal, a shift came over

the benevolent visage of the Primus. There was nothing holy in his aspect now; in fact, any who would have witnessed it would have found it quite the opposite . . . and likely feared for their very soul, then, too.

"West of the city . . ." he rasped in a voice now more like a serpent's than a man's. "West of the city . . ."

FIVE

As chaos overtook Seram, Achilios's first thoughts were not for himself nor even for Uldyssian. Rather, they were for Serenthia, caught in the open like so many others. The hunter dodged a spinning wagon wheel and what appeared to be the remains of a scarecrow on a cross as he rushed toward Cyrus's daughter.

From farther away came a shout. Achilios sighted the trader also running toward her. However, having stood nearer the hunter, Serenthia did not notice Cyrus nor could she hear her father.

At that moment, a massive fragment of roof suddenly tore off the Guard headquarters. It fluttered in the air like a gigantic black bird suffering its death throes . . . then dropped with all the accuracy of an executioner's ax toward the unsuspecting Cyrus.

Achilios shouted, but, as with the trader, could not be heard over the gale. A chill coursed through him. The hunter knew that there was only one choice left to him.

The moment that he could, Achilios leapt for Serenthia. He tackled her much the way he would have game seeking to escape one of his snares. The archer did not care; all that mattered was keeping the trader's daughter from witnessing the horrible scene to come. There was nothing he could do for Cyrus, who was too far away.

But although he managed to smother her view, Achilios could do nothing for his own. He watched in macabre fascination as the piece of roof caught Cyrus from behind. The force with which it struck the back of the man's neck ensured that there would be no hope for him. Indeed, the sharp edge severed bone and flesh with awful ease and despite the fact that he could not hear anything but the wind, the veteran hunter knew exactly what Cyrus's horrific beheading sounded like.

The rest of the broken piece collapsed atop the mangled body immediately afterward, thankfully obscuring it from sight. Serenthia chose that moment to finally struggle free. She looked up at Achilios, her expression one of surprise . . . and perhaps a little embarrassment, if her reddening cheeks were any sign. Achilios suddenly felt very uncomfortable and not merely because of having witnessed the fate of her father.

"Let me up, please," she called, her voice barely audible. "Have you seen Uldyssian?"

The hunter's own embarrassment grew. Unaware of Cyrus's tragic end, her first thoughts naturally went to the farmer and no one else. Certainly not Achilios.

Still, her concern for the farmer gave him a momentary reprieve from telling her what had just happened. Now was not the time for Serenthia to know. Besides, if she tried to uncover her father's body in the midst of this insane weather, it was very possible that she would merely end up joining him in death.

"I saw him run toward the smithy!" he finally shouted in response to her question. Despite his powerful lungs, Achilios had to repeat himself before the trader's daughter understood. He pulled her to her feet, careful to avoid turning her in the direction of the grisly sight. "Hold my hand tight or you may be blown back!"

To his relief, Serenthia obeyed without question. Achilios dragged her in the direction he had last seen his friend, the violent wind buffeting him as hard as any wild boar. He did not know what they would do if and when they actually located Uldyssian. The farmer was considered a prisoner, a possible murderer in the eyes of some, and Achilios's duty should have been to either convince his friend to return and face justice or, failing that, *force* him to do so. But the hunter had already seen enough of what passed for justice and the very thought of turning Uldyssian over to the Inquisitors— or even Tiberius—left Achilios cold.

More important, if he brought Uldyssian back to Seram to face the charges, the archer had no doubt that he would forever blacken himself in the eyes of Serenthia.

They raced for the edge of the village even as others ran past them in different directions. Planks tore off of buildings, adding to the dangerous debris flying about. A water bucket ripped from the village well smashed against the chest of one of Tiberius's men, sending him falling on his back. Achilios wanted to stop by the supine form to see if the other still lived, but feared that to do so would endanger Serenthia.

With much relief, he plunged Cyrus's daughter and himself into the woods. His attuned senses immediately noticed the difference between the weather there and the mad turbulence in Seram. It was almost as if he had shut a door behind him. The foliage barely shook and the howling had all but ceased.

Despite that, the hunter did not slow until the two of them were well away from the village's edge. Only then did Achilios pause, near a tremendous oak, and that more for his companion's sake than his own.

"Are you all right?" he immediately asked her.

Gasping for breath, Serenthia nodded. Her gaze shifted around the woods, seeking.

"We'll find him, Serry," he muttered, a little put out after having helped her escape the chaos. Then Achilios recalled Cyrus and guilt overwhelmed him.

"I wonder if—" the trader's daughter began, halting abruptly as an unexpected hush filled the area.

The two glanced back at their home. The lightning had ceased striking and the wind there had died down, too. Most astonishing, not only were the clouds thinning, but it actually looked as if the *sun* was already trying to peek through.

"Praise be! A miracle!" uttered Serenthia. Achilios, on the other hand, felt a peculiar dread inside him, a sensation he had experienced but one time before . . . when he had first touched the ancient stone.

Serenthia took a step back to Seram, but the hunter pulled her deeper into the woods. "Uldyssian!" he reminded her, though the farmer was not now entirely his reason for wanting to be away from the village. "This way, remember?"

The trader's daughter nodded, once more a look of determination across her beautiful face. Achilios wished just once that such an expression would be reserved for him.

Although he knew that he had seen Uldyssian head toward this part of the woods, Achilios found tracking his friend much more troublesome than he would have expected. Uldyssian had barely left any trace of his passing. In fact, the hunter had to guess half the time, for the farmer apparently moved through the woods with greater stealth than an animal. If not for that certain sense within Achilios, that sense that he had never mentioned to others but that always gave him the advantage when seeking a quarry's spoor, then it would have been impossible to keep after Uldyssian.

And that sense, that *knowing* that enabled Achilios to ever follow the correct trail, also told him that someone *else* had met Uldyssian in the woods. It was not a familiar trail and from its light touch, he suspected it to be that of the noblewoman. Who else? Whatever cloaked Uldyssian did so for her, as well. Her trail was even harder to maintain focus on than the farmer's.

For some reason, that made Achilios think of the stone again. Since he had discovered it, strange and unsettling things had kept happening, some of them undeniably unnatural in his eyes. Achilios recalled the symbols and wondered if, with time, Mendeln could translate them. Mendeln was clever. Perhaps he could even explain the terrible storm and what—

The hunter paused in his tracks, causing Serenthia to stumble into him. He looked behind them.

Thinking that there was someone back there, Cyrus's daughter also looked. "What is it?"

"Nothing . . ." He tugged her forward again. Achilios could not go back for Mendeln. Uldyssian's brother would have to fend for himself. Surely, wherever he was, he was safe. The archer could not even recall seeing him when Uldyssian had been brought out before Brother Mikelius.

He can fend for himself, Achilios repeated to himself. *Mendeln's very clever. Very learned. I have to worry about Serry. I have to find some way to tell her about her father . . . maybe when we find Uldyssian . . . maybe then . . . yes, Mendeln will be fine in the meantime . . .*

The hunter kept on repeating the last in his head, hoping that eventually he would believe that scholarly Mendeln would indeed stay out of trouble.

Hoping, but not expecting.

Mendeln had arrived at the outskirts of the village just as it seemed that the skies had declared war on his people. In contrast to the rest of Seram's inhabitants, he had stood where he was, watching in fascination as nature acted in a manner entirely contrary to what he knew to be correct. Storms did not without warning strike so particularly. Wind did not blow with tornadic strength within village limits, only to all but die at his very feet.

Only when the phenomenon had without warning ceased did Mendeln stir himself and enter Seram. The village center was in ruins and more than one person lay still on the ground. The enormity of what had taken place began to sink in . . . and so did the fact that it had proven most timely for Uldyssian.

That last point was further emphasized for Mendeln as he passed the burnt carnage that he somehow knew was all that remained of the robed figure he had recognized as a high cleric of the Cathedral of Light, a Master Inquisitor from the looks of him. The fearsome bolt had left little and the stench should have sent Mendeln retreating . . . yet some morbid fascination drove the younger son of Diomedes toward the ghoulish corpse.

But as he came within arm's reach, a violent sensation akin to a hard fist struck him full force. Mendeln staggered back and had the unnerving feeling someone was screaming fiercely at him. He continued retreating, suddenly not wanting to be anywhere near the burnt remains.

Then, someone behind him cried, *Where is she? I can't find her . . . I can't find her . . .*

Mendeln turned at the voice, but saw no one. Frowning, he gave up and started away in search of his brother.

Good Mendeln! Have you seen her? Have you seen my daughter?

Out of the corner of his eye, Mendeln saw a figure standing near a huge piece of torn roof littering the ground. However, as he turned, the figure seemed to vanish . . . or was never there in the first place.

But he thought he had recognized who it was. "Master Cyrus?" he called hesitantly. "Master Cyrus?"

There came no answer, but again Mendeln was filled with a compulsion, this time to approach the wreckage from the roof. As he neared, he sensed something beneath the wood. Reaching down, Mendeln tugged at the rubble. The wood proved even heavier than he had imagined, but by choosing to use his mass to slide it toward him, Uldyssian's brother managed to make some progress. Slowly, what had been hidden was revealed to the light—

At which point Mendeln let out a garbled cry and let the wreckage loose. He shook his head, a dismay he had not felt since the death of his parents and siblings rising up to overwhelm him.

And yet, at that moment, the familiar voice again asked, *Where is she? Where is my Serenthia?*

Only then did Mendeln realize that the voice was in his *head*. Trembling, he retreated from the roof fragment and that which it had shrouded.

A sharp point caught him in the small of his back.

He started to turn, only to be seized roughly by more than one pair of powerful hands.

The stern face of an Inquisitor guard came within inches of his. "You!" barked the figure. "You are kin to the accused heretic and murder, Uldyssian ul-Diomed? Admit it! Someone identified you earlier as his brother!"

Still struggling to comprehend what had just happened before, Mendeln mutely nodded. Unfortunately, that proved to be his captors' cue to drag him through the village toward where a group of locals stood pensively eyeing four other Inquisitor guards watching over them. Mendeln estimated nearly twenty people in the group, their wide eyes and movement reminding him of a herd of sheep heading to the slaughter.

Dorius stood arguing with one of the minions of the Cathedral. Of Tiberius, there was no sign. A few of his men stood near Dorius, but they looked uncertain as to what to do, if anything.

"But you've no right to be holding these good people!" the headman insisted.

"Under the authority granted by the signed agreements between Kehjan and the Cathedral, we have what right we need or desire!" responded the lead guard haughtily. To Tiberius's men, he added, "And in the scope of that, authority of your captain is ceded to us! You will obey all orders of the Cathedral and the first is to remove your headman to his quarters and confine him there!"

One of the locals put a tentative hand toward Dorius. "What should we—"

"I won't budge!" insisted Dorius.

"Then, if these will disobey, I will have no choice but to have some of my own deal with you . . . and them, afterward."

The headman glanced at the fearsome warriors, then at his own Guard. Shaking his head, he reluctantly turned and led the latter away.

With Dorius's retreat and Tiberius's absence—Mendeln

now suspected that the captain was one of those struck down—the fate of Uldyssian's brother and the rest of those gathered was squarely in the hands of the Cathedral's Inquisitor guards. Mendeln did not exactly share his sibling's loathing of the sect, but at the moment he could think of no worse fate for any innocent than that awaiting him now. The warriors were likely to think of this as some act of magic, a notion that even Mendeln could not entirely rule out. Certainly no reasonable explanation worked.

"Move into the circle!" growled one of those who had captured him.

Mendeln stumbled toward the others. Those nearest immediately shunned him, pressing against their fellows in their fear. Even those who had known him since childhood looked at Mendeln as if he were some sort of pariah.

Or rather, the *brother* of one.

"That's him," said the same guard who had shoved the younger son of Diomedes forward.

Mendeln turned to face a guard who, although he was a couple of inches shorter than the farmer, stared down the latter with ease. The broad, rough-hewn face looked more appropriate on a brigand than a representative of a holy order.

"The brother of the heretic and sorcerer, are you?" demanded the lead guard in a tone that indicated no response from Mendeln was necessary. "Where is Uldyssian ul-Diomed? Answer now and you may be spared his fate!"

"Uldyssian's done nothing!"

"His guilt is proved, his mastery of arts foul unquestionable! His soul is lost, but yours may yet receive absolution! You have but to give him up to us!"

The words sounded absurd to Mendeln, but the guard clearly believed everything that he said to the brother. Despite the fact that he would be condemning himself, Mendeln did not hesitate to shake his head.

"We will begin with you, then . . . and the rest here, all

known to have fraternized with the heretic, will learn from your example!"

Just as quickly as they had tossed him in among the others, the guards then pulled Mendeln out. They dragged him to an open space. As the farmer was forced down on his knees, he saw the lead guard stride over to his horse, there to remove a long, braided whip rolled up and attached to the saddle. The guard undid the loop binding the whip, enabling the full length of the sinister weapon to flow free. He tested the whip once, the crack it made shaking Mendeln worse than the harshest thunder.

Face resolute, the lead guard headed back to Mendeln, who squeezed his eyes tight and prepared for the agony . . .

It was a coincidence. That was all. A coincidence.

But as Uldyssian stared toward Seram, a niggling doubt ate away at him from within. He recalled again how terrible Lylia's ankle had looked . . . and then how unmarred it had appeared but moments afterward. There was the horrific storm that had assailed the village just as Brother Mikelius had begun condemning him. What were the odds of lightning striking so perfectly?

A coincidence! Uldyssian told himself again. *No more!*

Yet, even he was not entirely convinced of that.

The farmer continued to stand there, unable to decide what to do. Then, a face came unbidden into his thoughts, a face he knew as well as his own.

Mendeln's . . . and with it came a sense of urgency, of impending threat.

With a wordless cry, Uldyssian started back to Seram.

"Uldyssian!" called Lylia. "What is it?"

"My brother! Mendeln—" was all he could say. The need to reach the village before something terrible happened to Mendeln took over. Uldyssian did not question how he knew that his brother was in danger. All that mattered was preventing Mendeln from coming to harm, even if it meant being recaptured.

Without warning, figures appeared before him. Uldyssian prepared himself for a struggle . . . then recognized Achilios and Serenthia.

"Uldyssian!" blurted the trader's daughter. "Praise be that you are all right!"

The archer, too, started to speak, but, despite being glad to see them, Uldyssian did not slow. He sensed that time was running out. Without apology, the farmer shoved past the pair, each frantic beat of his heart a scream to hurry faster.

The edge of the village came into sight. His hopes rose.

But then, from further in echoed a sharp, cracking sound that sent a shock of pain through Uldyssian's heart.

Gritting his teeth, his breath now coming in pants, the son of Diomedes charged into Seram.

The sight that met his gaze filled him with loathing and anger. He saw many of his fellow villagers herded together like cattle, their expressions fear and confusion. Grim Inquisitor guards pointed weapons at them.

But worse, so very much worse, was what the villagers watched. Near the ruined well, the lead Inquisitor guard had Mendeln down on his knees. Another armored figure made certain that Uldyssian's brother could not rise. Someone had torn open the back of Mendeln's tunic and now a long, red ribbon decorated the latter's spine.

A red ribbon made by the long, scaled whip of the lead guard.

The officer at last noticed Uldyssian, then readied the whip for another strike.

"Surrender yourself, Uldyssian ul-Diomed, or you will force me to cause your brother more suffering!"

His twisted words—insisting that it would be *Uldyssian's* fault if Mendeln was again whipped—only made the farmer more furious. He wanted to lash out at them the way that they dared lash out at his brother—

The length of the officer's whip curled up in the air, as if blown by some sudden gust of wind. Startled, he tugged at it, trying to bring it down, but the sinewy cord instead tangled around his neck.

He reached to pull it off, but the whip suddenly tightened. The officer's eyes went wide and he let go of the grip in order to tear at the whip with both hands. A hacking sound escaped him.

The guard nearest Mendeln rushed to aid his commander, at the same time working to sheath his own weapon. However, his hand suddenly turned, causing the blade to rise above the sheath. Somehow, the blade bent— and buried itself upward, just beneath the breastplate.

Blood spilling over his hands, the stunned guard collapsed into the officer, whose eyes were bulging as he now clawed in desperation at the macabre noose. The wounded guard finally slumped next to Mendeln, who stumbled away in shock. A second later, the officer let out a last gasp and joined his companion. The whip remained tight around his throat.

"Uldyssian!" called Lylia from somewhere behind him. "Beware the others!"

He glanced to the side to see the remaining Inquisitor guards converging on his position. A part of Uldyssian wanted to flee, but his fury still dominated. He glared at the armed men, who terrorized in the name of their holy sect.

One man stumbled. His sword arm turned—

The edge of his blade expertly cut through the throat of the guard next to him. The second man let out a gurgle and fell. As he did, he dropped his own weapon, which somehow tangled the feet of another guard. That man spun around, then hit the hard ground skull-first. There was an audible snap and the Inquisitor stilled, his head now lying at an awkward angle.

But now the rest of the guards surrounded Uldyssian, who eyed them as he would have the vermin that sought to devour his crops. In his mind they were no more than that. The farmer recalled when once he had discovered a cache of grain infested with such. He had done the only thing that he could to keep the creatures from spreading. He had *burned* the cache, burned it with the vermin still inside . . .

Burned them . . .

The foremost guard cried out. He dropped his sword and stared in horror at his hand, which was blackening before the eyes of all. In but a single breath, the flesh cindered and the muscle and sinew turned to ash. Even the bone darkened and darkened until *nothing* remained.

And as he befell the fate of his hand, the guard himself suffered so. His face shriveled and his body shook, even his armor tarnishing as if tossed into a coal-fueled inferno. He screamed, but his scream was cut off as his tongue crumbled.

The eyes vanished then, melting into the sockets with horrible finality. The crumbling black figure collapsed in a heap of bones that further smoked away to dust.

His comrades had no time to gape in fear at his fate, for they perished at the same time. Their brief cries were shrill and their deaths were marked by the clatter of empty armor and lost weaponry.

Only after they were all dust did Uldyssian return to his senses . . . and stare at a monstrous sight he could not even at that point fully link to himself. Yet, neither could the farmer deny the fiery urge that had swept through him, the urge he had focused on the hapless men.

An unnatural silence filled Seram. Uldyssian finally tore his gaze from the macabre remains and looked at his brother, who stood but a few lengths from him. Panting, still obviously in some pain from the harsh lash of the whip, Mendeln gaped at his older sibling.

"Uldyssian . . ." he finally succeeded in whispering.

But Uldyssian now looked past Mendeln to where the rest of the villagers still stood packed together even though their captors were all dead. He saw no relief in their eyes, but only what the farmer recognized as *dread*.

Dread of him . . .

Murmuring arose from within the group. When

Uldyssian stretched forth a hand toward them, they moved as one away from his touch.

That, in turn, caused Uldyssian to retreat a step. He looked around and saw that other villagers had stepped out from hiding. Faces he had known all his life now eyed him as the former prisoners had.

"I didn't *do* anything . . ." he murmured, more to himself than others. "I didn't do *anything* . . ." The son of Diomedes protested louder.

But the people of Seram saw him differently, he knew. They now believed that he *had* slaughtered both missionaries. How could they not? Before their eyes, one man had been struck by lightning, another strangled by his own weapon, and the rest brought down in manners no one could ever claim ordinary.

Uldyssian spotted Tibion. He stepped toward the owner of the Boar's Head. The old man had been as near a father to him as anyone since the death of Diomedes. Tibion could at least see sense—

The stout figure backed away, his stony expression not entirely hiding the revulsion and anxiety. He mutely shook his head.

Someone tugged on his sleeve. Mendeln. Wincing from pain, his brother whispered, "Uldyssian . . . come away from here. Quickly!"

"I've got to make them see *sense*, Mendeln! They can't possibly believe—"

"They *believe*. I think even *I* believe. That doesn't matter! Look around! You're not Uldyssian to them anymore! You're the fiend that the Cathedral's Master Inquisitor claimed you to be! That's all that they see!"

Brow wrinkled tight, Uldyssian glanced from one direction to another. All he saw were the same dark emotions.

Dorius reappeared . . . and with him Tiberius. The captain had his arm in a sling and there was a gash on his right cheek. Behind the pair came the men who had been ordered to lock up the headman in his own quarters.

Captain Tiberius was the one who finally spoke to Uldyssian. "Keep perfectly still. Don't do a damned thing, Uldyssian, except put your hands behind you—"

"I'm not the cause of all this!" the farmer insisted, knowing all the while that his protests were as futile as ever. "You just have to listen to me—"

"There're archers positioned," Dorius anxiously interrupted. "Please listen to reason, Uldyssian . . ."

The farmer shook. No one would listen to him. He was surrounded by insanity. They saw in Uldyssian a murderer, a monster.

Distracted by his own turmoil, he almost did not notice a subtle motion by Tiberius. The headman's words returned to him. Archers. Those who had once been his friends would rather kill him than understand his predicament.

"No!" Uldyssian cried out. "No!"

The ground shook. People toppled over. Something whistled past his ear.

As the tremor overtook Scram, a hand pulled Uldyssian away. It was not Mendeln's, however, but Lylia's.

"This is our only chance! Come!"

Unable—and unwilling—to think anymore, he allowed her to guide him out of the village. Although those around them seemed unable to keep their footing, neither the farmer nor the noblewoman had any difficulty.

Someone shouted his name. Despite Lylia's tugging, Uldyssian looked back and saw Mendeln on all fours. His brother was trying to follow, but suffered the same trouble as the rest of Seram.

Ignoring Lylia's protest, he went back for Mendeln. Mendeln took his hand and suddenly found his footing. Holding tight, Uldyssian led his brother from the chaos.

"Horses!" Mendeln shouted above the din. "We need horses!"

Uldyssian was about to argue that they had no time to secure even one animal let alone five, when suddenly a horse raced ahead of them. It was followed by several more, all bearing the saddles of the Cathedral of Light. They raced directly into the woods . . . and straight into the waiting hands of Achilios.

Skilled in dealing with animals, the hunter easily brought under control three. Serenthia managed to catch another, but let a fifth escape.

Uldyssian paused before the hunter, the two lifelong friends reading into each other's gazes.

"We must be away from here," Achilios finally said, thrusting the reins of two horses toward the farmer. "Away until they come to their senses."

But both men knew that such a thing would never happen. Achilios and Serenthia could return, yes, and *would,* if the farmer had his way. However, Uldyssian—and by fault of blood, Mendeln—were likely saying good-bye to their home forever.

"We've only four mounts," the trader's daughter gasped. "Uldyssian, you and I could—"

"I shall ride with you, Uldyssian," interjected Lylia. "She is welcome to the other horse."

Serenthia looked ready to argue, but Uldyssian, reacting to the noblewoman's words, had already returned one set of reins. Achilios quickly handed them to Mendeln, who eyed the reins as if they had turned into serpents.

"Mount up!" urged the archer. "The tremor seems to be subsiding!"

Sure enough, all was slowly quieting in Seram. Uldyssian wondered if the tremor would renew its throes if he willed it so, then cursed himself for even thinking of such a thing. Whether or not he was somehow responsible, enough people had already been harmed or even slain due to events. To wish for something that might endanger others further was to him nearly as terrible as the crimes to which he had been accused.

He glanced around at the few who had stood by him. Of all of them, Serenthia was the most innocent. Surely, she at least could return *now* rather than later.

"Serry! Go back to the village! No one likely saw you! Go back to your father and brothers—"

She gave him a defiant look. "Not until I know that you're safe!"

To Uldyssian's surprise, Achilios added his support to her rather than to his friend. "She should ride with us for a time until things are settled. Now, no more talk!"

"To the southeast!" Lylia declared without warning. "Ride to the southeast! We will be safest there!"

Unfamiliar with that region, Uldyssian looked at the hunter, but Achilios only shrugged. He had not been much farther from Seram than his companions.

Lylia leaned near Uldyssian's ear, her breath warm and stimulating. "Trust me," she whispered. "The southeast . . ."

"To the southeast, then!" he growled to the others. "And away from this madness . . ."

With the noblewoman's arms locked around his waist and her soft head against his back, Uldyssian ul-Diomed urged his mount on. Behind him came the others, Achilios taking up the rear.

It would all resolve itself, the farmer insisted in his mind. It would all resolve itself. Somehow, sense would be made of everything and he would be able to begin his life again, albeit probably not anywhere near Seram. The ties he had had with the other villagers had been forever cut. He could never trust them again, just as they could never trust him. The accusations and the memories would always lurk in the background.

But Uldyssian could start over elsewhere, forgetting all that had happened in Seram. A farmer only needed a good patch of land and a strong hand. He had both. He could build a new home and, just perhaps, make it large enough for a family. Lylia had sacrificed much for him. He had to mean something to her, whatever the difference in their bloodlines. Together, they would put behind their pasts and make a new future.

If the Cathedral and the Temple let them, that is . . .

Six

They paused that night near the edge of a hilly tract that overlooked in the distant part of the vast jungles that surrounded the more tamed central regions of Kehjan the land. It naturally fell to Achilios to hunt for game. Mendeln worked on a fire while Serenthia, Lylia, and Uldyssian ventured out a short distance in separate directions to see if they could find water and edible berries. More than happy to focus on something other than his predicament, the fugitive farmer wended his way farther than agreed, the stillness of the rolling forest calming his heart for the first time in days. Indeed, he savored the silence so much that, for a good part of the search, Uldyssian forgot what it was he was supposed to be doing.

His peace was abruptly shattered by the sound of rustling leaves. Uldyssian instinctively reached for the knife that he had long lost.

But as he realized his folly, a form pushed through to him. His heart raced, but out of pleasure, not fear.

"I am sorry," Lylia murmured, looking up at him. "I was frightened by myself! I—I wanted to be with you, Uldyssian . . ."

His blood raced as she put an ivory hand on his own. Her eyes caught what light there was from the foliage-obscured moon, making them almost glow like stars themselves.

"There's nothing to be afraid of," he reassured her, savoring the touch. "Tomorrow, things'll be better. You'll see."

The noblewoman smiled. "How silly to hear *you* trying to calm *me!* 'Tis your life at threat, Uldyssian . . ."

"We're far from Seram now. They'll forget about me." It was obviously a lie, but the farmer had no idea what else to say.

"They will not. I think . . . Uldyssian, there is only one way to prevent us from having to run and run forever. I said something of it before and now that I have seen the wondrous gifts you possess, I think it more than ever."

He did not like where she was going with this. "Lylia . . ."

"Please . . ." Without warning, the blond noblewoman kissed him. It was long and lingering and filled Uldyssian with a yearning.

"We must go to the great city itself," she said once they had separated. "You must speak to the people! Not the mage clans or the nobles, but the *common* folk! They will understand you—"

He laughed harshly. "My own village didn't understand me! They saw me as some kind of horrible monster!"

"That was due to the awful circumstances, Uldyssian! If you go to the city, you start fresh! You have been given a gift most fantastic! They must be told!"

"And what am I supposed to preach to them? To follow me like some god or spirit or I'll tear them apart as I did the Cathedral's men? What could I give them except fear and loathing?"

Her expression turned solemn. She stared deep into his eyes. "You could give them the promise of becoming as *you* are! Of becoming more than the Cathedral or the Triune could ever claim for them!"

"Of becoming like me?" The farmer could scarcely believe his ears. Was she mad? "Why would they want to become like me? To suffer as I have? For that matter, I still don't even know exactly if I believe it all in the first place—"

Lylia put a finger to his lips. "Then test it again. One last time. Here and now."

"Test—"

"The final proof." She looked around. "There. Something small but significant. Impossible to deny."

The noblewoman led him toward a bush of the type for which they had been searching. However, this one was withered and, in addition to wrinkled leaves, had only a few shriveled berries to offer.

"What am I supposed to do?" growled Uldyssian anxiously.

"Touch it. Imagine what you want of it. That is all."

He recalled the last time that he had done as she had asked. It was still possible to question what exactly had happened then. Here, though . . .

But he could not deny her. *Imagine what you want of it,* Lylia had said. Uldyssian nervously shrugged. What *would* he want from the bush other than some fresh berries? But the plant was long past that and, in fact, looked near to dying. If it had been younger, full of life, surely it would have offered a bounty for them.

He let his fingers graze the dry bush. The leaves and branches were brittle to his touch. The plant was not dying; it was *dead.*

There was no point in continuing. "Lylia—"

She softly placed her hand atop his, keeping it on in contact with the dead bush. "Please . . . just this once more."

Despite his wariness, he wanted nothing more than to please her. With her hand still atop his own, the son of Diomedes thought of the bush and the juicy, ripe crop he would have liked to have found. Enough to feed them all. After the troubles he and the others had suffered in part due to these supposed powers, it was the least he could ask—

With a gasp, Uldyssian suddenly tore his hand back from the bush.

Unlike when he had concentrated on the storm over Seram, there was no hesitation between his desire and the fruition of it. Even in the dim moonlight, the transformation he now beheld could not be mistaken for anything short of miraculous.

The bush stood swollen several times its emaciated size and was now covered in lush leaves. From the few dried berries had burst a cornucopia of fresh, fat ones. They were not restricted to those native to the bush, either, for Uldyssian could easily make out more than half a dozen distinct variations. Blossoms also dotted the rejuvenated plant, filling the vicinity with a sweet scent.

In comparison to the storm, it was a small thing, this transformation, but it forever put to death for the farmer any doubt that *he* wielded powers beyond his imagination.

And that very realization made him tremble as he never had before, not even when facing the guards of the Cathedral.

"Why do you shake so?" asked Lylia, coming around him. "Look!" The beautiful noblewoman reached out and snatched some of the berries. She thrust them in her mouth, eating with gusto. Her eyes widened in merriment as she ate. "Delicious!" Lylia concluded. "Taste for yourself!"

Before he could decline, she had torn off another bunch and brought them to his lips. Her face she planted in his chest, eyes ever on his own.

Uldyssian could do nothing but accept the bounty. Lylia placed the berries into his mouth, her fingers lingering for a moment.

"Taste them," she repeated, slowly removing her hand.

Never in his life had Uldyssian come across such flavor. Each berry was a treasure unto itself, as sweet as the sweetest wine . . .

"The power within you should be feared only by those who envy you! When all others see the good it creates, they will understand . . . and then . . . then, you can teach them . . ."

"T—Teach them?"

"What I spoke of before! To see the potential within them to be as you! To show them that they need not cow to mage clans, Temples, or Cathedrals, Uldyssian! To know that within each is a glory beyond the conceiving of any would-be prophet or cleric . . ." She halted. "I speak from knowledge, my love. You *can* show them the way . . . I know it! Watch . . . watch . . ."

The noblewoman reached out to one of the blossoms, touching it softly with the tip of her index finger.

And from within the flower burst a tiny stem ending in an oval berry. The berry swelled quickly, then broke open, revealing a small, curled flower. That, in turn, opened wide. As Uldyssian gaped, a twin of the original blossom formed.

"It worked! I knew it! I felt it!" Lylia's laughter was music. "I have felt it ever since you healed me, as if what you did somehow stirred to waking a force within! It is not much, compared to what you have accomplished, but it is something . . ." She turned to him again, her voice taking on a determined edge. "You woke it in me, my love! Therefore, you can do the same for others! No false prophets will be able to fill their ears with lies after you are done! No one will ever be given empty promises, useless hopes! And all because of you!"

Her words swirled around him, both daunting . . . and tempting. In his mind, the farmer relived the deaths of his family and the cloying ways of the clerics who had come to take advantage of his grief. His anxiety and fear gave way to outrage again.

Lylia pulled his face down to hers, her lips barely an inch from his. "How many more are there who have suffered like you, my dear Uldyssian? You could see to it that it never happens again!"

No more clerics. No more Triune. No more Cathedral of Light. Men would depend upon themselves, guide themselves . . .

The son of Diomedes grinned. He liked the sound of that.

"And I . . ." Lylia breathed. "I will stand with you at all times. The two of us always together, always . . . *one.*"

She kissed him long and longingly . . . then led him to the soft ground . . .

Serenthia huddled by the fire, on a small cloth her meager find. Most of the berries were hardly edible, but at least they were there. She had found a few flowers worth eating, too.

Mendeln stood across from her, peering into the dark beyond the campfire. Achilios was not expected for a time, but Uldyssian and Lylia should have been back by now and both there knew it. Mendeln only worried about his brother's safety, while the thoughts of the trader's daughter were far more complicated.

"She's with him," Serenthia murmured, her tone hinting of an emotion that Mendeln ever found uncomfortable. Women in Seram had never found him of interest and he, in turn, had never figured out exactly how to change that.

"It is possible, I suppose." He tried to change the subject. "I hope that Achilios can catch at least one rabbit. There was little but dried rations in the guards' saddlebags."

"I worry about him, Mendeln," she went on. "When that woman is with him, Uldyssian loses track of reason."

"Surely not. I know my brother well."

Serenthia abruptly rose, causing her companion to step back in surprise. "All she's got to do is whisper in his ear and he follows her like a puppy!"

"Love will do that," he replied before realizing just what he had said. To his horror, Serenthia gazed at him as if he had just shoved a dagger into her heart. "What I mean to say is—"

Thankfully, his babbling was interrupted by the arrival of not Uldyssian, but Achilios. The hunter carried two rabbits and a bird in his left hand and wore a smile on his face that evaporated when he noted Serenthia's expression.

"Serry . . . what?" He looked from her to Mendeln and the burning gaze was enough to make Uldyssian's brother feel like the next quarry in Achilios's hunt. "You *told* her? Mendeln! How could you? Serry, I'm so sorry about your father—"

Mendeln sought to wave him to silence, but it was too late. Now the terrible expression that she had focused on the younger son of Diomedes was turned against the archer. "*What* about *my father?*"

Achilios suddenly started toward Mendeln as if not

hearing her. "Help me make these ready, Mendeln! They'll take a while to cook, so we'd better work fast—"

"*Achilios!*" Cyrus's daughter stepped around the fire, coming between the two men. "What happened to my father?" She glanced at Uldyssian's sibling. "You know, too?"

"Serenthia, I—"

She only grew more distraught. "Something's happened to him! I want to know what!"

Abandoning his catch, the hunter seized her by the shoulders. Mendeln had thought of doing the same, but, as was usual in dealing with women, he was generally a second behind the actions of other men.

"Serry . . ." All the merriment Achilios usually displayed had utterly vanished. "Serry . . . Cyrus is dead."

She shook her head vehemently. "No . . . no . . . no . . ."

"It is true," Mendeln added as cautiously as he could. "It was . . . an accident."

"*How?*"

Uldyssian's brother hesitated. "A portion of roof torn off by the wind."

The dark-haired woman looked down. "The wind . . ."

Mendeln feared she would blame Uldyssian, but instead Serenthia slumped down by the fire again. Putting her face in her hands, she began to cry.

It was Achilios who went to her side first. The archer put a comforting arm around his companion. There was nothing but compassion and concern in either his expression or his actions. Mendeln was aware just how much Achilios cared for Serenthia, more so than anyone including himself. Certainly in a different manner than Uldyssian, who had never truly ceased seeing her as the young girl tagging along.

But knowing Serenthia as he did, Mendeln pitied the hunter. Here was one quarry all his skills could not catch for him.

Feeling uncomfortable, Mendeln slipped away from the campfire. Achilios had brought them enough food, and once matters calmed, they could all get to work preparing it. For now, all he desired was to leave Serenthia in the care of the archer.

It was not simply out of respect that he left the trader's daughter to Achilios, no. As he slipped into the dark woods, Mendeln knew that he had departed as much for the sake of his own mind. What would he have said next to Serenthia . . . that her father had been calling for her *after* his death? That he could have sworn that he had seen Cyrus standing above the wreckage of his own *body?*

Slumping against a tree, Mendeln tried to understand what was happening to him. The blackouts, the dirt on his fingers, and finally the voice and the vision—they all pointed at madness.

Yet, what he had witnessed around his brother could have also been called that. Certainly, Uldyssian had appeared to think so.

And Uldyssian had clearly been wrong. Mendeln carried proof of that himself. The savage scar left by the whip was no more. It had healed, possibly during the brothers' flight from Seram. Certainly, by the time they had stopped for the night, it had utterly vanished.

Although the night air was cool, Mendeln felt the sweat dripping down his face. Wiping it away, he tried to calm himself. His brother needed him more than ever. He had to focus only on that. Only on—

He was being watched.

Mendeln spun to his right and in that moment glimpsed a figure in black robes and what seemed an odd, segmented armor. The face was utterly obscured by a tremendous hood.

Then, just as with the shade of Cyrus . . . the figure was no longer there.

It was too much for him. Whirling back in the direction of the camp, Mendeln started to run.

A huge shape dropped down from the trees, landing on all fours in front of the farmer. Even crouched, it was nearly as high at the shoulder as Mendeln was tall and when it stood, even hunched over it was more than half again his height.

The thing opened a mouth much like a frog's. The dim moonlight could not hide from the human the row upon row of daggerlike teeth and the thick tongue darting from within. Above, half a dozen black orbs glistened with an unholy light of their own.

"Meeeeaatttt . . ." it rasped, extending two append-ages ending in sharp claws as long as the human's hand. Behind the monstrosity, a thick tail thumped eagerly against the ground. "Cooommme toooo mmmmeeee, mmmmeeeeaaaatttt . . ."

Mendeln had no intention of obeying, but his body evi-dently had other, more horrific notions in mind. First one foot, then another, slowly, inexorably, dragged him toward the waiting talons of the fiend.

A stench filled his nostrils, the smell of what seemed a hundred years' worth of rotting carrion. The thing waited as he neared it. It could have already ripped out his throat or disemboweled him, but from its rapid breathing clearly enjoyed the fear rushing through its victim.

Mendeln wanted to cry out, but could not. However, as the creature loomed over him, its maw dripping with saliva, an image flashed through Mendeln's mind, an image of symbols familiar to him. They were akin to those on the ancient stone to which Achilios had led him, with some new ones mixed between. Oddly, where last time he had utterly failed to make any sense of them, now Mendeln knew how to pronounce each.

Which he did without urging.

The giant creature suddenly let out a snarl of confusion. It turned from Mendeln, looking past him. One taloned appendage thrust just next to the stunned human. The beast sniffed the air, its mood clearly much angrier.

Only then did the farmer realize that the fiend was now *blind* . . .

Mendeln also realized that he controlled his movements again. Not questioning his good fortune, he cautiously stepped to the opposite side. The beast turned, but away from him. Holding his breath, Mendeln took another step further on.

He must have made some sound, for the fiend spun in his direction and swiped the air with one massive paw. Although Mendeln moved as quickly as he could, the tips of one talon caught the sleeve of his garment. He twirled helplessly in a circle before crashing to the ground. At the same time, his mind for some reason took objection to the fact that the demon could hear. Somehow, Mendeln felt that the blindness should have been accompanied by a deafness as well.

The creature reached for him—

There was a shout and then the hiss of an arrow. Mendeln heard a thump, followed by a furious snarl from his inhuman attacker. He felt the beast turn from him.

"Move, Mendeln!" Achilios called. "Move!"

He obeyed, but not without shouting back, "The eyes! It is blind for the moment, but shoot the eyes!"

Likely he had not had to tell the trained hunter what to do, but Achilios had saved him and Mendeln owed his friend what little aid that he could give. The sudden sightlessness of the beast was the only advantage that they had at the moment, if even that could be called so.

"Mmmooorrree mmmmeeeaaatttt . . ." mocked the thing. "Wheerrre arrre yyyyooou?"

Achilios let loose with another arrow, but although blind, his target somehow sensed it coming and moved aside. The wooden shaft bounced harmlessly off its scaled hide. Mendeln saw only then that the first bolt stuck in the monster just under the arm, where the flesh was less covered. Achilios had been fortunate with that initial attempt; the rest of the creature's form was very much protected.

As the archer readied another shot, the abomination leapt like a frog in his general direction. However, from the monster's side, Serenthia lunged forward, gripped in both hands a thick, burning branch from the fire. Had the giant been able to see, she would have surely perished, but instead the blindness enabled the trader's daughter to bring the flames right against the vulnerable orbs.

A howl that tore into the very core of Mendeln's soul ripped through the area. A new stench filled the air, that of burning flesh.

The injured fiend swung wildly. Serenthia could not escape his reach. His talons slashed her back. She crumpled, then lay still.

"Serry!" Like a man possessed, Achilios fired upon the beast. This time, he caught it in one of the other orbs. The giant howled anew, then tore the shaft from the ruined socket.

As it turned again on the hunter, Mendeln realized that its sight had come back. With that also returned another danger, one of which only he was aware.

"Look not in its eyes, Achilios!" he shouted desperately. "It will draw you to it, then!"

His warning came too late. Achilios stiffened, the bow dropping from his hands. The hunter's arms went slack and he stood motionless before the oncoming horror. The beast laughed—a terrible, grating sound—then reached for the helpless tidbit.

But the talons halted just before Achilios, unable to touch the prey. The next moment, the earth beneath the fiendish creature seemed to liquefy. It tried to pull back, but its legs only sank deeper into the soil.

The beast looked around for an immediate cause, but found none. "Wwwwhatttt?" it roared. "Wwwhhhhooo?"

Its gaze fixed upon Mendeln, the only one in sight. Without thinking, he shook his head in denial of responsibility. Nonetheless, the scaled horror tried to turn toward him, the better to focus its hypnotic gaze.

As it did, the liquid earth now rose up its legs, as if impatient to take the beast. Mendeln suddenly forgotten, the creature struggled to remove itself . . . but to no avail.

The ground crawled ever upward, quickly enveloping the torso. One set of talons tore at it, only to become ensnared as if in solidifying honey. The trapped beast tried to use its other talons to pull free the one limb, only to have that also caught.

Within seconds, all that remained uncovered was the grotesque head. The creature twisted its head upward, then rasped, "Ggggrrreaaatttt Llllucionnnn! Ssssavvve yyyyyooourrr llloyyyyall ssssservvvvannnttt! Gggggreeeeaaattt Llllucionnn! Ssssavvvve! Grreeeatttt—"

With one last swift effort, the ground sealed over the froglike mouth, finally entombing its victim.

Achilios let out a grunt, shook, then dropped to his knees. Mendeln cautiously rose, not completely confident that the monster was no more. At last, he moved to Serenthia's side and gingerly inspected the wounds. They were horribly deep, but at least she was still alive. How long that would be, though—

"I'll see to her, Mendeln, don't you worry," Uldyssian's voice suddenly said.

The elder brother stood on the opposite side of the stricken woman. Mendeln eyed his brother with almost as much surprise as he had the beast. Despite the night, Uldyssian stood perfectly visible, as if a light within illuminated him. He was bare-chested, but seemed unmoved by the cool air.

There was a look in Uldyssian's face, a look that Mendeln could not read but that somehow made him feel more insignificant than ever. As his brother knelt down by Serenthia, Mendeln involuntarily slunk back, as if not worthy to be so close at such a time.

Seemingly ignorant of his brother's reaction, Uldyssian placed his hands palm-down an inch or so above Serenthia's torn back. He then stared at the wounds, while Mendeln watched in wonder and curiosity.

And as the younger brother watched, each of the terrible, crimson valleys healed themselves. The ends first tapered, drawing the wounds together as if by invisible needle and thread. The slashes themselves then shrank rapidly, in many cases going from over a foot long to a bare scar in less than three beats of Mendeln's racing heart.

One more beat . . . and Serenthia's back became completely unmarred again.

A slight moan escaped her. She started to move. Nodding in satisfaction, Uldyssian stepped back, the light within seeming to fade now.

It was Achilios, naturally, who proved to have the presence of mind to remove his own shirt and cover Serenthia as she started to rise. Mendeln, meanwhile, stood up to face his brother.

"What . . . what did you just do?"

"What had to be done, of course." Uldyssian looked at him as if Mendeln had asked why crops needed rain.

"But . . . *how?*" The younger son of Diomedes shook his head. "No, that is not what I mean . . . Uldyssian . . . everything that happened in Seram . . . *was* that you?"

Now seeming more as Mendeln knew him, Uldyssian slowly nodded. "It must've been." He nodded toward the macabre monument that was all that remained of the abomination. "And that, I won't deny doing."

"What *was* that thing?" snapped Achilios, still holding a stunned Serenthia. "Those talons . . . and those eyes . . ."

It was Lylia who answered, Lylia appearing behind Uldyssian almost as abruptly as he had moments earlier. The noblewoman wrapped her arms possessively around Mendeln's brother, saying, "It is the murderer they sought in Seram, obviously. The fiend that slew the two missionaries. What else could it be?"

Uldyssian, Achilios, and Serenthia took her answer to heart and even Mendeln had to admit that it was an obvious statement. Certainly, the condition of the one acolyte's corpse made sense when seeing the horrible talons. The creature was also cunning, even speaking the tongue of men with ease. Surely it had frozen each victim with its gaze, then done its foul work. It also moved extremely fast, which would explain the short time between the murders.

Yet, he found himself not entirely convinced. More to the point, something else about the abomination disturbed him. "But how does it come to be here? We are far from Seram."

"Why, it followed Uldyssian, naturally! After all, everyone thought that he was the one to blame. If it slew him, then no suspicion of its foul existence would remain!"

Again, another reasonable explanation, but for some reason Mendeln could not see the creature pursuing Uldyssian so far just for that. There had never been any suggestion by either the village or the Master Inquisitor that such an unnatural beast could be responsible. Everyone had thought of the murderer as human and far too many had assumed it to be Uldyssian.

Something else came to mind. "It *called* to somebody," he blurted. "At the end, it called to somebody."

"Aye," interjected Achilios as he helped Serenthia to stand. "I heard it, too."

Lylia's grip on Uldyssian tightened. "It was nothing."

But the elder son of Diomedes nodded to Mendeln. "I heard, too, but the name escaped me."

Mendeln concentrated, reliving the moment. "Great . . . Great *Lucion*. Lucion." For some reason, merely speaking it made him shudder. "That was the name."

Unfortunately, knowing it meant nothing to him, nor did he see any recognition on the faces of anyone else. Not even when Mendeln studied Lylia's as close—and as surreptitiously—as possible did he see any hint of knowledge.

"He must be with one of the mage clans," Uldyssian suddenly declared, his eyes brightening dangerously. "The murdered ones were emissaries from the Temple and the Cathedral. Who else would hunt such?"

"Yes," Lylia immediately agreed, sounding to Mendeln's ears almost pleased with his brother's quick thinking. "The mage clans. Surely them. Do you not agree, Mendeln?"

She gave him a smile such as he had seen her so far reserve only for his brother. Mendeln felt himself flush.

"The mage clans," he blurted, nodding at the same time. "Of course." Yet, Mendeln wondered why any of the mage clans, so desperate to hold their own against each other, would bother with two lowly emissaries in a backwater village.

Everyone else seemed satisfied. Uldyssian looked around at the others as if they were his children. "We can worry about that later. This only proves my decision the right one."

Mendeln had a bad feeling. "Your decision?"

"Seram is part of my past now, not my present or future." As Uldyssian spoke, Lylia—leaving one arm around his waist—moved to his side. "I never asked for this, but something's granted me a gift—"

"A gift? You call what happened a gift?"

"Hush, Mendeln."

He looked in surprise at Serenthia, who was the one who had spoken. Of all people there, Uldyssian's brother would have expected her to call the things that had happened horrible, certainly not a gift. Yet, now she spoke with what he realized was awe . . . awe of Uldyssian.

Mendeln looked to Achilios, but the hunter did not appear willing to contradict the emotions of the woman he loved. He kept his expression set.

"A gift, yes," Uldyssian went on, as if Mendeln were a small child in need of simple words. "Something inside *all* of us, in fact." He paused, smiling. "Let's get back to camp. I'll explain everything. Then, as soon as we're done eating, we need to get some rest. After all, the journey to Kehjan will take several days' riding."

"Kehjan?" Mendeln nearly choked on the name, so unexpected was it. They were now going to *Kehjan*? "But . . . but what about the sea?"

"Kehjan," Uldyssian repeated, gazing down at Lylia. "Where best to begin changing the *world*?"

As he and the noblewoman drank in one another,

Mendeln looked in dismay at Serenthia and Achilios. *The world?* Had he just heard his brother correctly? He looked to the other pair for some understanding, even help, but, to his dismay, the trader's daughter seemed caught between her awe of this new Uldyssian and her jealousy of Lylia, while the hunter only stared longingly at *her*. No one but Mendeln seemed to grasp the enormity of the moment properly.

No one but he seemed to understand that his brother was surely heading toward his certain doom . . . and very likely taking the others with him.

Malic angrily shut the tiny, jeweled box he had been given by the Primus. The green, circular gem situated in one of the four slots had crumbled to ash but a moment before, signifying its sudden worthlessness to the high priest. The hunter he had summoned was no more.

But anger mixed with growing interest, for he had been sent to investigate emanations felt by his master, investigate and, if it proved that they came from some person, bring that one back to the Temple for study and possible conversion. Now, at least, Malic knew that he was not on some wild chase.

Still, frowning, the tall cleric thrust the box back into the pouch on his belt, then returned to his horse. A hooded, armored Peace Warder handed Malic the reins, then retreated to his own mount. Behind them, a full score more well-armed warriors of the faithful sat ready to ride wherever their leader commanded and do whatever was necessary. They, of course, did not understand the entire truth concerning the Temple of the Triune, but they did understand *enough* to know, like Malic, that to not succeed in this mission was unthinkable.

Malic eyed them, seeking any weakness or hesitation, then looked ahead. The dark of night did not affect him, a gift of the Primus. Malic saw the path ahead as perfectly as he did during the day.

Soon, the high priest thought. *Soon.* They were not far

from their goal, the steeds granted them by his master swifter than any. Their appearance might be that of sleek black stallions, but that was mere illusion for the foolish masses. No mortal animal could have covered so much ground in so little time.

"Forward," Malic commanded, urging his own beast on.

The prize was not far. A demon might fail, but the high priest would not. Malic had not risen to be the Primus's right hand without effort. His hands were stained with the blood of his rivals, both figuratively and truly. He *would* succeed.

Again, there was *no* other choice.

SEVEΠ

Uldyssian rode a changed man. Never in his life had he considered himself a champion of the people, a transformer of a world. He had been content to be a farmer, tilling the soil, raising his crops, and seeing to his animals. How short-sighted, how simple, that all seemed now. He did not question his almost overnight shift in thought and purpose any more than he now questioned the force swelling within him. It had happened and that was all that mattered.

A great part of the change in Uldyssian could be attributed to the woman riding behind him. When he listened to Lylia, everything made sense. Everything seemed possible. Uldyssian was grateful not only for her presence, but her knowledge and experience. She knew the world outside of Seram, especially the pitfalls and other traps. She also understood the yearning of the masses to no longer be subject to the mercurial machinations of the mage clans or corrupt sects such as the Triune or the Cathedral. With her at his side, Uldyssian felt as if he could do *anything*.

It was all planned out, at least in his mind. Ride into the vast city and seek a place in the great public square, where many would-be prophets came to preach. However, where they were looked upon as fools and madmen, matters would be different for Uldyssian. He could *show* the people the path, the gift, that he offered. They would see that he was no charlatan. Once his first audience saw the truth, the word would spread like wildfire *everywhere*.

He glanced to his right, where his brother rode. Mendeln

watched the path ahead, just like the others, but Uldyssian knew that his sibling was one person in the party who did not fully appreciate what he intended. Mendeln had been hesitant from the beginning, bringing up suggestions and reasons for caution.

But Lylia had countered those concerns with strong words of her own, further empowered by her tragic tale. Caution and hesitation only allowed those who would be jealous of Uldyssian's gift to act. Innocents might suffer, then, as had happened with the noblewoman and her family.

No, Uldyssian was absolutely certain of his course. He loved his brother, but if Mendeln continued to fail to see things as they should be, then Uldyssian would have to deal with him somehow. It would not look good for his own blood to seem less than an absolute believer in what Uldyssian was doing—

The farmer grimaced. What sort of thoughts were these? His brother meant *everything* to him! Only Mendeln's presence had kept him from losing his mind when the rest of their family had perished.

Shame filled Uldyssian. He could not imagine life without his brother . . .

He'll come to understand, the older son of Diomedes assured himself. *Mendeln will come to understand . . .*

He *had* to.

They rode that day and the next toward their destination without so much as meeting a soul. To Uldyssian, life in Seram seemed more and more merely a bad dream as anticipation of the city grew.

Achilios went ahead to scout the way, something that Uldyssian felt unnecessary—considering his power—but did not argue against. The archer did not return to the party until well after they had made camp, bringing with him a pair of good-sized hares for food.

"I sighted smoke far in the distance just before sunset," Achilios remarked, giving the hares to Mendeln and

Serenthia. "A town, maybe." With a smile, he added, "Perhaps somewhere where we could get a good ale!"

Mendeln closed his eyes for a moment, then said, "Partha. I think that there's a town in this region called Partha."

One of Mendeln's favorite pastimes when in Cyrus's establishment was to listen to where travelers came from and to inspect the trader's collection of maps. In regards to the latter, Mendeln had an almost perfect memory.

"A good-sized place?" Uldyssian asked with growing interest.

"Larger than Tulisam, I believe, yes. On a direct route between the great city and the largest seaports."

Partha sounded ideal to Uldyssian in more ways than one. It had occurred to him, somewhat belatedly, to test himself on a simpler place than Kehjan. A few days in Partha would remove any doubt, especially from Mendeln, about Uldyssian's ability to show people the gift.

So far, despite the fact that each night Uldyssian tried to show them, only he and Lylia seemed able to draw upon whatever it was within. Serenthia appeared on the edge of making the leap, but something held her back. As for Achilios, he looked content with his skills as a hunter, which, for the first time, Uldyssian believed drew in a different manner from the same source as the farmer's abilities. Certainly, Achilios had always been a very, very fortunate hunter. There was still hope there, but long-term.

As for Mendeln, he seemed furthest of all from realizing his own abilities. Uldyssian did not understand why, having assumed that his brother would be the most adept other than himself. Lylia had, the night before, come up with what appeared to be the best answer so far. As with Achilios, it was very likely Mendeln's own personality that held him back.

But that was a matter that could also wait, at least for the moment. The town offered many, many new options.

"Partha . . ." he murmured.

Lylia leaned close, then, almost nuzzling his ear. Uldyssian did not miss Serenthia's brief look of dejection at this.

"We should really continue straight to the city," the noblewoman whispered. "The sooner the greatest number of people can hear and see you, the sooner the transformation of the world can begin . . ."

"Yes, you're right," Uldyssian returned, immediately seeing her point and wondering why he had even bothered thinking of a tiny, insignificant place such as Partha. "Straight to the city. That's best."

Achilios looked disappointed, but nodded. Serenthia's face was a mask. Mendeln appeared perturbed, but Uldyssian was used to seeing his brother so. No one protested; that was all that was important.

Still, Uldyssian needed to test himself. He finally rose from Lylia's grip. "Serry, would you come with me?"

Her eyes momentarily brightened . . . then the mask returned. She also rose. "Of course . . . of course . . ."

"Uldyssian—" Lylia called.

"I won't be long," he assured her.

The blond woman turned her gaze to the fire and said nothing.

Taking Serenthia's hand, Uldyssian led her past an uncomprehending Achilios and Mendeln. He guided the trader's daughter into the forest until the light of the camp could no longer be seen, then turned her to face him.

Serenthia waited expectantly. Uldyssian considered his words carefully before saying, "I'm sorry again about Cyrus, Serry. So very sorry."

"Uldyssian, I—"

He put a finger to her lips. "Serry, he may have died because of me—"

She pulled back. "No!" Lowering her voice, Serenthia added, "No, Uldyssian. I've thought about it a lot while we've been traveling. Perhaps . . . perhaps the storm came from you . . . I still don't know . . . but you never meant harm. Brother Mikelius was condemning you as a heretic! If you somehow caused the storm, then it was because *he* forced it on you! You were only *defending* yourself!"

He looked at her in surprise. Hearing this from one he knew who had cared deeply for her father—and had long respected both major sects—Uldyssian felt tremendous relief. Until then, he had not realized how much he had still worried inside about how the trader's death had affected her.

"Serry, even thinking that . . . why didn't you return home instead of following me into the unknown? Your brothers . . . they'll fear for you . . ."

"I am old enough to find my own way in the world," she said with some of her old defiance. Planting her hands on her hips, Serenthia added, "Thiel and the rest will know what I did and they'll leave me to my own actions, as always."

She said it with such finality that Uldyssian could only smile ruefully. Even now, he would not try to dissuade her. Besides, it still comforted him to have her around, just as it did to have his brother and Achilios. "All right. I had to ask. I had to know. I won't say any more."

"But, *I* must say something . . . if you permit . . ." Once again, Cyrus's daughter became the awed follower.

"You don't need my permission."

"Uldyssian . . . I understand what you do and believe wholeheartedly in it." She cleared her throat. "But perhaps Mendeln's concern has some merit. I know Lylia says to ride straight to the city, but—"

He frowned. "Is this about Lylia, Serry?"

Although she shook her head, he could tell that it both was and was not. Uldyssian doubted that Serenthia could separate matters.

"No . . . I mean . . . Uldyssian . . . I've spoken with missionaries from both the Temple and the Cathedral and not all of them are like Brother Mikelius. I do think that there's some good in them—"

"Hardly," the son of Diomedes returned, growing stone-faced. Memories of the Master Inquisitor raced through his head.

Serenthia paused, visibly seeking a different tack. "It's just that . . . I know Lylia has experienced far more than us, but not everything she says is what we should do."

Her words only made Uldyssian defensive. "I listen to Lylia just as I listen to all of you. It just happens that her advice has made the most sense to me more often."

"More like all the time—"

"Enough." Uldyssian felt an unreasoning anger rising, but managed to smother it. He could see no reason to continue with the conversation. It had been his notion to clear the air between them in regards to her father and that had been done. Obviously, Uldyssian thought, putting to rest any emotions Serenthia had toward him would take longer. He would have to be patient. Yes, patient.

Reaching up, he placed one hand on her head as he had done when she had been only a child. "Serry," he whispered. "You said you believe in what I've become, right?"

She nodded, her eyes still reflecting her thoughts on the previous subject.

"I know that what's been awakened in me is trying to stir within you, too, but so far it's not been able."

"I've tried . . ." the young woman insisted.

His hand went to her shoulder, which he patted. "I know. Let me try to help guide it to awakening. Take my hands." When she had obeyed, Uldyssian continued, "If this works, it will better help me understand how to show others once we reach Kehjan."

"But what are . . . oh!"

Lylia had suggested to him that it was their closeness, their melding to one, that had stirred the latent force within her. Obviously, Uldyssian could not share in that same manner with others—especially Serenthia—but he could try to come as close as possible. He focused on the woman before him, trying to see into her heart, into her soul. He tried to let the power flow from him into those places in the hope of igniting the flame.

It certainly felt to him as if what he did worked. A warmth entered his hands, a warmth he seemed to feel spreading from his companion. Serenthia, in turn, began to breathe rapidly and her eyes now looked up to the point where Uldyssian could see only the whites.

Then, to his surprise, Uldyssian felt stirring from her direction something akin to that which lurked within himself. He focused on Serenthia and was able to verify that it came from within the woman. It was slight in comparison, but the more he reached out to it, the stronger, more awake, it became.

He was awed by his own, swift success. Lylia had been correct again. Uldyssian had managed to stir to life within Serenthia the same force.

Without warning, her body began to quiver uncontrollably. The whites were still the only thing visible of her eyes. She let out a small moan . . .

Uldyssian grew worried. Serenthia had just passed a mighty threshold, although the enormity of it would not be evident for some time. Still, it behooved him now to stop and let her move ahead on her own. Too quickly and something might happen to her.

As Uldyssian released her hands, the trader's daughter let out a gasp and fell toward him. He caught her in his arms, holding her while she recovered.

"It felt like . . ." she finally managed. " . . . *feels* like . . ." But words failed her after that.

"I know . . ." he finally replied, hoping to comfort her.

Serenthia suddenly stiffened. She pulled away from Uldyssian as if he was a leper . . . then rushed toward the direction of the camp.

Uldyssian stood baffled. He had expected something akin to the euphoria Lylia had told him that she had felt.

Serenthia vanished among the trees and shadows. Uldyssian, still confused, stared after her for a few seconds more before starting back himself. He was certain that he had done everything right. Why, then, had she reacted so?

When at first he stepped back into the camp, he saw no sign of her. Concerned, Uldyssian started to ask his brother, but Mendeln mutely shook his head, then nodded toward his right. There, half-obscured by the dark, lay Serenthia. She had one of the blankets procured from the Cathedral saddlebags around her and faced away from the camp.

Uldyssian took a step toward her, only to have Lylia come up and gently take his arm.

"It would be best to leave her be," the noblewoman whispered.

He opened his mouth to reply, then clamped it shut again. It seemed that, even with all that he had gained, there were some things that Uldyssian would never understand.

Come the morning, Serenthia acted as if nothing had happened, yet Uldyssian could with his own burgeoning powers sense that the force within her had grown stronger. She evinced no sign of this, though, and he finally decided that he would let *her* choose when to accept her gift. It was enough to know that she did wield it. That meant that he *would* be able to guide others toward the same direction and with practice the effort would surely grow quicker and easier.

They rode under an overcast sky that Uldyssian at one point bemusedly wondered if he could clear. He did not try, though, for fear that, if it did indeed worked, he would only be announcing his presence to those who might wish him to never make it to the city. Lylia had suggested to him that it would be better if he waited until in Kehjan before revealing himself so. Then, she said, it would be too late for them to hide the truth from the people.

Despite the continuous gloom, it did not rain and so once more they made good time. Partha remained a faint spiral of smoke in the distance, the only change the direction in which they had to look for it. By Mendeln's calculation and Lylia's confirmation, they would see a similar hint of the great city in three or four more days at the utmost.

The five finally also crossed paths with other travelers, in this case, a wagon heading the opposite direction. The driver, a bearded elder with trade dealings at the seaports, greeted the party warily at first. His apprentice, a gangly, carrot-haired youth with watery eyes, anxiously kept his hand near a well-worn sword at his side.

As he still wished to reach Kejhan as soon as possible, Uldyssian decided that there was no use in revealing what he was to the pair. Instead, he sought from the trader news concerning the state of affairs in the legendary city.

"The mage clans have a truce going on at the moment, aye," declared the stout figure as he lit a long, clay pipe. "It'll last as well as the others, which's to say not long at all. Possibly even over, already. The nobles, they watch and wait while they plot to their own advantage and the clans let'm keep some control over the city's functions so's that they can free up themselves to figure out how to get around the truce." He chuckled darkly. "So, one might say all's pretty much as always in Kehjan . . ."

His words verified for Uldyssian the importance of what Lylia had said about heading directly there rather than turn to Partha or any other lesser settlement. Uldyssian graciously thanked the trader, then led the others on.

They settled for the night on the bank of a sedate river coursing along the region. Here the line between woods and jungle blurred some. For the first time, Uldyssian came to understand just how small the forested region was in comparison with the great jungles said to be covering much of the realm. He had even heard traders pausing at Seram remark that it seemed that the jungles were gradually swallowing up all else. Obviously that could not be the truth, but, eyeing the odd, almost unnatural shift in environment, Uldyssian could not help still wonder a little.

He had hoped that the day's ride would ease the tension between him and Serenthia, but the raven-haired woman yet again found reason to be away from him.

"It is best to let her work it out herself," Lylia finally whispered to him as she nuzzled his cheek. "She will come to accept matters. You will see."

Nodding, Uldyssian forced his attention to more important matters. Now that he was so near the city, his nerves had begun to act up. He admitted this to Lylia, who suggested that he retire early and let the rest of them see to things.

"You must be at your peak come the day we enter. Go, sleep. When there is food ready, I will bring it to you."

She kissed him again, then departed. Uldyssian immediately followed her good advice. The ground beneath was soft and the night warmer than previous. A short nap, he decided, was indeed the right thing for him. As usual, Lylia knew best. He could not imagine a future without her. It was as if Uldyssian had always known her.

With those comforting thoughts, he drifted off.

Serenthia knew that she had to come to grips with her conflicting emotions concerning Uldyssian. She believed in the goodness of what he had become, believed it enough to not even consider him at fault for her father's terrible fate, but at the same time she could not separate what he was from what he had once been . . . the man whom she had loved as no one else.

And who now loved another . . . a woman he had met only a short while before.

"We need more wood for the fire," Mendeln commented.

Seizing on the opportunity to be even more by herself, Serenthia quickly replied, "I'll go and gather it. You make certain that the fire doesn't die in the meantime."

She slipped out of the camp and began collecting small, broken branches. The search required little attention, which allowed her mind to wander to less confusing—and less painful—subjects. But Cyrus's daughter had gathered only roughly half an armful when a prickling sensation on her neck made her look over her shoulder.

"Lylia!" The presence of the noblewoman out here so startled Serenthia that she dropped several pieces of wood. She stared in disbelief at the blond figure.

The other woman strode up to her with footsteps as silent as a cat. "Forgive me," Lylia murmured. "I did not mean to scare you . . ."

"What . . . what are you doing out here? I don't need any help with the wood."

"I wanted to speak with you, that was all."

"Speak with me?" The trader's daughter feared that she knew the subject. "There's no need—"

Lylia moved closer. "But there is *every* need, dear Serenthia, every need." As she stared deep into the other woman's eyes, she set a soft hand on her arm. "You are special to Uldyssian and, thus, special to me. I want all his friends to be comfortable around me. I want you to think of me not just as his love, his future mate, but as *your* friend as well . . ."

If Lylia expected her words to comfort Serenthia, they had the opposite effect. An unreasoning distress filled Serenthia and the words "love" and "mate" rang in her head over and over. She felt utter shame that Lylia knew how jealous she had been. Serenthia struggled against her swirling emotions, insisting to herself that they were exaggerated . . . but, in the end, they still proved too much for her.

Eyes tearing, she whirled from Lylia's grip. The kindling fell unnoticed from her arms. Serenthia ran, not caring which direction she headed. All that mattered was to be away, away from everyone who knew what she had been thinking.

Tree limbs snagged at her clothing. Serenthia stumbled several times on the uneven ground. She tripped once across an upward-turned root. None of these impediments caused her to pause and thus possibly regain her wits.

Serenthia simply righted herself each time and continued running. Wild emotion clouded her mind.

A silhouetted form stepped out in front of her. Paying it no mind, she kept moving. Only when it seized her in a grip of steel did she start to come back to reality.

At which point she opened her mouth to scream. One gauntleted hand quickly smothered her cry. Serenthia struggled to free herself, but another figure came up behind her, securing the trader's daughter.

The first figure leaned forward, his hooded form almost ghostlike. "Be silent, girl . . ." he hissed. "Or else you must be punished!"

She began to notice other, similar figures, men in hoods and armor. At first she took them for Inquisitor guards, but then a symbol on the breastplate of the foremost momentarily glittered in the moonlight, revealing the familiar triangle symbol of the Temple.

Serenthia tried to speak, to explain, but her effort garnered her only a swift and painful slap across the face.

"Brother Rondo! Have a care with the child!"

The voice was low and smooth and its kind tone reminded Serenthia of her father. A dark figure atop a monstrously huge stallion rode up to where the two men held her. As the tall rider dismounted, the hardened warriors surrounding Serenthia released her, then fell down on one knee. Although now not held, she felt a compulsion to follow their example.

"Forgive me, Eminence," grunted the one called Rondo anxiously.

"Your enthusiasm is commendable, your tact in need of work, brother." The gloved figure touched Rondo atop his covered head, then turned his attention back to Serenthia.

"My child, shiver not so at my coming. I am friend, not fear." Up close, his features became visible. In contrast to his pale skin, he had thick, wavy dark hair and a deep brow. An elegant mustache gave him a regal dignity. His smile, like his tone, reminded Serenthia of her father. "I am Malic, high priest of the Order of Mefis—"

"Of the Temple of the Triune," Serenthia finished somewhat breathlessly. Instinctively, she bowed her head.

"A believer! How delightful!" Malic stretched out a hand to her, which, after a hesitation, the woman took. "And, I do apologize for the zealousness of Brother Rondo here. We are all eager to conclude our quest . . ."

His last words set Serenthia on edge. She instantly recalled everything that had happened in the village and how the Cathedral had immediately condemned Uldyssian without hearing his side. Suddenly, Malic's presence no longer eased her mind.

Somehow, he must have read that, for the high priest cocked his head and remarked, "But come, my child! I told you, I am friend! I sense your withdrawal . . ." Without permission, his hand touched between her breasts. "And I sense, also . . ." Malic frowned. " . . . that you are *not* the one we seek. There is the spark of something within you, but it is too weak . . ."

Without meaning to, Serenthia blurted, "Uldyssian—"

Malic's thick, dark brow rose. " 'Uldyssian'? Is that his name? And you think him the one we seek?"

She clamped her mouth shut.

Brother Rondo stirred from his kneeling position, but Malic waved him down again. The high priest leaned forward, until his face, and especially his eyes, filled Serenthia's view.

"You are fearful. But why . . . unless . . ." He smiled wider, revealing perfect teeth. "Ah! The Cathedral! It surely must be! Inquisitors, no doubt!"

Still Serenthia said nothing, although his accurate guesswork made her wonder if he could read her thoughts.

"The Cathedral . . . small wonder you show such distrust. Brother Rondo, was there not news from one of our messengers of the deaths of not only one of our own, but also a servant of the Cathedral as well?"

"Aye, Eminence. In the village of Seram, it was said. The murder of our missionary was especially brutal—"

"Yes, yes." Waving him to silence again, Malic said to Serenthia, "And the Cathedral did condemn your Uldyssian, did they not?"

"Yes," she finally answered, some of her distrust fading again.

"Typical of their ways. If they cannot fathom something, they must be rid of it. Woe betide the day that the Prophet began preaching his blasphemies . . ." The high priest stepped next to Serenthia, his arm wrapping around her shoulder in a comforting manner. "But we are not the Cathedral, child. The Temple of the Triune has always preached a peaceful resolution to matters, you understand that? Good! I would not have you believing that we come to do as they did! Rather, we are here just to do the *opposite* and surely it must be a sign for both you and I that we should meet at this fortuitous moment! You can lead me to your Uldyssian and then all of our problems will be over . . ."

"But—" Serenthia found it hard to think. Her mind suddenly felt as muddled as when Lylia had spoken with her. Still, she still recalled some things. Uldyssian wanted to go to the city . . . and he certainly wanted nothing to do with *any* sect, be it the Cathedral *or* the Triune. "No. I can't. Uldyssian wouldn't want me to—"

Malic's body tensed. Serenthia suddenly felt his arm slide back until his gloved fingers rested near the back of her skull. She felt a painful force there and tried to let out a cry, but her mouth would not work. Neither would her body. Only her mind functioned, but it was now a prisoner in an immobile shell.

"A shame you would not listen to reason, child," the tall figure remarked in a voice no longer comforting. "But you will *still* lead us to your Uldyssian . . ." He looked at the Peace Warders. "To your mounts! Hurry!"

As the men rushed to their beasts, Malic led Serenthia to his own. Up close, something about the creature put her ill at ease, but her body, subject to the high priest's will, would not let her pull back. Instead, she mounted up in front of her captor, who took the reins with one hand and held her tight with the other.

"Now," he whispered in her ear in the same kind tone that he had first used, a tone that Cyrus's daughter knew he used to mock her helplessness. "Now, my child. Show me the way."

Serenthia's left hand rose, pointing unerringly in the direction of the camp.

"Very good. Very good. Be sure to smile when you see your friend. I would hate to make him uneasy . . ."

The corners of her mouth rose. Malic chuckled quietly . . . then urged his mount forward.

EIGHT

A sense of disquiet pervaded Uldyssian in his sleep. He felt as if some malevolent presence suddenly hovered over him, seeking his soul while he lay undefended.

His uneasiness became so great that Uldyssian started into waking. However, instead of some fiend such as had attacked the party, he looked up into Lylia's perfect face. The noblewoman knelt at his side.

"Are you ill, my love?" she whispered.

"How long—how long have you been there?"

"I just returned. You looked so peaceful I did not wish to disturb you. I apologize if I did."

Uldyssian frowned. Now that he was awake, the disquiet magnified . . . only it seemed to have something more to do with their surroundings.

"Lylia . . ." he muttered. "Go join the others by the fire. Go right now."

"Why?" Her eyes widened. "What is the matter?"

"Just do it . . ." Rising swiftly, Uldyssian all but pushed the blond woman toward the center of the camp. As he did, he saw to his dismay that only Mendeln was present.

"Where's Achilios?" he demanded of his brother. "Where's Serry?"

"Achilios has gone hunting." Mendeln glanced about. "I believe Serenthia should be nearby. She only went to gather a bit more wood—"

"I am sure that she will be back shortly," interjected Lylia, attempting to calm the tall farmer. "There is no cause for concern, Uldyssian . . ."

But he felt otherwise. Something was close, very close. Something was—

There was a rustling sound from behind Mendeln. Startled, Uldyssian's brother scurried toward the others.

Serenthia stepped into the campsite.

Uldyssian began to exhale . . . and then another, dark-haired figure joined the trader's daughter. He was even taller than Uldyssian and, while slimmer, clearly very fit. The newcomer wore a kindly expression and his manner reminded Uldyssian in some ways of his father . . . but all that became moot as he realized just what garments the man wore.

They were those of a *cleric* of the Temple of the Triune. A high-ranking cleric, at that.

"Uldyssian," Serenthia called. "I have a friend with me. His name is Malic and he wants to help."

Uldyssian hid a frown. She of all people should have known how he would react to a cleric's presence, especially after the chaos in Seram. True, Serenthia had always been something of a believer, but he had thought that behind her now. What was she thinking?

"I have come to offer the protection of the Triune," Malic graciously added, spreading his gloved hands as if to show he carried no weapon. The flames of the campfire reflected brilliantly in his gaze, which fixed upon Uldyssian's with an almost magnetic pull. "This child has told me of the terrible injustice perpetrated on you in the name of the Cathedral of Light. The Triune frowns on such monstrous behavior. We would keep you from threat from the agents of the Prophet . . ."

Despite everything that had happened to him, despite his deep abhorrence of Malic's ilk, Uldyssian found himself half-wanting to listen to the man. There was just something understanding about the cleric. He seemed to feel the pain still buried deep in the farmer's gut. Uldyssian opened his mouth to welcome the man to their camp—

But, at that moment, the fire *erupted*, briefly bursting to a height greater than that of the cleric. Malic instinctively pulled back from the wild flames . . . and as he did, he also tore his gaze from Uldyssian.

The farmer felt as if a blanket had been torn from over his head. It was as if he had been blind and could not *see* again . . . and only then did he understand that Malic had briefly *mesmerized* him.

"Serry!" Uldyssian roared, his rage immediately swelling. "Come to me! Hurry!"

There was a hesitation, as if at first she either did not hear him or for some reason could not obey. Then, with a violent shiver, the dark-tressed woman cried out and fled from Malic's side. The cleric took a belated grab at her, then glared at Uldyssian.

And no sooner had Serenthia escaped than the camp filled with hooded and armored figures either on horseback or on foot. Uldyssian had seen their like before, seen them and been repulsed by them as he had by the Cathedral's Inquisitors. "Peace Warders" they might call themselves, but the warriors of the Triune were no better than the cut-throats commanded by the unlamented Brother Mikelius. All they sought was control of the minds and souls of the people. Those who did not kneel to them—those like Uldyssian—they found ways to condemn.

In the blink of an eye, the farmer relived the calamity in Seram. He saw the hatred and heard once more the lies . . .

"No!" he growled at the oncoming figures. "Not again!"

The air rippled.

As if struck by an invisible hand, the Peace Warders went flying back in every direction. Two crashed against the nearby trees, striking so hard that they wrapped around the trunks like vines. Another warrior flew up several yards above the ground, disappearing in the foliage. The rest lay scattered and stunned around the outskirts of the campsite.

"Impressive," declared Malic in the same fatherly voice. Unlike his minions, he stood untouched by what-ever force had acted. "What you could be taught, with just a little conditioning. What you could be taught . . ." His eyes narrowed, once more the flames reflecting strong in them.

A heavy weight all but crushed Uldyssian to his hands and knees. He felt as if it would soon bury him in the hard soil. Every muscle strained, every vein pounded. His head seemed ready to explode. The farmer turned his gaze aside, but still could not break free of whatever spell the cleric cast. He saw that Mendeln and Serenthia suffered worse than him, for they were already flattened against the earth. Of Lylia, Uldyssian could see nothing, but the thought of her also fighting to live gave him at last the impetus to push himself up on one knee.

"A very strong will," the robed figure remarked. "The master will savor breaking it further."

The force pushing at Uldyssian amplified. This time, his face smashed into the ground. A sharp pain exploded from the bridge of his nose and he had no doubt that it was broken, for blood already began dripping from the nostrils.

"Bind him," the cleric commanded. There was the scuffling of boots, Malic's servants rushing to obey. "We have no need of the others."

No need of the others . . .

With a pain-racked shout, Uldyssian forced himself up into a crouch. His head pounded and his heart strained, but a sense of triumph filled him. He found himself standing before two very startled Peace Warders. Before the pair could recover, the son of Diomedes reached out and seized both men by the throat.

His fingers barely wrapped across, yet the cracking of bone was very audible. The Peace Warders twitched, then collapsed at his feet, their necks broken by something other than mere strength.

Despite Uldyssian's resurgence, Malic appeared only mildly impressed. He glanced at the fire that had broken his mesmerism, then looked again at Uldyssian. "This could have been handled with so much more pleasantry, my child.

There is a place for you in the Temple. The Primus has sensed your power and would welcome you as a son . . ."

"I want nothing to do with either you or him!"

"A shortsighted choice, my child. The future of this land, of all lands, is the Temple of the Triune. Those who do not see the light shall fall forever in darkness . . ."

But darkness was all that Uldyssian saw when he looked at the high priest. There was that surrounding Malic that by no manner could the harried farmer link to any noble "light." In fact, Malic radiated a presence that repelled Uldyssian as nothing else ever had and he felt certain that it was the high priest's nearness that had earlier forced him to waking.

The Peace Warders had quickly regrouped and now surrounded the area. Serenthia stood near Mendeln, who seemed lost in thought. Uldyssian finally located Lylia near his left. She appeared as calm as Malic, but her calm evidently came from confidence in her lover. The noblewoman's face was filled with utter trust . . . trust in Uldyssian's ability to save them.

Strengthened by that, he looked from her to his brother and the trader's daughter before finally facing the cleric again. "I said I don't want anything to do with the Temple. Leave *now* or else."

"I truly regret the course you force me to, my child," Malic returned, glancing past his quarry. "That the others must *suffer* more than they need to because of your recalcitrance is so sad." The eyes narrowed dangerously. "So sad . . . and entirely your doing."

The Peace Warders moved. At the same time, several pieces of burning wood leapt out of the fire. They fell to the ground just before Uldyssian, where they immediately grew longer and thicker. Flames still surrounded them, but did not appear to burn them any longer.

Now several times their original size, the gathered sticks took on a new shape . . . a shape that mocked that of a man. Two lengthier branches for legs, two shorter ones for arms, and the knob of a broken piece acting as the head.

It stood as tall as the farmer, a stick figure from night-mare. The knob turned toward Malic.

"Take him," the cleric dispassionately ordered.

The fiery golem lunged at Uldyssian, its searing arms wrapping around his own in a hold worthy of a hangman's noose.

The heat was unbearable. The flames all but blinded him. He shut his eyes, but the light of the fire seemed to cut right through the lids. Uldyssian gasped for air, but all he received for his efforts was a searing sensation throughout his lungs.

Yet, for all the agony, it should have been far worse. Uldyssian should have been burned to death by now, his flesh melted away and his bones blackened . . .

But Malic did not *want* him dead, Uldyssian slowly recalled. Malic wanted him pliable, a willing convert to bring before his master . . . the Primus. He might torture the farmer, might bring him to the edge of despair, but the high priest would not dare chance killing the one for whom he had been hunting.

That knowledge turned the struggle for Uldyssian. Doing his utmost to push the pain from his mind, he let out a defiant roar and tore himself free of the golem's grip.

There was a sudden, intense chill, followed by a great clatter. Uldyssian shook. As his eyesight cleared, it was to see a pile of smoldering sticks in front of him, all that remained of Malic's creation.

That was not all, though. As Uldyssian looked at his scorched arms, the burnt areas started *healing*. The skin quickly turned from a horrific black and crimson to a fresh pink unmarred by even a freckle. Even his garments no longer showed any sign of smoke, much less fire.

Uldyssian's pleasure at overcoming the high priest's lat-est trick faded as his fear for Lylia and the others once again overtook him. Unprotected, they could hardly have stood against the trained and bloodthirsty Peace Warders.

But all three were *untouched*. Warriors of the Triune did indeed surround them, but that was as much as the villains could manage. All else ended in futility. Uldyssian saw one blade come at his brother, only to bounce away several inches from its target. A Peace Warder sought to seize Achilios, only to nearly break his hands against the very air near the hunter's neck. The same was the case for Serenthia, whose gaze at that moment caught his own. *She* understood, even if her attackers did not. Eyes round, Cyrus's daughter nodded in acknowledgment to Uldyssian's power.

And as for Lylia . . . the noblewoman stood just behind him, also under a furious but futile onslaught of weapons by the zealous servants of the Temple. She stood in their midst, her expression one of calm, of expectation, and, as with Serenthia, Lylia looked at Uldyssian with the understanding that he would keep her from harm.

It was enough to make him smile despite the circumstances, and that smile remained in place as he focused his attention on the cause of their troubles.

For the first time, Malic no longer smiled or even acted disinterested. A frown cut across his face and in his dark, dark eyes Uldyssian read a barely held fury. The high priest held in his gloved hands a small, jeweled box whose lid was turned so as to open toward his oafish adversary.

"You bring this upon yourself. The master will have you alive, if only it is your barely beating heart I present to him, my child."

He opened the box.

Uldyssian instinctively flinched . . . only to see that the box merely contained three glittering gems. Despite the flickering light of the campfire and the distance between the two men, Uldyssian was somehow able to identify them individually as a blue, oval stone, a gold, rectangular one, and—largest of all—a teardrop-shaped white diamond. The manner in which the gems were situated also indicated that there should have been a fourth, but that slot was empty.

"Do you think to bribe me into becoming a convert?" he finally asked, curious.

In answer, Malic ran a finger over each stone. "No. I think to make you *beg* me to let you."

Without warning, the Peace Warders abandoned their efforts, fleeing in the direction of the cleric. Malic paid them no mind, more interested in the open area between Uldyssian and him.

An area now filling with noxious smoke unlinked to the campfire . . . or any other source that could be seen.

Uldyssian had faced mesmerism, crushing force, and animated flame. He was not afraid of smoke. Taking a deep breath, he stepped forward. Once he was through the smoke, it would be a short distance to the cleric's throat . . .

But from behind came an uncharacteristically shrill and worried cry from Lylia. "No, Uldyssian! Not like that! Beware the lurkers!"

No sooner had she called out than a macabre shape formed just before the farmer. Uldyssian caught glimpses of razorlike appendages above what passed for *three* arms and a bulbous head that looked too heavy to be supported by any natural body. Four glistening orbs burned a sinister ivory. The thing took a step toward Uldyssian—

And then, in the blink of an eye, a silver aura shone around the monstrous form. The creature raised its various appendages high and gave out a low, gasping sound . . . then simply *faded away*.

But even as Uldyssian was somehow relieved of that horrific adversary, two more shapes coalesced in the smoke, in their own ways more grotesque than the one that had just vanished. One was a thing whose body looked to have been freshly flayed, a body consisting of two legs ending in clawed hands and a sinewy, spiked tail attached to a tube-like body. There was no head, just a gaping hole atop, out of which nightmarish, toothy projections snatched at the air just before Uldyssian.

Its hellish companion was a skeletal figure with the face of a hungry bird of prey. Two leathery, vestigial wings thrust up from its shoulders. Its arms ended not in hands or claws, but in multiple suckers, and its legs were bent backward, like those of a grasshopper.

From somewhere farther back, somewhere beyond the smoke, Malic uttered a single word. *"Lucion."*

The avian leapt forward with a swiftness unbelievable. One second, it stood before Uldyssian and the next it was upon him. Even as he fell under the force of its jump, he heard a deep grinding sound from the direction of the second beast.

The suckered appendages sought for the human's chest and throat and it was all Uldyssian could do to prevent them from reaching their targets. With his hands, he held the creature's horrific limbs by the wrist, shoving the upper part of the beast up as high as he could.

Above the sounds of the struggle, Malic almost nonchalantly commented, "They will keep enough of you left alive, my child, for the Primus to work with. Just enough."

Uldyssian tried to dismiss them the way he had the fire golem, but these were creatures more like the hunter in the forest. No, they were even more than that. Without understanding how, Uldyssian was certain that the fiend he had previously destroyed had been far inferior to these vicious horrors.

The long, sharp beak poised above Uldyssian's head. He expected the creature to snap at him or even try to spear him in the skull . . . but instead it opened wide and let out an ear-piercing shriek that rattled every bone in the farmer's body, a shriek without end or even respite.

It was all he could do just to keep from passing out under the intense onslaught. Ears pounding, Uldyssian finally released one of the avian's arms and went for the beak. However, as he did, the suckers dropped down across his chest.

A ghastly, gnawing sensation arose wherever the creature's suckers touched, but Uldyssian could not let that pain stop him any more than the previous. Straining, he seized the beak and, screaming himself, clamped it tightly shut. The avian shook its head, seeking release even as it continued to absorb what the human could only assume his life force.

Still feeling light-headed, Uldyssian attempted to shove his adversary off. Only then, though, did he realize that something now had hold of his feet, something that began dragging him . . . and the avian, in the process . . . toward where he last recalled the other demon to be.

Not at all wanting to know what horror the second creature offered, Uldyssian doubled his struggles, but could not free himself of his initial foe. The force that had so far protected him well now failed utterly and he could only guess that it was because he was not used to wielding it for so long in such a desperate manner. Given time, Uldyssian had no doubt that he could have learned how to easily overcome either abomination, but that time was now not his.

He did not fear death, for, again, he knew that Malic wanted him alive, but the high priest no longer cared what condition Uldyssian was in otherwise. A ragged, bloody stump that still breathed apparently would suffice to please the mysterious and clearly not so compassionate Primus.

The avian's vampiric suckers began to have a debilitating effect. Uldyssian feared what would happen to the others if he failed. Lylia's trusting face in particular burned in his memory. They would all be slaughtered . . . if they had not already been. He had no idea if any of the three were still protected or, for that matter, what had happened to Achilios, who had never returned from his hunt. It was likely that the archer had been the first to die, slain by the Peace Warders while in the woods.

A numbness began to spread from his feet up, a chilling numbness that Uldyssian knew was not the result of what the avian was doing. So, both demons had him now. Surely he was done for.

"L-Lylia . . ." he murmured. "Lyl—"

His body suddenly shook, but not because of anything

that his monstrous foes were doing. A tremendous, *glorious* strength filled the son of Diomedes. In an instant, he felt not only refreshed, but more powerful than *ever* before. The combined might of the two creatures seemed so utterly insignificant now. It made Uldyssian laugh that he had been so worried about being defeated by the likes of them.

Invigorated, Uldyssian tightened his grip on the first demon's beak. This time, though, he had no intention of merely trying to turn it to the side.

One squeeze was all it took to crush the beak. The demon let out a garbled sound and sought to rip itself free. Dark, green ichor flowed from its shattered maw, dripping all over Uldyssian. He ignored the burning caused by each rancid drop, eager to see what else he could do. The power surged through him like a roaring river, feeding him continuously. He felt his body swell. He was a giant in comparison to his foes, a titan.

A *god*, even . . .

Malic frowned as, not for the first time, he sensed something amiss. First there had been the nigh instantaneous attack by the fool just as the demons had first been materializing. Uldyssian's destruction of the razorlike pyrioh, the most foul of the servants given into his service by the master, had stunned the high priest more than he had let on. He had not even sensed the farmer's power rise up, so immediate had been the results.

But the other two demons had acted according to his desires and had looked ready to make short work of the prey. Malic had kept his own heightened senses at their peak in order to make certain that the creatures did not get carried away—as demons were wont to do—and kill Uldyssian. Indeed, the high priest had almost been as much a part of the struggle as if he had been physically involved . . . and that was why he, too, noticed the astounding and impossible surge of power abruptly coursing through what, a breath before, had been a flailing, lost buffoon.

Noticed that surge . . . and could not comprehend just *how* it had come about. It almost seemed to Malic as if it had been fed to Uldyssian from another source . . .

Tearing himself from the struggle, he glanced at the three other figures. The cleric immediately dismissed Serenthia, who barely sensed the force growing within her, and the perplexed-looking fool, next to the girl, whom he had determined to be Uldyssian's brother. There *was* something peculiar about the brother, but he was not the source.

And then Malic looked at the only person left, the one he had taken at first to be the least of interest to him. He looked at her very close, seeing her as only one of his skill could.

Seeing something that he could never have guessed that he would see.

"Great Lucion!" he blurted, for once unable to maintain the appearance of complete confidence and disdain. One hand came up to point and the words of a spell formed on his lips—

A sharp pain struck him in the back next to the left shoulder blade. Well-versed in the human body and the various points of lingering or instant death, Malic's mind routinely calculated that if what had hit him—an arrow, he surmised—had gone an inch more to the center, then even his power might not have been enough to save him. As it was, he immediately set about using the gifts of his master to keep himself from not only bleeding to death, but passing out as well.

Unfortunately, that meant that he could no longer maintain control over the battle or deal with the other, shocking discovery. Malic teetered back, trying to maintain focus. As he turned, though, it was to witness Brother Rondo instead falling, the Peace Warder slain by a bolt through the throat. The cleric caught a glimpse of a lithe figure darting along the edge of campsite, a mere *archer* of all things. It insulted Malic to think that he had come close to perishing because of someone without *any* skills in the art whatsoever.

Then, from where Uldyssian struggled, there came an

odd and unsettling sound. Malic at first thought that perhaps one of his creatures, now rid of his control, had torn the farmer asunder. Instead, though, Uldyssian once more stood *free*. Worse, in his left hand he held the limp form of the beaked demon . . . but who now had no beak whatsoever. As the cleric watched, Uldyssian tossed aside the dead monster and used both hands to seize the third demon by its thick, sticky tongue. That tongue Malic had last seen wrapped around the fool's legs, there to inflict such cold as would have frozen most mortals solid in a heartbeat.

Yet, not only had Uldyssian survived that cold, but now he had dragged the last of Malic's infernal minions to him. The grinding teeth of the demon clamped down upon the farmer's wrists and for a moment the high priest thought that Uldyssian had made a fatal error.

Instead, the savage teeth *shattered* like brittle glass against the human's bare flesh.

Gritting his own teeth, Uldyssian pulled one hand free, then grabbed the gore-soaked pieces of beak from the first demon. Wielding the long, pointed fragments as he might a dagger, Uldyssian plunged them into the fleshy area just above his foe's monstrous maw.

The demon squealed . . . then dropped in an ungainly heap. Thick, black fluid coursed down over its body from the great wound.

As that happened, the arrow in Malic's back—forced by his will—popped free. The cleric felt the last of his wound seal shut. Some pain remained, but most of his weakness now came from the combination of his healing and his previous efforts to control the demons.

This was not how it was meant to be, Malic thought as he watched the finish of his final demon. The Primus would be enraged with him. The high priest shuddered at what form that fury might take. He particularly recalled witnessing the form his master's anger had taken against one of the previous high priests of another order. There had not been much left to dispose of afterward.

But what should have been a simple task was not. Malic still could not say where things had gone awry, but he could not help feel that there had been a piece in the game that not even the Primus had sensed, impossible as *that* should have been.

Uldyssian looked up at the cleric, and spreading across his sweat-soaked countenance was an expression that reminded Malic very much of the anger of which he had thought only the Primus capable.

Unmindful of his minions, Malic quickly sought to protect himself.

The force that struck him and his Peace Warders was a hundred times greater than that which had earlier thrown the warriors. This time, bodies went flying as if shot from catapults. Men screamed as they collided with tree trunks or tumbled through the woods. One Peace Warder struck so hard that the oak's trunk cracked and the tree crashed into its neighbors.

Only Malic remained standing . . . if barely. He watched in disbelief as Uldyssian grimly strode toward him. There was blood in the farmer's eyes and the cleric knew that his would-be prey intended something far worse than anything unleashed so far.

And knowing that, Malic did the wisest thing he could.

The dust devil whirled to life just in front of Uldyssian, swiftly raising up whatever loose fragments of dirt and debris it could. The makeshift storm filled Uldyssian's face, momentarily blinding him.

The cleric concentrated . . .

Uldyssian swatted away at the thick cloud, angry at himself for having not expected something of the sort. Blinded, he prepared himself for the worst, certain that Malic had a second and far more insidious attack to follow.

But the dust settled almost immediately . . . revealing in its aftermath no sign of the high priest.

The son of Diomedes stood bewildered, awaiting some

trick, yet Malic did not suddenly reappear and attack. Instead, slim hands took hold of him from behind and Lylia's voice declared, "You have done it, Uldyssian! You have saved us all from the cleric and his demons!"

He surveyed the scene around them, seeing only the corpses of the Peace Warders and the two abominations. At least three of the former lay with bolts through them, a sign that Uldyssian had not been entirely responsible for protecting the party. Achilios even now stood at Serenthia's side, giving comfort to the trader's daughter.

"Forgive her carelessness, my love," Lylia softly added. "She did not mean to endanger us."

Uldyssian wanted to go to Serenthia and explain that he understood that Malic had seized control of her mind, but decided to leave the situation in the hands of the hunter. Achilios would do everything he could to see to it that the distraught woman calmed down.

"You were amazing!" the noblewoman continued, breathless. "Do you see now, my love? Do you see that nothing is beyond you, that nothing can prevent you from achieving what we dream?"

He had seen everything, naturally, and was still awed himself by the abilities that he had displayed. A high cleric of the Triune had set spellwork, men, and monster against him and had failed. What more could *anyone* fearing his existence do? Surely nothing . . .

But they *would* try . . . and the others, especially Lylia, would have to depend upon him until they, too, learned to fully awaken the force within them.

"Let them come," he muttered without realizing it. "Let *him* come," Uldyssian added, thinking of Malic.

Lylia came around to his side, her eyes glowing in the light of the campfire. "Uldyssian! Did you hear what the cleric said? Did you hear the name?"

"Name?" He tried to recall, but failed. "What name?"

Her lips drew close. *"Lucion,* he said. The cleric called out the name *Lucion* to the demons!" She turned her gaze to

Mendeln, who was just approaching. Uldyssian's brother started. "You. You heard, did you not?"

Mendeln visibly paused to regroup his thoughts, then nodded. "Yes. I heard that name from him. I did, Uldyssian."

Lucion. The same name that the first demon had called out to before perishing. Now Malic had used it, too.

Was there some connection between the Temple and this Lucion? Between the *Primus* and this master of demons?

Uldyssian felt an intense uneasiness creep through him at the thought. Demons at the beck and call of the Temple. What did it mean?

And who, then, *was* the Primus, whose name might also be *Lucion?*

Πίηε

Malic screamed again . . . and again . . . and again . . .

He screamed even though no one else could hear him, not in the sanctum of his master. He screamed for a release from the agony, even though he knew none would come until the Primus chose . . . assuming that ever even happened. It was within the master's power to see to it that Malic's pain became eternal.

That fear fueled the high priest's screams anew.

Then, without warning, the pain ceased. With a gasp, Malic tumbled to the stone floor. The solidity of the floor amazed him, for he could have sworn that he had been floating in a sea of needles and flame.

"I could have sent a first-year novice in your place and achieved just as splendid results," came the Primus's voice. There was none of the gentle calm in it for which the elder cleric was known to his faithful. Malic, however, knew that chilling tone well. It had always been focused on others, though, *not* upon him.

And those upon whom it *had* been focused had, without exception, never left this chamber again.

"I am so disappointed in you," the Primus went on. "I had such high hopes for you, my Malic, such high hopes! Who has been my favorite for far longer than any other mortal?"

The question was not a rhetorical one, Malic knew. "*I* h-have, Great One . . ."

"Yes . . . yes, you have, my Malic. Your life has lasted double that of any human and in that time you have witnessed the premature passing of several others, you may recall . . ."

Now the high priest of the Order of Mefis truly expected his end to come. He looked up, determined to face his master at the last.

The Primus gazed down at his servant from his grand chair, silent so long that Malic began to shiver despite his attempt to seem confident even in the face of death or worse. When the master deliberated so, it was generally to devise something particularly horrific.

The scholarly figure rose and with measured steps joined his failed minion. The Primus viewed Malic as if debating something. For the first time since he had managed to cast himself back to the Grand Temple, the high priest allowed himself a shadow of hope. Was he to be granted a reprieve?

"I have invested much in you, my Malic." The Primus's voice darkened further. Each syllable was venom, each word doom. The high priest hung his head again, certain that the sword would yet come down after all.

Instead, it was his master's hand, reaching for his own. Trembling, Malic extended his. The Primus guided him to his feet.

"I am *his* son, my Malic, and answer to *him* as you do to me! I will give you your life this once, for there is in my mind a question that even you could not understand, one that might have bearing on this creature called Uldyssian . . ."

"I am truly grateful, master! I live only to serve you! I swear!"

Still holding Malic's hand in his own, the Primus nodded. "Yes . . . you do . . . and to remind you of that, I give you a lasting gift."

The high priest screamed anew as his trapped appendage flared as if on fire. To his shock and dismay, it then twisted and curled, transforming. Gone was the soft flesh and sinew and in its place a thing warped and dripping green. Thick scales scored the limb well past the wrist. The fingers grew gnarled and clawed, the last two digits fusing together to become one.

The agony continued long after the spell had finished.

The Primus would not let Malic drop to his knees. He made the cleric stand and face him, the master's gaze keeping the servant's prisoner.

"My mark is upon you now, my Malic . . . my mark and that of my father." The Primus finally released his grip. "Now and forever."

Malic shook but refused to fall. Weaving back and forth, he kept his gaze down and gasped, "G-Great is Lucion, all-powerful and all-knowing . . . and greater still is—is his father, the glorious and benevolent—" The human dared look up again. *"Mephisto!"*

Lucion smiled, his perfect teeth suddenly ending sharper, more pointed. His aspect became shadowed in a manner having nothing to do with light. Although it was but a glimpse of his true self, even still it was enough to make the high priest pale more than ever.

Then, as quickly as he had changed, the Primus once again looked his kindly part. He reached out and put his hand on Malic's shoulder. The cleric managed not to flinch.

"You have learned your lesson well, my Malic! That is why you remain my *favorite*. For the moment. Now, come! We will better pursue this matter below, I believe . . ."

"As you wish, Great One." Clutching his twisted, throbbing hand, Malic fell into place next to the Primus. He said nothing more, not wanting to revive his master's anger toward him.

He whose true name was Lucion, son of Mephisto, led Malic not to the doors of the sanctum, but to the wall behind his throne. As they approached, the Primus drew an arc in the air.

A blazing crimson arc formed on the wall. It quickly lengthened, the ends reaching the stone floor before Malic could draw a second breath. As they did, the area within faded away . . . revealing a torch-lit corridor that descended into the ground as if toward some ancient tomb. More sinister, the walls themselves were flanked by row upon row of stonelike guards whose fearsome armor did not in the least resemble that of the Peace Warders.

As Lucion and the high priest of Mefis entered the subterranean corridor, the grim guards cast their gazes toward them. Immediately the ranks came to attention. Within black helms shaped to resemble the skulls of hornless rams, black pits—not eyes—stared out. The warriors' flesh was the color of gravestones and their breastplates bore the emblem of their unholy calling, a bleeding skull transfixed upon twin swords entwined by serpents.

Malic knew their kind well—indeed, had chosen many for their ranks. Unlike their master, they did not frighten him, for their lot was to be led by the high priests in the name of the Primus on that day when the Temple would fully control Sanctuary and all pretense could be dropped.

Sanctuary. It was a name known only to a few, most of whom were not of mortal flesh. Malic had learned the truth about his world from his master, who was in a position to understand the reality better than most. After all, was he not the blood—if such a simplistic term could be used—of the Lord of Hatred, whom some would call a demon and who was, with his brothers Baal and Diablo, master of the Burning Hells?

The concepts of good and evil had long ago become unimportant to Malic save in their most scholarly senses. The high priest understood only power, and that which the Primus represented was the ultimate power in *all* creation. Had it not been the Three who had come together to form the realm of Sanctuary and people it with the products of their imagination? And had not they been tricked by one they thought an ally and cast out of Sanctuary for centuries? Yet, despite that treachery, they now had a foothold back in the world of their making and soon they would rip it free from the one who had stolen it. That cursed figure believed that he now had a kingdom all his own, its inhabitants his to play with as he chose. But he had underestimated the Three and, in Malic's august opinion, the son of one—Lucion—most of all.

It had been Lucion who had, after all this time, forced the betrayer to come out of hiding, to make his presence known to them. That was the first step toward retaking Sanctuary and returning it to what it had been intended to be . . . a place from which those few worthy—such as himself—would be raised up to help the Three transform *all* existence into a reflection of their true glory.

And for those like Malic, that meant more power than the entirety of the mage clans and petty nobles combined.

What exactly the Primus sought of this Uldyssian in this regard, even the high priest did not fully understand. To Malic's mind, it was most likely that Uldyssian was to be the first of a new legion of warriors for the Three. What other use could there be? Malic saw the potential—had *felt* the potential—and so believed he was correct. His will properly broken, the farmer would readily succumb to Lord Lucion's will. He would then become a perfect servant, obeying all commands no matter how dreadful.

Just like the morlu, the cleric thought.

As if to reinforce that last thought, the corridor finally came to an end. A shimmering veil of poison green that Malic knew well confronted the pair.

Again, the son of Mephisto gestured. The veil faded to so much smoke, and dissipated . . . and, with a sudden, jarring clash of metal against metal, the lair of the morlu lay revealed.

This was the name that Lucion had given his ram-masked soldiers. The morlu. It was a word of power, two syllables steeped in the magic of the Primus's sire. The morlu were more than just fanatical; they lived and breathed the desire of the Lord of Hatred. They did not sleep, anymore; they did not eat. All the morlu did was *fight*.

And as Malic and his master entered the vast, bowl-shaped chamber dug well beneath the grand temple, they came upon the morlu indeed doing just that. Illuminated by thick, scalding rivers of molten earth flowing randomly through the huge cavern, the scene was one out of a night-

mare worthy of a demon. A tremendous sea of armored figures hacked and slashed and sliced and thrust away one
another with utter abandon and absolute glee. Every warrior bled from scores of deep ravines across their bodies.
Limbs lay strewn upon the ichor-soaked rock floor. Corpses
by the scores littered the vicinity for as far as the eye could
see. Malic beheld heads lolling far from torsos, the
mouths—if the jaws were yet attached—still open in their
death screams. Many of the faces lacked an eye or two or a
nose or ear and they looked not at all different from most of
the living, who, though likewise maimed and disfigured,
were so caught up in the battle that they paid their wounds
no mind. Bits of other body parts floated or lay on the banks
of the lava rivers and each breath more were added by the
zealous combatants.

A quick study of the scene below revealed that there was
neither rhyme nor reason to the struggle, no identifiable
sides in the conflict. The morlu did not have such. Every
warrior fought for himself, siding with his brethren only
long enough to accomplish some common goal . . . at which
point they tended to turn upon one another. They cheerfully slew one another with the same titanic effort with
which they would have any outside foe. Only against such
were they truly united, for that was what their lord desired
most of them. They were to be a plague that would strike
down those who would not be converted, who very likely
served the betrayer, be it willingly or as a dupe.

Lucion glanced up at the ceiling, although Malic knew
well that the mighty figure was not at all interested in the
rock formations there. The Primus looked beyond mortal
sight into a place that all the training in the world could not
reveal to the high priest or any other mere human.

"We have timed our visit well. The hour is nigh, my
Malic," murmured the Primus with something approaching the fondness a proud father might have for his children.
"Let us pause and savor the beauty of it all as it refreshes
itself . . ."

Turning his eyes back to the cataclysmic sight below, Lord Lucion gestured toward the very center, where the worst of the carnage had and was still taking place. In the midst of everything, a black gemstone nearly as large as a man sat embedded in a triangular column of red-streaked marble. "Blood marble," it was named, naturally. The stone was called by Malic's master the Kiss of Mephisto, although the cleric had, from past comments, reason to believe that it had once been named for another of whom Lord Lucion would not speak.

"Behold, my Malic . . ."

As if time itself ceased, every morlu warrior abruptly froze where he was. Blades paused halfway into guts. Severed heads halted in their tumble from the ruined necks. Utter silence reigned over the humongous lair.

The Kiss of Mephisto let out a burst of black light. Not darkness, but completely, utterly black *light*.

And as that light rushed over both the fighting and the fallen, they twisted and turned as if their bones had become fluid. Lost limbs flew up to reattach, gaping wounds sewed together. Mangled corpses shivered with renewed animation. Malic felt a twinge of remembrance concerning his own recent change and clutched his disfigured hand anew as he watched events unfold.

The ranks of the morlu reconstituted themselves. Even from the steaming, red depths of the magma rivers, the warriors emerged resurrected. Their armor momentarily glowed bright from the searing heat in which their corpses had bathed, then faded to the dour black.

It was a miraculous sight to Malic, this raising of the dead and healing of the wounded, even though he knew that in some sense it was not what it appeared. The stone did *not* have the ability to bring life back to the mortal remains. Those morlu who had been slain either this day or previous were not, in fact, even human anymore. Rather, they were cadavers animated by Mephisto's foul majesty through the will of his son, Lucion. What existed within was a demonic

essence that mimicked the life that had once existed. Every
new morlu warrior quickly joined the ranks of the animated—so harsh was the constant battling—but they
thought this an honor, believing that their souls were somehow still a part of all this.

But what truly happened to those souls, only the Lord of
Hatred surely knew, or so Malic at least thought.

Within moments, the field was again filled with restless
fighters in their prime. Several growled at one another or
brandished swords, maces, axes, and the like at potential
foes. The blood that had covered much of the area had
faded into the rock. To all apparent purposes, it was as if the
battle had never taken place.

"Damos . . ." Lord Lucion whispered.

From far off in the cavern, from deep within the ranks, a
particularly large and grotesque morlu turned and peered
up at the pair. He suddenly raised his massive sword and
gave a guttural cry, a salute, to his master.

The Primus nodded, then raised one hand with all fingers spread wide. Damos nodded and began barging
through the rows of heaving bodies. Without warning, he
seized one by the collar and dragged him from his position.
That morlu followed behind Damos as the Primus's chosen
commander sought another. In this manner, five soon followed Damos up the edge toward where Lucion and Malic
awaited them.

"Great master . . ." Damos croaked as he bent down on
one knee. His voice was akin to that of every other morlu
who had been slain once. It was as if, despite its best effort,
the dark essence within could not completely mask itself as
human. Damos's voice could never have passed for mortal.

Behind the lead morlu, the five others also knelt. Lucion
touched Damos on the top of the ram helm, giving his blessing. Damos then turned his head toward Malic. "High
priest . . ."

Malic repeated his master's gesture.

"Rise, Damos," commanded Mephisto's son. When the

lead morlu had obeyed, the Primus said, "You are at the high priest's command. You will obey him in all things."

"Yes, Great One . . ."

"There are prey of both life and death involved, Damos. You understand the difference."

The helmed figure nodded. Malic knew Damos from past need. The helm only partially obscured a face that looked as if the Kiss of Mephisto had failed to completely remake it. Not much remained of the nose save two gaping holes, and Damos's lower jaw seemed to have belonged to another, even larger creature, perhaps a bear. The pits that had once been eyes were misaligned. However, other than the fact that his eyes were no more, Damos looked very much as he had when first being initiated into the *living* ranks of new morlu. He had been one particularly ugly human inside and out and his dark soul even then had disproven the adage of not judging a book by its cover. Indeed, there was little difference now between the mortal Damos and the thing currently inhabiting his shell.

"The high priest will mark the one to salvage, the others to slay," continued Lucion. Then, to Malic's surprise, the demon lord added, "but you will also have to be on your guard for another."

"Another?" blurted the cleric, suddenly recalling some of what he had blathered to his lord in defense of his failure as the Primus had punished him.

There came an edge to the Primus's voice that Malic had never noted in all the years that he had served the great one. Almost it sounded like . . . *uncertainty?* But *no*, the human quickly decided, that could not be. Lucion was *never* uncertain.

Never . . .

"I have sensed . . ." the son of Mephisto said after an equally unsettling silence. ". . . that all is not as it appears on the surface. There is some intrusion, some . . . other . . ." He trailed off, suddenly caught up in thought.

The morlu stirred uneasily and Malic grew more perturbed. This was not how the master acted. He never paused so, never hesitated.

What was happening? *Who* was this other?

Malic again recalled his own suspicions during the debacle against the farmer. He had been overwhelmed by the incredible power wielded by the simplistic Uldyssian, power combined with skill that the fool should not have had. The high priest had wondered then if there was something else going on behind the scenes, that things were not as they had appeared.

And now . . . and now Malic suspected that Lord Lucion thought the same. Lord Lucion, it seemed, *believed* his tale.

Mephisto's son shook his head, his expression darkening monstrously. "No . . . it could never be." The expression passed away, leaving in its place the look of utter assurance to which Malic was more used. "You will know it," the Primus went on suddenly and calmly to both the cleric and Damos. "This time, you will know it. It must be obliterated. The farmer—this Uldyssian ul-Diomed—must be preserved, but *it* and all else around him shall be no more. Is that *understood*?"

The lead morlu bowed his head in acknowledgment. Malic nodded, his human hand still clutching the transformed one.

Lucion noted his action. Smiling benevolently, he said to the human, "It *is* a gift I give you, my Malic. You will see. You will see . . ."

The pronouncement encouraged the high priest. Malic eyed the macabre appendage anew. His master did nothing without thought. An actual *gift*, after all? He could flex the digits as easily as he could the old ones and in some cases in manners not previously possible. The pain had finally begun to subside, too. Curiously, the cleric also felt stronger than he had.

Steepling his fingers, the son of Mephisto concluded, "Now it is time to seek anew the one called Uldyssian. I will in this brook no failure; is that understood?"

Again, there was mute acknowledgment from both Malic and Damos.

"Then that is all. You will depart immediately."

The chosen morlu gathered behind Malic, who bowed to the master. Eagerness had replaced fear in the heart of the cleric. He silently swore that he would bring Uldyssian ul-Diomed to Lord Lucion even if it meant beating the farmer until there remained just enough spark of life for the Primus to use.

As he led Damos and the other five away, Malic also thought about this other intrusion of which his master had spoken. Despite whatever power it wielded, Lord Lucion wanted nothing of it. He wanted it destroyed, not preserved. It very much felt to the high priest as if his master *did* know what—or *who*—it was.

Malic was not the type to betray his master. No such fool was *he*. However, it would certainly do no harm to find out just *what* this other thing was. Then, once his curiosity was satisfied, he could let the morlu destroy it.

All that mattered was the fool of a farmer . . .

Lucion did not watch Malic depart. He knew that he could trust the cleric to obey this time. The mortal had no other choice.

The legions of morlu continued to chafe at the bit, but Lucion let them wait. He had not told his servants all, not given them true indication of his thoughts.

It cannot be, he argued with himself. *It cannot be . . . her. She cannot be here . . .*

And that made him think of the other, of the one with whom he played this game of control of the minds and souls of mortals. The one was as little like them as he was. Could it be that his foe had some part in this? Was this all a ploy to put Lucion and his father off balance? That certainly made more sense than the possibility that *she* was here.

He would not tell his father just yet. As Malic rightly feared punishment by the Primus, so, too, did Lucion fear the wrath of his sire. His own monstrous nature paled in comparison to that of the Lord of Hatred. No, for now, Mephisto would not be told.

But if it *was* her . . . then sooner or later Lucion would have to confront his father.

I must find out more. What he had not told Malic was that, live or die when next he confronted the farmer, the cleric would reveal to Lucion the truth about this second force using the human to shield it from his presence. Malic was bound by his new hand to his master more than he knew. There were abilities to the hand that could destroy even *her* . . . at the cost of his human vessel, of course. Lucion found Malic particularly useful, but his loss would mean little if it meant securing Sanctuary, especially from her.

Trying to ease his mind, the Primus nodded at the waiting warriors below.

With a collected cry, the morlu went at each other again. Metal rang out against metal. A hundred warriors were slaughtered in the first breath. Blood splattered the floor of the vast chamber and the cries of the wounded echoed, the last being music to the ears of their master.

Yet, despite reveling in the endless carnage created by his eager servants, Lucion's thoughts continually rebelled by returning to the previous subject. It could *not* be her; it could *never* be her. She was gone, either banished forever or dead. It was not within even her power to overcome either. He knew her well enough, did he not? Had he not once been as close to her as nearly any other? Only two had possibly known her better than Lucion, and one of those was his father.

The other was his adversary . . . who had been the reason for her downfall.

Which brought to prominence again the question that Lucion would have liked to know the answer to.

If this is not some plan of his . . . does he *sense her possible return, too?*

Ten

There was no disagreement when Uldyssian decided that the party could not stay where they had been camped. Serenthia wanted to at least gather the bodies of the Peace Warders together for some sort of respectful burial, but Uldyssian cared nothing for the corpses. These men had intended capture for him and death for his companions and so he felt justified in leaving them out in the open to be feasted upon by the carrion eaters of the forest.

They searched for the Peace Warders' mounts, but, oddly, there was no trace of the animals. No one could recall when last any of them had been seen and even the sharp-eyed Achilios could find no trail. They quickly gave up and, mounting their own for steeds, raced off into the dead of night.

Uldyssian remained tense throughout the ride, not because he feared for himself so much, but for the others . . . especially Lylia. Malic had surely noted her closeness to the farmer and the high priest would no doubt seek to take advantage of their relationship even more so than the blood ties between Uldyssian and his brother.

Thinking of Mendeln, Uldyssian glanced back at his sibling's shadowed form. What little he could make out of Mendeln's countenance revealed the same anxiousness the older brother had noticed before. Mendeln appeared particularly struck by the carnage, even more than Serenthia. Uldyssian had caught him standing near one body after another, shaking his head and reaching out into the darkness. The shock of the incident clearly continued to haunt Mendeln even now . . .

With a grunt, Uldyssian returned his gaze to the black path ahead. Perhaps it would be better to leave Mendeln somewhere along the way. He wished no harm to come to his brother nor did he want Mendeln's fragile state to cause any difficulty for him later on. Uldyssian had always known his brother was not as strong physically as him, but he had believed Mendeln of a sturdy mind. Evidentially, he had been wrong.

He took another glance over his shoulder. Yes, Mendeln looked like a man haunted. Something would have to be done if that did not change . . .

Faster and faster they rode, racing like the wind through the shrouded night. Mendeln tried desperately to stare only ahead, but even in that direction he could not entirely escape *them*.

They were five, he, his brother, and the rest. That was all that there should have been. Five people, four steeds.

But with the five there now traveled nearly a *score* more riders that only Mendeln could apparently see.

The translucent wisps of white and gray fluttered along each side of the party. They shimmered in and out of existence. They had gaunt, pale faces and wore the helms and breastplates of Peace Warders. When he did dare glance in their direction, it was to be rewarded with the same unblinking, hollow-eyed stares, as if the ethereal figures awaited some word from him.

But Mendeln had no words for these ghosts of the men his brother and Achilios had slain, no words save a silent plea for the shades to depart. Yet, not only did they not leave, it seemed to Mendeln that they clustered nearest to *him*. The phantasms kept perfect pace with the anguished farmer, riding astride invisible mounts. Mendeln supposed that if any of the animals had been killed in the process, then they, too, would have joined the ghostly charge.

That notion made him chuckle nervously, which brought a concerned glance from nearby Achilios.

He thought of telling the archer what was happening, Achilios perhaps the only one who might understand. The hunter would recall the unsettling stone and would make the connection just as Mendeln had.

But if Achilios had any good sense—which Mendeln believed he did—then the blond archer would immediately keep his distance from the hapless farmer. Mendeln certainly would not blame him. He wanted to be as far away from himself as possible. However, since it was not possible to do that, all he could hope was that, with time, the shades would go to whatever rest they were supposed to go.

Yes, he could *hope* that would happen . . . but Mendeln *doubted* he would be so lucky as that.

Night gave way to a mist-covered day, but although Achilios suggested that they stop, Uldyssian chose to press the horses and his companions until what he believed nearly noon. Only when they came across a stream surrounded by high, canopied trees did he finally call a halt.

Even Uldyssian felt weary by this point. Dismounting, he immediately went to help Lylia down. Achilios did the same for Serenthia. Mendeln slipped off his own mount and rushed to the stream to drink.

However, barely had Uldyssian's brother started to thrust a hand toward the clear water when suddenly he withdrew it as if bitten. The younger son of Diomedes stared off into the distance, then, blinking, looked back to the rest.

"This water is tainted," he said somewhat hesitantly. "Best not to drink it. At the very least, we would become very ill."

"How do you know?" asked Serenthia.

Mendeln frowned, acting to Uldyssian like a child caught in a lie. "I saw . . . I saw some small fish . . . more than one . . . float by. They were dead and mottled. Looked like they died of sickness."

"I've seen the like," interjected Achilios. "If what Mendeln describes is accurate, then we'd be best not to drink."

"But there is nothing to fear," declared Lylia, stepping from Uldyssian's side. She looked up at him. "You can surely deal with something so simple as this."

"Deal with it?"

"Make the water *pure,* naturally!"

The others eyed her in disbelief. Even Uldyssian had some trouble with what she said, but the longer she held his gaze, the more he considered the possibility.

"All right." He strode to the stream, glancing only briefly at his brother. Mendeln put out a warning hand, but Uldyssian sensed Lylia watching and so continued past his brother without a word. He could do this for her, he decided. Each time, it had been her confidence, her *love,* that had shown him the way. This would be no different.

His fingers touched the water. Droplets fluttered over his hand as he concentrated, willing the stream to be clean of taint. Uldyssian repeated the desire over and over in his head until finally deciding that either he had succeeded or it had all been a waste of time.

As he drew back his hand, Serenthia asked, "But, how will we know if it worked?"

Once again, Lylia proved her faith in Uldyssian. Without hesitation, she slipped past him and knelt by the stream.

This was too much even for Uldyssian. "Lylia! No—"

But in one swift motion, she brought her cupped hands to her lips and drank fully the contents.

Uldyssian stood ready to help her, fearful that he had failed this time and thus risked the life of the one most dear to him. To his surprise, though, it was Mendeln who sought to ease his concern.

"The stream . . . Uldyssian . . . the stream . . . is clear of taint now. No need to worry, I swear, brother . . ."

Uldyssian did not ask how Mendeln knew this. Yet, something in his sibling's voice made him believe.

"He speaks the truth," the noblewoman declared. "I am all right, my love. Trust me."

He seized Lylia, holding her tight. "Don't ever do that again!" he breathed in her ear. "Especially not because of me . . ."

"But I knew that your power protected me . . . protected all of us. Was I not correct?"

"Just . . . don't . . ."

"Well, I for one, need a drink after that," Achilios uttered loudly, leading the horses forward. "As do these fine creatures . . ."

His action brought normalcy back to the party. Uldyssian and the rest moved upstream of the animals and began to take their fill. Achilios took care of the horses, then joined the others.

But as he rose from satiating his thirst, the archer suddenly looked past the stream, clearly staring at something in particular. Uldyssian peered after him, but saw nothing.

"I'll be back shortly," Achilios muttered . . . then the hunter darted across the stream, vanishing a moment later among the trees.

Serenthia stepped up next to Uldyssian. "Should we go after him?"

The farmer knew his friend too well. Even he would have been hard-pressed to keep pace with Achilios when it came to seeking some prey in the woods. "Likely he just saw some rabbit or something he wants to bring back for our dinner. Nothing to worry about. You heard him. He'll be just fine."

But it was a tense several minutes that passed before Achilios finally reappeared. Despite the fact that surely he had run a good pace, the hunter was not at all winded. His expression, though, was anything but pleasant.

"There's a town nearby, barely an hour's pace on foot, much less that by horse."

Lylia, who had been sitting on a rock, leapt to her feet. "A *town?* That is not possible!"

Achilios cocked his head as he glanced at the distraught noblewoman. "Not only is it possible, milady, but it's *Partha.*"

Now, everyone else's expression mirrored that of Lylia.

"How can that be?" blurted Mendeln. "We did not ride that direction!"

"I *know* that . . . but it's definitely Partha. I spoke to one of the young locals."

At least one thing now began to make sense to Uldyssian. "Is that the reason you ran off?"

"Aye. I saw a bit of movement and didn't want to take the chance of losing him. Thought it was a bandit, but it was only a boy . . . Cedric, he said his name was. He was out trying to hunt." For the first time since his return, Achilios allowed himself a brief smile. "And he's not bad. Took me a bit to keep on his trail. The boy's light-footed."

Paying the archer's judgment of the boy's skills no mind, Uldyssian tried to determine just how the band could have possibly come around in what was nearly a circle at this point. Partha should have been far, far behind them by now.

"Malic . . ." he finally muttered. As the others looked to him, Uldyssian said, "Don't you see? It has to be the high priest! This smells of some spell! Who else could it be?"

Lylia joined his cause. "Yes, surely him! And knowing that, we must certainly *not* fall into his trap by going to the town! We must flee from its vicinity immediately!"

"But Cedric hardly seems the cleric's tool," argued Achilios. "And the people of Partha have the reputation of being good and fair folks—"

"It matters not what the people are like," she insisted in turn. "They will be pawns for him to use against Uldyssian; that is what we need to keep in mind."

Somewhat to the surprise of Uldyssian, Serenthia supported the other woman. "She's right, Achilios. There's nothing natural about this turn. Malic must intend something awful."

He looked to his brother, but Mendeln was conspicuously

mute on the subject. Curiously, rather than be of a mind to follow Lylia's sound advice and leave the likely trap behind, Uldyssian found himself *eager* to enter Partha. If Malic hoped to surprise him there, he would find his supposed quarry more than willing to finish their previous encounter.

"We go to Partha."

His declaration was met with a variety of expressions, Achilios's most eager, Lylia's most damning. A fire such as Uldyssian had never witnessed burned in her eyes. However, it lasted but a breath before the noblewoman caught herself. Trembling, she exhaled, then nodded.

"To Partha," Lylia agreed, finally smiling. "To the edge of an abyss and beyond, so long as with you, my love."

He was grateful for her change of heart. Her anger had only been fear for him, Uldyssian surmised. After all, it was he whom Malic desired to capture.

But it was she and the others whom the high cleric seemed to think expendable. Uldyssian would make certain that, should Malic strike, they were again protected. He could do no less since it was because of him that they would also ride into potential danger.

With Achilios taking the lead, the five rode toward the town. As the hunter had indicated, the party had stopped just beyond sight of Partha. Indeed, it took them less than the hour Achilios had suggested to reach the edge of town.

Partha was much larger than Seram or even Tulisam. For the first time in his life, Uldyssian beheld buildings four stories high, dwarfing even the barns of the wealthiest of his neighbors. Their stone and wood exteriors had been smoothed over with plaster to give them an extravagant look. Roofs were arched and made of wood tiles overlapping one another. The streets—

The streets were made of stone, not mud. Wagons and horses clattered along their way, raising a racket akin to thunder. There were more people in Partha than Uldyssian had probably seen in all his life and many were dressed in outfits that made him feel like a beggar. In fact, of all five of them, only Lylia looked at all appropriate to be seen by the inhabitants.

Someone called out to them. Aware that none of them had ever been to Partha, Uldyssian stiffened in the saddle. However, it was no trap, but rather a youth who ran directly up to the side of Achilios's steed.

"Ho, there, Cedric!" the hunter called down. He tousled the boy's mop of hair. "I told you we'd be along soon!"

"An' I called Father, I did!" Cedric returned breathlessly.

Sure enough, behind the lad came an august gentleman at least a decade older than Uldyssian and dressed in flowing brown and black robes that immediately stirred distrust in the farmer. Was Cedric's father a cleric of some sort?

"Calm yourself," Achilios quickly said. "'Tis a trader much like Cyrus. Probably even knew him, in fact, if the boy was correct."

"This them, Ced?" asked the would-be hunter's parent. The steely-jawed figure swept back silver and black shoulder-length hair and studied the newcomers. His eyes paused on Lylia, but froze on Serenthia.

"I know you, though you be all grown up! You'd be Cyrus's little girl . . . Sara, was it?"

"Serenthia," she responded, her face becoming overcast.

Cedric's father immediately noted this. His tone more formal, he said, "I am sorry, lass. I shall not ask you about it."

A silent Serenthia nodded gratefully.

Other townsfolk had begun to pause in the vicinity, curious about the new arrivals. Part of that curiosity clearly had to do with the man greeting them, whose status in Partha was surely prominent.

"Friends, my name is Ethon ul-Garal, and although I regret the passing of my old comrade, I heartily welcome those of kin and companionship to him."

Uldyssian eyed Achilios. "They both seem very certain that we were coming."

"I took a chance that you'd say yes, that was all. When Cedric mentioned that his father was an important merchant, I used Cyrus's name—my apologies for that, Serry—because I recalled how he seemed to know everyone in the region who shared his trade. Cedric said that he would run and tell his father about us and tell him what I said about the old man—"

"Many's a good haggle I had with Cyrus," threw in Master Ethon, eyes twinkling at old memories.

"Anyway, after our path led us so near, I figured Destiny wants us here."

"*Malic* wants us here, Achilios. Remember that."

"My friend," called the merchant, clearly seeking to prevent an argument between the two. "Is there something wrong?"

"Nothing that can be spoken of here," Uldyssian remarked in a low voice. "It'd be best if we spoke in private, Master Ethon. Your headman should also hear."

"As I am also elected leader of Partha, that shall be a simple matter to deal with! But come! Who do I have the pleasure of meeting? I knew dear Serenthia as a child and there is no mistaking her beauty even now. You—" He gestured at Uldyssian. "—have a vague familiarity about you, too, but the others do not." Ethon's eyes again lingered over Lylia. "Some, especially not, and I am known for my memory for faces."

"I am Uldyssian ul-Diomed—"

"Ah! Diomedes of Seram! A strong-hearted, outspoken man of the earth! You look his part, too. You'd be his first-born, if I'm not mistaken."

Acknowledging the older man's excellent memory, Uldyssian introduced Mendeln and Achilios, then, grudgingly, Lylia. He expected the merchant to fawn over her, but Master Ethon merely bowed and said, "By the garments and the face, you would be from the north of the great city, yes?"

She dipped her head in turn. "Yes."

Cedric's father clearly expected more of an answer, but when Lylia remained quiet, he took it in as much stride as he had Serenthia's silence. Instead, he looked to the group as a whole. "Well, now that we are friends, you shall come with me to my humble home!"

At first, Uldyssian wanted to turn Ethon's offer down. The man meant well, but this was not a social visit. Yet, if he was both its most prominent citizen and its leader, then there was no one better to warn concerning any possible threat to his people.

Uldyssian only hoped that Cyrus's old friend would not throw his daughter and the rest into a cell once he learned the truth. After all, it was they who brought the danger, in a sense.

As Ethon was on foot, the party dismounted, then led their horses after him. Uldyssian noted that the populace now treated the five as if they were visiting dignitaries, bowing as they passed. Master Ethon was clearly a man highly respected not only for his position but for himself.

That the man had come without a personal guard bothered Uldyssian. Were the people of Partha *that* trusting? Or was there something more sinister involved? If this was Malic's doing, it was a very convoluted trap. Uldyssian could see neither rhyme nor reason to it. These seemed *good* people, honest people. In addition to bowing, many of them also nodded pleasantly at the group. Some of those behind the party had already begun returning to their own tasks, clearly not at all suspicious of the strangers.

"I have not been in Seram for many years," announced Ethon to his guests as they walked through the busy streets. "How fares it? It was always a tranquil stop. I admit I used to go there in part because I savored the peaceful nature of it as much as the heated bargaining with Master Cyrus!"

"There was a fierce storm there recently," Mendeln interjected. Uldyssian quickly glanced at his brother, but saw that Mendeln intended no further comment.

"Indeed? I suppose that would be the most exciting thing to happen in Seram, lucky for you! I love Partha, but there are so many, many matters on which to keep a careful eye, you know. At times, I would have gladly exchanged places with your father, Mistress Serenthia."

Uldyssian decided to check something. "And do the clerics of the Temple and the Cathedral offer any help with guiding your efforts here?"

"Them?" Looking over his shoulder at Uldyssian, the merchant chuckled. "Hasn't been a blessed one of them in Partha for over a year. They've nothing we want. We're quite satisfied with our lot. They can save their words for someone who wants to hear them, if you'll pardon me for saying so."

Uldyssian nodded in appreciation, Master Ethon's words verifying what he had so far noted about Partha and its inhabitants. He saw robust men and women cheerfully going about their chores or taking a break to eat or converse with friends. He saw clean streets of stone and well-kept structures of both wood and rock. There was no one who was not dressed neatly, whether in simple robes or in more elegant garments. It was a good town with good people.

That was not to say that all was perfection in Partha. There were infirm and maimed among the inhabitants. An elder with barely a tooth remaining hobbled along on one leg and a crutch. Uldyssian also saw a young boy whose left arm was a shriveled version of his right, clearly a defect at birth. Another man with the look of the farmer that the son of Diomedes knew so well from his own face bore savage scars across his arms and neck from what had likely been some accident.

None of them appeared to be shunned by their neighbors and, in fact, all had companions assisting them. Partha under Ethon was evidently a very tolerant town, something even Seram could have learned from them.

He looked again at the child. The poor limb reminded him of his youngest sister, Ameli. In her case, the right arm had been of proper length, but it had been bent back and had always been as thin as a piece of straw. Yet, Ameli had been the most cheerful of the family, the most wanting to help—

The boy passed out of sight. Uldyssian gritted his teeth at the bitter memory. Men like Malic walked the earth living as lords while children suffered because of either chance or some capricious spirit, perhaps—

He stopped in his tracks. "Mendeln."

His brother hesitated. "What is it?"

"Here." The older brother thrust the reins of his animal into Mendeln's hand, then whirled back in the direction from which they had come.

Unaware of what was taking place behind him, Master Ethon started pointing out some of Partha's landmarks. "It may interest you to look upon that crested building yonder . . ."

Lylia said nothing as he passed, but Uldyssian caught a smile of understanding. Serenthia and Achilios barely had the chance to register him before he was far behind the party.

Making the best of his height, Uldyssian looked among the locals. Most paid him no mind, but a few watched the stranger with mild interest.

Uldyssian grew frustrated as the object of his search evaded him. He tried to recall just where he had last seen—

There! Heart pounding, the son of Diomedes pushed past a startled shopkeeper in the midst of arranging his wares. Ahead stood a woman he recognized from earlier.

As he neared, she turned. Next to her, the young boy with a ruined arm followed suit.

Now ignoring the woman, Uldyssian knelt down in front of the child. "May I see your arm . . . please?"

With the innocence of his age, the boy stretched it forward as far as it could go. However, his mother naturally looked concerned and pulled him back out of the newcomer's reach.

Uldyssian glanced up at her. "Please. I mean no harm. My sister was like this. I won't harm him. Just let me study it for a moment."

She had no reason to do as he asked, yet, the woman's expression softened and, with a nod, she allowed Uldyssian to examine the arm.

His fingers gently probed the limb. Up close, he saw that it was in even worse condition than his sister's had been. Thinking of Ameli again brought a sudden rush of emotion to Uldyssian that only at the last did he understand had been bottled up inside him for those many years. Tears drowned out his vision. He wished that he could have done more for his sister . . . for his *entire* family. With all the power that he seemed to wield now, he could have perhaps saved *some* of them from the monstrous wasting disease . . .

Tears drenched his face. Without realizing it, he kept his hold on the boy's withered limb. To Uldyssian, though, it was as if time had turned backward and he now clutched Ameli's arm. She, of all of the family, had been most mistreated by life. First being born so, then dying before she could even have had much of a chance to experience *anything*.

His mind filled with images of his lost sister, but with one difference. She had a healthy body now. Two healthy arms. He imagined her catching things or, better yet, hugging him tight.

Only belatedly did Uldyssian sense that someone *was* hugging him. That brought him back to the present . . . where he realized it was the young boy.

With *two* good arms . . .

Uldyssian looked past the child to his mother. She, in turn, stared at him with an expression of disbelief. Tears ran down her cheeks. Behind her, several other townsfolk had gathered, they, too, eyeing the farmer with astonishment.

Disengaging himself from the child, Uldyssian looked at the people surrounding him. Harsh visions of the reactions in Seram haunted him and he stepped back in concern. "I didn't mean—I didn't meant to—"

But he *had* meant to. He had noticed the child and had been filled with the sudden desire to see if he could do for the boy what had not been possible for Ameli. As it turned out, Uldyssian had been able to do just what he had hoped.

And now, Partha, too, would turn on him, call him a sorcerer or worse . . .

The boy's mother lunged at him . . . and covered the stunned farmer with kisses and hugs. "Thank you! Thank you!"

Beyond her, one man in the forefront of the growing throng bowed. Another followed suit, then another, and another, and another . . .

Someone then chose to go down on one knee. That became the impetus for the rest to do the same. Within moments, everyone around Uldyssian knelt before him as if he were a king.

Or more . . .

Eleven

Clad in floor-length robes of white, their heads lifted high, the six golden-skinned young women sang his praises as he lounged on the down couch in his private chambers. Although none were related or even physically looked like one another, there was that in their fanatic expressions that somehow made them all still seem identical.

Their adoration for him was absolute and each would have gladly accepted his advances . . . not that such would ever happen. That they were beautiful meant nothing to him save that they were as the vast murals on the walls and ceiling or the intricate vases standing atop the crested marble stands. They were part of an overall design, one to help him relive, in some minute—*very* minute—way, the wondrous past that he had willingly left far behind.

The Prophet's luminous silver-blue eyes gazed up at the masterfully-painted images of ethereal winged figures fluttering through the sky. The artisan had been excellent by most standards, but he could never have understood the true depth of what his patron desired. Still, the results of his long labor let the Prophet imagine a little of what had been . . . and of what he had forsaken.

He barely looked old enough to be called a man, though looks could be and were most definitely deceiving. His ivory skin was unmarred by even the least stubble and his golden locks flowed well past his shoulders. The Prophet was lithe and very fit, although not overly muscular like the Inquisitor guards standing at attention outside his sanctum doors. He was, by the opinion of all who had seen him, simply *perfect*.

He wore a look of innocent contemplation, yet tonight he was anything but serene. The impossible had come to pass and he would not stand for it. He was too close to achieving his desires, too close to re-creating the paradise he had lost.

Near the area of his repose, four senior clerics clad in the collared silver-white robes of their station knelt with heads down in prayer. Each man looked old enough to be his father or even grandfather, yet, just like the women, they treated *him* with the utmost veneration.

The Prophet suddenly found the many voices annoying to his ears. He raised one hand and the singing ceased. The praying stopped a moment later as the clerics became aware of the shift in mood.

"I must compose myself before the next sermon," the Prophet declared, his own voice flowing like the music of a lyre.

The singers filed dutifully out of the chamber, followed immediately by the clerics.

The Prophet waited for a moment, then reached out with his thoughts to make certain that his sanctum was sealed off from any who might wish to enter or attempt to hear within. Satisfied, he stared again at the fantastic images above, especially those of the magnificent fliers. A slight frown escaped him as he studied the details. Their wings were feathered like a bird's, the closest a mortal mind could come to the truth . . . and yet so very far from it. The countenances were akin to his own, youthful and unmarred, but somehow, at the same time, ancient and knowing. He credited the artist for that touch, it perhaps being the most accurate portrayal, even if also wrong in so many ways . . .

It had been years—nay, *centuries*—since he had revealed the truth, even to himself. Part of the reason had to do with his ongoing attempt to forget the past, to go on only forging a future that would be rid of any taint, any imperfection.

But a greater part of it had to do with *her* . . . and her terrible betrayal. He had never wanted to be reminded of what had been or what might have been. It had taken him several lifetimes just to thrust her to the back of his thoughts, then twice as many to bury her memory deep to pretend, on occasion, that she had never existed.

Yet . . . now it seemed that all his efforts had gone for naught.

So be it. He would unleash his righteous fury and she and the others would learn what it was to dare plot against him. They would be reminded of just *who* and what he was . . . just before they were annihilated.

The Prophet raised his hands high . . . and both he and the chamber were enveloped in light. The paintings, the murals—everything on the walls—faded away as if dew caught by a hot morning sun. Vanishing in their wake was literally *all* else—the intricate vases and the grand marble stands beneath them, the long, tapering rugs, the garlands of fresh flowers draping every wall . . . even the very couch upon which he had reclined. There remained *nothing* but the Prophet.

With but another thought, he next reshaped the chamber itself. From the very top of the ceiling to the floor beneath his feet, every inch of the room took on a gleaming, mirror-like finish. The Prophet stood reflected a hundred thousand times over, his glory undiminished no matter how great the distance the image was from the original.

But it was still not the true him. Unfamiliar emotion filled the Prophet. Desire. The desire to gaze upon his long-relinquished form. It suddenly became too much to bear. He stared at the foremost reflection, remembering, then, in the next instant, made his memory reality once again.

The light he had earlier summoned focused upon him. It grew so bright that any normal man would have been immediately blinded no matter how well he covered his eyes. Even then, the light continued to strengthen, first taking on an aspect akin to searing white flame . . . and then becoming it in truth.

But the flames did not harm the Prophet, for they were a part of him as he was a part of them. He bathed in the white fire, let it melt away the false image of a youthful human that he had worn for far too long.

And in its place there stood revealed a towering, hooded figure with wings of that same flame, a figure who had no face as mortals understood it, but rather a wonderful radiance beneath long flashes of silver light that in their shaping somewhat resembled a magnificent mane of hair shadowed by the hood.

The other flames receded, allowing him to fully view his glorious image over and over. His long robe was pure sunlight, his great breastplate the shine of copper. Some would have recognized his as resembling a knight, but clearly of no mortal order. Even if the fiery wings that now stretched almost the full width of the chamber had not been a part of him, it would have been clear to any that his kind did not generally walk among something so lowly as Humanity. The light shimmering from within the hood was the true him, a unique combination of pure energy and tonal resonance that marked him as one distinct being even among his own illustrious kind.

And slowly he whispered the name that he had left behind on that fateful moment, the name which had once been sung in praise by the highest of the high.

The name she had oft murmured in love.

INARIUS . . . INARIUS . . . came a voice that was not a voice, but rather a sensation simultaneously experienced in mind, ear, and soul. *I AM INARIUS AGAIN.*

And in announcing it to himself, he felt a rush of jubilation. He was again *Inarius,* once of the Angiris Council, once a commander of the Heavenly Hosts!

Once a rebel against both the High Heavens and the Burning Hells . . .

The last remembrance doused much of his pleasure. Much, but not all. He had done what he had because both sides had become so mired in conflict that they could not see the ultimate futility of their struggle. Since the dawning of reality, when the two celestial realms had come into existence and, shortly thereafter, discord, their vast forces had fought one another for the control of All. Anything of value became the focus of attack and counterattack, generally to its destruction. Angels—as his kind would have been called by humans—and demons alike perished by the legions, all in the name of the Angiris Council—they who ruled the High Heavens—and their eternal adversaries, the Prime Evils.

But Inarius had grown sick of the endless battles, the plotting and the counterplotting. Nothing was gained. Had he been in charge of the Council, he would have done things differently, but even his brother—brother in the sense that their resonances, their beings, held a distinct similarity compared with others'—would not see reason. Even Tyrael, he who was the essence of Justice, could not or would not understand the truth.

And so it was that Inarius at last chose to abandon his part in the struggle. Yet he could not help feeling that there had to be others like him, even in the Burning Hells. Making contact with such—either those of his own kind or, especially, the demons—proved a tricky situation, but Inarius had not been an advisor to the Council for nothing. He understood the machinations not only there, but as they would be in the Burning Hells, and that allowed him to circumnavigate the watchdogs of both. He soon began to locate those others and gather them secretly to him. To his surprise, there were far more than even he had dreamed, far more who saw no sense in battering away at one another throughout eternity. Even more astonishing, there had been among the demons one who had thought like Inarius long before the angel himself had dared to do so.

Her. The one who would awaken love in him as he would do in turn. The one with whom he would help forge a world, a place known to his band of rebels as *Sanctuary*.

The one who would turn his dream of a paradise into a nightmare of blood.

Inarius gazed at the mirrored images and saw her at his side again. She would not be wearing the form he recalled, not now. If she had truly found her way back, it would have been in a masked shape, female likely, but possibly male. She was cunning, beguiling . . . and a threat to all that was by right *his*.

YOU SHALL NOT TAKE FROM ME SANCTUARY, Inarius reprimanded her memory. *I WILL NOT LET YOU AGAIN DESTROY MY DREAM! SANCTUARY AND ALL IT CONTAINS WILL NOT BE YOURS, EVEN IF I MUST DESTROY IT MYSELF . . . AS IS MY RIGHT . . .*

After all, it had been Inarius who had kept it all from collapsing after her heinous betrayal. It had been he who had countered the plots of the Prime Evils and Lucion when they had discovered the realm and he who continued to keep the Angiris Council ignorant of all. The fate of this world and all the brief lives on it were *his,* no one else's!

The angel dismissed the vision of her with what in humans would have been bitterness but what in Inarius was certainly no such base emotion. He was above all that, of course. He reacted only as events demanded, no more.

In fact, Inarius had *already* set into motion steps against her return. She kept herself veiled well, but not well enough. She could not hide from him; he knew her even as her brother did not. Having divined that she had in fact returned to Sanctuary, Inarius had then calculated where she had to be located. That had turned out to be no difficult matter, not given her obvious plan, a continuation of her ancient obsession.

I WILL NOT BROOK THE STIRRING OF THE NEPH-ALEM AGAIN, he thought, recalling what had happened last time. *SUCH AN ABOMINATION WILL NOT SEE FRUITION AGAIN!* He suddenly swelled up in size. His wings filled the vast chamber and the entire Cathedral shook with his anger, though his followers would blame that on a mere tremor. *YOU SHOULD NOT HAVE DARED RETURN, NOT DARED TO INFLUENCE THAT WHICH SHOULD HAVE BEEN LEFT BURIED SO DEEP . . .*

Inarius stared at his reflections. Humanity did have one

advantage and he chose to use it again. With a thought, the angel altered his appearance, re-creating beneath the hood glimpses of a face akin to that of the gold-tressed Prophet. The eyes were still pure energy, but the rest had some semblance of mortal life.

More important, Inarius now had a mouth and on that mouth he set an angry edge, a scowl. It better allowed him to display for his own satisfaction his fury.

"You should not have dared return," the angel repeated, savoring the harsh movements of the mouth and the coarse tones that accented his words better. The scowl deepened in a yet more satisfying manner as Inarius added, "And you should not have dared try to cross me again, *Lilith . . .*"

They brought him gifts of flowers, food, and goods. Many of the gifts were simply discovered at the gates surrounding the estate of Master Ethon, left there by anonymous folk who had heard the tale from others.

"Partha has had its share of preachers and clerics talking of healing the body and soul," their host told Uldyssian. "Yet none of them were ever able to back their words with anything but emptiness!"

"I only did—I only did what I wished that I could've done for my sister," the son of Diomedes explained helplessly, not for the first time.

The tale of the boy's healing had spread like wildfire throughout the town. Without exception, it was called a miracle, especially by the grateful mother. According to Ethon, she had gone from place to place, showing off what he had done for her only child and singing Uldyssian's praises to the heavens.

"I know the woman. Bartha is her name. That child's her treasure, her only love. His father died just before he was born. Fall from a horse." The merchant and headman smiled sadly. "She always feared for the lad, though I know she never let him see that. Tries to teach him to be strong . . ."

"They have to stop leaving all these things," Uldyssian interrupted, staring out the window overlooking the gates. Even as he watched, a furtive figure in a cloak dropped a basket that appeared to contain loaves of bread and a flask of wine. The guards there pointedly looked the other way, not helping Uldyssian's situation. From what he had seen, they were as awed by him as the rest of the citizenry.

"My people are a generous, appreciative lot. They seek to honor you for your good deed, nothing more."

"It would be best if we left before this gets any more out of hand, Uldyssian," remarked Lylia. "We must be on our way to the city."

The party had originally agreed to just stay overnight at Ethon's estate. However, that single night had turned into two, then three. Ethon made no attempt to ask them to depart and Uldyssian had quickly found that he had missed such simple comforts as clean beds and proper meals. He liked Partha, liked the people, especially the kindly merchant. He was only embarrassed by the excess of generosity, something he felt he did not deserve.

"I can't," Uldyssian finally said to her. "Not yet." Without warning, he started for the door.

The others rose to their feet. Achilios was the first to ask, "Where are you going?"

"Out to do what I must. Wait here."

Uldyssian gave them no chance to argue with him. He especially worried about what Lylia would say if he hesitated. The plan was still to head on to Kehjan . . . just . . . not yet.

He all but flew down the stairs, but as he headed toward the doors, a slim figure caught up with him. Cedric, eyes wide, stepped up next to Uldyssian and began keeping pace.

"Are you finally going out? Are you? Will you do anything like the last time?" he asked excitedly.

The farmer grimaced. "I'm going out, but alone. Stay here, Ced. Stay for your safety."

"Safety? Safety from what?"

Instead of answering, Uldyssian picked up his pace. He crossed the threshold just ahead of the boy. However, when Ethon's son attempted to follow, it was to have the door shut right in front of him despite no one touching it.

Outside, Uldyssian breathed a short sigh of relief. He had hoped that the door would do as he wished, but actually having it happen still astounded him. No one would be able to open it again until Uldyssian was well into the town square. By then, it would be too late to stop him . . .

Unfortunately, if he had hoped to make it there unnoticed, in this his abilities failed him. Even before Uldyssian stepped beyond the gates of the estate, people began to gather in his vicinity. It was as if they had been waiting for him to finally come out . . . very likely the case, he mused. None of the faces he saw gave any indication of malice or fear, though. Something far different. Something he thought approached . . . reverence?

It was not the emotion he wanted of them. He had experienced it to a point with Serenthia and still felt uncomfortable. He was a simple man. He came to offer them something to put them on a level with himself and to free them from the control of the nobles and the mages . . . and, most of all, the Temple and the Cathedral. Uldyssian had no desire to be worshipped.

But first, he would have to show them that what he had done was not so much a miracle, not if they could learn to do it for themselves.

By the time he neared the town square, there followed in his wake a substantial throng. Uldyssian continued to sense nothing threatening in anyone around him. Perhaps he had overreacted in keeping his friends from coming with him immediately, but it was still possible that there would be one person around who might choose to see him as a thing of evil, a monster, as his own village had declared him.

The center of Partha consisted of an open, stone-paved area where, in the morning, merchants and farmers with wagons sold various wares, especially food and meat. They ringed a wide, round fountain in the middle of which stood a statue of a scholarly figure with a long, long beard and bearing twin scrolls under his arms. Master Ethon had called him Protheus, one of the founders of Partha and the man who had preached kindness and understanding. Uldyssian thought Protheus's shadow a good one to have cast over him when he began his task.

Four leaping fish spouting water marked the outer edge of the fountain and directly between two of these was the location that Uldyssian chose. Protheus would be staring at the crowd from right behind him.

The market had still been active, but a hush spread through the townsfolk the moment he stopped. Uldyssian suddenly felt nervous. His mouth went dry and he was tempted to thrust his head in the fountain not only to try to quench his sudden thirst but to hide from the very audience he had sought out.

But then Uldyssian spotted a very familiar figure in the crowd. The woman, Bartha. He had only to glance down to discover her son, who beamed at the man who had healed him as if Uldyssian were his own father.

That gave him the heart that he had momentarily been lacking. Unconsciously mimicking the statue's stance, Uldyssian surveyed the crowd, then proclaimed, "What I've done is no miracle!"

His words were met with disbelief by some, confusion by others. Bartha smiled as if he had told some gentle joke. *She* was absolutely certain of what she had witnessed and her son was proof of that.

However, Uldyssian shook his head at her, then continued, "It is no miracle . . . because it lies within each of you to do as *much,* if not more!"

Now a murmur arose among the people, many of them clearly not believing this suggestion any more than the last.

"Hear me!" the son of Diomedes shouted at the top of his voice. "Hear me! Only a short while back, I was no different from the rest of you! I toiled in my farm, concerned only with my day's work. I thought of little else. The vicious bickering of the mage clans was not for me, save that I hoped it would not spill over into my village! Nor was I concerned with the empty words of missionaries from the Temple and the Cathedral, knowing how they had done *nothing* for my family, who first suffered long from plague, then withered slowly into death!"

Here, he received sympathetic glances and nods of understanding from several in the crowd. Uldyssian spied at least a handful of people who wore the pockmarked faces of plague survivors. Partha might overall be very prosperous, but its individual citizens suffered their black days, clearly.

He shook his head. "I said that what I did was no miracle, but for me there *did* come a miracle one day, an awakening of something *within* me . . . a force, a power . . . call it what you like! Things began to happen around me. Some feared them, some did not." That was as far as he would go into the story of what had happened in Seram. If the townsfolk discovered the truth later on, so be it. By then, either Uldyssian would have convinced them or proven himself a madman after all. "I was able to *do* things, *help* others . . ."

He gestured at the boy—whose name he realized he still did not know—urging the child to come to him. Bartha patted her son on the back, sending him off to Uldyssian. The child ran up and hugged the tall figure tight.

"I was able to help him," Uldyssian added, letting everyone see the arm. The boy smiled at him. "And what I did, you can do, too. Perhaps not immediately, but you *will*."

Many shook their heads or frowned. It was one thing for them to believe that he could perform miracles, but still they could not conceive of such abilities in themselves.

With a sigh, Uldyssian considered. Perhaps he moved too swiftly even for the understanding people of Partha. Perhaps he just had to show them.

"Bartha," the son of Diomedes called. "Come up here, too. Please."

Beaming, she rushed up. "Yes, Holy One?"

Her use of such a title caused him to wince. He did not wish to be put in the same category as Malic and his ilk. Never that. "I'm just Uldyssian, Bartha, a farmer by birth, like many you know." Her expression immediately told him that his words passed by unnoticed. With a sigh, he finished, "Just call me Uldyssian, please."

She nodded, which was all he could hope for at this juncture.

"Stand beside me." When she had obeyed, he looked for the man whose face had most been ravaged by disease. "You there. Come to me."

There was a moment of hesitation, then the sandy-haired figure stepped up before Uldyssian. He held his cap in his hand as if it were a form of security.

"What's your name?"

"Jonas, Holy One."

Uldyssian tried not to react again. He would get them to stop . . . eventually. "May we touch your face?"

Again, there was a pause, but finally the man nodded. "Yes. Yes, Holy One."

Uldyssian reached to Bartha, taking one of her soft hands in his own. She allowed him to guide it up to the ruined flesh, unfearful of touching it despite its grotesque appearance. That impressed him. It was one thing to see someone disfigured so, it was another to actually *feel* that scarred skin beneath one's fingertips. He had chosen the right person with which to start.

As both his fingers and hers made contact with the man, Uldyssian closed his eyes and tried to imagine the flesh whole. At the same time, he also reached out to Bartha, trying to see inside her and let her feel what he was doing.

He felt her abruptly shiver, but she did not pull away. Grateful for that, Uldyssian focused on the figure before him. The man was understandably anxious, perhaps most of all from being the center of attention. Uldyssian knew that he had to hurry, if only to prevent Jonas from growing faint of heart and retreating.

Uldyssian tried to recall the emotions that had flowed through him when he had healed the boy's arm. It proved easier to bring them to the forefront than last time, something that surprised him.

The pain, the loss, coursed through him. He knew others who had suffered disfigurement as this man had, people in his village whom he could not help now. Perhaps . . . perhaps if all went as hoped, Uldyssian could someday return to Seram and make amends . . .

Then, as if such thoughts were the key, the force within suddenly poured out of him. He sensed Bartha's renewed astonishment, an astonishment mixed with immense pleasure.

He also sensed the man feel the power flowing into him, and, specifically, his ravaged face.

A gasp of wonder rose from those watching. Uldyssian dared open his eyes—

His fingertips had already given him some hint of the results, but seeing them still amazed Uldyssian at least as much as it did the throngs. The damaged skin was pink and whole . . . in fact, there was no longer a blemish or mark *anywhere* on the man's countenance.

"Another miracle!" Bartha breathed.

The subject of Uldyssian's experiment put his own hands to his face, marveling at the feel of his skin. He turned toward his fellows, giving them a good view of the results.

Before they could start praising him again, the son of Diomedes loudly interjected, "Bartha, did you feel everything? Did you?"

Her expression turning confused, she replied, "I felt you heal him—"

He cut her off. "What do you feel inside *yourself*? Do you sense it yet?"

She touched over her heart. The crowd—including the healed man—looked at her.

"I feel . . . I feel . . ." She smiled beatifically at Uldyssian. "I feel as if I've just awakened, Holy—Master Uldyssian! It . . . it's . . . I don't know how to describe it . . ."

Nodding, he looked to the others. "That's how it begins. The feeling will continue to grow. It may take time, but slowly . . . slowly . . . you'll come to be everything I am . . . and possibly more. Possibly much more."

It was a weighty promise and one that Uldyssian in great part regretted the minute that he uttered it. Yet, now it was too late to turn back. As he learned more about what he was able to do, he would try to teach the others, at least until someone else could do better.

That meant that Kehjan would have to wait even longer than he had initially intended. Uldyssian could not very well leave the people of Partha until they understood better.

Immediately, he thought of Lylia. She would be upset at first, surely, but, as in the past, she would come around. When the noblewoman saw how the Parthans reacted, it would make absolute sense to her to stay as long as needed.

At least, he hoped that she would see it that way.

The man he had healed came up to him again. "Master Uldyssian. . . could you . . . could you show me?"

Uldyssian started to reach forward, then hesitated. He smiled, surprised himself not to have sensed it sooner. "I guess I don't have to. You should know that. Just look deep. You'll see . . ."

Jonas's brow furrowed . . . then suddenly joy filled his face again. It had nothing to do with his mended skin. He nodded eagerly, all but shouting, "I feel . . . I think . . . what Madame Bartha said! I feel . . . awakened . . ."

His awestruck words were enough to cause the crowd to break into excited babble. Someone stepped toward Uldyssian. That caused the entire crowd to flow forward. Each person wanted to be the next.

Caught up in the moment, Uldyssian accepted one after another, spending what time he needed with each. Hands stretched toward him, seeking his touch. Not all of them would feel the awakening as quickly as Bartha and Jonas had and he said this to every person before trying, but it *would* eventually happen. Uldyssian truly believed that and because he believed that, so, too, did those to whom he ministered.

As each new supplicant stepped up, he also grew more and more confident with his decision. Partha was indeed a perfect place to prove himself. If he was able to do this well here, it staggered Uldyssian's imagination to think just how matters would fare in the city.

No, a short respite in the town would surely not endanger matters . . .

Surrounded by so many, Uldyssian did not notice that, far back, the one whose thoughts most mattered to him watched him now with veiled eyes. Lylia stood at the base of a set of steps overlooking the fountain, drinking in the sight. Oddly, despite the noblewoman's arresting appearance, not one among all those there so much as noticed her.

But *she* noticed everything, including that what Uldyssian had set into motion here would keep him occupied for quite some time to come. *Too long,* in fact. He should have nearly reached Kehjan by now. That was how she had planned it. Not this highly suspicious turn to Partha, of all places.

Yet, after a moment's consideration, Lylia suddenly smiled. Plans were made to be adjusted constantly.

"If not Kehjan, then by all means here, my *love,*" the blond woman whispered to herself. "In the end, the location does not matter. You will yet bring to me what is rightfully mine, Uldyssian . . . you will . . . even if you must *die* to do it . . ."

Twelve

Achilios found Serenthia not where he had expected, that expectation being that Cyrus's daughter would be assisting Uldyssian with his task. Instead, the hunter discovered the dark-haired woman sitting where she could see the proceedings, but was far enough away not to be a part of them. Her eyes were, of course, on Uldyssian—to ask otherwise would have been unthinkable even to Achilios—although as the archer approached, his own keen gaze noticed hers surreptitiously shift to Lylia, then back to the son of Diomedes again.

"I brought you some water," he said as way of interjecting himself into her private world. He offered her the sack he had carried with him, freshly filled at Master Ethon's estate. Ever practical—save when it came to love—Achilios had first paused to gather something to drink before chasing after his friend.

Serenthia took it with a nod of thanks. She drank far more from it than Achilios assumed that she would, which meant she had been sitting out here for quite some time, just watching. Likely Serenthia had run all the way here, fearing some imagined danger, whereas he had taken his time, somehow aware that Uldyssian was utterly safe.

When she was done, he took the sack back and remarked, "It's truly astonishing, isn't it, Serry?"

"Yes, it is."

"I've been his friend since we were children." Without asking, he took up a place next to her. It was as forward as he dared get. Despite his sometimes gregarious appearance,

Achilios was much more at home in the forest, alone with his quarry. In social circumstances, he felt only one step above Mendeln and, where the woman next to him was concerned, as awkward.

His comment caused her to look at him with such intensity that Achilios wondered what he had said wrong. Serenthia appeared poised to say something, but it was almost a full minute before a single word escaped her lips.

And when she did speak, it was not on the subject that he assumed it would be. "Why *are* the two of you friends, Achilios? You seem so different in so many ways."

He had no answer save "Because we just are, I guess. We were friends the moment that we met." He shrugged. "Children are like that."

"I suppose." Serenthia thought for a moment, then asked, "Is she what *you* would dream of?"

Now the subject he had expected was at hand. Serenthia had merely taken a more circuitous route to it. "Lylia? She is fair, to be honest, and no man would let his gaze pass over her without noticing that, but the same could be said for others, not merely her."

He could barely have been more blunt—in his eyes—but she seemed not to understand that he meant her. "I know that to us she is exotic and I can understand why Uldyssian would fall for her, but it was all so quick, Achilios."

"It can be like that." It *had* been like that for him . . . in a sense. One day, he had known only Serry the impish child. The next day, there had stood the beautiful woman. Achilios had been so lost in amazement of the change that, for the next week, he went without a single catch to his credit.

Serenthia was silent for a time and Achilios satisfied himself with being in her company . . . which was how such situations generally ended. They watched as Uldyssian greeted one Parthan after another. Each time he succeeded in doing whatever it was he did, Achilios noticed both his friend and the one touched share a look of immense satisfaction.

"Is that the way you felt?" he finally dared ask Serenthia. "Like them?"

"Yes." But the way she said it made the hunter not so certain.

"Have you been able to do anything?"

This time there was a pause, followed by, "I don't know."

"How could you—"

Her tone grew more adamant. "I *don't* know."

Normally, Achilios would have left it at that, but this time, he could not. "Serry, what do you mean?"

Her gaze shifted not to him, but rather her hands. "I feel it, just as I know many of them do, but that's all. I haven't noticed anything else different around me. I've tried to think of things, make them happen, but . . . but as far as I know, nothing *has.*"

"Still? I would've thought by now that—"

Now she looked at him. Her eyes were steely. "So would I. Believe me, so would I."

It made no sense to him. Lylia had already displayed several instances of ability, such as making flowers and berries bloom on bushes or healing some minor cuts suffered by one of the mounts. She had also summoned a rabbit to them, saving Achilios from having to hunt but leaving the archer feeling as if somehow the animal had been cheated of its chance to survive.

"What about *you?*" his companion asked without warning. "I haven't seen anything from you, either."

In truth, Achilios did feel something within him seeking to grow, but he had done his best to smother it. He had told no one of that decision. Many might desire the gift that Uldyssian offered, but not his best friend. Achilios was satisfied with being who he was. A hunter and a simple man.

"I suspect that I'm not the best student for Uldyssian," he returned. "Not at all."

"But no one taught *him,* not really! With Uldyssian, it came as suddenly as the storm over Seram . . . which apparently was caused by him, too!"

"Uldyssian was pressed on all sides, Serry. He was accused of brutal murder by Brother Mikelius. The Inquisitors would have dragged him back off to the Cathedral, probably to burn as a fiend! He had no choice!"

She was not convinced. "It was all terrible, but why at that time? Why not when his family slowly and horribly perished from plague? Why not then? Why even him, for that matter? There are so many others who've suffered worse and yet we've never heard of such an astounding thing before! It would've even reached Seram, you know that!" Even as he nodded his agreement to this argument, Serenthia went on, "And why not Mendeln, then? He suffered as much, too! His family was wiped out and his brother was accused of a terrible crime! It could've been him, but it wasn't! I've seen nothing unusual about Mendeln, have you?"

Her mention of Mendeln made Achilios flinch. Serenthia noticed his reaction and her eyes narrowed.

"What is it, Achilios? What about Mendeln? Is he manifesting abilities like his brother?"

It was not the suggestion of that which had caused the archer to flinch, but rather a brief and unexpected recollection of another time, another place. As Serenthia had spoken of Uldyssian's sibling, Achilios had *relived* the moment when he and his other friend had inspected the mysterious stone near Seram. Not only had the archer seen again Mendeln freezing in place before it, but he had also reexperienced touching it himself . . . and the awful emptiness that had overwhelmed him until he had managed to pull free.

"No . . ." Achilios finally managed. "No . . . nothing like Uldyssian."

She was not convinced. "Achilios, what—"

Without warning, a tremendous sense of fear overcame the hunter, but not fear for himself. He had the awful feeling that something was happening to Mendeln at this very moment.

Achilios leaped to his feet, startling his companion.

"What is it? What's wrong?"

He wanted to answer her, but the urgency he felt was too strong. Without a word, Achilios began running. He ignored Serenthia's concerned call after him.

But barely out of sight of the woman he loved, Achilios came to a dead stop. The fear for Mendeln had not lessened any, but the archer hesitated to begin his run anew.

The truth was, Achilios had no idea just *where* Uldyssian's brother had gone.

The streets through which Mendeln moved were oddly empty and the buildings around him had suddenly taken on an unsettling gray cast. There was no wind whatsoever and not the slightest sound. Mendeln would have felt very alone save for one thing . . . he was still surrounded by the shades of the guards Uldyssian had slain.

Since their arrival, it had taken monumental effort on his part to keep from screaming out the truth to the others. Either these shadows of men existed or he had gone mad . . . or both. Mendeln did not know which would be worse. He only knew that he just wanted to tell *someone* what was happening to him.

But he had not. He had said nothing even when they had arrived in Partha, where his hopes that the ghosts would leave him had dissipated the moment the first of the shades had passed through into the town. Until then, Mendeln had believed that his haunting would be temporary. Now, he feared that the dead would always be with him.

"Fear" was perhaps no longer the right word, though. Certainly, they kept him anxious, but the more they were around him, the less frightened he became. They did nothing but stare. Not in condemnation, but as if awaiting some word from him. So far, though, Mendeln had said little directly to them. He had asked them to please kindly go away, but since they had not obeyed, he had seen no reason to continue any further attempt at conversation.

At the moment, they were the least of his concerns. As he continued through the town, Mendeln began noticing peculiar signs of age on the buildings, as if Partha were some ancient place long abandoned. The shift became more apparent with each step. The grayness grew darker, veering toward the black . . .

This was not right, he realized. Where was everyone? Where was Uldyssian, after whom he had been chasing? Mendeln was worried about his brother, especially what the Parthans might do. He recalled too vividly what had happened in Seram, where people who had known Uldyssian all his life had turned on him . . .

But then there arose a sight ahead that made Mendeln falter in his steps and forget all about his brother. He spun around with the intention of fleeing . . . only to find himself facing the very direction he had just abandoned.

A direction that led to a long-neglected cemetery. A cemetery that, from its ancient state, surely could not be Partha's.

With the shades of dead men already surrounding him, Uldyssian's brother could see nothing but ill coming of entering the overgrown burial site. Yet, when he tried to back away, the cemetery only drew nearer. Nevertheless, Mendeln tried one more step back—

And in the next breath found himself standing *within* the ruined grounds.

A choking sound was all he could muster as he tried to come to grips with what was happening. He prayed that it was only a bad dream, but knew otherwise. Mendeln then thought of his blackouts and wondered if this was some bizarre continuation of them. He certainly had no other answer.

He suddenly noticed another very curious—and unsettling—thing. The shades of the dead guards had not entered with him. They drifted beyond the arched gateway, as if the winged gargoyle he saw above it kept them at bay. For the first time, Mendeln would have liked their company, if only because of their comparative familiarity. Now he was completely alone, facing who-knew-what.

As he started to turn his gaze back . . . what felt like a *hand* pushed him deeper into the cemetery. Stumbling several steps, Mendeln glanced over his shoulder. He immediately swallowed. Naturally, there was *no one* there.

The farmer glanced down at the first of the graves. A crescent-shaped stone marked the spot. The grave had been dug so long ago that it was infested with generations of weeds and grass and had even sunken in a bit. Mendeln started to look away again, then eyed the marker one more time.

Barely legible in the odd, gray shadows, was the same script that he had seen on the stone near Seram.

Despite himself, Mendeln grew fascinated by the revelation. Keeping respectful to the grave, he knelt to the side, then leaned toward the stone. Up close, Mendeln was able to verify what he had seen. Many of the very same symbols ran along the crescent, but in patterns that he did not recognize.

Without hesitation, he ran his fingers over the first line. Immediately, he sensed some sort of power emanating from the symbols. Mendeln had heard of words of power, such as the mage clans supposedly used at times, and he could only surmise that these were such.

Looking up, Uldyssian's brother surveyed the seemingly endless field of stones. The graves were marked in a variety of manners. In addition to the crescents, there were star-shaped slaps, squat rectangular ones, and more. Surveying the landscape ahead, Mendeln even spotted one over looked by a towering, winged statue bearing a weapon in one hand.

Drawn by that statue, he slipped among the graves in order to get a better look. Fascination replaced dread. He had to learn more. Was this some repository for the dead of the mage clans? If so, did they have some tie to what was happening to him . . . and to Uldyssian, for that matter? Until now, he would have doubted it, what little he had gleaned from merchants indicating that the once-powerful clans had all but shut themselves off from the world as they continued their arcane duels of wit against one another. They would hardly have the time to bother themselves with a pair of farmers far from the city.

Although the statue stood deep in the cemetery, it seemed that Mendeln had barely begun toward it when suddenly it loomed over him. He paused, trying to understand what it was supposed to be. A winged being, with a face hooded save for glimpses of the mouth and some cascading hair. It wore a robe and breastplate somewhat akin to that of the Cathedral's Inquisitors, but sculpted to resemble some finer material. The breastplate also had script upon it, more words in the same mysterious language.

Mendeln glanced at the wings again, realizing that they were different from those of birds. What he had taken for feathering looked, when studied closer, more of an artist's rendition of *flame*. Mendeln had never heard legends of any creature or spirit with such wings, not even in the stories his mother had told him when he had been a very young child.

In the giant figure's left hand it held a great sword whose tip rested on the base beneath the statue. The other hand pointed down, not merely, it seemed to Mendeln, indicating the grave beneath, but also those around it. He had the distinct impression that this was supposed to *mean* something to him, but what, Uldyssian's brother could not say.

And so, despite his situation, Mendeln grew frustrated beyond belief. He was a patient man in general, but someone appeared to be trying—very successfully—to draw him past his limits.

"All right, then!" he shouted, his voice echoing over and over and over in the silence. "If you want something from me, then tell me what it is! Tell me, I demand it!"

The moment that he finished, a grating sound filled his ears. Swallowing, Mendeln watched in horror as the statue's pointing hand turned enough so that it now indicated what was written on the base.

Mendeln waited for it to do something else, but the

winged guardian froze once more. Slowly, he built up the nerve to look down at what was below.

The same ancient script greeted him. He had hardly expected otherwise, but still this added to his frustration.

"But I cannot *read* it!" he muttered. "I do not know what any of it says!" Squinting, Mendeln attempted to recall the words that had come unbidden to him that frightening time when the demon had caught him alone in the woods. He remembered the images in his head and the sounds of those words, but they were still not enough to help Mendeln with what now lay before him.

Weary of the futility of this nightmare, Mendeln finally dared lean on the grave as he studied each mark. His mouth formed shapes, but that was all. Nothing, absolutely nothing, made sense.

"What does it say?" he growled under his breath. "*What does it say?*"

The Dragon has chosen you . . .

Mendeln jerked to his feet. He had heard a voice like that once before, back in Seram. It was akin to the voice of Cyrus . . .

Cyrus, *after* he had been killed.

Part of him wanted to scream for this new one to get out of his head, but another part fixed on what had been said. *The Dragon has chosen you . . .*

He stared at the ancient script and read it anew. "The Dragon has chosen me—you . . . the . . . Dragon . . . has . . . chosen . . . you . . ."

And suddenly, Uldyssian's brother could read that line. More important, *other* symbols now made more sense. Mendeln felt that he was now on the verge of discovering the meanings of all of them and, in doing so, discovering the truth about what was happening.

But what did the phrase actually relate to? Kneeling close again, Mendeln studied the symbol representing the most important word . . . Dragon. A loop twisting into itself, a thing without beginning or end. Mendeln knew what a dragon was from legends; why would this mark represent such a creature? And why such a creature at all?

"What happened?" Mendeln quietly asked . . . then frowned when he noted how he had phrased the question. He had meant to ask *what is happening*. Why would he—

The dirt beneath his hand suddenly shifted . . . as if something beneath was seeking to dig its way *out*.

Eyes round, Mendeln scrambled back. In doing so, he inadvertently threw himself atop another of the graves, where, to his further dismay, something *also* began to stir beneath.

Worse, it began to register on him that graves *everywhere* were shifting, stirring. Mounds of upturned dirt decorated many already and Mendeln's imagination pictured skeletal figures readying to emerge.

But just as it seemed that his imagination would become a monstrous reality, there formed in the shadow of the winged statue a figure entirely shrouded in black. Mendeln had a momentary glimpse of a face not unlike his own in that it was studious in nature, but otherwise very, very different. It had an unreal handsomeness to it, as only a sculpture or a painting could achieve.

The figure drew a single symbol in the air, a daggerlike mark that for a single blink flared a bright white. What sounded like a great sigh swept through the cemetery—

The graves stilled. The cloaked form vanished . . . and, at that point, Mendeln's surroundings changed.

He was still in Partha, that much even his jolted mind would have guessed, but Uldyssian's brother no longer stood within the cemetery. Instead, Mendeln was poised at its gateway, the gargoyle's grinning maw seeming to mock his sanity. The cemetery no longer looked ancient and overrun, but well-kept, as one would have expected in Partha.

But no matter how hard he squinted, Mendeln could see no winged statue.

Something touched his shoulder, causing him to yelp like

a kicked hound. Strong fingers grasped Mendeln and turned him around.

To his relief, it was Achilios, not some fiend from the dead.

"Mendeln! Are you all right! What are you doing *here?*" The hunter looked almost as pale as Uldyssian's brother felt. Achilios's eyes darted past Mendeln to study the cemetery with utter loathing. "Did you go in there?"

"I—No." It seemed best to Mendeln not to try to explain, since he himself was not quite certain just what had taken place. A delusion? A dream? Insanity?

Instead, Mendeln focused on a new and intriguing question. "Achilios, my friend, why are *you* here? Did you follow me?"

This time, it was the archer who hesitated before replying with an equally suspicious "Yes. I did." Achilios gave Mendeln a sudden grin, then slapped the farmer on the shoulder. "Don't want you getting lost, eh, Mendeln? Town this size, lots of things to distract you, hmm?"

Mendeln was not certain whether he was supposed to be insulted by such comments, but chose to ignore them for the sake of both men. Perhaps another time, he could share his secrets with Achilios and the hunter could do the same with him. Those secret, he believed, all focused on that fateful stone back home.

"You need to come with me back to the square. Uldyssian—"

It shamed Mendeln that he had not been concerned about his brother. Nervously rubbing his hands together, he blurted "Uldyssian! Is he all right?"

"More than that," replied Achilios. "But you'll have to see to understand—" He happened to look down at Mendeln's hands. His brow arched. "Your hands are covered in dirt! What—?"

"I tripped in the street just before here and had to use my hands to keep from striking the stone with my face," Mendeln quickly explained. "There was dirt there," he added rather lamely.

To his relief and surprise, the blond bowman took this answer at face value, too. "A fall in the street! You're getting too absentminded for your own good! Here, let's find something to wipe your hands off with and be on our way . . ."

With nothing else around, Mendeln finally had to brush his hands against his garments. As a farmer, he was used to doing such, but felt a little embarrassed to be seen so in Partha. Yet, they could not very well return to Master Ethon's home first. Mendeln dearly wanted to see what was happening in the square.

He started to follow Achilios, only to falter but a few steps later. Making certain that his friend was not looking his way, Mendeln spun in a quick circle, searching.

The ghosts who had been with him since the battle in the wild were nowhere to be found. It was as if that, when the shrouded figure had sent the spirits of the graves to their rest, it had also done the same for the shades of the Temple's guards.

"Thank you," he whispered.

"Did you say something?" asked the archer, pausing to let him catch up.

"No . . ." Mendeln replied with a vigorous shake of his head. "No."

Achilios took this answer as he had the others, for which Uldyssian's brother was grateful. Yet, as they hurried along, Mendeln's mind stayed not with his sibling's situation, but the unsettling, indeed, even *sinister*, episode through which he had just suffered.

One thing about it haunted him most of all. Not what had happened, not exactly. No, it was a new question that the strange vision had raised . . . or rather, *two* new questions bound together.

What *was* the Dragon . . . and why had it chosen *him?*

Despite Achilios's genial appearance, his mood was actually darker than when he had gone off in search of

Mendeln. The archer had not at all expected to discover Uldyssian's brother standing at the very entrance to such a place. It had brought back full-blown for a second time the horrific sensations that Achilios had suffered after touching the stone.

He had tried to cover up his abrupt anguish immediately and was thankful that Mendeln had been so preoccupied that he had not noticed. Unfortunately, that preoccupation had drawn the hunter's attention in turn . . . and was what ate away at Achilios even now.

When asked if he had entered the cemetery, Mendeln had denied doing such a thing. Yet, Achilios did not have to have a master hunter's honed senses to know that the dirt on the other's hands was not what would have been found in the street. It had a drier consistency, an aged look, and there had been some bits of weed and grass mixed in, too.

The sort of dirt that would have been more likely found—very easily—in a cemetery.

That, in turn, caused Achilios to remember another time, back in Seram, when Brother Mikelius had wished to see the grave of the murdered missionary . . . and had proclaimed to the archer and the others there that someone had desecrated it. The Master Inquisitor had believed Uldyssian somehow responsible. Uldyssian or someone near to him.

And now here was Mendeln at another cemetery, with dirt on his hands, Mendeln, who had been curiously absent during much of the events in the village.

Mendeln . . . who in some ways was beginning to frighten Achilios even more than Uldyssian.

Thirteen

Day followed after day in Partha with no end to Uldyssian's task. It was not that he could not sense the forces stirring within most of those who came to him, but that their progress beyond that did not leap forward—as his and even Lylia's had done—mystified Uldyssian. He spoke of it with her as they lay in bed in the elegant quarters granted them by the generous Master Ethon, but Lylia seemed not at all bothered by the lack of results.

"It shows that you are even more special, my love, as I already knew," she cooed, her hand running over his chest. "But give it a few more days. I think you will begin to see what you desire."

"I'm glad you think so," he returned morosely. "I also appreciate it more since I know you weren't happy when we found ourselves here instead of nearly in Kehjan."

"I am, if nothing else, very adaptable, dear Uldyssian. I have been forced to be."

Uldyssian would have questioned her remark, but when he looked at her again, it was to discover that Lylia had just drifted off to sleep. A few minutes later, he fell asleep, too, for the next few hours happily relieved of his concerns.

The noblewoman's prediction came to pass barely two days later. By this time, Uldyssian had touched nearly everyone in the town. There were astonishingly few people hesitant about awakening the gift within themselves and fewer yet that he could deny.

It was Master Ethon who suggested those who should be

forbidden time with Uldyssian. They were criminals all, the most suspicious and untrustworthy. As lead justice of the Parthan tribunal, the merchant knew most of them by face. He made certain to stand by Uldyssian once he knew what was happening.

"That man there," Ethon had declared. "Be wary of giving him anything . . ." He then pointed to another. "He's likely to slit your throat while you greet him, so watch that one, too."

In the beginning, Uldyssian had dutifully obeyed, but on this day, he saw again the first man in question, an unsavory, bearded soul by the name of Romus. A wicked scar ran across a good portion of his bald pate, a result, no doubt of his nefarious activities. The moment that Romus saw that he in turn was being observed, he started to leave. However, Uldyssian suddenly decided that he *wanted* to speak with the disreputable figure.

"Romus! Romus! Come to me!"

Hundreds of pairs of eyes fixed on Romus. He had no choice but to step forward despite scowls from the town Guard and many others.

Master Ethon, too, was not pleased. "Uldyssian, I know you mean well, lad, but such as *him* would be more of a danger if given the gift—"

Lylia put a soft hand on the merchant's arm. "But dear Ethon! How do you know that some others like Romus have not already received Uldyssian's aid? Can you claim to know *every* villain to walk Partha?"

"No, my lady, but I know a damn lot—pardon my saying so—and this one's among the worst!"

She would not be dissuaded. "You have seen the faces of those who have been awakened. You yourself have experienced it, too. Look deep. Do you think that you could ever use it for ill?"

Ethon faltered. "No . . . never . . . but . . ."

"No one *could*," Lylia insisted. "No one could."

Not bothering to wait to see what his host might say next,

Uldyssian reached for Romus, who looked less like a threat and more like a frightened child. The bald man was surrounded by a good many townsfolk who considered Uldyssian something of a holy figure.

"Don't be afraid," said Uldyssian. To the crowd, he added, "Give him some room. It's all right."

As they obeyed, the son of Diomedes drew him closer. Romus frowned but let himself be guided.

Still at Master Ethon's side, Lylia leaned forward, her gaze intent.

The rest of the townsfolk watched warily, Romus's reputation apparently well known. They were ready to defend Uldyssian if anything happened.

But Uldyssian himself had no such fears. The moment that he touched the other man's hands, the force within him surged forth. Uldyssian immediately felt it stir something within Romus. The bald man gasped and a look of wonder spread across his face. It made him look like a completely different person, one whom Uldyssian would have trusted with his life.

"It's—It's—" Romus stammered.

"Yes, it is."

Uldyssian stepped back, as ever, giving the person a chance to come to grips with the change themselves. Romus chuckled like a child and a tear slid down his cheek. With both hands, he rubbed the top of his head as he tried to comprehend.

As the hands came away, Lylia abruptly called, "Uldyssian! See what he's done! Look at the scar!"

Uldyssian could *not* look at it . . . for it no longer existed. The skin where once the jagged cut had lain was now as healthy and as pink as that on Jonas's restored face.

And it had not been because of any effort by Uldyssian.

That was not immediately apparent to the townsfolk, who applauded this latest work as his. Quickly raising his hands high, Uldyssian waited for the crowd to quiet, then shouted, "What you see was none of my doing! None at all!

What you see before you . . . the miracle you've witnessed . . . Romus did himself!" When cries of denial arose,
he grew more stern. "I say this and I know this! Who here
would call me false?"

No one there *could*. Many began looking in amazement at
Romus, who shook his head over and over, trying to deny
the truth as much as his neighbors had a moment before.

But Uldyssian would not let him. "Romus, come join me
here by the fountain! Let the others see!"

Wordlessly, the bearded man obeyed. Others crowded
forward, murmuring to one another and pointing at the
healed area. Romus began to turn a deep shade of crimson.
There was nothing about him that looked like the hardened
criminal Master Ethon had first identified.

"Uncanny . . ." muttered the merchant from the background. "Is it possible?"

Lylia clutched their host's arm tight. "It is!" she breathed
to Ethon. "Do you understand *now?*"

"Yes . . . yes . . . I suppose I do . . ."

Meanwhile, Uldyssian had gathered the people's attention again. "It may be some time before anything manifests
again, but you see now what is possible! Let no one doubt
that *everyone* will be able to do the same . . . and more!"

That was enough to send the throng into a roar. Many fell
to their knees and thanked Uldyssian, who looked
extremely upset by this reaction.

"Get up! Get up!" he insisted. His fury shook his followers. They stared fearfully.

He did not care. They had to understand. "No one bows
to me! I'm no king, no patriarch of a mage clan! I was and
still am a simple *farmer!* My land, my home, may be lost to
me, but that's what I remain even with what I've been
granted! I offer to share, not to command! Never, ever, kneel
to me again! There are no masters here! Only equals!"

Even as he said it, Uldyssian knew that they did not
entirely see it that way. They would look to him for
answers, for direction. He consoled himself with the

thought that he acted as teacher, as guide. One day soon, most would no longer need him. There was even the possibility that some would surpass Uldyssian and that he, in turn, would have to learn from them.

For the time being, though, it was all up to him. Romus's startling act, though, gave him renewed hope. Each person was individual. As a farmer, he understood how growth varied. All he had to do was be more patient.

He had the time. Kehjan was not expecting him. He could stay here until he was certain. That would make it all the better when he did present himself to the inhabitants of the city.

Feeling better about matters, Uldyssian turned to the next supplicant . . . and the next . . . and the next . . .

Malic was being more cautious, this time. Not because he felt any concern about facing Uldyssian, but because he wanted the mission to go very cleanly. The morlu could be a double-edged sword in some respects. They were very capable, but their tendency for bloodshed almost rivaled that of demons. Fortunately, the master had chosen a capable servant in Damos and Damos had chosen well in his five warriors. Collectively, they were a far more potent force than the demons and guards that the cleric had led previously.

Damos even now stalked ahead of the party, sniffing the air like a beast on the scent. The other morlu sat eagerly in the saddle, awaiting word of the prey.

"This way they came," grated Damos. He raised his ram's skull helmet up to the sky and sniffed again. "And in this place, they turned . . . that way."

Malic's gaze followed the outthrust arm. "Are you certain?"

The lead morlu grinned, revealing sharp, yellowed teeth. "I smell the blood, high priest . . ."

"They were heading toward Kehjan. When last I encountered them, they were well on their way to the lowlands and the jungles. Veering off in *that* direction means an extreme detour."

Damos shrugged. To his kind, such considerations were unnecessary. All that mattered was where the prey could be found, not what direction it had run before the hunt.

The cleric stroked his monstrous arm, a motion that had, in the short time since the transformation, become an unconscious habit. The clawed fingers twitched. Just before the party had left, the master had finally told him what the hand could do. Malic was now eager to try it . . . but to do that he had to reach his quarry.

"We go that way, then," the high priest finally declared.

Grunting, Damos returned to his dark steed. That following the trail was what they needed to do was very obvious to all the morlu, but they knew their place and so did not make anything of the cleric's unnecessary comment. The high priest could send them to their deaths if he so desired, so long as it served the Temple. They would not question his leadership unless commanded to by the master.

With Malic in the lead, the band rode on at a furious clip. Curiously, their mounts left no trails of their own and, indeed, even the clatter of hooves was missing. Had there been any other person there to witness their passing, they might have noticed that the hooves did not even quite touch the ground . . .

Night settled again upon the town of Partha. An exhausted Uldyssian fell into his bed. He barely noticed Lylia slide in beside him before sleep overtook the farmer.

Dreams soon invaded his slumber, pleasant interludes in which he was able to help the sick and maimed everywhere learn how to heal themselves or bring burnt lands back to bloom. Uldyssian watched the world become a paradise and its people reach a point of perfection undreamed . . .

Then, in the midst of the harmony and love, calamity broke out. Fissures opened in the ground and even the sky developed cracks. It was as if his home was hidden inside a vast egg now being broken open by something *outside*.

And in the next breath, the heavens filled with fiery-winged figures and from the fissures rose monstrous, scaled hordes. The two fearsome armies immediately collided with one another, with Humanity caught in the middle. Men, women, and children were torn to bloody gobbets by the unnoticing warriors of both sides. Thousands lay strewn dead in an instant.

"Stop!" Uldyssian roared. "Stop!"

None of the combatants paid heed to his cries and when he sought to use his gifts to make them listen, nothing happened.

"They're all over us!" shouted Achilios, suddenly at his side. "Do something! I'm almost out of arrows!" Indeed, the archer had apparently managed to bring down nearly a hundred of the fighters, but still the tide flowed toward where Uldyssian and he stood. "This is your fault!" Achilios insisted, growing angry. "Your fault!"

"No!" Uldyssian whirled from the hunter and his accusations, only to find Serenthia gazing at him from afar. She stood surrounded by a sea of furious warriors, oblivious of the surmounting threat to her. Blades already slashed past her head, but all Cyrus's daughter did was continue to stare at Uldyssian as so many in the audience had this day.

"I have faith in you," she declared. "I do—"

An ax already scarred from heavy use neatly severed her head. Blood poured forth like a fountain from the open neck. As Serenthia's head toppled over, Uldyssian saw that the look of trust yet remained.

"Serry!" he choked. Uldyssian tried to push forward, but a hand suddenly pulled him back. He looked at the one preventing him from reaching her and discovered it to be none other than his own brother . . . but a Mendeln of the likes of which made him shiver.

"Do not worry about her anymore," the cadaverous fig-

ure intoned without emotion. Mendeln's face was drawn
and gray and he seemed half-shadow. A dark cloak surrounded him, a cloak that twisted and turned despite no
apparent wind. "Do not worry about her, anymore. She's
one of mine, now."

Only then did Uldyssian see that there were figures
behind Mendeln, faces he recognized from both Partha and
Seram. However, they, like Mendeln, had drawn faces and,
when he looked close, jagged wounds and torn flesh.

They were all dead.

Having made his declaration, Mendeln drifted past
Uldyssian as if a shade himself. In his wake, the corpses
of the innocent rose to follow. The fighting separated
around Serenthia's body, which still stood despite its
death.

Mendeln gestured and the torso also turned to join him.

"Wait!" called Achilios, leaping forward. Throwing
down his bow, he seized Serenthia's bleeding head and
rushed after Mendeln. "Wait!"

Uldyssian attempted to follow, but for him the battling
legions would not make room. The winged warriors and
their bestial adversaries pressed tight against one another,
yet, despite heavy losses on both sides, the numbers
seemed undiminished. An endless flow of replacements
continued to come, filling the world to overflowing.

There was no longer even a hint of the paradise that had
once stood all around Uldyssian. The ground was a blazing
slaughterhouse, the sky burnt and smoke-ridden.

Then, when he had nearly given up hope, he heard
Lylia's voice call to him. Desperately he looked around for
her, at last spotting the noblewoman—her finery gleaming—gliding toward him from across the carnage. The battle did not touch Lylia in the least; in fact, the combatants
seemed eager to be out of her way. She ran directly into
Uldyssian's arms, holding him as tight as he held her.

"Lylia . . ." he gasped, relieved beyond belief. "Lylia . . . I
thought I'd lost you, too . . ."

"But you will never be without me, my love, never . . ." she cooed, holding him tighter yet. Her face was planted in his chest. "We are bound to each other forever . . ."

Grateful, Uldyssian leaned down to kiss her. Lylia raised her face to his—

Choking, he tried in vain to disengage from the noble-woman, but Lylia's embrace was unbreakable. Uldyssian stared in horror as her mouth moved closer to his.

"Will you not kiss me, my love?" she asked with a smile . . . a smile filled with sharp teeth. Her eyes had no pupils, merely a sinister shade of crimson covering the entire area under the lids. Her skin was scaled and her ears beneath her hair long and pointed. That hair still hung long, but now consisted of harsh quills colored emerald green.

Despite the macabre changes, there was that about her that still filled Uldyssian with desire, a desire so deep that it frightened him. The grand dress that she had worn was gone, utterly gone, and although similar scales covered her flesh, they did not hide what the human garments had often hinted of.

"No!" he blurted, shoving her back with all his might. "No!"

Lylia laughed at his antics. Her tail, which ended in three daggerlike projections, slapped merrily against the bloody soil. She took a step back on hooved legs like those of the goats Uldyssian had kept on the farm and displayed herself fully for his wide eyes.

"Am I not everything you dreamed? Am I not all you desire?" The demonic woman laughed again and even though that laugh sent chills through the hapless farmer, it also heightened his desire for her. "Come, my love," Lylia continued, her clawed hands inviting him toward her. "Come . . . you are mine, body and soul, soul and body . . . come to me . . ."

As she said this, the armies suddenly halted their strug-gle and turned to face Uldyssian. They marched slowly toward him, their steps matching the rhythm of Lylia's voice.

" . . . body and soul . . . soul and body . . . body and—"

With a wordless cry, Uldyssian woke up. He twisted to the side to find Lylia stretched over him, her face—her beautiful face—filled with concern.

"Uldyssian, my love! Are you ill?"

"I saw—the others—you—" Planting his face in his hands, he slowly pulled himself together. "I dreamed . . . dreamed. That's all. Nothing but a bad dream."

"A nightmare?" Lylia reached a smooth—unclawed—hand to his cheek. Uldyssian instinctively flinched, recalling her appearance in the vision. "And what a horrible nightmare it must have been," she added. "if it makes you so afraid of me!"

"Lylia . . . I'm sorry."

She shook her head, letting her loose blond hair cascade around her naked form. Even shadowed by the darkness, she was arresting. Desire again filled Uldyssian and the foul dream began to slip into forgetfulness.

Snaking her delicate arms around him, Lylia whispered, "Let me help ease your mind, let you see that you have nothing to fear from me . . ."

"Lylia, I—"

"Hush!"

Their lips met and stayed that way until Uldyssian was well out of breath. As he inhaled, the noblewoman giggled, a sound not only extremely pleasant, but not at all like the seductive yet mocking laughter of the nightmare.

"And that is just for the beginning, I promise you." Her hands caressed his arms, ran over the hair on his chest, and worked their way down.

The last vestiges of the dream faded. With a playful growl, Uldyssian lunged forward and filled his arms with her. The two of them rolled to the other side, where the son of Diomedes worked relentlessly to make certain that no memories of the vision would ever return . . .

*   *   *

When Uldyssian again slept, it was in a mood that could only bring to him enjoyable dreams, not nightmares. With lusty snores, he lay on his stomach, one arm draped casually over Lylia.

But Lylia did not sleep. Lying on her back, she stared without blinking at some place in her own memory, a place far from the bed and Uldyssian.

There were many among Humanity who believed that dreams were portents and Lylia knew that they were not far from the truth. Dreams *could* be portents; she knew that better than most. Throughout their lovemaking, Lylia had managed to gather little snippets that Uldyssian did not even realize he mentioned. Those combined to create a vision that had caused her at one point to nearly forget herself. Fortunately, her powers had quickly healed what would have under other circumstances left the farmer with a deep and hideous scar on his back.

Yes, dreams could be portents and there was that possible aspect to Uldyssian's. However, there was another reason for them, one that concerned Lylia far more.

Dreams—and nightmares, especially—could be *warnings*, too.

Lylia knew just what those warnings concerned. What she did not know was the source. She had done her utmost to veil her presence to those who would recognize it. To be sure, they now had their suspicions, but they, too, had to tread carefully. To not do so would reveal the entire situation to the High Heavens. No one, not even *he*, desired them to discovery Sanctuary's existence.

Which still left her at the advantage, at least as far as she could see.

But this dream continued to disturb her. It did not sound like an attempt by any of those who would seek to prevent her from fulfilling her goal . . . yet, what else could it be?

It does not matter, she told herself. She was mistress of this situation. She was the one who had awakened the power of the nephalem in the fool beside her and through him she would raise it up in *every* mortal possible. Nothing would stand in her way.

And if Uldyssian ul-Diomed failed at some point to remain a docile puppet, then Lylia would simply *kill* him and find another dupe. After all, there were so *many* men . . .

FOURTEEN

Four more days passed in Partha, days in which Uldyssian became ever more comfortable with his surroundings. Kehjan remained a focus of the future, but that future stretched further ahead with each passing day.

In addition to the townsfolk, others from the farmlands and smaller communities within a day's ride began filtering in, the news spread to them by those who had already been touched. Naturally, Uldyssian greeted each newcomer and did what he could. Although progress was slow, at least now he had proof that what he had told them was true; in addition to Romus, nearly two dozen others had manifested some sign of powers. Those signs varied wildly, from healing minor injuries or causing flowers to blossom to a child's sudden ability to call birds to her hand. No two were exactly the same. That in itself fascinated Uldyssian further and he spent some of his time trying to decipher why what worked for one did not for another.

He suffered no repeat of the nightmare and, with matters demanding so much of him, soon even forgot it. Meanwhile, the ranks now swelled in another, unexpected manner. Partha was a trading town and so visitors and merchants en route elsewhere would stop there on a daily basis. They could not help but be swept up in the excitement going on all around them and many who came merely out of curiosity left touched by Uldyssian. Not all did, of course, even as not all in Partha had yet. However, the reluctant shrank in numbers with each new "miracle," such as the elderly man whose daughter healed his failing vision, initially without even realizing it. Again, it was an act she could not repeat, but Uldyssian could not help thinking that many more were on the threshold of joining him.

Despite the monumental change going on inside them, most of the townsfolk tried to continue their normal lives. What else *were* they supposed to do? Crops still had to be harvested and children fed. Master Ethon freely admitted that he enjoyed his own work, especially since the death of his wife several years earlier and the departure of his two older sons for Kehjan the season before.

In fact, it was because of that enjoyment that he had to abandon his guests come the following evening. "I will be apologizing to you, good Uldyssian, for my absence tonight. An old friend and fellow merchant would have me visit his caravan to show me some of his latest items! Like me, he had been touched, but, also like me . . . well, he, too, is a merchant at heart!"

"There's no need to apologize, Master Ethon. You've been more than generous. You've done so much."

"*I? I?*" The older man laughed. "Oh, Uldyssian, you are likely the most *humble* person I've ever known! *I've* done so much! You've merely altered forever the lives of everyone here!"

Ethon left still laughing and with Uldyssian feeling somewhat embarrassed.

Lylia later sought to sooth Uldyssian's feelings. "You should be full of cheer! You are just being yourself, my love! Nothing to be ashamed about!" She kissed him. "But it is true, you are wonderfully humble, considering the truth."

"Perhaps . . ." He suddenly felt restless. "I need to walk."

"Where shall we go?"

His discomfort increasing, Uldyssian replied, "I'd like to walk alone, Lylia."

"In Partha?" She sounded amused. "I daresay you will not get very far, dear Uldyssian, but I shall let you try. I wish you the best of luck."

He knew what she meant. The moment even one person

sighted him, a crowd would form as if by magic. Still, nighttime was his best opportunity. Most people would have by now returned to their homes. The inns and taverns would still be open, but Uldyssian intended to avoid those areas.

"I'll just walk down the street to the right side of the estate, then probably return right after that."

"Poor Uldyssian! You do not have to tell me everything you do!" Lylia gave him another, lengthier kiss. "I wish you a relaxing excursion!"

From anyone else, he would have thought such a reply hinting of mockery, but from her Uldyssian sensed only concern and love. Not for the first time did he think how fortunate he had been to find her. It was almost as if Fate had planned it.

With yet an even more passionate third kiss, he left her in Master Ethon's study. Uldyssian was tempted to first locate his brother, but suspected that, as in previous tries, he would not find Mendeln around. While everything else seemed to be coming together, Mendeln and he continued to grow more distant from one another. What made the situation worse was that the few times when Uldyssian might have been able to talk with his sibling, he was without exception interrupted by new supplicants. Unwilling to turn down such requests, he had let the precious chances slip away.

But there's got to come a time. Mendeln was not well. Uldyssian felt certain of that. The younger brother was hiding something important. What it was, perhaps only Achilios knew, but the hunter was also good at being absent when Uldyssian sought to confront him. Even Serenthia's presence at the gatherings did not seem to keep Achilios nearby.

Not for the first time, Uldyssian swore to himself that all that would change as soon as possible. Somehow, he would find out the truth. For now, though, he needed to clear his own head and relax.

The night air helped him almost immediately. As he reached the outer gates, Ethon's men silently saluted him. Like so many, they had experienced the awakening within, but still felt most comfortable keeping their normal routine. Fortunately, they also already knew to respect Uldyssian's privacy.

"I won't be long," he told them.

"As you wish, Master Uldyssian. We will be here for you when you return."

He had given up trying to make them or anyone else cease calling him by such a title. Better that, at least, than being declared a "holy one" or the like, as some still did.

He chose the least lit avenue and quickly headed into it. The darkness comforted him, its shadowy veil giving Uldyssian a sense of anonymity that he truly needed at the moment. He began to think of his farm, surely either in utter disarray or in the hands of some opportunistic neighbor who had recognized the value of its soil. Uldyssian hoped that at least someone had taken care of the animals properly.

Faint voices warned him of someone coming from the other direction. Preferring to be alone, Uldyssian turned down an even darker side street and hurried off before the others would see him. What little he could make out of the tone of conversation indicated that they were merely two members of the Partha Guard making their rounds, but even they represented too much interaction with the townsfolk at this point.

Uldyssian had no idea where the new street went, but its seductive solitude was enough to keep him on it for some distance. The voices soon faded behind him. He began to relax as not even sleep could help him do. For the first time since before the calamity in Seram, the son of Diomedes felt like an ordinary man again.

Then, another voice, this one whispering, caught his attention. Uldyssian looked to the left, where he thought the source lay.

But from his right came a second whisper. Like the first,

it was just low enough to be unintelligible. There was something about its tone, however, that raised his hackles.

"Who's there?" Uldyssian called. "Who's there?" From the left, the first voice began anew. Wasting no more breath, Uldyssian leapt toward the sound . . . but his groping hands found only shadow.

A *third* voice came from somewhere ahead. With a growl, Uldyssian whirled in that direction . . . and once more nothing of substance could be found.

Carefully, he retreated several steps, then glanced over his shoulder. There should have been some glimpse of another street a short distance back, but Uldyssian saw only darkness.

Suddenly, *all* the voices renewed their mad muttering. Worse, now they were quickly joined by several more, all speaking in the same intense tone that set Uldyssian's nerve on edge. He spun around in a circle, seeking either one of the speakers or an exit, but finding neither.

"Show yourself, damn it!" he finally shouted. "Show yourself!"

He tried to summon the power to his command . . . and failed. Trying a different tack, Uldyssian specifically imagined bright illumination—the better to ferret out his stalkers—or even some great wind that would carry him away from this area. Yet, these, too, came to nothing.

Nothing . . .

One voice suddenly seemed to come from right by his ear. He started to turn toward it . . . and a thick limb from the opposing direction wrapped around his throat.

Choking, Uldyssian struggled to free himself from whatever had snared him. He could not even tell if it was an arm or some sort of tentacle, only that its grip was stronger than iron.

As the lack of air took its toll on him, Uldyssian's thoughts went to Lylia. He could only assume that this attack had to do with Malic and so he feared that the high priest would next go after her. Yet, even that concern did not give him the might to escape—

Then, from out of nowhere there came a hiss, followed by

a snarl like that from the throat of a foul beast. At the same time, some instinct took over in Uldyssian. Every muscle in his body tensed.

The air rippled. A guttural exclamation filled the night, followed immediately by a crash.

The tightness around Uldyssian's throat vanished, along with it the insidious whispering. Suddenly, there was only the sound of him trying to catch his breath, that, and the soft padding of swift boots.

"Uldyssian!" came a voice very familiar to him. "Uldyssian! I thought I saw . . . damn! I don't know *what* I saw . . ."

But, despite that little obstacle, Achilios had evidently managed a masterly shot. In the blackness, it could have just as easily been Uldyssian whom he hit and certainly that would have been a high probability had it been any other archer. However, Uldyssian knew his childhood friend's skill well and so understood that his life had never been in danger, at least from an arrow.

"Th-Thank you . . ." he gasped.

Achilios, bow over his shoulder, helped Uldyssian straighten. "Don't thank me for anything. I'm sorry I didn't manage to kill whatever had you . . . though I'm damned if I know why not! I had it or him right where the back of the neck should've been! If it was an assassin, he should lie dead at our feet right now." Making certain that Uldyssian could stand on his own, the hunter knelt. A moment later, Achilios muttered, "There's something here, but it doesn't feel like *blood*. Not fresh, anyway. Couldn't be from your attacker . . ."

Recalling all too well the sort of fiends that had been so far thrown against him, Uldyssian was not so certain. For the moment, though, he would trust Achilios's knowledge.

Rising, the lithe figure rushed off in the direction of the crash. A minute later, Achilios returned, what little was visible of his expression revealing his disgruntlement.

"Something heavy struck the side of that building," he said, gesturing at the darkness from which he had come. "Cracked it good . . . but whatever it was got up right after and ran off."

That, too, did not surprise Uldyssian. Malic would have sent servants far more capable than the previous ones. They had planned their little trap better this time, waiting for him to venture out on his own. The high priest had read him well. He had known that his prey would eventually seek private time.

Then it occurred to him to wonder just what the archer was doing here, too. Uldyssian had long given up believing in coincidence.

But before he could ask, Achilios said, "I'd suggest we leave this area for somewhere a little more populated. You might enjoy your privacy, but surely not *that* much, anymore."

With a nod, Uldyssian followed his friend back the way they had come. Achilios apparently could see in the dark much better than him. The hunter soon had them back in the vicinity of Master Ethon's house. Only then did both pause to breathe normally.

"Much better," commented the blond man.

"Thank you again," Uldyssian returned. "Now tell me how you happened to be right there when I needed your help."

Achilios cocked his head. "And why *did* you need my help, Uldyssian? What happened to you back there?"

Uldyssian would not let the questioning turn to him, not just yet. "Answer me, Achilios."

There was a long hesitation, then, "I *thought* you were going to be in danger."

His phrasing left Uldyssian puzzled. "What do you mean?"

"I just had a feeling that something was going to happen and so I followed a hunch. That's all."

"And managed to follow it all the way to where I was."

The archer shrugged. "It's nothing new. Just an instinct, Father would've said." Achilios's father had been a hunter like him, one whose reputation had never been dwarfed until his own son. "What makes me a good hunter, I guess."

But Uldyssian was thinking that it was much more than merely an instinct. He refrained from saying anything, yet suspected that Achilios had turned the very same gift that Uldyssian carried into something honed to his particular talents. More to the point, it was possible that the archer's family had been doing so for at least two generations.

That meant that there was more to the powers growing within them than even he had believed. Uldyssian realized that he was likely not even the first to learn of the gift, merely the first to understand that it was something astonishing.

"What *was* that thing back there?" Achilios asked. "Did you see it?"

Deciding not to pursue Achilios's situation—for the time being, at least—Uldyssian replied, "A pet of the high priest's, I'd say." He considered further, then added, "It wore the guise of a man, I think. I also thought I felt armor."

"Well, my arrow didn't hit armor. I heard a healthy strike. It should've done more damage . . ."

Uldyssian did not care about that. He had something far more important on his mind. This attack, so deep within Partha, had made him determined to do something. "Achilios, I've a favor to ask you. Promise me that you'll do it."

"Not until I hear what it is, old friend! You know me better than that!"

"Then listen carefully and think even *more* carefully. Achilios, you're the only one I can trust to do this. I've decided that the others are only in danger here. I need you to lead them to somewhere *far* away from me. Will you do that?"

"When you say the others, you mean specially Lylia, I presume?"

"*All* of you . . . but, yes, I hope you can help her, obviously."

Achilios glanced around to see if anyone was nearby. However, the streets were empty. "I understand why you would want Lylia, Serry, and Mendeln away from here . . . and you know that I most of all want Serry to be safe."

"Achilios—"

The hunter waved him to silence. "I can never be you in her eyes, but I live with that. Still, even though we agree that they shouldn't be here—and I understand that you'd like me safe, too, naturally," he added with a chuckle. "I know that not *one* of them would agree to go. Not even your brother. They'd fight me, fight you, Uldyssian."

"This isn't safe for any of you! You've the proof of that tonight!"

"Aye, and telling them of it would just make them all that more stubborn . . . which I can't say I blame them for! You won't be getting rid of them or me, old friend! There's no way . . ."

But there *was* one way, Uldyssian thought. The worst way of all.

Although he knew the futility of continuing the argument, Uldyssian opened his mouth to try . . . only to shut it at the sound of hooves. Both men immediately tensed, Achilios freeing his bow.

However, the figure riding out of the black street turned out to be none other than Master Ethon. The merchant sighted the two men and reined his horse to a halt just before them.

"Uldyssian. Archer. What causes you pair to stand out here, looking so filled with distrust?"

Achilios grinned. "Just nerves, Master Ethon! Just nerves, that's all!"

With a quick nod, the son of Diomedes agreed. "I needed a breath of air."

"And I am not surprised about that." The older man dismounted. Reins in one hand, he slapped Uldyssian on the shoulder with the other. "Much you have done, Uldyssian

ul-Diomed! Much you have done . . ." He hesitated, then
added, "And if there is *anything* I can do to be of service to
you beyond what I already have, please do not hesitate to
come to me."

Uldyssian felt embarrassment. Fortunately, Ethon unex-
pectedly turned his attention to Achilios. "Have I told you
what a fine bow that is, archer? I have had my eye on it
since first I saw it."

"'Twas my father's, Master Ethon! He kept it as good as
the day it was carved and I've done my utmost to see it
stays like that! Half a man's skill depends on the bow he
wields . . ."

"So much, you think? May I hold it?" the merchant
asked, extending a hand.

"By all means." Achilios let their host inspect the
weapon. Ethon ran his fingers expertly over the finely
crafted piece. Uldyssian, who himself had admired and
even fired the weapon several times over the years, saw it
anew. Few there were who could have surpassed the work
of Tremas, Achilios's father.

But had Tremas's exceptional talent with carving *also*
been some variation?

After giving the bow a very thorough inspection, Master
Ethon finally returned it to its owner. "A splendid piece,
yes. I look forward to seeing it in action again."

His comment caused the other two to briefly exchange
glances. The leader of Partha had no idea just what he was
asking. Uldyssian felt certain that the attack in the street
had just been the very beginning of something far more
sinister . . . something that could engulf the entire town.

Something that could very well *destroy* it and everyone
within . . .

The sheep poured out of the temple, unaware that they
were one step closer to losing their souls . . . and more . . .
to Lucion.

No . . . not to him, the Primus quickly thought, his pious

expression hiding sudden concern. Rather, to the greater glory of his father and the other Prime Evils.

Yet, the son of Mephisto did not mind basking in the reflection of that glory.

But for that to continue, for the eventual control of Sanctuary to happen, all had to proceed as Lucion had planned it . . . and recent events no longer guaranteed that such would happen. Matters had to be set properly back in place. For a demon, Lucion was a very orderly being. He liked things just so.

The other two high priests, Herodius and Balthazar, came up to him and bowed respectfully. Generally, after the Primus had given a sermon to all three orders, he and his most loyal followers met in private for further discussion of the Triune's progress toward domination.

Not this evening, however. Lucion had to focus on restoring the situation. While his servants were useful, when it came to the planning, he relied most on himself.

"We will speak together tomorrow eve, come the moon. Go and see to your duties . . ." Those duties included indoctrinating the faithful who had reached the point where they had begun to turn to the true doctrines of the Temple . . . Hate, Destruction, and Terror. The methods by which the Primus and his servants slowly manipulated the fools toward that end were many and ranged from the mundane to the magical. Some of the faithful were more attuned to this—the *weak-minded* ones—and they were carefully picked out of the throngs and invited to special sermons. There, the subtle shapings of the Primus's private sermons delved deep within the mortals' minds, seeking that which lay in the darkest recesses.

But Lucion could rely on the two humans before him to handle such matters for a time. He dismissed them and hurried back to his private sanctum. It galled him that he had to do his work in secret, but some sacrifices had to be made . . . especially if *she* was indeed involved. Malic's efforts would make for a good distraction in that regard, causing her to be unaware of what Lucion also intended.

The four guards snapped to attention as he passed them. They wore the semblances of Peace Warders, but were morlu. Anyone foolish enough to attempt entry without permission would quickly learn the difference . . . a moment before they were cut to pieces.

Shadows filled the chamber, Lucion's work now more suited for the dark. He looked to where two more morlu stood sentry over a cowering young man in the gray garb of a novice cleric. In the first part of their study, those chosen by the high priests did not wear the robes of any order, for it was by the Primus's decision which one they would best serve.

"Ikarion . . ." Lucion entoned. He wore his most kindly expression, which was lost on the youth in front of him, who knew who and what his master was.

"G-Great is my lord," Ikarion stammered, going down on one knee. "Merciful is m-my lord . . ."

This brought a chuckle from the Primus, who knew himself much better than the mortal obviously did. He reached down to the kneeling figure, stroking the chin of his chosen. "Dear Ikarion. You know the sacrifices you make to take on the mantle of a cleric, do you not?"

"And I have accepted them gratefully!"

"Have you? Your sisters were to be brought to us, to be made our loyal handmaidens . . ." Lucion had a very earthy taste for human women, especially untried ones. It was a mark of how devoted his acolytes were that they willingly sold their own to prove their love for him. "But they appear to have left for a long journey . . ."

"Master, I—"

The hand that stroked the chin now painfully clamped the mouth shut. Still speaking in the same kindly tones, Lucion continued, "They did not travel far, though, thanks to the very dedicated Brother Tomal, your good friend. I had the pleasure of discussing their talents with them only last night . . ."

"Nggh!" Ikarion made the mistake of trying to leap at his master.

One of the morlu drew his great ax and, in a single swift motion, removed the rebellious youth's head.

The head tumbled into Lucion's hand. He turned it upside down to preserve the contents. The son of Mephisto preferred to do his own slaying, but could not fault the warrior for his enthusiasm.

"Leave the carcass," he commanded the morlu. "You are dismissed."

The armored figures bowed and departed. Lucion paused, then glanced up at the deepest shadows above. "Astrogha! I know you watch! I have a tidbit for you . . ."

"And what the cost?" came a hissing voice. "What the cost, oh, Lucion?"

"Nothing you cannot afford, dog of Diablo . . . we shall speak of it later. Take the carcass . . ."

Something white and like rope shot down to where the body lay. It resembled the webbing a spider might shoot, only much, much larger, as if a creature at least as great as the son of Mephisto somehow hid in the recesses of the ceiling.

The headless body shot up, pulled by the webbing into the shadows. A moment later, there was a horrific slurping sound.

He has been bought, Lucion thought to himself. *That leaves just one more.*

With his free hand, the Primus drew a triangular symbol not unlike that of the Triune in the air. The pattern flared a savage crimson, then drifted to the floor, sealing there.

Lucion tossed Brother Ikarion's head into the center. It landed perfectly, the bulging eyes staring up, the mouth slack as if in midscream. Blood puddled around it, in actuality feeding the burning symbol with power.

"Gulag . . . I have something for you. Come and get it."

The stone floor beneath the head began to shift as if suddenly liquid. The magical pattern remained intact, as did the stones beneath, but they rolled and twisted as if part of a turbulent sea.

Then . . . a gap reminiscent of a whirlpool opened up just to the right of the pattern. Although it was circular, within, one could see ridges of teeth. The "mouth" swirled around the pattern twice, then sought to engulf it.

Dark sparks arose each time it attempted. At last, the toothy gap paused.

"Stupid is Gulag," came Astrogha's monstrous voice from above. "Like his master he is . . ."

"You have your treat, arachnid," reprimanded Lucion. "Be still . . ."

The demon above grew silent, save to renew the slurping that marked his eating. The macabre mouth attempted once more to take in the head and once more the pattern kept it away.

"Rise up, Gulag . . ."

The floor began to swell. It took on a shape vaguely humanoid, vaguely porcine. Its body still maintained the stone design of the original floor, but approximately where the head should have been, three eyestalks suddenly sprouted.

"LLLLLuccccionnnnnnnnn . . ." it said, the voice akin to the last gasp of a dying man. "Wwwwaannnnntttt . . ."

"And so you shall, servant of destruction, servant of Baal, but in a moment. You and Astrogha must assist me with a spell. Will you?"

Above, the slurping ceased again. "Expensive is this meal, this one thinks now . . ."

Lucion's expression grew sharp. His eyes seemed to sink into the sockets and he was suddenly half again as large as before. "You accepted it, spider, just the same. A bargain made without thought is still a bargain . . ."

"So it must be . . ." the other demon replied reluctantly.

Looking slightly more like the genial Primus again, the son of Mephisto focused on the second demon. "And you, Gulag, do you have any reservations about accepting what I offer even before hearing the price?"

"Dessssstrucctionnnnnn?"

He smiled at the simple question. "Yes, there could very well be some."

"Hhhheadddd . . ."

It was as close to an acquiescence as Lucion would get from one of Baal's minions. He gestured at the pattern, removing it.

Gulag's mouth suddenly expanded to nearly his entire length. The skull of Brother Ikarion tumbled into the bottomless maw, vanishing.

The demon shut his mouth, then formed a crude smile out of the stone pattern.

Lucion nodded. Steepling his fingers, he closed his eyes in thought. "Excellent. Now . . . this is what I seek from the two of you . . ."

Fifteen

The illusion of peace shattered, Uldyssian lived in a constant state of high concern. Malic was nearby, no doubt plotting something more heinous. As ever, Uldyssian did not fear for himself so much as he did Lylia and the others. However, as Achilios had said, they would not leave him of their own free will and he had no idea how to make them change their minds.

Noticing his darkening mood, Master Ethon pulled him aside after dinner the next evening. "You are not yourself. Does something ail you?"

"There's nothing."

The dark eyes burned into his own. "Yes, I think that there is, but you do not wish to talk now." Ethon frowned. "The other night, I offered whatever additional help I could to you. I think this is just such a situation. Perhaps, if we met alone when the others sleep, I could at the very least pass on some advice."

Since the death of his parents, Uldyssian had more or less relied on his own advice over the years, only now and then turning to the likes of Cyrus and other friends of his father. Still, the merchant had seen much and lived through more and surely had a view of matters far exceeding that of the farmer.

Uldyssian finally nodded gratefully to his host. "Thank you. I'd like that."

"Later, then," murmured Master Ethon. "Say the hour before midnight?"

Nodding again, Uldyssian returned to the company of

Lylia and the others. It was all he could do from that point on to hide his impatience. The minutes took hours to pass, the hours an eternity. When at last he excused himself from Lylia—the noblewoman becoming used to his late-night walks—Uldyssian almost ran through the house, so eager was he to reach the study and pour out his concerns.

On his way, he nearly collided with a smaller figure. Cedric looked up at him, the youth's face oddly pale.

"Ced! What do you still do up?"

The boy glanced past, as if impatient to be away from the man before him. "Father . . . my father wanted to see me. Now I'm going to bed."

Already feeling late for his own meeting with Master Ethon, Uldyssian patted the merchant's son on the shoulder. "Of course. Off you go, then."

Without waiting for a reply from the boy, he continued on. The halls were dimly lit, only a few oil lamps marking the nighttime. Uldyssian passed no guards, the merchant obviously feeling very secure in his own domain. That would certainly change once he heard what his guest had to say.

The door to the study was closed and no light shone through the bottom. Uldyssian looked around the empty hall, then knocked once.

From within, Ethon's voice bid him enter. Relieved, Uldyssian slipped inside, quickly shutting the door after him.

The only illumination in the room came from a single candle situated atop a small, mahogany table to the side. Next to the candle sat a decanter of wine and two goblets, one of which Uldyssian's host—seated in a leather chair next to the table—took up even as the farmer's eyes adjusted to the gloom.

"Tonight, I find the quiet of the night much more relaxing," explained Master Ethon after a sip of wine. "The better to think, also."

Uldyssian slipped into another chair that Master Ethon indicated. "Thank you for seeing me."

"How could I not? After all that has happened? Uldyssian,

I could not refuse this moment to you!" He gestured at the other goblet. "Please . . . I would recommend it."

Although he wanted to keep a clear head, Uldyssian suddenly felt parched. He allowed Master Ethon to pour him some wine. The liquid flowed like delicious fire down his throat.

"A strong vintage, but one that touches the soul, I say." Ethon put down his own goblet. "You are very troubled, my son."

Clutching his wine in both hands, Uldyssian leaned forward and explained his concerns for his friends . . . and Partha itself. The older man listened quietly, nodding now and then in understanding.

When Uldyssian had finished, Master Ethon rubbed his chin in thought. The flickering candlelight danced in his eyes, catching the farmer's attention.

"Your fears for my people and your own comrades does you justice, Uldyssian. I would hope to do no less myself in your situation . . ."

"But what can I do to keep them—*all* of you—from harm? I don't know if I can protect *everyone*, not from the might of the Triune. I thought I *could* once, but after the other night . . ."

The leader of Partha rose and began to pace slowly in front of Uldyssian. His mind was visibly at work.

"Yes . . . the other night, as you describe it, shows an inconsistency in your gift I would not have expected. It was a telling moment." Ethon paused, looking down at him. "You may be correct; what you wield might not be enough against such a force as the Temple. Their tools are legion. I have heard through trusted sources that they have fanatic warriors who make the Peace Warders seem pacifists. Some claim that these dark, armored fighters cannot even be slain by mortal means—"

His description struck home with Uldyssian. "Yes! The attacker in the street! As I said! Achilios should've slain him with that bolt, but it only startled him . . ."

The older man stepped from the vicinity of the

candlelight, all but disappearing in the shadows in the far corner of the room. "So, the stories have merit. It almost makes me suggest . . . but, no, you would never do that."

"What?" Uldyssian was willing to try almost anything, if it would at least protect the woman—the *people*—he loved. "Tell me!"

Master Ethon turned to face him again. If not for the fire of the candle reflecting yet again in his eyes, Uldyssian would not have been able to read *anything* of his expression. In that gaze, though, he saw determination and that strengthened his own resolve.

"There is one way to protect them . . . and my beloved Partha, but I feel much guilt even suggesting it."

"Please! I won't hold anything against you, Master Ethon! You've been nothing but a good friend and host!"

"Very well. It may be, my young Uldyssian, that you can only accomplish what you wish by leaving them without any notice. Leave them in the dead of night and ride out of Partha as if the hounds of the Temple are nearly upon the town. Ride out and meet with this Malic—"

Uldyssian leapt to his feet, the goblet dropping and the chair falling backward. *"What?"*

"Hear me out! Malic came for you! He wants only you! Whatever the outcome of your encounter with him, by abandoning Partha and the others, you remove them from the situation entirely! The Triune will trouble them no longer!"

The terrible thing was, what he said had not gone unconsidered by Uldyssian already. Yet, to hear it said so bluntly put a solid weight to it that pressed down hard on his heart.

But it would keep them all safe, especially Lylia . . .

Still, there was something else to think about. "But the high priest's minions are already in Partha. It may be too late to undo that."

"They watch for you. They will assuredly see you leave, even if you choose to do so this very minute. Such creatures will immediately follow their prey . . . or does that not make sense?"

To Uldyssian it made dreadfully perfect sense, and yet, there was that about Master Ethon's suggestion that did not sit right with him.

But it's the only way! his mind insisted.

The merchant stood silent, letting Uldyssian battle this out himself. Leaving the others behind was the only true course of action. This was strictly between he and Malic.

"They would all follow me, you think? The creatures of the high priest, I mean?"

"I would guarantee it. To do anything to the contrary would be absurd."

That finally settled it for Uldyssian. "I've got to do it, then."

His host bowed in acknowledgment of the heaviness of his decision. "I will assist you to the best of my ability. In any way I can."

Ethon reached out a hand. Uldyssian instinctively did the same, but just before the two men could shake, a sense of urgency overtook the son of Diomedes. He pulled his hand back and stared at the merchant's eyes. There was something wrong about them . . .

He tore his gaze from the merchant's, suddenly needing to look toward the ceiling.

It was too late. From the darkness above, a heavy, armored form fell upon the farmer. It brought him to the floor, their combined weight cracking the boards beneath them.

"There is ever *something* that causes the best plans to somehow go awry!" snapped a voice that was not the merchant's. "I begin to wonder if it has to do with your curious and unpredictable abilities . . ."

Even as Uldyssian struggled against his opponent, he recognized the new voice. It was *Malic* speaking. Malic, in the guise of Master Ethon . . .

"All so very simple . . . or so it was supposed to be.

Lure you out into the wild, where this could be handled without further complications. But as with last time, *nothing* can go simple where you are involved, farmer, can it?"

His face almost crushed into the floor, Uldyssian gasped, "Where—where is E-Ethon?"

"Why, right here," replied a voice that was now both Malic's and the merchant's. "Let him see," the cleric ordered Uldyssian's guard.

From behind, a thick hand grabbed the captive by his hair and pulled hard, forcing him to look up. The image of the merchant still stood before Uldyssian. "Right here, in the flesh," Ethon said, once more using the high priest's voice. The figure chuckled, then added, "Or, at least *wearing* his flesh."

He reached up and touched his cheek with the palm of his right hand. Where the hand came in contact with the face, the skin there suddenly *dripped* as if melting. In large portions, it started sliding down to his chin, where it hung in gobbets.

Uldyssian's stomach turned. He struggled to free himself, but the monstrous warrior had him in a tight grip.

Through the macabre display, the high priest's own dark countenance began to peek out. Malic pulled his hand away, which caused the horrific melting to cease. He showed Uldyssian his palm.

Revealed there was a sight more terrible than the face, for it was no human hand that Malic had, but rather something that matched his demonic heart well. The high priest flexed what passed for fingers and it amazed Uldyssian that he had not noticed the misshapen appendage despite the disguise.

"A simple use of misdirection and illusion," explained Malic, reading his expression . . . or his thoughts. He thrust the limb closer. "Granted me by my master to assist in this hunt. I tested it twice before the merchant, whom the morlu caught as he was returning to his home. He was an opportunity that I could not pass up."

Uldyssian spat at the man, unfortunately coming up

short with his effort. His guard—a morlu, the high priest had called him—rewarded the captive's attempt by slamming Uldyssian's face in the floor again.

"That will be enough," Malic commanded, whether to his prisoner or the guard, it was impossible to say. "Raise the fool up."

Another pair of powerful hands took hold of Uldyssian's right arm. The original morlu shifted to the left. The two armored giants held Uldyssian in viselike grips.

"Not as I originally intended, but this will do—"

The door opened. Glancing there, Uldyssian saw in horror that Cedric had returned.

"Go!" he shouted at the youth. "Run!"

But instead of obeying or at least looking fearful, Cedric ignored the warning. To Malic, he said, "The woman's not in the room."

The blood drained from Uldyssian. The voice emerging from Ethon's son was no more that of the boy than Malic's had been the merchant's.

"No . . ." he gasped. "No . . ."

"She must be there!" insisted the cleric. "I sense her there even now. The arm, too, verifies that. It is drawn to her, as the master said. You looked in the wrong room."

Cedric shook his head. With a dismissive shrug toward the gaping Uldyssian, he grunted, "This one's scent is all over the room . . . and the bed. Nothing of her. No smell, no trace."

Malic reconsidered. "I see. This is a wily prey. Certainly more so than this buffoon . . ."

Uldyssian could not make sense of everything the pair said, but one bright point stuck out. Malic had sent this abomination—tears streaked down Uldyssian's face as he thought of what had happened to the lad—to hunt for Lylia. That, thankfully, had so far ended in failure.

"Find her quickly, Damos," the high priest continued. "You will leave nowhere untouched. The spell I cast will continue to muffle any sounds within the house only. Recall that at all times."

"I will hunt her down, Great One. And she will not live long after that." The false Cedric accented his dire statement with an animalistic snort, then left again.

Malic smiled at his captive. "We will salvage this yet, it seems. Then, you will be on your way to a long-overdue audience with the Primus."

"They'll not let you out of Partha, cleric!" Uldyssian snarled. "The townsfolk loved Master Ethon! They'll stop you! They'll tear you apart for what you've done!"

"But why should they stop me?" asked the malevolent figure, putting his monstrous palm to his face. As Uldyssian watched, stunned, the flesh moved to cover the revealed areas. In seconds, Malic once more completely resembled the merchant, even to the difference in height. The spell that allowed him to walk in Ethon's flesh was an astonishing if grisly creation. "Why should they stop their dearly beloved *leader*?"

Indeed, there was no reason and Uldyssian now saw that. The guards and any bystanders would be fooled just as he had been, especially in the dark.

"She must be with one of the others," Malic went on, turning back to the question of Lylia. "Perhaps she is already seducing one of them to take your place—"

The high priest could not have said more terrible words in front of Uldyssian. His blood boiled and a mindless rage swept over him. He shoved back in an attempt to free himself from his guards' grips.

But instead of the few steps back, steps during which he had hoped his captors' feet would trip, Uldyssian and the two morlu *flew* across the study.

Across the study . . . and through the window.

Debris rained down on Uldyssian as he and the morlu fell. Despite their predicament, the bestial warriors clung to him as if their lives depended upon doing so. Uldyssian, in turn, tried to fold himself up as much as possible, aware that the ground was not all that far.

They collided with a thud and a rush of dirt. The crack

of bone echoed in Uldyssian's ear. One of the morlu let out a rasping cry and his fingers slipped from the captive's arm.

Uldyssian immediately tried to pull free of the other warrior, but the morlu held fast. As the two rolled over, they came face to face. The night shadowed the morlu's counte-nance much, but not enough at such close range to prevent the son of Diomedes from seeing the black pits where the eyes should have been.

A fist in the morlu's chin did nothing. Uldyssian grabbed for the throat just as his foe did the same. The warrior's fingers all but threatened to crush his windpipe, yet, for some reason, the morlu held back.

It took Uldyssian several precious seconds to understand why. They still wanted him alive after all this. Why else try to take him in secret?

However, while that gave him some hope, he could not completely discount the morlu forgetting orders and finally simply killing the man with whom he struggled. What stared at him from within the unsettling ram-skull helmet was not human, not anymore. At any moment, his foe might become lost in bloodlust.

With all his will, Uldyssian attempted to summon the same strength that had thrown him and his two bulky adversaries so far away. Gritting his teeth, the farmer swung at his foe again, this time aiming at the only target, the heavily armored chest.

The morlu blocked his wrist, slowing the strike. Uldyssian's fist splayed open. His palm slapped lightly against the breastplate, hardly enough to do any damage.

The morlu went sinking into the ground as if a huge, invisible hammer had struck him. He sank so deep that there was not even a trace of him to see.

Another hand seized hold even as Uldyssian sought to recover. Shouts erupted from elsewhere, likely Master Ethon's guards coming to protect their employer and his property. Uldyssian wanted to warn them of Malic's horrific masquerade, but the remaining morlu, having recovered from the fall, now fell upon him in earnest.

Perhaps "recovered" was not quite the correct word, for as the warrior spun Uldyssian to face him, the son of Diomedes found himself staring at a head bent completely to the right. A good portion of the morlu's neck stuck out in an obscene and impossible manner. Yet, none of this appeared to matter to the furious creature.

Once again, fingers clamped around Uldyssian's throat. The morlu squeezed, but not enough to kill. Uldyssian's air was cut off. He knew that all his foe had to do was wait for him to pass out. Then, Malic would have his prey ... and no one would be able to save Lylia.

Reaching up, Uldyssian grabbed hold of one side of the morlu's head. Gritting his teeth, he pulled as hard as he could.

With a horrible sucking sound, the head came free. The morlu's body shivered and the fingers released. They grasped blindly for the head, which Uldyssian pulled back.

Like something out of a ghastly puppet show, Uldyssian led the torso several steps toward the wall surrounding Master Ethon's estate. Then, with as much strength as he could muster, he threw the head over.

The torso lunged, only to collide with the wall. It repeated the attempt, but with the same results. On its third try, the headless body stumbled, then slid to the ground, where, at last, it stilled.

Exhaling, Uldyssian quickly looked back at the house. There was no sign of any activity in the study, but around the grounds, guards scurried. Two of them closed on Uldyssian.

The moment that they recognized him, the pair slowed. He gestured at the house. "Inside! There's more inside! Beware! You must cut off their heads!"

They looked at him with somewhat fearful expressions. Uldyssian did not care if they believed him. He ran past, already fearful that Malic had located Lylia ... or any of the others, for that matter.

Bursting through the front doors, he stumbled over something in the dark. Twisting around on the floor, Uldyssian discovered to his horror a corpse that surely had once belonged to one of the merchant's household servants. Once again, the contents of Uldyssian's stomach threatened to come up, for the body had been completely and perfectly *flayed*.

First Ethon and his son, now this poor soul. Uldyssian was caught between revulsion and bitterness. Each of the horrible demises could be tied to him. Yet Uldyssian was not foolish enough to blame himself alone. Malic was the culprit who had done the foul work. Malic, at the bidding of the Primus.

Anger again overwhelmed him. There was nothing that Uldyssian could do about the mysterious Lucion, but he could try to see about making certain that the high priest troubled them no more, even if he had to sacrifice himself in the process.

The guards he had spoken to stopped at the entrance, the torch in the hand of one illuminating the grisly scene for them. They stared round-eyed at Uldyssian.

"Beware anyone in the house bearing a weapon or anyone with the semblance of your master and his son. If they are truly Ethon and young Cedric—" He had to choke back the emotions swelling up or else the guards would suspect the truth. "—then they will understand that you locking them away is for their own safety!"

"Lock them away?" blurted one man in surprise.

"For their own sake and yours! Trust me!"

If Uldyssian had been any other person, the men likely would have rejected his commands, but they knew of his miracles. Uldyssian cursed silently, wishing that more than a handful of people had exhibited some abilities akin to his own. At the moment, he would have been happy with Romus or Jonas at his side.

Or *Achilios*.

The archer was his only hope. Achilios had nearly slain

Malic once and could have killed one of the morlu if aware how.

As the guards sought to catch their wits, Uldyssian raced up the steps to the next floor. Already he pictured Lylia lying dead in the corridor and the fear of that coming true urged him on despite his injuries and exertion.

The room he shared with her lay directly ahead. Mustering his strength, Uldyssian threw himself at the door.

With a crash, it fell open. Uldyssian immediately rolled to his feet, ready to face a hundred Malics.

But the sinister cleric was not there . . . and neither was Lylia. Instead, a frightened young woman huddled in the far corner. Uldyssian recognized her as one of the women Master Ethon had commanded to see to the noblewoman's needs while she was his guest..

"Where is she?" he roared, ignoring her fear. "Where is Lylia?"

The woman wordlessly pointed at a huge oak clothing cabinet. In addition to what she had been wearing on her arrival, she now had other garments procured for her by their host. The same went for all of Master Ethon's guests. The man had shown nothing but courtesy and care and what had happened to him was a true nightmare that Uldyssian would never forget.

And worse, he now feared that it had also happened to the woman he loved. Why else would the servant point at the shut cabinet and shiver with such horror?

Then, something struck a chord. A servant . . . a household servant . . .

Uldyssian recalled the false Cedric and how, despite his diminutive appearance, some spell surely hid from sight another monstrous morlu or the like.

Could it be?

He whirled around . . . almost too late.

It leapt across the bed at him, a thing swollen beyond the proportions of the skin it wore. Rips and tears spread through the fragile flesh and beneath them could be seen armor. The face was a contorted mask no longer fitting and even as the horrific figure fell upon him, Uldyssian could not help but again marvel at how Malic's spellwork made size and shape of no consequence to the guise.

The two crashed into the cabinet, reducing it to splinters. Scraps of stolen skin dropping from his ghoulish countenance, the morlu raised his hand . . . a hand in which he now wielded a savage, curved ax.

With a grating laugh, he brought it down upon Uldyssian.

Sixteen

Achilios woke with a start. He reached for his clothes, throwing them on as quickly as he could, then snatching the bow and quiver from a nearby chair. The archer heard not a sound, but something set him on edge. He crept toward the door, pausing there to listen.

At first, all was silence, but then Achilios heard faint movement, either of someone very slight or very sure-footed. Looping the bow over his shoulder, he retrieved the hunting knife he always carried on his belt. Then, with the utmost caution, Achilios opened the door a crack.

The dim light of a single weak oil lamp mounted in the wall gave his expert eyes just enough illumination to see down the corridor. Someone moved at the very edge of the lit area, but not a figure tall enough to be Master Ethon or one of the household servants.

In fact . . . it looked like young Cedric to him.

The boy slowly moved along, pausing now and then before various doors. He stopped in front of the one leading to Serenthia's chambers, then moved on. For some reason that caused Achilios to exhale in relief.

What exactly the merchant's son was doing, the archer had no idea. There was nothing normal in Cedric's behavior. Achilios began to fear that the boy's mind might not be all right . . . or that, considering the events of the recent past, something or someone had control of it.

That decided it for him. Moving as silent as a cat, Achilios stepped out into the corridor. He kept the knife ready . . . for what, he did not know. Not to use against the poor boy, certainly. Ethon's son was an innocent.

Cedric continued to study the doors, but also peered at alcoves and even, at times, the ceiling. Achilios wondered what he expected to find above, then decided that he would prefer not to know.

Eyes well-adjusted to the dimness, the archer kept pace with his unsuspecting quarry. Achilios reached Serenthia's door. He hesitated there, leaning his ear close. Within, the soft sounds of her steady breathing reassured him that she was unharmed.

Straightening, Achilios focused on Cedric again . . . or would have, if the youth had been anywhere to be seen. Somehow, in the brief seconds when the archer's attention had been on Serenthia's safety, Cedric had vanished from his view.

Frowning, Achilios pushed forward. Master Ethon's son had to be somewhere ahead, unless he had managed to slip into one of the last rooms without Achilios noticing. That was highly unlikely. The hunter could not have missed such an obvious action.

But as he neared the end, it seemed to Achilios that entering a room was the *only* possibility to explain Cedric's disappearance. Yet, the most likely of the doors proved locked and surely he would have heard the rattling of the handle.

A few more steps took Achilios to the far wall. Perplexed, he ran a hand across the area, thinking that perhaps there was a hidden door. Unfortunately, he discovered nothing. The wall was very, very solid.

Then, some inner alarm made him look up at the ceiling . . . only to find that, while it was dark there, it was also empty of any nightmare. Achilios frowned, briefly wondering why he had suddenly felt as if danger had lurked above him.

Still perplexed by Cedric's disappearance, he turned back—

Master Ethon's son stood only a yard away from him, gazing up solemnly at the tall archer.

Achilios all but jumped. "Ced!"

"I was looking for her," the youth remarked quietly and steadily. "The one with Uldyssian."

"Lylia, you mean? Why would she—"

"Lylia," Cedric repeated, almost as if memorizing it. "Do you know where she is?"

"I'd imagine with Uldyssian, as you said, lad!" Achilios chuckled. "But I'd not disturb them now! Would probably be very inopportune!"

"She's not with him."

"And how would you know that?" For reasons he could not explain, the archer suddenly felt very cold. Achilios leaned toward the boy. "Ced, are you all—"

Master Ethon's son shoved him against the wall with such force that the hunter felt the wood crack.

Giving silent thanks that it had not been his *bones* that had made such a sound, Achilios let himself drop to the floor. Just above his head, Cedric slammed a fist into the wall, wreaking further damage in a manner impossible for one his size . . . or even Achilios's, for that matter.

The hunter kicked out, hoping to knock his attacker off balance, but it was as if Achilios struck solid rock. The impact vibrated through his body. Cedric appeared unaffected. In fact, Achilios could almost swear that the boy smiled at his puny effort.

As the small figure reached for him, the hunter reprimanded himself for still thinking that it was the merchant's son with whom he battled. This was not Cedric; this was possibly not even anything human. Achilios recalled too well the demons in the wild. Surely, this had to be one of them.

With an agility born from keeping on the trails of the most wily animals, Achilios managed to avoid the grasping hands. He shoved himself forward, slipping past the false Cedric.

Unfortunately, as the hunter tried to get to his feet, one hand finally snagged him by the collar. With a triumphant grunt, Cedric threw Achilios down the corridor.

Achilios landed hard, but the sound of his collision was oddly muffled. He doubted that anyone other than he could have have even heard it. Clearly another spell at work and one which concerned Achilios as much as the creature masquerading as the boy. It meant that an army—led by the high priest Malic, of course—could walk the entire house and no one would even know until it was too late.

The villains would be after Uldyssian. It was possible that they even had him captive already. But why, then, would they want Lylia? He could only assume that either he was wrong and his friend had escaped the high priest's grasp—which meant that they wanted to use the noblewoman for bait—or Uldyssian *was* a prisoner as Achilios had first supposed and Lylia was to be used to force him to remain compliant.

But whatever the reason, she had not been with him. Achilios gave thanks for that stroke of luck even as he scurried to his feet to avoid being fallen upon by his assailant. Her escape meant there remained some hope.

He had no more time to concern himself with Uldyssian and Lylia, for suddenly Cedric wielded in his hand a pair of vicious swords nearly the length of his body. Achilios had no idea where those weapons had come from, but the creature used them with tremendous skill, cutting arcs in the air and through a wooden railing too near. Fragments of wood went flying.

There was also something *else* different about the figure before Achilios. He was larger, bloated, as if something sought to burst free from under the skin. The cold Achilios had felt within grew worse as he imagined the fate of the boy whom he had befriended, the boy who had wanted to be an expert hunter like him.

Jagged tears spread all over Cedric's face and form. The right side near the jaw snapped away, revealing underneath something as pale as death and clad in black metal. What had once been Master Ethon's son now stood nearly as tall as Achilios and wider yet.

And even as the transformation took place, the blades came at the archer. Achilios dodged one after another, barely even able to draw a breath between leaps. Most other men would have long been cut to shreds and he knew that one lapse would see him dead. His concern was not so much for himself as it was for the rest and he worried what would happen to Serenthia and Mendeln if he failed. He dared not even warn them for fear that they would step out of their rooms and be slain. For that matter, it was possible that they might not even be able to hear his cry, if what he suspected about a spell was true.

One of the blades sank deep into the rail again, this time momentarily catching. The hesitation was all Achilios needed. His knife he had lost when smashed against the wall, but with practiced ease, the archer slipped free his bow and notched an arrow. At such a range, he could hardly miss, but the exact target was what mattered. This was surely a fiend similar to what had attacked Uldyssian in the street and so merely firing for a vital spot would not necessarily work. In fact, there was only one place Achilios was fairly sure would have an effect.

All this went through his mind in the matter of a single second. In the next, Achilios fired, aiming for one of the eyes. They now had an ominous darkness to them, as if there were no pupils, merely sockets. Still, the thing *had* to see . . .

He should have easily hit the spot. Even the creature seemed to think that, for it moved the twin blades up to protect the face. Yet, not only did the arrow miss the area of the eye, it flew entirely against all logic, burying itself deep in the wall *beside* his foe.

The bestial figure laughed. It tore away the last of poor Cedric's countenance and, as it did, it expanded in height and girth again, becoming an armored giant upon whose head was a macabre helmet that looked like an animal skull.

Swearing, Achilios stumbled back a step and notched another arrow. Keeping the last bolt's direction in mind, he fired again.

This time, it bounced off the armored shoulder.

The fearsome warrior grinned. "Not so good," he mocked in a voice that sent shivers through Achilios, for it sounded of the grave and reminded the archer of that moment when he had touched the stone near Seram. "Not so good for you . . ."

The blades came like twin whirlwinds. This time, Achilios moved too slowly. One cut into his thigh. He let out a cry and fell to the floor.

"You would make a good morlu," the armored behemoth grated. "Not as good as I, Damos, but still good. Maybe I bring your body back for the master . . ."

He raised both swords—

From behind Damos, someone quietly spoke. Achilios thought that he recognized the voice and yet, at the same time, there was that about it that made it sound as unnatural as when the morlu had spoken.

The huge warrior jerked as if a puppet tugged by the strings. With a hiss, he spun to face whoever stood there. Achilios reached for his bow, but did not know where to fire. The only open area was near the neck, a target where his arrow had failed to slay last time.

"Who are you?" demanded Damos. "What is it you speak?"

The other said something in a tongue Achilios did not recognize.

The morlu let out a howl. He doubled over, dropping one of the swords.

"Stop it! Stop!" Damos lunged with the remaining weapon, only to come up short. He gasped, then fell to one knee. The second sword joined its brother.

The dark figure beyond the morlu uttered a single syllable.

Damos let out a howl. His body shivered. A stench suddenly arose from the morlu's direction, a carrion smell.

With a last, mournful sound, the armored giant collapsed in an ungainly pile. The stench grew stronger.

Covering his nose and mouth, Achilios stared at the one standing over the body.

"Mendeln?"

Uldyssian's brother stared at Achilios as if seeing *through* him. There was a presence around Mendeln that made the hunter shiver almost as much as when he had realized what had become of Cedric. It was not evil, but so *different*, and it once more put Achilios in mind of the stone and what he had felt.

"*Kyr i' Trag 'oul discay,*" Mendeln finally said to him, as if this gibberish explained everything.

Rising, Achilios glanced at the morlu. From the smell and what he could glimpse, he would have sworn that the creature had been dead for many days, even weeks. The flesh almost seemed to be putrefying before his very eyes.

He looked again at Mendeln, pale as the corpse. The younger brother suddenly blinked. Life returned to his expression, followed a moment later by utter bewilderment and horror at the tableau before him.

"Achilios . . . what . . . where . . . ?"

At that moment, the house filled with noise. There was a crash and voices both below and nearby. A tremendous thud came from the direction of the chambers shared by Uldyssian and Lylia, a place that the archer had assumed vacant from the false Cedric's remarks.

A door nearby flung open and Serenthia, a dressing gown given to her by Master Ethon closed tightly around her throat, burst out. She saw Achilios first, then Mendeln, and finally noticed the grisly form on the floor. To her credit, the trader's daughter smothered a cry and instead immediately asked, "Where's Uldyssian and Lylia? Are they all right?"

Before Achilios could answer, there came another crash, this one from the very direction of Uldyssian's chambers. The hunter spun about and headed toward the noise. As Serenthia started to follow, he shouted, "You two stay! Do as I say!"

He had no idea whether they obeyed or not, but hoped that at least Mendeln would have the good sense to keep Cyrus's daughter out of danger. How Mendeln had done what he had to the vicious morlu, Achilios did not understand—nor did he understand *exactly* what had happened to the creature—but hopefully that same power would come into play if they were attacked. There was no telling how many more of the foul warriors there still were.

Two guards raced up the steps, obviously heading for the same destination. The first to reach the door gripped the handle—

From the chamber *next* to Uldyssian's, the massive form of a morlu burst through into the hall. He rammed into the two startled guards, sending one falling down the stairs. The second tried to turn to fight, but the monstrous warrior cut through his chest with an ax, spilling blood everywhere. The corpse went tumbling back, the eyes of the hapless guard ending up staring at Achilios.

The archer already had his bow unslung and ready to fire, but he remained well aware how his previous attempts had failed. With a swift calculation honed by having to adjust for wind and the sudden darting of animals, he finally released the arrow.

By all logic, the bolt should have flown far past his target, but it swerved at the last, just as Achilios hoped. He was certain that some spell had been cast on his weapon, although when that might have happened, he could not say. The only one other than him to touch it of late had been Uldyssian and Master Ethon . . .

The shaft buried itself exactly where he hoped. The morlu let out a howl as he reached to pluck the arrow from one of the dark eye sockets.

Achilios had a second shot ready by then. He fired immediately and watched with grim satisfaction as the new arrow hit directly in the other socket.

The armored behemoth slumped to his knees. The hand pulling at the first arrow dropped loosely to the floor, followed by the one wielding the bloody ax. Yet, the morlu did not completely collapse.

Racing up to the fiendish warrior, Achilios snagged the ax.

The morlu weakly sought to grab at him. The hunter dodged, then, bow looped over his shoulder, raised the ax high.

A moment later, he let it sink deep into the morlu's neck, cutting the head off cleanly. Only then did the body fall forward.

Keeping the ax ready, Achilios looked to Uldyssian's door. To his dismay, Serenthia—a sharp, broken piece of railing in one hand—already stood there, Mendeln on her heels.

"I told you to stay—"

Heedless of his warning, she flung open the door. Achilios leaped after her, fearful for her life.

As they entered, it was to see Uldyssian and another morlu with their hands around one another's throat. Serenthia let out a gasp, then ran up behind the morlu. Achilios expected her to try to club him with the piece of wood, but instead she turned it point first and aimed for the back of the neck.

By right, it should have cracked harmlessly or, at most, caused some shallow wound. Yet, as Serenthia thrust with all her might, the point flared white . . . and sank into the morlu's flesh with the utmost ease.

Uldyssian's adversary hacked. Releasing his hold, the morlu tried to pull the rail free. He fell to his knees, clutching desperately at it.

Serenthia stepped back, obviously awed by what she had done. Uldyssian, on the other hand, simply bent down over the morlu, then seized the wood. With powerful effort, he twisted it so that he nearly tore the head off.

The morlu dropped.

"The head . . . the head is the key," Uldyssian declared. "The head . . ." He looked up. "Lylia! Is she with you?"

"No!" Serenthia quickly responded.

"One of these creatures was looking for her," Achilios added. "He seemed to be having no luck in this area."

"I don't understand, unless—" He pushed past them, shouting, "She must've gone to look for me! She must've headed to the study . . . where I last left Malic!"

*   *   *

Mendeln did not follow after his brother and the others as they rushed to rescue the noblewoman. It was not that he did not wish to help, but something made him pause and look again at the morlu, both the one just slain and the other in the hall. A sense of foreboding rose within him as he moved to the nearest. He almost felt that, despite appearances, some spark of animation—not life—remained in the hideous corpse.

Without knowing why, he stretched a hand out over the back of the body. In his head, symbols appeared. This time Mendeln had some vague understanding of what they meant and, as with times previous, their pronunciation was obvious to him.

As he said the words, he felt a coolness emanate from his downturned palm. A faint glow like moonlight shone down on the region below his hand.

The morlu's body shivered, almost as if intending to rise again. It was all Mendeln could do to keep from pulling away. Yet some inner sense warned him that if he did, it might prove catastrophic.

The morlu's corpse shook violently. Then, a black cloud no larger than an apple rose from the body. It hovered briefly, then drifted up into his palm . . . where it promptly dissipated.

The morlu stilled again. The corpse looked as if it had deflated some. Mendeln no longer sensed anything.

He went to the one in the corridor and performed the same ritual. Glancing over his shoulder, Mendeln eyed the first one that he had encountered with Achilios. He could still not recall how he had gone from his bed to the hall and why that morlu had fallen at his feet. All that Mendeln knew for certain was that he had uttered words to that one, which made it unnecessary to perform the ritual used on the pair.

Curiously, Mendeln also suddenly recalled that he had not felt alone when he had dealt with that creature. He could have sworn that there had been a figure behind him, someone who had first whispered the needed words just in time.

But who? Mendeln asked himself. *Who?*

Then he remembered that there might be more of the helmed warriors, either those in wait or those believed dead. Whichever the case, Mendeln knew that he had to see to each one of them, make certain that the ritual was done. Only then could it be insured that none would rise again . . .

Shivering at the thought, Uldyssian's brother hurried along.

It had to be the study. Somehow, Uldyssian knew that Lylia had gone there. She would have entered without hesitation, certain that her love and Master Ethon were inside, discussing some matter.

Malic would take her, then, use her as leverage against the son of Diomedes. He knew that Uldyssian would do anything to save her from harm.

Uldyssian's blood suddenly boiled. But if she *was* harmed . . .

The doors to the study were shut. That seemed very odd considering that now household servants and guards ran all through the building, trying to make sense of what had happened. That none of them had gone to the study in search of their employer boded ill, for it smelled of the cleric's manipulations.

His thoughts growing more turbulent, Uldyssian threw himself at the entrance.

The doors crashed open, one flinging back so hard that it broke off. Uldyssian landed on the floor, immediately rolling to his feet and trying to muster whatever he could from within.

"*Malic!*" he roared, awaiting the worst. "This is between you and—"

But as he drank in the sight before him, Uldyssian faltered. There was another morlu in the center of the study, his head cleanly separated from his body and a dark, burnt area across his chest. The head, still within the ram's-skull helmet, seemed to peer angrily at the ceiling.

That scene, though, was nothing compared with what lay sprawled a little farther inside. It was another corpse stripped cleanly of its flesh, blood spilling from a thousand ripped veins. The body was tall, athletic in build—as ruined muscle and sinew still managed to indicate—and somehow yet clad despite its flaying.

It was the body of Malic, high priest of the Order of Mefis.

Seventeen

Malic's monstrous hand clutched his chest just below the throat. The demonic limb twitched twice, as if not quite dead despite its host's sorry condition.

Behind the macabre sight, a trembling Lylia stared at Uldyssian.

"My love!" she called, running to him and wrapping her arms tight around his body. She smelled of lavender and other flowers, a thing in utter contrast to the horrendous scene. Uldyssian inhaled deeply, wishing that all else had been nothing but a terrible nightmare.

Unfortunately, it was all too true. Pulling away from the blond woman, he eyed the late cleric. "Lylia . . . what happened here?"

"It was . . . it was part luck, and part the gift you awoke. I found you gone from the bed and came this direction. I thought I heard something and knocked." She shivered. "I heard the voice of dear Ethon and when I entered, the merchant stood waiting for me—" The noblewoman planted her face in his chest. "Oh, Uldyssian, please do not make me go on!"

"Just take a deep breath. We need to hear. There may be something important that you don't realize."

Mendeln slipped past the others and knelt by the morlu's body. Uldyssian found himself slightly annoyed with his brother's morbid interest, but chose to ignore it for the moment.

"I-I will try." Lylia pulled herself together. "The door I stepped through . . . it shut immediately behind me. I leaped

away and saw that abomination—" She pointed at Malic's
servant. "And then noticed that the window was completely
shattered. Ethon laughed suddenly and his voice *changed*. I
recognized the high priest's. Then . . . then . . . oh, Uldyssian,
he was wearing poor Ethon's *skin*."

"I know, Lylia, I know. Cedric and one of the servants
suffered the same fate."

"The boy, too? How horrible!"

He held her tight. "What then?"

Recovering, the noblewoman continued, "Malic . . . he
started to reach for me with that . . . I have never seen such
a hand! . . . and it came into my head somehow that it would
do the same to me as had happened to Ethon! I found the
strength to throw myself at him and *thrust* his arm back into
his chest!"

Rising from the morlu, Mendeln went to the cleric's
corpse. "And it caused this?" he asked. "So quickly?
Against his will?"

"It was as if someone tore off a cloth cover in order to
unveil a new statue beneath! I will *never* forget it! He did not
even have time to scream, much less think . . ."

Uldyssian appreciated the justice in the situation. He
hoped that Malic had suffered at least as much as any of his
victims, especially young Cedric.

"And the morlu?" asked his brother, abandoning the
flayed form. Mendeln's eyes were wide with curiosity.
There was no longer even a hint of revulsion at what he had
seen. "You managed *that*, too?"

Her expression hardened. "That beast came at me just as
his master died! I do not know exactly what I did, but I
waved my hand at him as if slicing with it . . . and you see
what happened."

Uldyssian understood exactly what had happened. The
stress of the situation had stirred up the powers within her
just as it had him. Her instinct for survival had taken over
and, fortunately, her action had dealt with the morlu in the
only certain way.

"His chest is burned, too," remarked Mendeln. "Deeply, I might add."

"It must have happened at the same time. I do not remember. I do not *want* to remember."

A commotion arose outside. Uldyssian tightened his hold on Lylia. "That's enough now," he told his brother. "We were all fortunate to survive . . ."

Mendeln nodded, but then asked, "Did you fight any others, Uldyssian?"

"There are two outside. One buried deep in the ground, the other minus his head by the outer wall."

With a nod, the studious figure abruptly walked out of the chamber. Uldyssian blinked, not certain why that information should be so relevant to Mendeln.

A guard suddenly appeared at the doorway. He looked aghast at the sight. "Master Ethon! Where is he?"

"Master Ethon is dead, as is his son," explained Uldyssian. "The bodies are hidden away somewhere. They'll look like—they'll look like this one," he added, pointing at Malic.

"By my soul! Master Uldyssian . . . w-what happened here?"

There was no time to start repeating the entire story. "Evil, that's what happened. Let's clear things up and pray that we find the merchant and his son so that they can be given a proper burial. I fear Master Ethon might be found somewhere beyond the town . . ."

Another guard joined the first. The two exchanged quick words; then the second man left. "I'll stand watch here," the first told the party. "Others will be told the dire news." His expression revealed his anguish. "Master Uldyssian . . . is there nothing you can do for them?"

It took Uldyssian a moment to understand just what the man meant. "No . . . no, nothing." He swallowed, disturbed even by the notion. "I'm sorry."

The guard nodded morosely, then took up a position in the corridor.

Achilios put a hand on Uldyssian's shoulder. "It might be good if we left here."

"It might be good if we left Partha completely," Uldyssian returned, scowling. His fears had come to pass. Friends and innocents had lost their lives horribly because of his presence. "As soon as possible, in fact . . ."

It did not take long to find the remains of Ethon's son. Cedric lay in his bed, the notion accepted by most—and pressed by Uldyssian—that the boy had died in his sleep. No one wanted to think otherwise.

The corpses of the morlu and the high priest were unceremoniously burned. No one considered contacting the Triune, although the unspoken thought was that sooner or later someone would come seeking the fate of the missing cleric. However, that was a situation that all were willing to put aside for the time being . . . or forever, if possible.

As was the custom of the Parthans, Cedric's corpse was burned with honor, the ashes placed in the family mausoleum the day after the travesty. No one spoke at the ceremony, but nearly all of Partha came to mourn.

It was not until two days later that they found Master Ethon himself. The morlu had hidden him well and if not for Achilios noticing a massing of carrion eaters, there might not have been anything left to burn. Ethon's ashes were set next to his son's and his wife's, and for days afterward, mourners wore across their chest a dark blue sash, the Kehjani symbol for honoring a great man.

Uldyssian wanted to leave, wanted to make certain that no more happened because of him, but there was always something requiring his attention. First it was dealing with Cedric, then speaking with all those who came to be comforted. No sooner had he finished that than Ethon was found and the cycle started over. Everyone turned to Uldyssian for guidance—Uldyssian, who still considered himself just a simple farmer.

Curiously, there emerged another source helping the Parthans cope with the loss of their beloved leader. Mendeln. When a handful of people came to the house to see Uldyssian—who had departed to speak with others— Mendeln suddenly brought it upon himself to talk with them. His message was an unusual one that, when his brother first heard of it, caused much concern. Yet, to those who had listened, it brought some closure.

Mendeln spoke of death, but not as a finality. He declared it only a state. Master Ethon and his son lay not just cold in their graves; they existed now on another plane. They had gone beyond the struggles of mortal existence to face new and exciting challenges. Death was not to be feared, Uldyssian's sibling insisted, but to be better understood.

No one seemed more surprised at these suggestions than Mendeln himself. When questioned, he could not explain just when they had occurred to him. They just had.

The inhabitants of Partha knew nothing of Uldyssian's intention to leave them. That was the way he wanted it. If they discovered the truth, he feared that there would be an upheaval and many would simply give up their lives and follow him. Lylia seemed to think this a good thing, but enough trouble had been caused here. Uldyssian wanted to reach the great city without further loss of life. In the city, he told himself, things would be different. No one could attack him surrounded by so many people.

It was a lie, of course, but he preferred to believe it.

To his surprise, however, Uldyssian discovered that his party would be much smaller than he imagined. The news came from Achilios and dealt with an unexpected situation.

It was only two nights before their intended flight. Lylia still urged him to forget sneaking away. If the people wished to follow him, the noblewoman had said, was that not what he wanted? Did he not want to give Kehjan proof of what he offered? What better than scores of willing witnesses, including some who could show their own abilities, however meager at this point?

Rather than argue with the woman he loved, Uldyssian had walked the dark streets again. He always made certain to stay within sight of more populated areas, not desiring any repeat of the attack. It was doubtful that there were any more of Malic's creatures about, but one could never tell.

Still, despite his precautions, he had sensed someone quietly following him. Only when Uldyssian had turned a corner, then waited, did he discover it to be the archer.

"Ho, there!" Achilios blurted much too loudly. "I'm no morlu, I swear!"

"You knew I'd hear you and wait," Uldyssian returned. "Otherwise, I'd have never noticed a sound."

His friend grinned. "True! I'm that good."

"What do you want?"

Achilios immediately sobered. "I wanted to talk with you, but in private. This seems the only way. I apologize if it's wrong."

"You can talk to me about anything, Achilios. You know that."

"Even . . . Serenthia?"

Like Uldyssian, the hunter had always called Cyrus's daughter by the shortened version of her name. That he now called her differently made the farmer's brow arch. *"Serenthia?"*

The other man cleared his throat. Never had Uldyssian seen Achilios look so uncomfortable. "She prefers that."

"What do you want?"

"Uldyssian . . . all that there is between you and Lylia . . . it remains strong?"

The course of the conversation began to make sense. "As strong as the spring storms. As strong as a raging river."

"There is nothing between you and Serenthia."

"She is a beloved sister to me," Uldyssian stated.

Achilios managed a slight grin. "But far more to me. You know that."

"I've always known that."

This caused the archer to chuckle. "Yes, I've been pretty obvious, except maybe to her."

"She knew." Of that, Uldyssian could swear. Serenthia had been no fool when it came to the lovesick Achilios. "Now tell me what this is about. We've only got all night."

"Uldyssian . . . Serenthia wants to stay behind when you leave. I want to stay, too."

That she wanted to stay startled him, but that Achilios wanted to remain with her was not so surprising. Uldyssian found that he was relieved by the news, even though there was a part of him that ached at the loss of friends. "I wanted all of you to stay behind. That Serry—Serenthia—wants to do so now, I've no problem with. I'm also glad that you'll be there for her, Achilios, but . . . does she know and, if she does, do you expect anything to change between you?"

That produced a wider smile. "I've recently had some hint that it has."

This was even better—no, joyous—news. "Then I'm doubly happy. I've wished that she could see you as you are, Achilios . . . and that the two of you will be safe makes me glad, also."

"There is that last. I *shouldn't* abandon you, of all people. This is not the end of the danger. There will be other Malics! I should be standing with you—"

Uldyssian halted him. "You've done more than you should, just as Serenthia and Mendeln have! I told you before, I wanted all of you far away from me. You spoke the truth; there'll be other Malics, especially as long as the Primus still commands the Triune. I want none of you near me when the next comes . . . not even Lylia."

"But she'll never leave you!"

"I know . . . but I've got to try to make her see sense. If I do, please watch over her for me . . . and Mendeln, too."

The hunter extended a hand, which Uldyssian clasped tight. "You know you can ask anything of me," Achilios muttered. "Even to stay."

"You could do me no better favor than to leave and keep the others with you."

"What about the Parthans? What do I tell them when they discover you missing? They won't like it."

Uldyssian had considered this for quite some time, but all he could say now was "Tell them to keep growing."

It was the words of a farmer and so the truest he could speak. He hoped that they would understand. He also hoped that they would forgive him for forever altering their lives. There would be no peace for them now.

No peace at all . . .

Mendeln remained outwardly calm, but inside he was very much on edge. He had come to realize many truths in the past few days, but those had also opened up the road to a thousand more unanswerable questions. He still had no idea what was becoming of him, save that it seemed sharply different from that affecting his brother or any of the rest. Their paths seemed pointed toward an expansion of life, a growth.

His appeared fixed upon death.

He did not entirely mind that. Not anymore. In truth, Mendeln found himself more comfortable than at the beginning, so comfortable, in fact, that he could spend much time away from other people. The solitude and the shadows seemed to beckon him. There was someone watching over Uldyssian's younger brother. He knew that now. Who it was had yet to be revealed. That stirred Mendeln's curiosity in more ways than one. True, he wanted to know the other's identity. However, Mendeln also found it interesting that he did not fear the answer.

And by all rights, he *should* have.

With his gradual understanding of things came changes. Mendeln had always dressed a bit more subdued than Uldyssian, but now he found he favored the colors of the calming night. He also noted how people treated him with more veneration, but also a little

uncertainty. Everyone appeared to see the transformation slowly taking place, but the rest understood it
even less than he did and likely assumed it had to do
with his brother's gift. Thinking that, they came to him
for comfort concerning their lost leader and he told
them what he believed. To his relief, most took his words
to heart, even if they did not completely understand
what he truly meant.

The shadows more and more became his companions.
He began spending excessive time awake at night. It was at
that point that Mendeln first started hearing the whispers.
After two nights of listening, he finally became bold
enough to try to follow them.

And, sure enough, they led directly to the cemetery.

This time, Mendeln did not hesitate to enter, despite the
fact that there was no moon this eve, and no stars. He was
not in the least afraid, for what lay before him was not the
mysterious, endless place of his vision, but merely the final
repository for the locals' loved ones. As such, it was a location mostly of peace, of murmured thoughts and eternal
dreams.

But there was something else, something far more
ancient in the very center. The thing that stirred the whispers and enticed him forward.

Mendeln had noticed that his night vision had grown
acute of late. In truth, he felt he saw almost as well now as
he did during the day. Even Achilios could not have
matched him.

He neared the area that felt the source. Here the whispers
grew more pronounced. Most of them were from the graves
nearby and they talked of their lives as if those lives continued to this very moment.

*Must get the beans cooked, then the bread in the oven. The chil-
dren need their shirts mended . . .*

*That mare'll breed a fine colt, yes, indeed, then I can sell it once
it's old enough to Master Linius . . .*

Poppy says not to go play by the river, but it sparkles and the fishes dance under it. I'll just go and look a little and I'll be real careful . . .

On and on they went. If Mendeln squinted, he even thought that he could see vague shapes above the graves, shapes resembling those whispering.

But while all this fascinated him, it was not the reason for his presence here at this time. That had to do with what lay at the heart of the cemetery. Yet when Uldyssian's brother first looked there, it was to see nothing but an overgrown old stone with faded markings.

He leaned close. Disappointment filled him. The markings were in an old but legible script, not the ancient symbols for which he had hoped. Mendeln almost left, then, but suddenly recalled something else about his current location.

It was the very same place where, in his vision, the huge winged statue had stood.

That brought him back to the gravestone. With tentative fingers, he touched it where the name had been inscribed —

A tremendous force tossed him back more than a yard.

Mendeln landed against another stone, the collision jarring him. His vision blurred . . .

A huge, half-seen shape suddenly stood above the stone. It was nothing remotely human but neither did it seem anything demonic in nature. Shadow and starlight—starlight coming from somewhere other than the sky—formed what *was* visible. What Mendeln thought a long muzzle like that of a reptile turned his way.

You must stay with him . . . , it intoned. *The brother reveals the secret of the sister and she will kill for it . . .*

Mendeln's vision finally cleared . . . and the shape vanished. All was as it had been before he had touched the stone.

Somehow, though, he knew that it was not the marker itself that had been summoned this . . . *whatever* it was . . . to him. No, the true source was buried *beneath* the grave there. The marker had merely acted as a conduit of sorts.

But what did it mean? Mendeln ran the words through

his head. *You must stay with him . . . The brother reveals the secret of the sister and she will kill one for it . . .*

"The brother? The sister?" None of it made any sense to him save that the shadow creature had warned him that death would come of some conflict between them. Oddly, this "death" disturbed Mendeln as none other had of late. It would cause even more terrible things to go into motion, he felt.

You must stay with him . . .

He jerked to his feet. The key lay there. The warning could refer only to one person, for who else would Mendeln first think of other than his brother?

"Uldyssian!" He raced from the cemetery, urgency over-whelming his respect for his surroundings. Whatever the message spoke about would take place very, very soon.

If it had not already . . .

In the dark of night, the Cathedral was literally a gleaming beacon that welcomed all to it. No matter what time, there was always someone to greet a late-traveling pilgrim or lost soul. The Prophet had decreed it so, saying that the salvation of the masses could not cease merely because the day was over.

The Prophet could often be seen in those late hours, for Inarius did not require sleep. However, although he would have denied it, the angel did grow restive and so, unable to go out among the mortal throngs in his full glory and take flight, he instead paced the length and breadth of the spiraled edifice, sometimes appearing where his followers least expected it.

This night, the radiant youth stood at the top of the highest of the towers. From here, one could overlook the landscape for mile upon mile. It was as close as he could come to soaring through the sky.

Inarius was not afraid, but he was cautious. The game he played against Lucion required tact from both in order not to upset matters and reveal Sanctuary to his brethren. He felt more than adequate to handle the demon, even with Lucion able to summon all the might of the Burning Hells. After all, this world was *Inarius's* creation. No one could take it away from him . . . not the demon, not her, and not even some simple farmer whose life span was less than the blink of an eye compared with his.

And they would all soon find that out.

EIGHTEEN

Uldyssian heard the shouting just as he was building up the nerve to tell Lylia that she had to stay behind no matter what she desired. He had already failed twice this evening and the fact that both attempts had ended up in lovemaking had not assuaged his guilt much. Now, just as his breath and strength had finally returned and he had been determined not to fail a third time, what sounded like his brother's voice echoed throughout Master Ethon's house.

The people of Partha seemed to consider it Uldyssian's now, but he planned to use it only for a day or two more . . . and even that with much guilt. Once he was gone, Lylia and the others were welcome to make it their own long enough to sort out their lives.

Unfortunately, it seemed that Mendeln needed sorting out immediately. Uldyssian rose from the bed to see what was the matter.

"Do not be long," Lylia murmured, her tone seeking to entice him anew.

With a nod, he put some clothing on and stepped out . . . at which point he nearly collided with his brother.

"Uldyssian! Praise be! I feared the worst!"

Mendeln's tension was contagious. "What? Is it Peace Warders or morlu? The Cathedral's Inquisitors?"

"No! No!" Mendeln looked him up and down. "Uldyssian! You are well?"

"I am." The older brother did not bother to mention his intentions just now. Mendeln could learn about them later. "Now, what's this all about?"

"I feared . . . I thought . . ."

"What?"

With a look of chagrin, Mendeln shook his head. "Nothing. It was a nightmare, Uldyssian. Just a foolish nightmare . . ." His eyes glanced past his sibling, to where Uldyssian realized an unclothed Lylia could be partially seen in the bed. "I *am* sorry. Forgive me . . . I do not know what to think."

Mulling it over, Uldyssian suggested, "You've been up all hours, Mendeln, day and night. That's not good. You've helped me a lot in soothing the spirits of the Parthans after Master Ethon's slaughter. I think you just need some rest."

Uncertainty tinged his brother's voice. "Perhaps . . ." Again, the eyes flickered past Uldyssian. "I am very sorry to have intruded . . ."

Before Uldyssian could say anything, Mendeln whirled and rushed off to his room.

Shutting the door behind him, Uldyssian returned to Lylia. She smiled languidly as he slipped in next to her.

"Your brother is all right?"

"He's overexhausted."

The blond woman ran soft fingers over his chest, toying with the hair. "And are you?"

"Not in the least," Uldyssian returned, taking her in his arms. "Let me show you."

Three hours passed. Three hours in which he had drunken deep of Lylia again. Three hours since they had lain side by side.

Three hours that now saw Uldyssian just finishing the saddling of his horse.

It was the only way to resolve the situation. No more thinking. No more explanations. After assuring himself that the noblewoman was asleep, he had cautiously risen and dressed. With soft footfalls that would have made Achilios proud, Uldyssian had then slipped out of the room and through the house. When he had come across the few guards on duty—they swearing to watch over him as they had their former employer—none saw him sneak past. They could not be faulted for that, however, for it seemed that Uldyssian's gift worked for him without trouble this time. He wished the men to look the other way . . . and they had.

It was with growing guilt that Uldyssian rode quietly through the streets and, at last, out of Partha. The people were just beginning to understand what was happening to them. As recent as he was to his own abilities, the son of Diomedes knew that he understood them far more than anyone else did. Uldyssian was also the one responsible for their transformations. All *that* demanded he return to the town immediately and take responsibility.

But always weighing more heavily were the deaths. It was possible that he was making a terrible decision in abandoning everyone and riding to Kehjan himself, yet . . .

Uldyssian shook his head as he rode on. He could ill afford to think of any more "yets."

The trees surrounded him like silent sentinels. The night seemed blacker than usual. Uldyssian tried to encourage his mount to a swifter pace, but the animal moved tentatively, almost as if it feared something lurking in the shadows.

The trail wound around a series of low hills. There was a well-traveled road leading from Partha to Kehjan, but Uldyssian wanted to make it less simple for anyone to follow him. Other than Achilios, who would understand his sudden departure, there were probably few who could track him. Taking a lesser trail would also guarantee less possible encounters with other travelers.

His belongings were meager, consisting mainly of the clothes on his back, a worn but workable sword, and a few bits of food he had managed to gather on his way out. His impulsive departure had given him little time to do much else. He had one sack of water—filled near the stables—but assumed that somewhere soon he would pass another source.

Thinking of the water sack, Uldyssian suddenly felt very thirsty. He tugged the pouch free from the saddle and drank his fill. The contents were a bit brackish, but tolerable.

As he swallowed the last, Uldyssian, eyeing the dark path ahead, considered his trek. The lowlands and Kehjan awaited to the east. The beginning of the jungle regions was not that far off; if he continued riding in his present direction, he would soon descend into the warmer climes. Cyrus had spoken in the past of the abrupt change that took place down there, almost as if some great mischievous spirit had divided up the world at whim, not planning. One day, Serenthia's father had told him, you would be wearing a nice, sensible coat that kept you safe from the snow . . . and the next you would find yourself gasping in the sweltering heat, slapping bird-sized mosquitoes every step.

Uldyssian had never entirely believed the man's tales, although some of the traders who had come to Seram *had* proven the exotic did exist in the east. There had been a handful over the years with the swarthy skin and long, narrow eyes which were supposedly predominant the farther into the jungles one went. Rumor had it that there were men darker yet, with flesh like coal. Others were supposed to be golden in color.

The mage clans were said to be filled with such strange races of men, and Kehjan itself was supposedly a melting pot. Lylia was proof of that, Master Ethon having even guessed just where her family would have been from. The very thought of approaching the vast city by himself suddenly proved very daunting to the simple farmer. He wished that he could have at least been accompanied by the noblewoman—who knew Kehjan best—yet she was also the one he least wanted near him should trouble arise. The fear that something terrible might befall her had been the most driving reason for his abrupt flight.

Her face filled his mind. Perhaps one day they would be able to reunite, but not after Uldyssian made certain that it was safe to do so. Yet, Lylia would always be with him, even if only in his memories and his heart—

"Uldyssian . . ." came a soft voice suddenly. "My love . . ."

He dropped the water sack, then twisted in the saddle. Behind him, to his disbelieving eyes, was the noblewoman herself. She was completely dressed and riding a large, dark steed that he did not recall.

"Lylia! What're you doing here?"

Her smile alone began melting his resolve. "I've come to be with you, naturally."

"You should've stayed in Partha," he insisted, trying to gather his strength. "I left you with the others for your own sake . . ."

She urged the huge mount forward. "You may leave the others, but you can never leave me, Uldyssian. I began this with you and I will end this with you."

He was touched by her dedication and wanted to take her in his arms, but recalled the evils of Malic. If she stayed at his side, Lylia would forever be a target of men such as the high priest . . . or, worse, their masters. No matter how much he yearned for her, Uldyssian had to let her go.

"No, Lylia. It has to end here for us. I don't want you hurt. I don't want you dead."

"But you saw what I managed against Malic and think how powerful *he* was! I can defend myself, my love, especially from those who would separate us!"

It was a powerful argument, Uldyssian himself having been hard-pressed against the servant of the Primus. Still, he understood from his own abilities that Lylia might very well have been merely lucky, that next time she could discover herself entirely defenseless against some murderous foe.

The thought of what would happen then was all he needed to regain his determination completely. "No, Lylia. I can't afford to think like that. If anything would happen to you, it would be too much! You've got to go back. No argument. Stay with the others, but don't consider coming after me again."

Instead of obeying, the blond woman dismounted. "I will not go. I will follow you wherever you ride."

"Lylia—"

She left her horse behind, not at all concerned, it seemed, that it could wander off. Stretching her arms to Uldyssian, Lylia continued, "Come hold me once more. Kiss me once more. Prove to me that you can leave me behind. Perhaps, if you say you can, I might reconsider."

Although he knew that it was foolish to do so, Uldyssian also dismounted. Just one hug and kiss. It would give him something to remember. He would still insist that she return to the town. He would not weaken in any way.

But as she melted into his arms, as her lips found his, Uldyssian's will drained away again. What if Lylia *did* ride after him? Would she not be more likely in harm's way searching for him rather than being at his side? Surely, with how he was learning to control his gifts, he could keep her safe . . .

A shiver suddenly coursed through him as the kiss continued. Eyes closing, Uldyssian pulled back. A momentary weakness overcame him and it was all he could do to stand.

"Uldyssian! Are you ill?"

Almost as quickly as it had vanished, his strength returned. He shook his head. Opening his eyes revealed his vision to be blurred. Uldyssian blinked several times, trying to restore it.

"I think . . . I think it's passing," he muttered. A vague shape that had to be Lylia began to coalesce in front of him. Uldyssian frowned as she took on more definition. Something was wrong. She seemed different, almost as if—

He managed to stifle a shout, but could not keep from stumbling farther away from her. Without meaning to, the son of Diomedes collided with his mount.

The animal turned. Uldyssian heard it snort, then the horse began to shy away, as if it, too, saw something unsettling.

"What is it?" Lylia asked anxiously. "Uldyssian! What is it?"

He could not tell her, for he was not certain himself.

What stood before him was no longer the blond noble-woman. Rather, it was taller and hideously scaled, with a mass of fiery quills for hair, quills that ran down the spine to . . . to a reptilian tail ending in savage barbs. Where the delicate hands had been were now clawed fingers—four, not five. Worse, the feet were like hooves, yet splayed, too.

The body was unclad and, although monstrous, still very, very female. The lush curves enticed, drawing his eyes despite his dismay. But most horrific of all was that, when he looked up into the face—the face with its burning orbs that had no pupils and teeth designed for shredding—he could still see the features that he recognized as that of the woman he loved.

"Are you ill?" the creature asked in her voice, a black, forked tongue darting in and out with each word.

It was and was not the image from his nightmare and, for a moment, Uldyssian prayed that he had been asleep the entire time. Yet, sense told him that this was reality . . . and that what he saw of Lylia was no illusion.

"What—what *are* you?"

"I am your Lylia!" she declared, sounding confused and slightly irritated. "What else could I be?" Her tail slapped the earth angrily.

His eyes shifted to it, then quickly back to her face. However, she noted his reaction and her expression grew more terrible.

A word escaped Lylia before she could stop her self. *"Lucion . . ."*

"Lucion? What does he have to do with this?" asked Uldyssian, trying desperately to make sense of things.

"It is obviously a spell of the Primus! He has transformed me into this!" Lylia reached for him, imploring, "Only your love can save me!"

He started toward her . . . and then some instinct bade him hold back. Uldyssian recalled how she had glanced back at the tail with little surprise, as if its being there was a perfectly natural thing.

A great pit opened up in his stomach. He shook his head, trying vehemently to reject what he was beginning to believe. This could not be happening! There had to be an explanation. Lylia could not be . . . *this*.

"Uldyssian!" the demonic figure beseeched. "Please! Hold me! I am frightened by your coldness! My love, only you can restore me!"

"Lylia . . ." Again, he stepped toward . . . and again his instinct was to retreat a moment later. Uldyssian stared closely at her, noting minute details that seemed to show a comfort, a familiarity, with her current form.

Next to him, his mount continued to grow more and more anxious. The horse began struggling with him. Uldyssian could barely hold on to the reins.

In contrast, though, Lylia's steed stood still. *Too* still for one so very familiar with animals. It was almost as if the black horse was mesmerized . . .

His frantic mind raced for answers. Maybe this was not Lylia at all! Maybe she was still in bed and this demon had assumed her role. Yes, that could very well be it, he supposed.

Drawing his sword, he growled, "Keep away from me, demon! I've slain others of your kind! You'll not fool me with that voice!"

The figure looked perplexed. "Uldyssian, it *is* Lylia! Remember our first meeting? How you found me admiring the horses? Remember how I insisted on coming to you when you were unjustly locked away? Have you forgotten everything?"

She went on to name a half-dozen more incidents with enough detail to drain away his hope that this was not her. In doing so, she might have thought that she would pull him back to her, but all Lylia actually succeeded in doing was reinforcing the fact that Uldyssian had been cavorting with something monstrous.

Yet, despite that growing horror, the farmer could not

keep his eyes off of Lylia. There was an unnatural seductiveness to her, so much so that his body desired to crush itself against hers despite what his mind knew. Her every movement enticed, as if, as she pleaded innocence, she also sought to use her wiles to ensnare him.

Shuddering, Uldyssian forced himself to look away. As he did, he heard a sharp, furious hiss.

"Look at me, Uldyssian!" Lylia abruptly cooed. "Look at what you have had and what you can have again . . . and again . . . and again . . ."

Something told him that if he looked, it would be his undoing. His will was only mortal, whereas that with which he had lain could never be called such.

"Get away from me, whatever you are!" he demanded, still looking slightly to the side. "Leave or . . . or I'll do with you as I did the other demons!"

He expected anger or perhaps fear, as she would surely recall how he had disposed of the foul creatures sent forth by Malic—

Malic . . . suddenly *that*, too, made more sense. Uldyssian had been stunned by the swift ending to the cunning cleric, but that Lylia was more than she seemed explained much. Poor Malic had not known exactly what it was he had faced. Perhaps he had suspected, but even that would not have been enough. The irony might have made Uldyssian smile if not for his own circumstances.

A strange sound came from Lylia's direction. Not a hiss, not a snarl . . . but *laughter* that tore at his soul.

"Poor little Uldyssian! My sweet darling! So naive, so believing! You were ever too trusting when it came to what I said . . ."

That almost made him face her, which was perhaps as she wanted it. "What do you mean?"

"Have you not wondered at how quickly your vaunted abilities have blossomed? Have you not wondered why all others—save your loving Lylia—have so far shown so little progress?"

He had, and the implications in her tone set the hair on his neck stiffening.

"Yes, he sees the truth *now*, or at least a hint of it. Yes, dear, sweet Uldyssian . . . I have guided you every step of the way! What you do, you do in great part because of *me*, not yourself! *I* it was who brought forth the storm, who guided the lightning, who caused most of your desire to become reality—"

And more than that, he knew suddenly. "And who slaughtered one missionary, then slew another with a knife of mine!"

This caused her to giggle, a sound once musical to the human but now filling him with loathing. "The stage had to be set for you, my love! And what were they, *anyway*, but pawns of a treacherous lover and a fool of a *brother*?"

Uldyssian tried to digest the last. If she was to be believed, both the Primus and the Prophet were known to her very well. One was of her blood—assuming that such flowed through her—while the other had assumed the same role as Uldyssian, but before him. The knowledge only made Uldyssian's consternation grow. His entire existence was nothing but delusion. He was not this powerful force, but rather a puppet. Her puppet.

But . . . a small part of him rebelled at that thought, reminding Uldyssian that this encounter was surely not as she planned matters. She had spat the name of Lucion out before she could help herself. Yet, if Uldyssian was only a weak pawn, why take this action? Why had Lucion just not destroyed him? Uldyssian could only assume that he was either of some value to the Primus or that Lucion could not do away with him. At the moment, Uldyssian doubted the latter, but the former still made some sense, based more than once on Malic's words.

And if it did, it had to be because there was *something* to the power growing within the farmer. Why else would Lylia—if that was what this demoness was called—have chosen him in the first place?

"I told you before," he finally said, trying to sound confident and defiant. "Leave now or else!"

Again, she giggled. "Ah, my darling Uldyssian, how I have come to adore your little stubborn streak! I would say it was from my side, but it could also be from his, they so arrogant, so righteous!" When he said nothing, Lylia continued, "You do not even know about that, do you? You do not even know your history! All of this I would have revealed to you in time, when you were ready! Shall I tell you now? We can still be together! You can still hold me, caress me . . ."

Feeling his will crumbling, Uldyssian ducked back. Unfortunately, the horse, still fighting with him, used that moment to pull the reins free. Uldyssian spun around, chasing after them, but the horse was already too far away. He watched the animal race off into the night.

"Poor Uldyssian . . . but you do not need that weak creature! I can teach you to fly or materialize *anywhere!* Once more, the nephalem will rise and, this time, they will assume their rightful place! Ha! *I* will assume my rightful place, no matter how the High Heavens and the Burning Hells cry out against it!"

There was a manic tone in her voice, a hint of madness that he had never heard. Without thinking, Uldyssian looked at her.

Her eyes immediately snared his. Her lips parted and her tongue flashed out, licking as if about to devour a tasty tidbit.

"When he cast me out for what he thought eternity, he underestimated my resolve! I had slain all of them for the sake of the children; why would I then let the children be his to mold forever in his imperious image? They were special. They were more than either demons or angels! I saw then that they were to be the future, the true end to the infernal struggle!"

Lylia raised one clawed hand and Uldyssian felt his right foot slide forward. She beckoned with a single finger and his left followed suit. With effort, he slowed his momentum, but it was only a matter of time before he would stand directly in front of her.

Obviously aware of this, she continued to talk as if all was well between them, as if he was happy to know that he had lain with a monster. "What you have called a gift, my love, is that and much more! You . . . *all* humans . . . are the spawn of our coupling! From demon and angel came the nephalem, greater than anything ever created in the cosmos! The force I stirred within you, the force which I found begging to be released, is nothing less than your *birthright!* He would see it smothered and all of you kept as so much docile cattle to serve his vanity . . . but I . . . but I can offer far more!" She reached toward him. "Much, much more . . ."

Gritting his teeth, Uldyssian growled, "The only thing you can offer me is a way to forget what happened!"

"Do you *truly* wish to forget everything, my darling? Do you truly wish to forget *me?*"

He finally managed to stop dead in his tracks. Face contorting from effort, Uldyssian retorted, "Nothing would please me more . . ."

"Is that so?" Lylia's eyes flared darkly. "Is that so, my love?"

To his horror, Uldyssian discovered himself stumbling toward her at almost breakneck speed. His best efforts proved laughable and it suddenly came to Uldyssian that all this time Lylia had been toying with him. Not for a moment had he truly been able to stand against her power. His "birthright," as she had called it, was nothing more than a hollow lie.

Her arms embraced him as he reached her. He, in turn, wrapped his own around her scaled form, the quills running down her back stabbing his flesh. Her body was a furnace, yet so very soft in the places that mattered. Uldyssian felt his lust rise up to do battle with his repugnance.

"Let us kiss and see how much you wish to forget," Lylia mocked.

He could do no less than obey. His body reacted with a passion he could not quell.

No! Uldyssian shouted in his mind, even as he and Lylia pressed against one another. *No! I won't become hers again!*

A sharp pain in his lower lip made him wince. She had bitten him. Uldyssian felt her tongue taste the blood and the action caused him to shiver.

Lylia finally pulled back. Her expression said it all. She knew that while part of him was utterly disgusted, another was entirely under her domination.

The demoness chuckled. Uldyssian experienced a sense of foreboding—

A tremendous force *struck* him full, sending the human flying through the air as he had once thought he had done to Malic's Peace Warders. Uldyssian let out a cry as he soared among the trees, certain that he would hit one.

However, despite the odds so against him, he did not so much as graze a limb. Instead, Uldyssian finally dropped to the ground, tumbling hard and rolling several yards farther. Every bone felt as if it was breaking, every muscle shrieked. When the son of Diomedes finally came to a rest, he could not even so much as move a finger.

However, despite the distance Uldyssian had flown, he immediately sensed Lylia's presence close by. Sure enough, she loomed over him but a breath later.

"The great Uldyssian, changer of worlds! I think you understand now just how *great* you truly are . . ."

"D-Damn . . ." was all he could say, his lungs still pleading for air.

"Still defiant?" She knelt down, giving him, despite the darkness, a very close look at her charms. "A worthy trait, sometimes . . ."

He could do nothing when she kissed him again. Well aware of his conflicting emotions, Lylia stretched it out longer than the last.

"I think you will come around," the demoness cooed afterward. "But first, one more lesson to be learned, my love. The lesson of just what you are *without* me."

The wind suddenly raged, howling like a pack of wolves as it tore through the region. The quills atop Lylia's head shook as if alive. The demoness stood and raised her arms, clearly the cause of the shift in weather.

"Yes, let us see just what you are without me," she repeated with a laugh. "Let us see how long your defiance lasts! Not so very long, I think, eh, my love?"

Summoning what strength he could, Uldyssian made a desperate lunge at her ankles. What he hoped to do beyond toppling her, the human could not say, but he felt that he had to try.

His attempt was as pitiful as his earlier arrogance. His fingers barely grazed her scaly hide. Lylia merely stood there, watching his antics.

"Not yet, not yet, dear Uldyssian! You can hold me again when you have been properly chastised . . . if, of course, you *survive* the lesson!" She cocked her head. "If . . ."

He snarled and tried again to reach her, but the wind trebled, shoving at him with such ferocity that Uldyssian was rolled back. The world spun around him for a moment and once more he was left gasping for air.

Without warning, the terrifying gust died. Silence fell over the area. Uldyssian's lungs gradually filled. He managed to twist his gaze back, wondering what the temptress would do to him next.

But Lylia—if that was indeed her name—was *gone*.

Let us see what you are without me, she had said. He shuddered, knowing that her absence presaged dire events to come. The demoness had proven quite readily that Uldyssian had no true power, that everything had been a hoax perpetuated by her.

Visions of Inquisitors and Peace Warders filled his head. He imagined demons and morlu already waiting in the dark, their thirst for his blood only held in check by their masters. It mattered not which sect; both the Primus and the Prophet apparently wanted him for his vaunted "birthright." However, once they discovered that he was merely an empty shell, a pawn, they would have no further use for him.

Worse, those he had led into this would also see him as a man of false promises. They would lose heart, turn against him. His friends would realize that they had given up everything for nothing.

Let us see what you are without me.

He knew what he was already . . . the greatest of fools and a *condemned* man.

Nineteen

Someone was calling his name. He knew the voice, but could not answer it.

"Uldyssian!"

He tried to wave a hand, give some sort of call, but failed. His mind sluggishly attempted to recall what had happened. Slowly, Uldyssian recalled Lylia and the revelation of her nature. That horrifying memory proved enough to enable him to let out a primitive shout, a garbled sound that proved sufficient, for the searcher's own calls became more pronounced.

"Uldyssian! I know you're here somewhere! Where—"

It was Achilios's voice, Uldyssian finally realized. Good, faithful Achilios. He tried to say the hunter's name, but it only came out as a rasping sound.

"Here! Here he is!" said what sounded like Serenthia. As grateful as he was to know that she also searched for him, Uldyssian suddenly grew concerned. Lylia would take special pleasure in tormenting Cyrus's daughter.

Soft hands took hold of his face. Uldyssian instinctively jerked away, thinking that Lylia had returned. However, that fear was quickly squashed as Serenthia said, "Praise be! You're alive! Achilios! Mendeln! Here he is!"

The sounds of figures thrashing through the brush alerted him to the others' nearby presence. He heard an oath which had to have come from the archer.

"Is he wounded?" asked Mendeln, sounding more curious than concerned.

"He has bruises," Serenthia returned. "But I see no cuts, no slashes! I don't feel any broken bones."

Another figure leaned over the fallen farmer. "He looks as pale as death," Achilios rumbled. "Or worse."

More and more details came back to him. He remembered fearing for his friends and his brother. He also recalled starting to walk back, but then, as if Lylia had taken even his will to live from him, Uldyssian had, without warning, just blacked out. Had the others not come in search of him, he wondered whether he would have ever awakened again. He supposed he eventually would have. After all, Lylia had not seemed to want him dead, merely . . . broken.

"How—" He swallowed hard, then tried again. "How did you know—"

It was as if he had asked them to join together to commit some terrible crime. All three grew oddly perturbed. Their silence added to his unease.

Mendeln finally spoke. "We knew that your life was in danger."

Uldyssian remembered his brother running through the house earlier, shouting his name. "You did?"

"We *all* did."

The hunter and Serenthia nodded. "I thought it was a nightmare," she added. "But it was so terrible, I had to go check. That was when I noticed Achilios also up."

"And barely had she and I met, when Mendeln came, insisting that he needed to see you a second time."

The younger son of Diomedes frowned. "The notion would not go away, Uldyssian. I knew that you might be angry with me, but I was determined to try to warn you again . . . only to have all three of us discover you . . . and Lylia . . . gone."

"Lylia!" gasped the raven-tressed woman. "We've forgotten about her! Uldyssian! Isn't she with you?"

"She was." His answer came out as a croak . . . not because of his condition, but rather the repulsive memories.

And yet, a part of him *still* yearned for her.

His companions anxiously looked around. He quickly shook his head.

"No . . . don't look . . . for her." Uldyssian forced himself to a sitting position. "With our luck . . . you might find her."

He sensed their confusion. With help from both Serenthia and Achilios, Uldyssian next stood. As he did, his gaze met that of his sibling. Curiously, the nightmarish vision of his brother struck Uldyssian once more. He stared with such intensity that Mendeln finally looked away, as if guilty of something.

"Uldyssian," murmured Achilios. "What do you mean? Why wouldn't we want to find Lylia? Why wouldn't *you* want to find her?"

Had they not already been confronted with the reality of demons and spells, he could never have told them. As it was, Uldyssian's shame was so great that it took him a long pause before he could finally begin.

And by the time he was through, they looked as horrified as he felt.

"You must've imagined it!" the hunter insisted. "It can't be true!"

"A demon?" Serenthia blurted, with a shake of her head. "A demon?"

Only Mendeln, after his initial shock, nodded in understanding.

"It explains so much," he finally uttered. "If one looks back at all that has passed."

Uldyssian was not so certain that he shared his brother's opinion. He only knew that he certainly had been blind, deaf, and dumb. He had let Lylia command him around as if he were a dog. People had died because of her madness, because of her intent to create a world of magical beings.

It was to their credit that they took his story to heart. Uldyssian had left nothing out—not even the part where Lylia had claimed the world was called Sanctuary and had been created by rogue demons and angels. It was important to him that someone else understood that the demoness had some mad plan that had stirred up the Temple and the Cathedral, both of which somehow had ties to her.

That brought him back to her final declaration. She had left him on his own to teach him the penalty for defying her. That meant that they were *all* in immediate danger. "We have to leave Partha!" he blurted. "We have to flee for our lives! The jungles in the lowlands are our best bet—"

"Hold, Uldyssian!" Achilios demanded. "What do you mean? We can't flee! To flee means to become the hunted and there is no defense in that!"

"Achilios, all that I thought that I could do turns out to be a lie! It was all *her!* Everything!"

The archer shook his head. "I don't know if I believe that. It doesn't ring true!"

"And it isn't," insisted Serenthia. "Uldyssian, I've watched you. I've felt what you did. That could not have all been Lylia! What I sensed when you touched me was a part of *you!* I know that as well as I know . . . I know myself." Her face reddened as she said the last.

While he appreciated all that she said, Uldyssian refused to accept that his efforts had been anything but false spectacles directed in secret by Lylia. "You didn't see how easily she manipulated me, how easily she showed me that she could make me do whatever she wanted."

"Uldyssian—"

"No, Serry! Had she wanted to, Lylia could have just as easily slain me herself, there and then. You saw how I was when you arrived . . . and it takes all I can muster just to keep standing."

Achilios grunted. "There, he has a point. Let's get him to one of the horses."

As his friends assisted him, Uldyssian noted how he was practically a baby, so weak had his struggle with the temptress left him. Yes, Lylia had not been jesting when she had said that he was nothing without her. It would merely take the others a little longer to understand that.

Unfortunately, they barely had any time left as it was. Sooner or later, someone would come for Uldyssian.

"Your points would have much more merit," Mendeln

commented as he held the reins of the animal while Achilios hefted Uldyssian into the saddle. "If they could but explain how it is that Serenthia and Achilios knew that you were in danger."

The trader's daughter quickly seized hold of that point. "Yes! That certainly doesn't sound like a ploy to work in her foul favor!"

"You've all got to see the truth!" he growled, tearing the reins from his brother's fingers. "It was all a trick! This was some game between demons and others in which I played the biggest fool of all!"

Bitterness overtaking him, he kicked the horse into motion and took off in the direction he had originally been heading. Achilios gave a shout, but Uldyssian paid him no heed. He had intended to flee rather than risk his friends and loved ones any longer and that was more important than ever.

But behind him, he quickly heard the sound of hoofbeats. Swearing, Uldyssian urged his horse to a full gallop. The path was treacherous and made more so because it was beginning to slope downward, but he did not care. Had the animal tripped and tossed him to his death, it would likely have been the best of ends. Not only would he no longer have to fear being twisted inside and out by manipulators, but Mendeln and the others would surely be safe. They had never been suspected of being threats or potential weapons by the Temple or the Cathedral. They would have nothing to fear.

"Damn you, Uldyssian!" Achilios shouted. "Hold up!"

The nearness of the hunter's voice startled him. He glanced back to see Achilios barely a length behind. Much farther in the rear were the murky forms of Mendeln and Serenthia, who had to share one mount.

"Return to Partha!" Uldyssian shouted back to the archer. "Take them with you! I want no more deaths, save maybe my own!"

"Talk sense, Uldyssian! You know that none of us will

leave you now, not after knowing what Lylia was and what she did!"

The other two were no longer in sight. Looking ahead again, Uldyssian saw a fork coming up. The path to the left almost immediately narrowed dangerously. Achilios would not be able to come alongside him.

Veering, Uldyssian entered. His horse nearly stumbled as the terrain grew more wild and uneven. Very few had obviously taken this route in years, but he did not care. All he wanted was for it to slow or stop those behind him.

Achilios's voice rose as the hunter swore at something. Uldyssian did not look back, concentrating on his own course. The clatter of hooves behind him lessened. His friend was clearly falling behind.

Then, out of the night, a series of low, thick branches cut across the trail. Uldyssian barely had time to avoid striking the first one dead-on. As it was, his right arm received a terrible blow that reverberated through his entire body. It was only by sheer will that the collision did not stun him enough to make him unprepared for the next and thicker branch.

A third and fourth one came in rapid succession. Uldyssian ducked left, then right, then right again. The last of the branches scraped the top of his head. He felt a trickle of moisture, undoubtedly blood.

But despite his injuries, Uldyssian's hopes rose. Achilios would see the branches and be forced to slow. It was a chance for the son of Diomedes to either gain on his pursuer or lose him altogether, for there were places coming into the dim moonlight that promised Uldyssian such cover that even the skilled hunter would be unable to track him.

Then, a crashing sound nearly caused him to steer his horse directly into a tree. Without thinking, Uldyssian slowed the animal. The noise had come from back up the path, about where the treacherous branches would be.

The branches . . . and if he had not slowed, *Achilios.*

Uldyssian reined the horse to a halt and listened.

Silence . . . no . . . the snorting of a horse. Not a horse in motion, though.

He started to urge his mount forward, then hesitated again. Still no sound other than the animal.

With an oath, Uldyssian turned back. He had wanted to lose Achilios, nothing more. If something worse had happened . . .

The dark path proved just as haphazard to climb as it had to descend. Bits of earth and rock broke away under the hooves. At one juncture, the horse's shifting nearly caused Uldyssian to slip.

Ahead of him, a massive form loomed. Achilios's horse, but without the hunter. Where—

A groan arose from somewhere to the left, where the path dropped precariously. Uldyssian's fears increased. He pulled up and, barely waiting for his mount to halt, leapt to the ground. Every muscle burned; in his anger, he had paid little mind to his own state and now his body was angrily reminding him that he could barely walk.

Yet, despite that, Uldyssian continued. He took both his mount's reins and those of the other horse and tied them to one of the very branches in question. Uldyssian then stumbled in the direction of the moan.

The irony of the situation did not escape him. Achilios had freely come to help Uldyssian and *this* was how his friend had been repaid. Guilt vied with shame now. He remembered even *hoping* that one of the branches would cause Achilios trouble, although not to *this* extent. Nevertheless, Uldyssian *had* been aware of the danger and yet he had not cared about anything but his own choices.

The descent was a slippery one, for the ground gave way with every step. There was still not a sound of the third horse and Uldyssian wondered just how far behind his brother and Serenthia were. He could not simply trust that if he dragged Achilios up to the path that they would come across him. Uldyssian had ceased believing in miracles, great or small.

Below him, he saw only darkness. It had been his hope that the hunter's blond hair would stand out, but that was not the case. Uldyssian grew more concerned. Was he even in the same area where his friend had ended up?

Then, some urge sent him toward the left, a place he would not have considered a possible location. Yet, when Uldyssian thought of turning back, he found himself unable to do so. Frowning, the farmer delved deeper.

A moment later, Uldyssian spotted a rounded form. He dove toward it, reaching out and cautiously turning it over.

As he did, a cough escaped the shape. "U-Uldyssian? Strange. I-I thought I was rescuing *you?*"

"I'm so sorry, Achilios! I never meant for this to happen! Can you stand?"

He heard the hunter grunt in pain. "Left leg's stiff, but I think it's just very sore. Give—give me a hand."

As Uldyssian did, his own body reminded him again of what it had suffered. The two men groaned simultaneously.

With a weak laugh, Achilios remarked, "W-We are a stalwart pair, eh?"

That brought a chuckle from Uldyssian. "I remember worse scrapes than this when we were children. We didn't groan at all, then."

"Children are more resilient than old men!"

They slowly wended their way back up. More than once, one or both of them slipped. As they finally neared the top, Uldyssian heard the slow clatter of hooves. Mendeln and Serenthia had finally caught up.

"I promised you that we would find them," his brother said with unnatural calm. "You see?"

But the woman did not waste time answering him, instead sliding down from the animal and racing, not toward Uldyssian, but rather *Achilios.*

"Are you all right?" she demanded, putting her arms around him.

"I'm fine . . . I am."

Serenthia did not seem convinced, but she finally turned to Uldyssian. "What happened?"

He opened his mouth to explain, but Achilios cut him off. "I was careless, Serenthia, that . . . that was all. Fortunately, my good friend realized something had happened and came back for me."

She ran her hands over the hunter's arms, chest, and face, not relaxing in the least until she was certain that his injuries were shallow. "Praise be. If something had happened . . ."

Uldyssian saw that Achilios had spoken the truth when he had said that Cyrus's daughter had finally turned to him. It was one of the few things to make him happy this night. The two were a good match.

He felt his legs starting to give. Keeping his tone level, Uldyssian said, "Let's get to the horses."

It took effort for both men to move, which caused renewed concern for Achilios from Serenthia. "Your leg!" she gasped. "Is it broken?"

"No, just bruised, like my pride. I should know to watch out for low branches."

"Give me your arm," Serenthia insisted. She all but seized the hunter from Uldyssian and guided him toward his horse. Despite all that he had been through, the scene momentarily made Uldyssian smile.

Other hands suddenly came to his own aid. "Let me help you," Mendeln said, appearing next to him as if by magic. "Put your arm over my shoulder."

His brother's presence both comforted and shamed him further. Uldyssian muttered, "Thank you, Mendeln."

"We are all we have left."

His words struck the older son of Diomedes to the core. He had concerned himself so much with Lylia that he had not truly considered Mendeln in as much depth as he should have. But with that renewed concern came again thoughts of what would happen to Mendeln and the others if they remained with him.

"The Torajan jungle," Mendeln remarked quietly, without warning. "The deepest of them all, southwest of Kehjan."

"What about the Torajan jungle?"

Blinking, his brother glanced at him. "Torajan? What do you mean?"

"You mentioned the jungle. Specified the Torajan one, southwest of the great city."

"Did I?" Mendeln pursed his lips, but did not otherwise seem startled at his lapse of memory. "It does strike me as a place to go, if we are not returning to Partha." He nodded toward his mount. "I have some provisions and water, enough for us to get started, at least. Admittedly, that and having two riders slowed us down during the chase."

Uldyssian could not hide his confusion. "You gathered supplies? When?"

"They were already prepared. I assumed that it was an extra mount you had to abandon at the last moment."

A glance at the horse ascertained for Uldyssian that it was not the dark beast ridden by Lylia. Yet what explanation was there for a fully laden animal found waiting just when his brother needed one?

Not certain whether this was a gift or bait of a sort, Uldyssian thought again of the jungles. There *was* merit in the suggestion, despite its questionable origin. Somehow, coming from Mendeln, he doubted that it had been planted by the demoness.

"The Torajan jungle," he muttered a second time, now with more conviction.

"You want to go there." It was not a question.

With a grim nod, Uldyssian replied, "I don't think I have any choice."

"*We* do not have any choice."

Uldyssian tightened his grip on his brother's shoulder, grateful for Mendeln's determination. "We."

"Do not mistake me, Uldyssian. I am referring to Achilios and Serenthia, too."

"What *about* us?" called the hunter from the saddle. Even as he asked, he pulled the trader's daughter up to him. No one questioned the change in riding partners.

"We plan to ride to the Torajan jungle," Mendeln answered bluntly before Uldyssian could properly phrase the suggestion himself.

"Torajan." Achilios cocked his head to the side. "The densest, most unknown, I've heard. Few folks there. Toraja is the only city, the people said to oil their skins black and file their teeth like daggers." He let out a laugh. "Sounds like a delightful place to visit."

Uldyssian thought of the journey ahead. They would first have to travel through other unexplored and possibly treacherous regions before reaching their destination. In truth, there was really only one, immense jungle, but, being territorial, men always divided up places and gave them different names. The Torajan jungle just happened to be a particular piece of the much vaster one. In fact, assuming they made it that far, it was very likely that they would not realize it for days after.

He could not imagine Serenthia in such a place. "Serry—"

"If you say one word about me staying behind, Uldyssian ul-Diomed, I'll teach you to regret it. There's no question as to whether I'm going."

Achilios grinned. "And you know that I won't argue with her, either."

Well aware of that, Uldyssian nodded. However, he needed them to understand the urgency of the situation. "If you come with me, there's no returning to Partha. I won't go back. There's too much of a chance that it'll be near impossible to leave again without arousing the entire town."

This brought an immediate acknowledgment from Mendeln. Seeing that, Achilios and Serenthia quickly acquiesced.

"I have some supplies and water," Uldyssian's brother informed them.

"I'll provide fresh meat along the way," the hunter

returned without a trace of conceit. All there knew that Achilios would be able to keep his promise with ease.

There really was only one thing left to say and Uldyssian had to say it now. "Thank you . . . I'd rather you all stayed back, but . . . thank you."

As Mendeln mounted, he said, "They will discover us gone come the dawn. We should be as far away as possible, by then."

No one could argue with that logic. When the Parthans realized what had happened, some of them would surely go out hunting for Uldyssian, at least at first. He hated abandoning them, but it was for their own good. They would soon find out that their gifts were, in truth, nothing. They would feel tricked and anger would replace adoration.

As he led the party off, Uldyssian thought of how violent that anger might become. Had he left the others in Partha, they might have become the focus of the townsfolk's ire. Certainly, they would have been run out of it. In a sense, Mendeln, Achilios, and Serenthia were better off with Uldyssian.

At least, for the moment.

Lucion stared into the bowl of blood, his gaze intense. He had seen everything occurring since first casting the spell in coordination with the other two demons. He had found *her*—Lilith—in the arms of the mortal knave and had planned well his sister's unveiling before the fool. What a delicious piece of work that had been. All her arrogance had been channeled into futile posturing and anger. She had turned on her own puppet, finally abandoning him.

And there, Lilith had made the greatest of mistakes.

The vision in the bowl finally began to fade, the result of the last of the life essence fading from the blood. Lucion could have redone the spell, but that would have required new bartering with Astrogha and Gulag, who would demand much more than the simple offering he had given them the first time. That was the trouble with both demons and humans; they always wanted more.

No, Lucion would handle this purely on his own, for the reward would be one too precious to share with anyone else. It would not be difficult to keep his two counterparts ignorant, for there was much that he had done since assuming his role as Primus of which they were unaware . . . of which even his *father* was unaware.

"Thank you for laying the groundwork, sister dear," Lucion rasped. He was also grateful to the late Malic and Damos, servants who had fulfilled their duties, whether they knew it or not. It had been a shame to lose both of them, but Lucion already had a notion as to a competent replacement for the high priest and there were always more vicious morlu. What was important was that by touching Malic's demon limb—which, knowing the cleric's greed and his sister's sense of irony, had been a foregone conclusion—Lilith had not only revealed herself, but had inadvertently removed, for a brief moment, any magical shields she had created.

It had been at that moment that a patient Lucion had cast the spell preparing the downfall of her plans. He had arranged so that when certain elements went into play, Uldyssian ul-Diomed would see her for what she actually was. It had all gone so perfectly. She had even played into it further, in her fury twisting the facts so that her puppet would not realize what was the truth and what was lies.

And leaving Uldyssian ready to be manipulated by him.

Lucion's grin widened—then faded as the sensation that he was being watched overcame him. He immediately searched not with his eyes, but rather with his mind, pretending to stare at the fading scene in the bowl while in actuality scouring the chamber of the other presence.

Yet, despite his best efforts, he found no one but himself. Still wary, the son of Mephisto quickly searched the temple for the other two demons. He found Gulag down below, the destructive beast tearing apart morlu for the simple pleasure of it. Other morlu attacked the demon with gusto, inflicting wounds that immediately resealed. This lack of success did not in the least dull their hunger; they simply attacked anew as Gulag ripped another of them apart. The demon of destruction knew that so long as he did not eat any of the broken bits, he could cause as much mayhem as he desired. The morlu would simply be resurrected with the end of the cycle, their slaughter only making them even more vicious warriors when next they fought.

Satisfied that it was not Gulag, Lucion sought then for Astrogha. The spider was a more cunning creature, being of Diablo's calling. If either of the two thought to spy upon him for their own goals, it would be that one.

But Astrogha remained in one of the shadowed corners he preferred, dining at this moment on what little remained of Brother Ikarion. Around the shrouded, multilimbed form, smaller arachnids scurried. They were of the essence of the demon, extensions of him that did his bidding while he waited.

Could it have been one of them? Lucion considered, but knew that even the Children, as Astrogha called the creatures, bore his taint. Lucion would have recognized him in them.

Still motionless, he surveyed the hidden chamber once more, but again found nothing. Demons, being what they were, were prone to unnatural distrust and Lucion knew that even he was not immune from that.

He finally pushed the incident from his mind. All that mattered was Lilith's puppet. She had set him on the path; Lucion would now complete his education.

Or, if the human proved to be nothing of value after all, *destroy* him.

In a place that was and was not real, a figure shrouded in black materialized. Around him there was nothing but absolute darkness, yet he showed no discomfort in being there. In fact, this was *home* for him, as much as anywhere had been in a thousand lifetimes.

He waited in silence, aware that the one with whom he needed to speak would come when it was right to do so. The shrouded figure understood that it might mean waiting for what seemed days, weeks, or even years, but that did not matter. In the other place, that which was called Sanctuary, no time would pass at all. He would return at the very moment that he had left.

Which still might be too late.

There was no sound, no wind. He felt solid ground beneath his booted feet, but knew that to be illusion. In this place, everything that existed was but the dreams of his teacher.

Then . . . from above there came illumination, a warm light that stirred his tired bones. He gazed up, his eyes immediately adjusting to the difference. Above him, what appeared to be an array of distant stars formed. At first, they clustered together, but quickly began to spread far apart.

As they did, they formed a vague shape. Like a constellation, the stars create a half-seen, gargantuan image that, to his trained eye, resembled a beast as mythic as himself.

"It is her brother that moves," the shrouded figure murmured. "*He* does not. That can only mean one thing . . ."

And in a voice that would have made even angels pause, the other replied, "*Yes . . . there will be death . . .*"

Twenty

Toward the jungles they rode, stopping only when necessity forced them. Uldyssian guessed that they made good time, although since none of them had ever been far from Seram before this insanity, they could judge only by Mendeln's recollections. Fortunately, Uldyssian's brother proved again that any map shown to him for a short period remained burned in his memory, for landmarks he told them to watch for started to appear.

The latest was a squat peak on the horizon, what Mendeln said the map's owner had called a volcano. None of them knew of such a thing, and when it was explained that this was a place where once burning rock had been shot out of the ground like missiles, the rest had looked at Mendeln as if he were mad. He, in turn, only shrugged.

Uldyssian often looked back, certain that this would be the time when he found the people of Partha hot on their trail. However, of the townsfolk there was still no sign.

"The volcano is the last landmark," Mendeln went on. "It, in fact, lies within the first portion of the jungle."

That caused Uldyssian to straighten in the saddle. "So, we're nearing the Torajan region?"

"No, we have quite a ride still, but at least we have reached the lowlands."

Indeed, they had all already noticed the change in climate. It was warmer and muggier. Uldyssian was covered in sweat and even Achilios and Serenthia showed signs of the heat. Only Mendeln appeared untouched. In fact, he seemed to bask in the change.

The two brothers had not yet discussed what was happening to the younger of them, the harsh journey leaving the entire party exhausted each evening. However, as Mendeln had indicated, the jungles would immediately offer some respite . . . even if also some new danger. Uldyssian hoped that, once they entered, he might find time to deal with his sibling.

The clothes that they had been given in Partha had begun to fray with overuse. However, since they had purposely avoided contact with civilization, there had been no opportunity to find new garments or at least properly clean their own.

Food and water were not a problem, just as Uldyssian had hoped. Achilios had supplemented their original supplies with game and the others had gathered berries. Most of the supplies from Partha were now gone, but in their place was bounty enough to keep them going for three days. In the meantime, they continued to gather more whenever and wherever possible.

The wooded lands with which they were so familiar had given way the past three days to brush. According to Mendeln, whom everyone assumed was correct, tomorrow would see the first hints of jungle vegetation.

With that in mind, they made camp just before sunset. Uldyssian felt very unprotected without even a few trees nearby, but the only other choices would have been either to retreat back half a day to a small grove or to ride night and day to reach the jungle. The others seemed just as ill at ease, which helped him not in the least. Aware that all he had believed himself to be had been false, Uldyssian knew that he could not help any of his companions should they now be attacked by Lylia or either sect.

Fortunately, the night passed peacefully, so much so that for once Uldyssian slept until dawn without once stirring. He rose refreshed, but also angry at Achilios, who had made certain not to disturb him even when it was Uldyssian's turn to take watch.

Ominous clouds covered the sky, but there was no rumbling nor did the wind pick up. Uldyssian eyed their surroundings with some trepidation, yet wondering if the clouds presaged something supernatural. However, their day's journey went so smoothly that, well before the sun fell, they not only reached the edge of the jungle, but, after several anxious minutes' consultation, the party plunged in.

The jungle both fascinated and repelled Uldyssian. He had never seen such bizarre plants or such lushness. The plant life seemed to be fighting with itself, each species seeking some sort of dominance.

"Everything's so green," marveled Serenthia.

Achilios slapped something crawling on his arm. "And so full of bugs. Never seen the likes of that thing."

"There is more life in one square mile of this realm than in twenty surrounding Seram," Mendeln declared.

No one asked how he knew, expecting that it was something he had learned from a passing merchant. Certainly Mendeln's comment struck Uldyssian as truth, especially as he swatted a variety of exotic and macabre insects from his own body. He began having great regrets for choosing the jungles in which to hide.

"Is there a river ahead anywhere?" asked the archer.

Mendeln gave it a thought. "Tomorrow. There should be one by day's end tomorrow."

"We should still have enough water."

The jungle canopy combined with the clouds to make them feel as if they traveled the entire day in twilight. The horses grew restive, not at all used to such terrain. Their tails constantly slapped back and forth as they did their best to also keep free of vermin.

Some of Lylia's story came back to haunt Uldyssian the farther he and his companions rode. She had said that the world had been created by a band of refugees gathered from both sides of a celestial conflict. Angels and demons together. Such a fantastic combination of power would definitely explain what he still considered an abrupt change in both climate and landscape.

It also reminded Uldyssian of just how tremendous the danger was to him and the rest.

When it finally grew too dark to risk any further movement, they simply stopped. Since the past few hours, they had been making their own trail, no easy task. Gathering their horses near them, they ate what food they had; then all but Achilios retired.

Uldyssian did not go to sleep for quite some time, the jungle continually unsettling in its differences from what he had grown up knowing. Strange creatures called out. Insects sang for mates. There seemed more noise now than during the day.

There came one moment when something of fairly good size passed within a short distance of their encampment. Achilios, still on guard duty, slipped into the jungle, but returned a few minutes later without a word. Still, Uldyssian thought that the archer acted a bit unsettled.

While the night was cooler than the day, it was still very humid. Uldyssian constantly felt damp. His hair clung to his head. The discomfort of the jungle fueled his misery and fears. Once more, he had chosen wrong. He should have kept to the regions he knew. At least the familiarity would have given him some respite.

By the time the light of another overcast day finally poked through the canopy, everyone was more than ready to move on. At the very least, the thought of reaching the river gave them hope. The river meant fresh water and a chance to see something over their heads other than thick leaves.

Again, they constantly swatted at insects. Everyone save Mendeln had welts, the denizens of the jungle for some reason not finding his pale flesh to their liking. Uldyssian's brother remained warmer-dressed than the rest, yet did not suffer as they.

Near midday, the party paused to eat and deal with other

necessities. The four shared what water remained, Uldyssian insisting that he be the last.

However, as he raised the shriveled sack to his lips, his eyes strayed to the surrounding jungle . . . and something thick like a tree that was definitely no tree.

He immediately lowered the sack for a better look . . . only to find no trace of the shape.

Serenthia noticed his reaction. "What is it?"

"I thought I saw . . . I don't know. I thought it was a tree, but . . ."

"But it wasn't?" asked Achilios, his expression unreadable. "Tall and thick of build, was it?"

It was enough to verify a suspicion of Uldyssian's. "You saw something last night. I thought as much."

The archer raised a hand in defense against his friend's words. "Hold on! I saw as much as you, which was little enough! Whatever it is, it's as much a part of the jungle as these trees and shrubbery!"

"Is it stalking us?" Serenthia asked, looking around.

Here Achilios looked contemplative. "At first, I would've said yes, but now . . . the more I think of it, the more it seems our friend is . . . *curious.*"

"That kind of curiosity, I don't like," muttered Uldyssian. "Do you think there's more than one?"

"I noticed only it. There could be more, but it strikes me as solitary."

"Like a predator?"

The hunter grimaced.

Their mood more pensive, they quickly mounted and left the area behind. For the rest of the day, the riders kept one eye on the path and the other on the thick vegetation. No one saw so much as a trace, but the consensus was that their mysterious companion had not yet abandoned them.

When at last they heard the rushing of water, Uldyssian greeted the sound with a contradictory mixture of relief and suspicion. He was glad to reach this latest landmark, but at the same time the river was a barrier of sorts. With something now tracking them, Uldyssian began to fear that all they had accomplished was willingly riding into another trap.

Achilios clearly thought likewise, for as soon as he had dismounted, he said in a low voice, "I'm going to find a place to cross quickly, if need be."

On the louder pretense of hunting, he hurried off. Uldyssian eyed Cyrus's daughter, who, in turn, pensively watched Achilios vanish into the unsettling wilderness.

"He'll be fine," the son of Diomedes said somewhat awkwardly, aware that his friend would not be in this situation if not for him. "Isn't that right, Mendeln?"

"Yes, he should be." But Mendeln's tone was distracted, which did not help the situation any. He seemed interested in something at the edge of the river, but what it was, Uldyssian could not say. Certainly not some huge creature such as he and the archer had noted. The only thing one generally found in rivers was fish.

As they filled their water sacks, Achilios made a swift return. Serenthia had to visibly hold back from running to him. The blond hunter smiled with more assurance as he reached the party.

"There's a *bridge*," he announced merrily. "Just a few minutes downstream. Looks worn and there are some planks missing, but the horses should cross over just fine."

Uldyssian took heart. Without hesitation, he said, "We make camp on the other side, then."

He received no objections. The four quickly remounted, this time Achilios taking the lead. They followed along the water's edge as the hunter dictated and very soon sighted the bridge in question.

It had been made from elements of the jungle around it. The planks had clearly been harvested from the local trees, the undersides still covered in bark. The craftsmen had skillfully shaved the other side flat. Three of the planks were broken or completely gone, but if the party guided their horses on foot, there would be little threat.

Strong vines and other long plants had been used to tether the wood together. Some sort of brown substance had also been added in between to keep everything solid. Considering their surroundings, Uldyssian thought that the builders had done the best possible. True, the bridge swayed a little under their moving weight, but otherwise held.

Once they were over, there was debate as to what to do next. Achilios wanted to remain near the bridge, and Serenthia seconded this. Uldyssian preferred a little more distance from it.

Mendeln . . . Mendeln left the decision to the others. As usual, he seemed lost in thought.

The archer finally pointed out that while Uldyssian was rightly concerned about their unseen companion, it was possible that something of a more immediate threat lurked nearby on *this* side. Conceding this, Uldyssian agreed to their remaining near the bridge.

They kept their campsite as compact as possible, huddling close to the animals and one another. Only Achilios left the vicinity, necessity forcing him to hunt. When he returned, the relieved greeting he received was more for his safety than the bountiful catch he carried.

The two creatures that the archer had brought with him were recognizable as reptiles, but none such as any had ever seen. They were huge—nearly five feet from the tips of their muzzles to the ends of their tails. One look at the terrifying teeth was enough to let the others know that these were generally predators, not prey.

Achilios quickly reassured them. "I was never careless. I assumed that there might be dangers by the river, but also game. I found this pair hiding among some reeds. I don't think that they were prepared for something like me."

Uldyssian studied them dubiously. "Are you sure that they're worth eating?"

"Some of the best meat I caught back home came from snakes and lizards! These, I suspect, will be like a feast in comparison!"

The two dead beasts had done what little else had . . . drawn Mendeln's attention. He touched one almost gently. "These are young. Juvenile."

"I thought as much myself," Achilios replied. "The big ones are probably three times the size." To Uldyssian, he added, "These were wet, as if they'd just been swimming. You wanted us to move farther away from the bridge and the river. I'd say that was an idea we should still act on."

They wasted no time in following the suggestion. Achilios, scouting ahead, located a place he believed far enough from the river reptiles' normal haunts. Even then, Uldyssian insisted that they ride a little longer, despite the darkness.

Achilios showed him another spot. Finally satisfied, they halted again. While Mendeln and Uldyssian gathered fuel for the fire, the hunter and Serenthia began the process of skinning and cooking the meat.

"Don't stray far from the camp," Uldyssian reminded his brother as they left, Mendeln's condition worrying him.

"I will take care. Do the same."

While there were plenty of trees, finding viable firewood was not so simple. The plant life had a constant moistness to it. Uldyssian picked what he could, cautious in his task lest some vermin or animal hiding in the bush took umbrage at his presence. Unfortunately, due to conditions, Uldyssian soon found himself disobeying his own orders to stay close; there just was not enough good fuel nearby.

In order to make up for the necessity of searching farther away, Uldyssian kept a careful eye on his position relative to the camp. This encouraged him to go yet farther afield, and gradually the pile in his arm grew to something useful.

Behind him, he heard the rustling of branches. Aware of how far out he had strayed, Uldyssian suspected that one of his friends had come in search of him. He turned around—

And dropped the firewood.

The behemoth stood half again as tall as him and more than twice as wide. At first, Uldyssian thought it a demon, for it had a vague resemblance to a man, in that there were two arms, a pair of legs, and a head, but beyond that was a creature so bizarre that surely it had not been born of his world.

Yet, if a demon, it was a very docile one. In fact, although its face was much in the shadow of the night, Uldyssian could for some reason sense that there was an intelligence there, one that was driven by more than the thirst for mayhem and blood.

The giant shifted slightly, but not in any manner that caused Uldyssian alarm. In that flash of movement, more details became apparent. The entire torso had a rough finish to it that reminded him of nothing less than wood. Indeed, one limb ended not in a hand or paw, but a great, thorny club upon whose flat head was etched runes of some sort. The other arm had a hand, but there was also a broad, sharply bent formation that started near the elbow and looked to the human like a living shield.

Two bat-wing horns rose above the head, which was squat and heavily browed. Uldyssian could detect no mouth or nose and the eyes were but deep crevasses.

The behemoth strode toward him at an oddly leisurely pace, and as it moved, there was not the least sound. Uldyssian understood that the rustling he had heard earlier had been purposely meant. The creature had wanted him to be forewarned.

"Are you . . . are you the one who followed us?" Uldyssian finally asked.

The figure did not answer. Instead, with astonishingly graceful movements, it went down on one knee before the human.

At that moment, Achilios's voice came from the direction of the camp. "Uldyssian! Where are you? Uldyssian—"

His gaze strayed toward the voice. A moment later, the archer appeared.

"Am I going to have to keep searching for you every time you stray away from a camp?" Achilios asked cheerfully.

Uldyssian's eyes widened at such a mundane question in

the presence of so astonishing a being as the jungle dweller. He looked to the creature for its reaction . . . and saw then why Achilios acted the way he did. The behemoth was gone, as if he had never been there.

The hunter noticed his tension and all humor vanished. "What is it?"

"It . . . *he*—" Yes, for some reason, Uldyssian knew his visitor had been male. "—was here."

"What . . . the thing tracking us?" Achilios started to ready his bow, but Uldyssian quickly put a stop to the action.

"He means no harm. He . . . he knelt there."

"Before you?"

Uldyssian wanted to deny that, but finally nodded. "He knelt before me." The farmer went into quick detail, giving even a cursory description of the creature. "And then, when I looked in your direction, he simply vanished."

"Which means that it was *you* specifically that he wanted to see, old friend. You."

"He may have never seen a human like us, that's all. It could've been Mendeln or you. Since Malic used her, Serenthia usually stays near the camp."

His companion did not see it that way. "There were plenty of chances to view me, especially that first time. Mendeln, too. He wanted to see you, Uldyssian. You must face that."

"There's no reason."

Achilios turned back toward the camp, but although he moved casually, the bow remained in his grip. "Only in your eyes, Uldyssian, only in your eyes . . ."

Despite their unusual night visitor having shown no hostility, Uldyssian did not rest well. He expected other strange beings to follow in the wake of the first, some of them surely with more sinister intent. Yet, the day came without incident. The party ate what was left of the meat, then set out again.

"How far is Toraja's region now?" he asked his brother as they rode.

"Several days yet," Mendeln replied. Further information, he did not supply and Uldyssian settled back into the saddle. He was already sick of the jungle and continually sick of himself.

Small creatures flittered through the branches, some of them recognizable, others almost as unsettling as the behemoth. However, Uldyssian sensed that these were simple animals, not some mysterious, intelligent being, such as had confronted him.

What did the confrontation mean? He refused to believe that Achilios was right. There was nothing to Uldyssian. He was a fraud, a mockery.

With such thoughts, he rode through the day and on into the night. They traveled late, it taking Achilios some time to find a clearing large enough for them to use as a place to sleep.

Uldyssian had no desire to leave the safety of the campsite, but, as ever, the hunt for firewood demanded it of him and the others. He tried to keep close, this time, but the pickings were slight and necessity once more demanded he widen his search.

With growing wariness, Uldyssian gathered one piece after another. Each moment, he expected the giant to confront him, but the closest he had come to an encounter so far was an irate toad the size of his head that leapt out from under a dead branch Uldyssian had just grabbed.

Uldyssian returned with his arms full and his mood as black as the night. He ate sparingly from Achilios's newest catch—some sort of huge rabbit—then slept fitfully until a hand shook him awake.

Believing it to be the behemoth, Uldyssian jerked back. However, it was only the hunter, awaking him for his turn on guard duty.

"Easy there!" Achilios muttered. "Are you sure you want to take watch?"

"I'd rather be up."

"As you like."

Uldyssian grabbed his sword and walked to the edge of the camp. As was the practice, he kept watch first from one vantage point, then, after a few minutes, quietly went to another. In this way, he also kept more alert.

Eventually, however, time did take its toll. When he was certain that he dared not stay on watch any longer, Uldyssian sheathed his sword and went to wake Mendeln, who was next. After Mendeln would come Serenthia and then Achilios again, if necessary. The three men would have preferred to rotate the night between them, but Serenthia had insisted, pointing out that she was just as capable with a sword as they were . . . a piece of training done at the insistence of her late father.

Uldyssian approached his brother's location . . . only to find Mendeln not there. That was not uncommon, necessity making its demands whenever it chose. He paused, aware that it could not be too long.

But after several minutes, there was still no sign of Mendeln.

Uldyssian tried to tell himself that it would only be a moment longer, but then that moment passed and still there was no hint of his brother's return. Uldyssian glanced at the ground and made out a single footprint. Not yet wishing to disturb the others, he drew his weapon and started in the direction that the print was pointing.

The way was troublesome. He was forced to hack at the branches. Twice Uldyssian whispered Mendeln's name, both times to no success.

His heart pounding faster, Uldyssian doubled his pace. Mendeln *had* to have come this way.

A slight sound from the side made him pause. When it came again, he turned toward it. It might be his brother, but it also might be something more sinister.

Or . . . it could be the creature again.

Despite the risk, Uldyssian pushed on. Mendeln was out

here; that was what mattered most. If it was the creature, then perhaps it could even help him. The thought seemed ludicrous, yet, Uldyssian knew that if he ran into the jungle dweller, he *would* ask it for aid.

From a slightly different direction came more movement. Uldyssian froze. A breath later, from yet a third direction there was a noise.

Whatever lurked out here, there was more than one.

Images of morlu swept through his head. Uldyssian considered retreating to the camp, but it was already too late. He heard more activity in the jungle, all of it converging on his location.

A murky form moved among the trees, then another, and another. Ducking low, Uldyssian closed on the nearest. Despite his failures, he had no intention of merely standing still as the fiends slaughtered him and his companions. Even if he could kill but one, it would be some small victory . . . and all Uldyssian could ask for.

The black form assisted him by veering his way. As the figure neared, Uldyssian noted that the head was unencumbered by the monstrous ram's skull helmet of the Temple's infernal minions.

Peace Warders, then. Or perhaps even Inquisitors. The Cathedral of Light had been oddly silent all this time, even though Uldyssian was certain that they were still interested in him.

His adversary was now so near that he could hear the rapid breathing. In fact, had Uldyssian not known better, he would have sworn that the warrior sounded uneasy, even a little frightened.

Taking some grim pleasure in that, Uldyssian maneuvered around the figure. A little more and they would both be in position.

The dark form abruptly changed direction again, this time striding directly toward where Uldyssian hid.

Unwilling to wait any longer, the son of Diomedes leapt at him.

What should have been a quick, mortal thrust failed utterly, his foe avoiding it by accidentally stumbling to the side. The two men became entangled. Their weapons fell at the same time. Uldyssian cursed, knowing that such a loss meant far more to him than it did the other. He was surrounded by enemy, his one chance to in some small way redeem himself now all but gone.

His fighting became more frantic. By sheer force alone, he managed to end up on top. His hands grappled for the guard's throat.

But before Uldyssian could make good his hope, other hands pulled him off of his intended victim. His arms were wrapped behind his back. The area filled with armed figures.

Someone brought a torch. It was thrust in his face, no doubt so that he could be identified for the sake of some high cleric of one of the sects.

"'Tis him!" a harsh voice declared.

Uldyssian expected to be clapped in irons . . . but instead his arms were released. The figures surrounding him stepped back.

And, one by one, they went down on their knees, leaving only the torchbearer. The man held the flames close to his own face as he stared at Uldyssian.

"Praise be! We've found you, Holy One!" blurted *Romus*.

Twenty-one

Mendeln had awakened with the feeling that someone had just called his name. At first, he thought it his brother and that made him stand up and look around. But when Mendeln saw no sign of Uldyssian, his suspicions grew.

Then, the voice called to him again.

This way . . . it beckoned. *This way . . .*

Somehow, he knew exactly which direction to go. Not for a moment did Mendeln hesitate. He had finally gone beyond fear of his situation. Fascination commanded him now.

Making certain that no one observed him, he slipped into the jungle. Curiously, Mendeln felt more at home here than he ever had back in Seram. It was as if this was a cherished place that Uldyssian's brother had forgotten until now.

Treading with a nimbleness generally absent, Mendeln dove deeper into the jungle. The voice kept urging him on, telling him where to turn. He followed its guidance with the utmost trust.

The insects kept their distance from him, just as they had since shortly after he and his companions had entered the lush land. They had quickly sensed the change in him, the *otherness*, that Mendeln was only just beginning to understand.

Despite the dark, he found it not at all difficult to see. Things were shadowed, true, but his vision was sharper than ever. Indeed, in some ways, Mendeln could see better than he did even during the day. His surroundings had more definition, more distinction.

Turn . . . turn . . . the voice commanded. Mendeln obeyed, took several steps, then waited.

But the voice gave him no more instructions.

Frowning, he took one more step—

And suddenly, in front of him stood a towering, glittering obelisk untouched by the incessant growth. It stood more than twice as tall as Mendeln and was made of what he suspected was obsidian. Mendeln had admired samples of the black stone that Cyrus had bought from a merchant and felt that what stood before him could be nothing else.

Yet, what drew his attention most was not the pointed obelisk itself, but what was carved on each of its faces.

More words in the ancient script.

They ran from the top to the bottom and as he eyed them, it almost seemed that they glowed faintly. Mendeln mouthed them as best he could, recognizing enough symbols to have some crude notion of what others might mean.

As he read, his understanding grew. Becoming excited, he poured over the first face again and again. Each time, the message proved clearer. His expression transformed into that akin to a child, for what was written there filled him with awe.

And so, Mendeln kept reading . . .

Uldyssian stared in disbelief at the man before him. Romus, the criminal. Romus, the converted.

"What—what're you doing here?" Uldyssian demanded. His gaze flickered to the few faces partially visible around them. He recognized most. They were *all* from Partha.

"When you were found missing, Holy One, we feared for the worst, especially after how it was for poor Master Ethon and his boy! Nicodemus, he's a good tracker and some of the others're, too! We took off as soon as we could after you!" Romus grinned. "But you're all right!"

"You shouldn't have followed," Uldyssian reprimanded the men. "You endanger yourselves . . . and what of your families?"

"All of us came willingly," someone else said. "And our families are all with us, of course! We'd not abandon them! Isn't that right?"

There was a chorus of ayes. For the first time, Uldyssian noticed that some of the figures toward the back of the dark throng were of slighter builds. Several were fairly short. He had not thought of them as women or, for that matter, children.

But *why* bring their families with them on such a desperate pursuit?

A sick feeling swelled up within him. *"Why* are you all here, Romus?"

"Why, to learn more from you, Holy One! To follow your path, wherever it takes you!" Others backed up his declaration.

"Don't *call* me that!" Uldyssian blurted. "Never that!"

Romus bowed his head. "Very sorry, Master Uldyssian! I'd forgotten, yes!"

Gritting his teeth, Uldyssian continued, "You uprooted your families to follow me? Are you mad?"

Almost as one, they shook their heads. He eyed the townsfolk, aware that his fury barely touched them. They were utterly insane, but could not see that fact.

But as it became apparent that he had nothing more to teach them, they would surely come to their senses . . . and then it would be *they* who would become outraged with him.

Mendeln still concerned Uldyssian, but he needed to deal with this band first. "How many are there of you, Romus?"

"A good quarter of Partha stands around you, Master Uldyssian, and others but await word of our success before they join us!"

The sick feeling swelled a hundredfold. Barely able to think, Uldyssian whirled back toward the camp. "Follow me."

"Always," murmured Romus.

Already regretting his choice of words, the son of Diomedes stalked away. Behind him came a mass shuffling of feet and the shaking of grass and branches.

As he neared the edge of the camp, Achilios—an arrow notched and ready to fire—stood sternly waiting. His face went through a contortion of emotions as he drank in what came in his friend's wake.

"What've you found out there? An army?"

"The Parthans . . . or, at least, a good number of them."

Achilios looked from one newcomer to the next. "Is there anyone *left* there?"

"Too few." Uldyssian looked around. "Where's Mendeln?"

"I assumed with you."

"I noticed him rise at one point," Serenthia piped up from near the fire. She, too, eyed the Parthans with wonder. "I fell asleep again almost immediately, though."

It was not what Uldyssian had wanted to hear. "He's been gone too long. I need to go back out and search for him."

Leaning close, the archer whispered, "Then, why not use this bunch? I can only assume that they came after you and, from the looks of those admiring expressions, if you asked them to hunt for your brother, they would!"

"And half of them would get eaten while the others would likely die of accidents or some disease! They understand nothing about the jungle!"

"Nor do we, but we chose to come here, nonetheless."

As the two argued, more and more people flowed into the tiny site. The women and children became apparent now, they moving closest to the single fire. Some of the men came bearing wood, which they used to build other fires for their numbers.

Numbers which continued to grow.

"You're certain that it's only a *part* of the town?" Achilios asked.

"For now . . ." Uldyssian spotted Bartha and her son. The woman smiled, then leaned down to point out him to her child.

The boy waved merrily. Uldyssian could not help but wave back, but his heart grew heavier. Their faith was based on lies.

Romus joined him again. There was absolutely none of the distrust and unsavoriness of the man Uldyssian had first viewed from a distance in Partha's square.

"Master Uldyssian, would it be permissible to have them start cooking meals and clearing more ground?"

"You have food?" He prayed that they did not somehow expect him to magically supply them with anything.

"Oh, yes! We knew that we might have to travel some distance to catch up to you! There are horses laden with packs just coming up now."

Sure enough, in addition to the throng of people, more than a score of heavily encumbered mounts were already in sight. Uldyssian could scarcely believe what he was seeing. How could such a large party have organized so quickly, much less followed him so expertly?

And they all expect the world from you, came the thought. *They all expect you to teach them to become more powerful than the mage clans . . .*

The immensity of what he was supposed to do— especially in light of the fact that it was utterly beyond him —struck Uldyssian so hard that he turned from the others without another word and stalked off into the jungle. He did not go far, naturally, but just enough to find some peace.

Or at least, attempt to. Even alone, Uldyssian could not escape his feelings of failure, of complete shame. They ate away at him with an intensity he had not experienced previously. In his mind, he heard the voices speaking so reverently about him, saw again the awed faces, both young and old. Bartha's son came unbidden to his memory, the boy and his mother seeing him as some mythic healer when the truth was that it had been a demoness who had given the child a new life.

Lylia. How she would have laughed at his situation. In

fact, it was very likely that she watched from somewhere, enjoying his torment and the eventual chaos when the Parthans discovered the awful truth about him. Lylia had called him *nothing* and he was seeing the truth of her words more and more with each passing moment.

Perhaps the temptress had even silently urged the towns-folk to this foolish trek, whispering in their ears that they had to follow. That could explain their swift and certain path. How better to ensure the greatest depths to his down-fall than to bring all the elements together herself? Once more, he had underestimated her retribution.

"You've got what you want!" Uldyssian shouted at the darkness. "Now leave me be!"

No one responded, of course. He had not expected it. She wanted him completely humiliated, perhaps even slain. If Uldyssian was torn apart by his enraged followers, Lylia would simply find herself a new puppet.

You thought that you would bring down the masters of Sanctuary. You thought that the Triune and the Cathedral of Light would fall, so that you could finally rid yourself of the demons of your past.

Uldyssian shuddered, thinking how he had even failed anew his lost loved ones. Their memories would be tainted by his debacle. When people recalled his family, it would be with curses and dark thoughts.

"I only wanted to help," the son of Diomedes muttered. "Only wanted things to make sense."

To his ever distraught mind, the calls of the jungle's nocturnal denizens began to sound like mocking laughter. Uldyssian almost turned and headed back to camp, but then recalled what he would find there. He looked at his shadowed surroundings, seeking *some* escape.

There is always the Triune. At first, the thought startled Uldyssian, but as he considered it, it made some sense. True, before it had been the suggestion of Malic, but now Uldyssian considered what would happen if he willingly walked into the main temple and gave himself over to them.

There would be no more running. The Parthans would initially grow angry when they discovered his duplicity, but then they would feel justice had been served. Uldyssian did not care what happened to himself at that point, only that no one else would be affected anymore.

Perhaps it would even be best to lead the Parthans to the Temple, too. Let them see the truth there for themselves.

Uldyssian grimaced. It said something for his state of mind that he had thought of such an outrageous thing for even a moment. Uldyssian shook his head, trying to clear it. What he chose to do concerning himself was one thing, but he would not lead the Parthans through any more deceit . . . and he would certainly not lead them to the Temple.

Yet, if Uldyssian intended to cut all ties with those following him, it behooved him to do so as quickly as possible. However, once he returned to the camp, they would be with him waking and sleeping. It would almost be better, Uldyssian thought, if he just never returned at all.

Never returned at all . . . Perhaps this time, it would work.

His feet began moving even before his mind registered the action. Uldyssian shoved aside the thick branches, pushing as fast as he could through the jungle. On the one hand, he knew that his abrupt flight was even more insane than the one from Partha, but on the other, it would catch everyone unaware. They would have no idea where to look, where to go. He defied their best trackers—Achilios included—to keep on his heels in this thick vegetation.

But as Uldyssian tore his way through the night, he began to wonder how far he would get without a mount. A horse could at least barge through the jungle easier and surely there would be emptier trails ahead where a rider could quickly pick up the pace. If only he had thought of taking one with him.

But that was something well beyond hope now. Unable

to do anything else and feeling as if all depended on him running and running until he could run no more, Uldyssian moved blindly through the jungle. Each moment, he expected shouts to arise and pursuit to begin . . .

A large form moved through the vegetation just ahead.

Uldyssian tried to slow, but the ground was soft and moist and his footing failed. He tumbled forward, landing on his face.

There was a heavy snort. A muzzle prodded his shoulder.

Wiping dirt from his eyes, Uldyssian beheld a towering white horse. Loose reins dangled under the thick neck. The animal was also saddled and Uldyssian could only surmise that this was a Parthan steed lost during the trek through the jungle.

Seizing the reins, he murmured to the horse, reassuring it that he was no danger. The mount actually seemed grateful to have him near, the unknown landscape no doubt putting it ill at ease.

Thanking his good fortune, Uldyssian started to mount—

"No! Keep away from it!"

Startled by the voice, his foot slipped free. The horse snorted violently, as if furious at the interruption. It moved away from the direction of the caller, pulling Uldyssian—who still gripped the reins—with him.

"Easy! Easy!" Forcing the animal to halt, Uldyssian turned to face the one who had spoken.

The face was so pale that even in the dark jungle he could make out some of its detail. The figure strode toward him with urgency, but also a smooth movement that seemed right at home in their surroundings.

"Mendeln?" Somehow, Uldyssian could not quite be certain that he was actually seeing his brother. This was Mendeln . . . but somehow, it was *not*.

"Uldyssian . . ." Mendeln's voice was low and so steady it again made the older sibling wonder if what he saw was truth or illusion. "Uldyssian . . . keep away from that creature. It is not what it seems . . ."

The only "creature" near them was the horse, which, to Uldyssian's eyes and hand, was certainly what it seemed. He could not entirely say the same for the figure approaching him. Memories of the foul work of Malic returned.

"Keep back!" he demanded of Mendeln. "Keep back!"

"Uldyssian . . . it is me."

"I don't know that . . ." His head pounded. *It cannot be him! It cannot be Mendeln! A demon, perhaps! Let him come closer. The knife . . . use the knife when he is in range . . .*

"Do not listen to him," the possible Mendeln quietly said. "I do not understand what he tells you, but I know it to be vile."

Uldyssian frowned. The pounding was becoming worse with each beat of his heart. "Who? Who are you talking about?"

"Yes, you cannot see him as he truly is. He leans at your shoulder, murmuring like a lover, but giving only hate. I think he knows her, Uldyssian, for he has a look to him akin to her."

Her. In Uldyssian's mind, that could mean only one person. "Lylia?"

"That is what you called her, yes. Do you also remember how you finally saw her?"

Uldyssian had once believed that he could never forget Lylia's true form, but now, no matter how hard he tried to summon it, he could not. "I . . . No . . . Keep away from me!"

"Uldyssian . . . it *is* me. Your brother Mendeln. Look closely. See my eyes. Remember all we have been through. Remember the pain and suffering of the plague as our father, mother, and our brothers and sisters were eaten away by it . . ."

As the figure spoke, his tone changed. It remained low and overall steady, but there were hints of deep pain that mirrored what lay within Uldyssian's own soul.

He knew then that this *had* to be his brother, not some demon wearing Mendeln's flesh.

That made him release the reins . . . or at least,

Uldyssian *tried* to release them. His fingers would not uncurl. In fact, if anything, they tightened their grip, defying his will.

The white steed snorted, then renewed its efforts to pull him away from Mendeln.

His brother uttered something unintelligible. The horse suddenly reared, shrieking as no earthly animal could. Its form twisted in a manner that should have snapped the spine in half. Yet, the creature seemed more furious than pained.

"Pull free now, Uldyssian! Lean against the reins and pull with all your will!"

Uldyssian immediately obeyed. His one hand continued to clutch the reins even as the enraged horse twisted as if made of soft bread dough. Its orbs blazed red and no longer had pupils. The mane coursing down its neck and over its shoulders had a thorny cast to it now. Despite its girth, the creature stood upon its hind legs as if more accustomed to moving in that fashion.

Still his fingers would not free themselves. Uldyssian tugged as hard as he could, using his strength to its utmost.

Then, something Mendeln had said came back to him. The younger brother had used the word "will," not "strength." Mendeln had been so specific . . .

Relaxing slightly, Uldyssian focused on wanting to be separated from the reins. He concentrated on his fingers, seeking *control.*

His grip loosened. He immediately whirled, his hand flinging free.

And as it did, the beast next to him lost all semblance of a horse. It reshaped, growing slightly smaller. The demonic aspects also transformed, at least, to a point, the thorns becoming hair and the body more human.

Before him now stood a tall, kindly figure with flowing, gray hair and a trim beard. As he smiled at Uldyssian, he extended his arms.

"You have proven very worthy, my son. Come and accept my blessing for your stalwart efforts."

"What—who are you?"

"Why, I am the Primus, of course." The smile dazzled. "But you may call me *Lucion*."

Uldyssian looked aghast. "The Primus! Lucion!"

The figure nodded. "Yes, Lucion . . . and I understand that the demoness Lilith has been spreading false witness concerning me."

"Lilith? You mean *Lylia*?"

"Lilith is her true name, an evil older than the world! She is the mother of deceit, the mistress of betrayal! You are indeed strong for having survived against her, my son."

From behind Uldyssian, Mendeln said, "Beware, brother. False images are legion where this one is concerned."

Before Uldyssian could respond, the Primus calmly replied, "Does that actually sound like the Mendeln you know? Have you not noticed the dark changes in him of late? There are more demons in the world than merely Lilith, my son . . . and one of them has cast his shadow over your sibling."

Uldyssian looked back. "Mendeln?"

"I am still me."

What exactly that meant, Uldyssian did not know. He considered all that he had seen happen to his brother. Mendeln had definitely changed, but was it for good or ill?

"I do not know you, demon," Lucion remarked, sounding much like a protective uncle to Uldyssian. "But your intent is clear. You would work at the soul of this worthy one, burrow into it through one of those nearest and dearest to him. That cannot be permitted. He is under my protection."

"'Protection'?" Mendeln returned. "As the high priest Malic sought to protect him with his spells of skin-flaying and his bloodthirsty morlu?"

"Exactly. Malic's. I regret his actions immensely. I was unaware that one so close to me had been seduced by demons. I had sent him to invite Uldyssian ul-Diomed to visit the temple as my guest. To be honored, nothing more." He considered further. "The morlu are an abomination created by what is called the Cathedral of Light, not the Triune. It must be from there that came the demon who turned poor Malic."

There was something about the Primus that made Uldyssian want to believe him. Yet, bits of what he said did not sound true.

"The only demon here stands before us, Uldyssian," Mendeln insisted, stepping between his brother and Lucion. "You must believe."

The master of the Triune shook his head. "His words are strong, embellished as they are by sorcery. For your sake, I fear I must remove the taint. I am sorry for your loss, dear Uldyssian, but there is no choice."

It took Uldyssian a moment to understand. When he did, he reached out in sudden panic. "No! Mendeln—"

A circle of silver light formed around the Primus, then immediately burst forth. It struck where Mendeln had been standing . . . and suddenly, Uldyssian's brother was no longer *there*.

Both Uldyssian and Lucion eyed the empty spot, then the Primus remarked, "Fear for your brother, Uldyssian. The demon is powerful. It has taken him away from here. It would be best if we joined together, fought him side by side—"

"No." Uldyssian was not quite certain what was going on with Mendeln, but he refused to believe that his brother had become some vessel for evil. He also now refused to believe much of what the Primus had told him concerning Malic. The high priest had been too adamant when it came to speaking about his master. Malic had been a loyal follower, not a betrayer, of the Primus. "No. Leave me alone."

"Dear Brother Uldyssian—"

Something pressed against Uldyssian's brain. Gritting his teeth, he stepped back from the glistening figure. "Leave me alone! I want nothing of you or the Cathedral of Light! Nothing at all!"

He spun from Lucion. Uldyssian was not certain just where he headed, but he knew somehow that he needed to be away quickly.

There was a flaring of light behind him, as he recalled had happened just before Mendeln's odd vanishing. Even as Uldyssian ran, he steeled himself for the inevitable.

The force that struck him was oddly cold. He felt as if his body was twisted inside out. His legs, his arms, refused to function, both the muscle and bone seemingly turned to jelly.

Uldyssian collapsed against a tree, then tumbled to the jungle floor.

"Perhaps you are actually nothing, as my sister said," Lucion commented clinically. "Perhaps there is nothing to Uldyssian ul-Diomed."

A tingling surrounded the barely conscious Uldyssian. The ground beneath him suddenly grew distant. Vaguely, the son of Diomedes realized that he was floating several feet above it.

"I shall have to test you and retest you to be certain. Let the morlu play with you, too. They tend to bring out the desire for survival, which should, in turn, bring out the power of the nephalem . . . if it is truly stirring within you."

"There . . . is nothing," Uldyssian gasped. "I am no . . . threat to you . . ."

"But you never were, human. I am Lucion, son of *Mephisto,* the greatest of the Prime Evils! Blood of my kind may flow through your veins, but it's watered down with the puerile emptiness of Inarius's ilk!"

Uldyssian's view shifted as he floated toward his captor. Lucion still wore the semblance of the Primus, but Uldyssian very much believed that the horrific glances he had seen during the earlier transformation had been nearer to the truth.

What had Lucion said of Lylia—*Lilith?* That she was his . . . *sister?*

"Yes, test you and retest you so that there is no mistake,"

the demon repeated. He smiled, and although his face was yet human, the sharp teeth and forked tongue were not. "And if you fail . . . then I will just feed you to the morlu . . . still alive, of course."

And although Lucion continued to smile, Uldyssian knew that he was not in any way jesting.

Twenty-two

Achilios had let Uldyssian go without hesitation, aware that his friend was under incredible pressure. The startling arrival of so many people from Partha was enough to even disturb the archer. He was astounded by their dedication, even to someone whom Achilios himself would have trusted with his life.

His thoughts were interrupted by Serenthia, who suddenly gasped and turned in the direction that he had last seen Uldyssian go. Barely had she done so when he, too, sensed that there was something terribly wrong going on.

Something involving Uldyssian *and* Mendeln.

"Stay here!" he shouted at her. Racing past startled townsfolk, the archer unlooped his bow. He knew that the jungle presented an even trickier environment than his native forest, but all he asked for was one clean shot. That was all he needed.

Providing, of course, that he was not already too late.

"I wanted to do this in quiet, in private, so that others with a possible interest in the nephalem would not take notice," Lucion remarked to his helpless captive. "There are so many others who would be interested, yes. And, besides, anything my dear sister takes an interest in is deserving of such caution."

His eyes were no longer human and reminded Uldyssian too much of Lilith's. They appraised the farmer again and again, seeking that which Uldyssian himself felt was not there.

"She is cunning and her mind is like a labyrinth. I wasn't too sad when I learned, centuries later, that the angel had cast her out into the endless void, never to return." He laughed. "Well, 'never' is a relative term with her. Inarius should've known better. He should have slain her, but his kind always was too sentimental."

A sudden crackle of blue energy engulfed Uldyssian. He let out a cry, but the sound was smothered.

If this told Lucion anything, he did not reveal it. Instead, the demon nodded to himself, then said, "There remains only the question of your brother and what has a hold over *him*. I lied about so many things, but not that. Something of a demonic nature does hold sway over him . . . and yet it's also something else. Perhaps, I'll make a study of both of you. Would you like that?"

"Damn you!"

"Thank you, I already am. Shall we go?"

Lucion smiled wider and the world around Uldyssian took on a hazy, insubstantial appearance. Somewhere in the background, the faint images of the interior of some great structure—the main temple, Uldyssian assumed with a shock—began to form.

And, at that moment—the scene illuminated by the energy surrounding Uldyssian—a feathered bolt struck the Primus directly in the throat.

Lucion's head swung back from the force. Blood spilled from the ugly wound. The head of the arrow lay embedded so deep it was a wonder to Uldyssian that it had not come out in the back.

"Uldyssian!" called Achilios. "Try to free yourself!"

He had been attempting just that since his capture, only to fail miserably each time. Uldyssian had used Mendeln's advice again, but to no avail. He began to wonder if it had merely been by chance and whatever power his brother had wielded that he had escaped then. As ever, Lylia's mocking words returned. He was nothing . . . nothing . . .

A whistling sound presaged another arrow soaring at

Lucion. Knowing Achilios's skill, Uldyssian had no doubt that it would hit exactly where the archer intended.

But at the last second, Lucion's hand caught the bolt just an inch from his chest. He easily snapped it in two and, as the pieces fell, reached up to take the one buried in his throat.

The Primus pulled at the arrow. With a horrific sucking sound, it came free. He inhaled and the blood dripping from his wound receded into the gap, which then healed shut.

From somewhere to Uldyssian's left, Achilios let out a curse, then growled, "Not again!"

Lucion eyed the blood still on the tip of the arrow. His tongue shot out and lapped up the red liquid, leaving the arrow perfectly clean. The demon chuckled as he tossed the shaft to the side.

"Able to make a perfect strike at night even from a bow enchanted to miss! A fine morlu you would make," he said. "Would you like to join us?"

The Primus gestured. Achilios grunted. Uldyssian heard the shuffling of feet and guessed that the hunter was being forced forward.

"I've not had this much activity in centuries," their captor mocked. "I'd forgotten how delicious it was doing it myself instead of relying on fallible mortals . . ."

Without warning, a different missile came at him. However, where Achilios's arrow had struck true, this one—a rock—bounced away after hitting what seemed an invisible shield around Lucion.

That, though, did not stop a storm of more rocks, bits of wood, and other, unidentifiable objects. Many were tossed with terrible aim, but several others would have hit their target if not for the same force that had repelled the first rock.

And from all through the jungle, completely surrounding the trio, the people of Partha, led by Cyrus's daughter, emerged.

"Let him go!" shouted Serenthia. "Let them both go!"

Others took up the shout, Romus among their leaders. The townsfolk brandished crude spears, axes, and pitchforks, the weapons of the common people. Several more objects flew at the Primus, with the same lack of result.

For the first time, something other than arrogance filled the demon's visage. He surveyed the throng with tremendous interest.

"Impressive!" Lucion boomed. "I didn't sense their coming until just before the first stone cast!" He eyed Uldyssian again. "Could it be you . . . or maybe your brother?" The gaze narrowed. "No, I think it has something to do with you, pawn of my sister! I sense a connection spreading between *all* of these others, but originating . . . yes, that would make sense . . . it would have to be because of . . ." Lucion trailed off in thought.

Apparently taking this for hesitation, Romus let out a yell and led several of his fellows forward.

Lucion stared at his oncoming attackers with bemusement.

The ground around him erupted. People, trees, dirt— nothing escaped. An explosion ripped apart the jungle for yards around. Screams filled the air and the night was momentarily blindingly bright.

Uldyssian did not fear for his own life, for not only would he have rather died at that moment, but the demon kept him protected. He was the only one, though, and his heart wailed at the thought of what was happening to all those who had come here because of him.

It seemed to never end and yet, Lucion's spell in truth lasted but the blink of an eye. When it was done, there stood not a tree within twenty paces and the ground not only crackled black, but underneath there was a fiery glow, as if the demon had, in the process, summoned up the anger of the world. The jungle had always been hot and humid, but now the very air burned.

"A taste of what is to come," Lucion stated to no one in particular. "When this world is made over in our image."

Moans arose. Uldyssian smelled something horrible, something that he had not smelled since his family's death. The acrid stench of burning corpses. Yet, these were not plague victims being incinerated to protect the living; these were innocent folk who had perished for no good reason but that they had believed Uldyssian's naive promises.

Something within him wrenched tight. An overwhelming tangle of emotions swept through Uldyssian. He relived every mistake, every catastrophe. With an anguished cry, Uldyssian struggled to free himself.

Struggled . . . and failed again.

"I see you're as anxious to return to the Temple as I am," jested Lucion. The towering figure surveyed the carnage he had caused. The fiery cracks in the ground illuminated his face with ghastly perfection. "And since there really is nothing of value left here, we might as well go now, don't you think?"

But even as he spoke, another shaft struck him in the chest. However, unlike the first, this one bounced off with no visible effect.

Out of the corner of his eye, Uldyssian saw Achilios quickly notching another arrow. The blond archer kept his gaze on the demon as he worked.

Lucion tsked. "I said that you would make a splendid morlu, but to do that, you must die."

Achilios fired.

"And so you shall," continued his target.

The arrow curved around in midflight. Achilios stumbled back, one arm going up in defense—

The bolt caught him through the throat, exactly where the demon had been hit . . . but where Lucion was a demon, Achilios was only mortal.

A scream echoed through the ruined jungle. However, it came not from the hunter, but rather Serenthia. As Achilios crumpled into a limp heap, Cyrus's daughter ran to him. She caught him just before he would have struck his head on an overturned tree.

"Oh, Achilios, no! No!"

The man in her arms had no words for her, and his gaze was empty. He had died instantly, although not due to any kindness on Lucion's part.

The Primus now extended a hand toward Serenthia. "How delicious! Come to me, my dear. Let me comfort you in your loss."

She struggled to maintain hold of Achilios as she was pulled forward by the demon's sorcery. Lucion's power dragged her across steaming, molten gaps and ragged patches of burnt ground. Serenthia was finally unable to maintain her grip and the limp body of the hunter was left behind.

It was all coming to an end now. Uldyssian's humiliation had brought with it the death of his friends and his brother—he had to assume that Mendeln was no more or else where *was* he?—and Serry was, like him, to be a victim of another sort.

It might have been different if the power he had thought he wielded had been truth. Then, Uldyssian could have at least tried to make a stand, possibly save his friends from sharing his fate. However, he was no threat to Lucion. He was nothing . . . nothing . . .

His gaze passed from the desperate Serenthia to Achilios's cold body and back again. They had fought for him, more than once. They had believed in him, just as so many had.

One of the Parthans suddenly ran up to help Cyrus's daughter. Romus, face disfigured far more than ever, took hold of her with burnt hands. Another Parthan joined him, then another. Their added mass slowed but did not halt her progress. Lucion merely laughed at their antics.

But as he laughed, a score more Parthans tried to charge him again. This time, they had weapons other than their axes and pitchforks.

They used what some would have described as magic.

Around the Primus, the air became a cornucopia of violent

energies. Rocks appeared out of nowhere. A tree limb went flying at Lucion's handsome face, only to go bounding back.

Among the fighters was Bartha, who had tears in her eyes and a grim set to her mouth. Uldyssian noted with dismay that there was no sign of her son. He prayed that the boy was somewhere farther back, unharmed.

"The potential is there," Lucion commented, nodding at his attackers in approval despite their dismal results. "But I think I'd prefer to test just the one and train others from scratch. Less to unteach!" He said the last with a dark gaze at the Parthans.

The jungle floor burst open around Bartha's group. The fiery, molten earth below it engulfed her and several of the others. Their screams filled Uldyssian's ears—

"NO!" he screamed at the top of his lungs. His eyelids clamped together tightly as tears coursed down over his face. He beat his fists against the soil, repeating his anguished call. "NO!"

It took Uldyssian a breath to notice that the rest of the area had fallen into silence again. He worried that the carnage Lucion had earlier wrought now faded in comparison to what had just happened. Tears continuing to streak down his face, the son of Diomedes opened his eyes.

To his surprise, he beheld Bartha and the others untouched. A wall of formerly molten ground rose around them, yet, it had obviously cooled completely, for one of the Parthans began cracking open the side with his foot and fist.

Uldyssian gave thanks for the miracle, then discovered two more. One was that Serenthia no longer helplessly moved toward Lucion. Instead, Romus and the others with him even now carried her away.

The final—and to him in some ways most astonishing—miracles concerned himself.

Uldyssian no longer floated in the air. Only now did it register with him that he had been pounding his fists, that he knelt on the ground.

That *he,* not Lucion, had made it so.

Lilith had lied to Uldyssian . . . which should not have surprised him. He could guess now that the reason he had been so unable to fight her had been because of what he had once thought her to be. She had used that to crush his spirit further.

Uldyssian pushed himself up on one knee. His gaze grew terrible as he looked at his persecutor. The treacheries of Lucion and Lilith combined in his mind to further fuel his determination.

"No more . . ." the once-simple farmer intoned, rising. "No more of this."

The Primus did not smile now and there was that in his face that hinted more than ever of his true, monstrous self. "You'd do well not to provoke me, mortal. This kind and civilized exterior is a shell, nothing more. You do not want to anger what lurks just beneath . . ."

Shaking his head, Uldyssian returned, "You have it all wrong, Primus . . . Lucion . . . brother of Lilith. You should be careful not to provoke *me,* anymore."

This caused the demon to howl with laughter, but Uldyssian could almost swear that there was something hollow to that laughter. There had been no reason why Lucion would have lessened his control over the human. Uldyssian had freed himself and that meant that the gift . . . no, *birthright,* Lilith had called it . . . flowed through him much as he had once believed it. Perhaps not as powerful and as malleable as it had seemed, but certainly Lilith *had* lied when she had said he was nothing without her.

"Leave now," Uldyssian suggested sharply. "Leave now or finish it here."

Lucion ceased laughing.

The ground erupted anew, this time the force of it all centering around Uldyssian. Hot ash rose up, covering him. Scalding earth bathed his body. As the ground crumbled, he started to sink beneath it.

Uldyssian took one stubborn step toward his adversary.

When that succeeded, he took another. He paid no mind to the ash, to the fire-hot ground . . . and because of that, they did not harm him.

In the back of his thoughts, Uldyssian sensed those who had survived the demon's assaults gaining their own strength from his renewed confidence. There were more alive and well than he could have hoped. That, in turn, gave Uldyssian the impetus he needed to take another step, then another.

And when he had crossed half the distance, it was to note with amusement of his own Lucion taking an unconscious step *back*.

"Will you not give me your blessing after all, Primus? A blessing such as your servant Malic gave the good Master Ethon, his son, and others?" The amusement vanished, replaced by disgust. "You seem to favor it . . ."

"I will give you my blessing," the demon croaked, his voice no longer at all cultured or even, for that matter, sounding human. "And then . . . I will dine on your entrails and drink your blood from a cup fashioned from your fragile skull . . ."

And as he spoke, the facade of humanity fell away. Lucion's aspect grew terrible to behold, even more so to Uldyssian because there was resemblance to Lilith after all. Lucion stood half again taller than the demoness and much broader, but he, too, had the thorns that acted as mane all the way down his scaled back. Yet, where she had only had one tail, her cursed brother had *three*, all spiked from top to tip with daggerlike projects longer than Uldyssian's hand.

Lucion took a step toward him again and, in doing so, revealed that he also had the hooved legs his sister did. His hands were different, though, for the fingers on each numbered more than five and the claws were like those of a badger, but dripping with what surely had to be poison.

And of the face, only the eyes were identical. Lucion, who played at being the handsome, schooled cleric, was a beast whose head more resembled a toad. His mouth was wider than the top of his skull, and row upon row of teeth greeted Uldyssian. The brother of Lilith had no nose, not even nostrils, and his chin was hooked so sharply in the middle that Uldyssian could almost imagine it being used as a weapon.

"Well?" rasped the demon, his grin literally growing from ear to ear . . . the latter long and wide, as if for a creature even larger than he. "Come, Uldyssian ul-Diomed . . . I'll give you a blessing, definitely . . ."

Yet, although Lucion was daunting, he no longer instilled fear in the man before him. Only loathing touched Uldyssian, loathing that any such abomination could be allowed to exist in his world long enough to taint it. Surely, it was wrong that such as Lucion walked Sanctuary's—yes, that was the name of the world—lands . . .

"Then give it to me," he demanded of the demon. "Give it to me."

Almost immediately, Uldyssian felt a churning in his stomach, as if the organ itself sought to escape. That sensation was joined by a similar one in his lungs, then his heart. He had no doubt that if he let it happen, then all of them would rip free.

He wondered if Lucion understood what the spell felt like. Would the demon suffer so?

As if his thoughts were action, he saw Lucion suddenly clutch his chest. The demon looked perplexed. Pain was recognizable in his unsettling eyes.

He stared at the human. The turbulence in Uldyssian's own system ceased. Lucion recovered simultaneously.

The demon hissed. "Little tricks for little creatures . . ."

Seeing no reason to reply, Uldyssian strode closer yet. He did not know what he intended to do, just that it had to be done and done quickly.

Curiously, the less distance between them, the less Lucion struck him as even a threat. Uldyssian felt a surge of strength adding to his own and knew it to originate from the Parthans and Serenthia. They not only had continued to believe in him throughout all of this, but more than ever were certain that he was what they had thought him.

Understanding and appreciating that, Uldyssian lunged for his horrific foe. What he did now he no longer did for himself in the least; all he cared about were those who followed him.

His audacious attack left the demon stunned, but only for a second. As the two collided, Lucion's tails flung forward like that of a scorpion's. They struck Uldyssian across the back—especially the spine—again and again, sinking all the way inside. Yet, each time, they were immediately repelled and the wounds would heal in scarcely a heartbeat. Uldyssian felt a slight discomfort, nothing more.

He managed to seize one tail and, despite the spikes thrust through his palm, tore it off. The demon let out a howl of both pain and outrage. Uldyssian contemptuously threw aside the appendage, then sought another. However, Lucion withdrew them, no doubt to use when it was less likely to lose one or both in the process.

"How was she, my sister?" the master demon murmured as the two of them locked together again. "Was she all that you ever dreamed? All you ever lusted for? Lilith is every creature's desire, you know. She had so many lovers besides you, but only one did she love . . . oh, but not you."

Uldyssian let Lucion talk. The pain of Lilith's false love still stung deep, but not enough to sway him from what he needed to do. He cared only about stopping his horrific foe.

"She loved only one, yes . . . and his name is Inarius! You recall it? Did she mutter it in bed when you were with her? Best to bend down before me, human, than before *him!* He would not be so gracious! No, not at all . . . you would be as nothing to him, nothing at all!"

Nothing. There it was again. Ever Uldyssian was nothing to such beings, just as all humans were nothing to them.

No more, he suddenly thought. *I . . . we . . . will no longer be* nothing *to such as this!*

"I—will—bend to *no one!*" Uldyssian finally retorted. He gripped the demon by the throat. Whatever he hoped to do, he had to do it now. The longer they struggled, the more likely that Lucion would find some weakness to exploit. "Least of all one who is nothing to *me!*" Lilith's words came back in a rush, only now he saw them as reversed. He was not the nothing; she and those like her brother *were.* "*You are nothing, Lucion, and that is all you deserve to be!*"

The demon started to laugh again, but the laughter turned into a hideous choking. Lucion clutched at the hand holding his throat, but not because Uldyssian squeezed tight. In fact, the human only gripped it enough to keep his monstrous adversary at bay. An overriding desire filled Uldyssian, a desire to see his words become fact.

"*Nothing,* Lucion . . . *nothing!*"

Uldyssian blinked. A pale cast swept over the demon. The harsh colors of his body grew faded, as if somehow bleached. Lucion's tails abruptly renewed their frenzied assault, but now they did not even pierce the human's skin. In fact, for all their effort, the tails felt like light touches of wind . . . and, gradually, not even that.

And then Uldyssian noticed that he could see part of the dark jungle *through* the demon. That encouraged him to press further. He utterly ignored Lucion's desperately scratching claws, which were no more than the least pinpricks now.

At last, the demon cried, "Beware, Uldyssian ul-Diomed! She is not through with you! My sister never lets go of a toy until it's chewed ragged! But I know her ways! I can help you! I can act as your guide! I will bow to you, call you 'master'! Just listen—"

"I hear nothing but the calls of the jungle creatures," Uldyssian replied with a shake of his head. "And the whisper of wind, now already dying down. *Nothing* more."

Lucion's mouth moved, but now no sound came from it.

Under Uldyssian's fingers, scale gave way to empty air. The demon was now transparent. His face wore a contorted look of fear, for he did and did not understand what was happening. What Uldyssian was doing was impossible for any human . . . but not for a nephalem.

And, at last, the demon became as Uldyssian had said . . . *nothing*.

The son of Diomedes stood there, his fingers still bent as if holding a throat. Slowly, Uldyssian straightened them, then studied the palms as if seeking some great truth there.

He belatedly sensed a figure cautiously approaching him from behind. Already aware just who it would be, Uldyssian slowly turned. Even then, Romus let out a squeak and stepped back several paces.

"Forgive me, Master Uldyssian! I meant no treachery, coming up on you that way! It's just . . . aye, it's just that you were standing so still there . . ."

"It's all right, Romus. It's all right."

"Is it over?" asked the Parthan "Is the demon dead?"

"No . . . he just *isn't,* at all."

Romus only looked more confused.

With a sigh, the son of Diomedes said, "The demon is gone forever. We're all right."

However, even as he said the last, Uldyssian knew that it was otherwise. Around him, still illuminated by the blazing cracks in the ground, lay the wreckage of the jungle and, worse, the bodies of too many who had followed him here. Some he could see were beyond help, but there were others still clinging to life . . .

Without thinking, he walked past Romus and went to the first of the injured. The man's face was vaguely familiar to Uldyssian, but otherwise he only knew him as a Parthan. Still, that was enough, and just the thought of what this one soul had suffered was enough to make an already drained Uldyssian shed tears again.

He reached down to try to better position the injured man . . . and a soft glow formed under his palms.

The Parthan gasped, his chest swelling to full capacity. Uldyssian nearly pulled his hands away, but then he noticed the bruises and cuts on the man's face begin to recede. A shoulder that had been bent as if the arm had become separated seemed to mend.

Uldyssian kept his hands where they were until the last of the wounds had faded and the Parthan breathed normally. As he rose, he suddenly noticed that there stood around him other Parthans, all staring in rapt awe.

Reaching out to one with a bleeding scar across her face, Uldyssian repeated the process. When he took his hand away, she, too, was healed.

And so he went from person to person, from those surrounding him to those lying prone on the ground. Uldyssian tried to find those most in need of his assistance and help them first.

How long he took, he only understood when the first light of day filtered through the thick foliage. Exhaustion filled Uldyssian, but so did excitement. He had managed to help all those who could be helped, despite Lilith's claims to the contrary. Doing so thrilled him more than even overcoming Lucion.

But that thrill evaporated when he finally confronted Serenthia. She still cradled Achilios's head in her arms. Uldyssian had almost approached her once during his night's work, but had felt guilty, knowing that his friend had perished trying to rescue him. Worse, he had known that Achilios was beyond his powers.

There stood another with her, one he had also almost thought dead. Mendeln, as pale as the dead archer, stood somberly over the lovers. He eyed his brother as Uldyssian neared, nodding once.

"You did it. She lied."

"She lied." He started to ask Mendeln about his part in the final moments, but Serenthia chose that moment to look up at the older brother.

"Uldyssian . . . is there nothing . . ."

In truth, he had tried once this night to do the unthinkable, tried once, and failed. Uldyssian was not so certain that had been a bad thing, even if it meant no hope for his friends. "I'm sorry. Nothing."

She nodded in understanding, which made his heart ache more for her ordeal.

Mendeln looked past his sibling, to where the Parthans were building a great fire. As was their way, they were preparing to burn the dead. "They should bury them." His gaze grew intense as he focused on the pair again. "At least, we should bury Achilios, do you not agree?"

Although slightly unsettled by Mendeln's determined expression, Uldyssian nodded. That was how it was done in Seram, save when disease demanded otherwise.

Still, it was not his decision to make. "The choice is yours, Serry—Serenthia."

She did not hesitate. "He would prefer to be buried, to be a part of the jungle, if not a forest."

Mendeln smiled grimly. "I know just the place . . ."

The brothers carried Achilios themselves, with only Cyrus's daughter following. When Romus and a few others sought to come, Uldyssian forbade them. This was a personal matter.

He allowed Mendeln to lead. After some trekking through the thick underbrush, Uldyssian's brother paused at a lush region nearby which could be heard a rushing stream. Tall, thick, and healthy trees surrounded the area. Uldyssian felt a sense of calm pervading the area and immediately approved of it. Serenthia, too, acknowledged Mendeln's choice as the correct one.

With tools borrowed from the Parthans, the pair dug the grave. Uldyssian considered seeing what he could do with his abilities rather than his hands, then thought how Achilios deserved more effort than that. The ground was soft and surprisingly easy to remove. They soon had a hole deep enough to make certain that no scavengers would dig the body out.

After gently depositing the hunter within and filling up the site, the sons of Diomedes and Serenthia stood in silence. No words were said, for words were inadequate for moments such as this, at least to them. Their souls spoke to the lost one, each bidding him farewell in their own way.

It was Serenthia who finally broke the spell, the dark-tressed woman suddenly turning to Uldyssian and crying in his arms. He held her much the way he had held his little sister during her last days. Mendeln politely turned his face away, at the same time muttering some final message to Achilios.

And then . . . it was over.

Twenty-three

It took the Parthans the rest of the day to deal with their own dead. Uldyssian and the others attended, naturally. The deaths all struck him hard, but worst were the ones he knew.

Despite his attempt to save her, Uldyssian found out that Bartha was yet among the victims. Her heart, broken by her son's death, could not survive the aftermath. They found her unbreathing, the boy cradled in her arms. In death, they had a peace to their expressions that was complemented by a love between them one could still see. The boy and his mother were laid on the pile together and burned as one.

And as they vanished in flame, the sadness in Uldyssian changed to fury again. Fury at Lilith, at Lucion, at those like the Triune and the Cathedral, who cared for nothing but their dominion over all else at such costs.

Try as he might, Uldyssian could not quell that fury. By the time the last body had been properly burned and the day had once more faded, he knew that there was but one course of action, a course that, for the moment, had a particular focus.

"The Triune must be brought down, Mendeln," he said when they were alone. "I may be mad to think it, but I plan to do what I can to see their temple crumble. They've done too much to too many of us."

He expected his brother to dissuade him, but, instead, Mendeln only said, "If that is what you wish. I will always stand by your side, Uldyssian."

Uldyssian was grateful, but could not let it just end there. "Mendeln . . . Mendeln . . . what's happening to you?"

For the first time, a troubled expression briefly crossed his brother's countenance. As Mendeln buried the emotion again, he replied, "I do not know. I can only tell you that I do not fear it anymore . . . and that, so long as I can, I will do whatever it allows me to help you."

Staring into his brother's eyes, Uldyssian saw no guile there, only honesty. He wanted to demand more of Mendeln, but also saw that to do so would tread on ground neither were quite ready for just yet. When he instead patted Mendeln's shoulder, his sibling looked both relieved and grateful.

"That's all I can ask," the older brother said. "That's all."

He expected Serenthia to condemn him for even thinking of such a plan—Achilios having already paid the price—but the hunter's death had, instead, galvanized the trader's daughter. When Uldyssian told her what he had decided, she showed no hesitation in agreeing.

"My father's dead because of them. Achilios, who foolishly loved me and who I loved for too short, is dead because of them. You want to bring down the Triune . . . and the Cathedral, too . . . and I'll be there, Uldyssian! All I ask is that you help me to learn as much as I can, so that I'll be able to stand up at the front of the struggle and pay them for what they've done!"

Her vehement response worried him, for Uldyssian did not want Serenthia throwing herself into danger so that she could rejoin her lost love. He would have said as much, but, Serenthia suddenly turned to the remaining Parthans and shouted, "Uldyssian has spoken! The Triune must pay for all this! We will tear down the temple! Who is with us?"

There was a moment of silence as Romus and the others drank this in . . . and then determined cheers broke out. "Down with the Temple!" and "Death to the Triune!" filled the jungle.

"Someone must summon the others!" shouted the former cutpurse. "They'll want to join us!"

And, with that, what had began as but a bitter notion in Uldyssian's head became the start of an uprising. He stared at what he had wrought, startled to also realize that he did not regret the fervor of those with him. They were not his followers, not in his opinion, but companions, comrades in suffering who had as much right as him to demand justice . . . even against demons and other forces.

"This world is ours," he muttered, his words drawing the attention of the shouters. They grew silent, wanting to hear him better. "We are its children! Our existences are intertwined!" He hesitated. "And, most of all, we are our own masters! Our lives are ours to control, no one else's! That is our *birthright* as much as the powers growing within us! Our birthright!"

This brought renewed cheers. Uldyssian let it go on for a time, then raised his hands for silence.

"Romus!" he called. "Are there still among you those who can track well?"

"Aye, Master Uldyssian . . . and if they can't, I can!"

"We leave at first light, with the city of Toraja as our goal! A good-sized city, Mendeln?"

His brother considered. "It is not Kehjan, but nothing is. Yes, it is a good first destination."

He knew what Uldyssian had in mind. To face the Temple and, very likely, the Cathedral and the mage clans, their numbers would have to be much greater. Uldyssian had no doubt that there would be those in Toraja who would be open to what he offered.

There would also be those who would oppose him . . . and so Toraja would in addition become a proving ground for his uprising. . . or a burial ground.

"We head to Toraja, then," he said to the rest. "The riders must go back and tell whatever Parthans wish to hear that they are invited to join us there! Tell them to head there!"

"I'll see to the message myself, Master Uldyssian!" replied Romus with increasing resolve. Three other men let out shouts of equal enthusiasm.

"The task is yours, then, you four. The rest of you remember! First light!"

They cheered again, caught up in the imagined spectacle of sweeping across the world and gathering with them throngs of enthusiastic newcomers. Uldyssian let them celebrate, knowing that it might very well be otherwise.

They might very well be slaughtered before they even reached the gates of Toraja.

"They would follow you anywhere," Mendeln commented.

"Even to the Burning Hells and High Heavens?" his brother returned, recalling the mythic places of which Lilith had spoken. He could scarcely imagine an eternal conflict between celestial beings, but even less could imagine he and his kind remaining potential fodder for whichever side triumphed.

Mendeln nodded. "Even there . . . if it should prove necessary."

He glanced in startlement, not certain whether Mendeln was jesting or not. Certainly, his brother did not seem the type to jest, not anymore.

They continued to let the Parthans cheer. If not the Burning Hells and High Heavens, at the very least there would be demons and more aplenty here in Sanctuary . . . chief among them Lilith. Lucion had been correct about one thing; Uldyssian had no doubt that she would find a way to come back into his life . . . and then attempt to either control or *take* it.

Whichever she desired, Uldyssian did not shy from facing her. She would find him far more than she thought. Much favored her in their struggle, but he was prepared.

"My birthright," he whispered. Then, thinking of all those there, Uldyssian corrected himself. "*Our* birthright. Our world." His determination grew greater yet as he thought once more of Achilios and those others who had perished for no good reason. "Our *destiny*."

"Yes," answered Mendeln, hearing Uldyssian despite how

quiet he had spoken. "That and more. That and *much* more."

And thinking about it, Uldyssian knew that he was right.

An uneasiness had spread through the main temple of the Triune. Few understood it, but all felt it. The high priests pretended as if all was as it normally was, but those who watched them close saw that even *their* eyes held some hint of concern.

In the private sanctum of the Primus, the demon Astrogha hung deep in an upper corner, his form completely shadowed from any who might enter. Around him scurried several eight-legged fiends, all moving with an anxiety he did not outwardly reveal.

But mixed with that anxiety was a growing thought. Lucion had not returned from wherever he had gone. It was far past any reasonable hour of return. While the son of Mephisto had said one thing concerning where he had vanished to, Astrogha had not taken that at face value. He knew that Lucion saw in this human something more than mere potential for the ranks of the morlu or any other force benefiting the Triune. Lucion had been on the verge of the unthinkable . . . perhaps wondering if the nephalem could raise him up above even his father and the other Prime Evils.

Yet, Lucion was not back and Astrogha now contemplated how that worked in his favor. Perhaps *he* should take on the aspect of the Primus. *He* should command the power of the Triune.

Yes, after all, it could certainly not be turned over to a fool such as Gulag. Gulag was pure chaotic force; he had no wit for commanding.

Suddenly, the demon sensed another presence in the chamber. He tensed, ready to spring if it turned out to be an intruder. Astrogha had eaten recently, but he always had a taste for blood.

But to his surprise, it was the one being he had not expected.

"Lucion is back," he announced. "And has Lucion done what he wished?"

"In some ways, yes, in some ways, no," the Primus remarked cryptically. "Astrogha?"

Lucion's tone almost sounded as if he was not certain who spoke, but that could not be right. The spider demon chose to move on with the conversation. "Was there sign of her? Of Lilith?"

The Primus was quiet for a moment, then nodded. "Some, but I do not think we shall see much of her for a while."

"Good, good . . ."

Lucion put a hand on the tall throne upon which he generally sat during audiences. As Astrogha watched, the towering figure settled into it, then looked up into the shadows where the other demon lurked.

"I would be alone, Astrogha."

"How long?" There were times when the son of Mephisto demanded this. Generally, the arachnid would retreat to one of the towers until Lucion was done with whatever it was he was working on. As the demon chosen to lead, Lucion had benefits that Astrogha often envied.

"From this point on," returned Lucion, expression hardening. "Find yourself a place to spin a new web. The towers, perhaps. If I ever need you, I will summon you."

He was being cast out of the chamber forever? Astrogha almost protested, then considered that Lucion was, after all, the *son* of Mephisto, whereas he was only a favored of the Lord of Terror. Diablo would not defend him against Lucion.

"As is wished," the shadowy arachnid muttered. "As is wished."

He summoned his children to him, then breathed upon the web so as to dissolve it. Then, with one last—and somewhat angry look—Astrogha vanished.

The figure on the throne reached out with sorcery to survey the room. No one was present, not even one of the spider's over-inquisitive pets. The chamber was magically sealed off from all others.

The Primus let out a slight laugh . . . one with what might have been called a *feminine* aspect to it.

"Come to me, my love," Lucion said with the voice of his sister. "I am waiting anxiously for you . . ."

And in the Cathedral of Light, the Prophet nodded.

All was going exactly as he had dictated.

The Sin War
continues in
SCALES OF THE SERPENT

About the Author

RICHARD A. KNAAK is the *New York Times* and *USA Today* bestselling author of some fifty novels and numerous shorter works. He has written for such well-known series as WORLD OF WARCRAFT, DIABLO, DRAGONLANCE, CONAN, and PATHFINDER and is the creator of the long-running, popular epic fantasy saga THE DRAGONREALM. He has also written comic, manga, and gaming material, and his works have been translated worldwide.